ABANDONED BY THE GODS

ABANDONED BY THE GODS

A Novel

MARK HENDERSON

Copyright © 2014 by Mark Henderson
All Rights Reserved.
Printed in the United States of America
ISBN: 978-0615976075
First Edition
Volume I

This is a work of fiction. Names,
characters, places, and incidents either
are the product of the author's imagination or
are used fictitiously. Any resemblance to
actual persons, living or dead,
is purely coincidental.

Cover and Interior Design by Sari Henderson
Cover Image: "A Young Family," Copyright ©
Shutterstock/Liga Lauzuma, 2014

For Carmen

*muse to the real, to the things that in each other
are included, the whole, the complicate,
the amassing harmony*

ABANDONED BY THE GODS

VOLUME I

CONTENTS

BOOK ONE: THE HAPPY SPRING

1	On The Discovery of Forgotten Photos, From Which Comes A Question of Color	5
2	Lost Scenes From A Family Album	6
3	When A Telling Is Formed By An Old Fear, One Beginning Necessarily Occludes Another	12
4	This Is The Beginning	15
5	The Temporal Distance Remains Between What Is Real and What Is Written	19
6	An Old War Story	24
7	The Priest Sends Forth The Dark Girl	28
8	Scenes From An Arabian Story	33
9	On Feelings Of Sentiment and Sentimentality	36
10	Two People Go On Together In A Telling	42
11	Then Everafter Everything Is Always To Be	45
12	In Search Of A Poetics Of Reverie, Not Dead Recollection	55
13	The Recorded Self Is The Authorized Edition Of The Self	58
14	A Sense Of Place Is Expressed In A Face	61

15	To Be Laid Along A Girl Alive In The Night, Is To Forget A Girl	65
16	A Kind Of Court	69
17	One Must Act To Relinquish The Past	74
18	Rank Is The Ritual Of Authority	76
19	How One Goes Home, and Goes Nowhere	81
20	The Fighting Is Finished	83
21	A Dark Girl Comes Forth With Children In Rain	89
22	An Intimation Of America	102
23	The True Story Of A Name	111
24	What Is To Come	120
25	The Women Were Storytellers, The Men Were Warriors	123
26	One Sees In Significances	129
27	A Question Of Convention and What-Happens-Next	145
28	The French Soldier	148
29	In The Tuareg Style She Follows Him To Kill Him	152
30	She Was Loving A Soldier	154
31	A Time Of Confession Is A Time Of Aversion	157
32	There We Lay Along Big Water	162
33	On The Philosopher-Priest	164
34	An Odd Juxtaposition Of Black and White Photos	168
35	A Girl and A Boy In The Night	174
36	Nothing Is Told In Goodbye	180
37	The French Priest, Her Letter, The Official Paperwork	182
38	The Remains Of Reverie	186
39	The Boys In The Bar	189
40	The End Of The Happy Spring	198

BOOK TWO: HOLIDAY IN THE COUNTRY

41	On The Advantage and Disadvantage Of History For Life	*203*
42	A Tourist In A Train Station	*208*
43	A Kind Of Travelogue	*213*
44	The Girls On The Train	*216*
45	The Unreal Actuality Of Arrival	*219*
46	One Is Ever and Perpetually Arriving	*223*
47	In A French House In A French Village	*226*
48	Reborn To Life	*233*
49	At Last Arrived In A Name In The Night	*236*
50	An Act of Waking Is An Act of Remembering	*241*
51	It Is Not A Question Of Color, It Is A History Of Color	*243*
52	She Came All Dark In Her Dress	*246*
53	The First Look Of Her Parents	*249*
54	A New Little Story Of Her Parents	*251*
55	Pieds-Noirs	*256*
56	A Kind Of Homecoming	*262*
57	Interlude Of An Old Indian Tale	*265*
58	A Kind Of Homecoming, Continued	*269*
59	On Learning A Language	*276*
60	A Serious Lunch	*286*
61	The Things To Be Done To Make A House A Home	*289*
62	An Elegant Girl In Her Blue Dress	*294*
63	A Boy and A Girl A Little In Love	*298*
64	Gone North In Country Between The River and The Rock	*301*
65	Finding Books In English and A Very Happy-Beautiful Girl	*304*
66	It Is Like That In The South	*309*
67	Walking Up In The Light	*311*

68	A Kind of Undeclared War	317
69	In A French Café	323
70	Hurt Good	327
71	There Is A Certain Peace	329
72	The Fighting Is Finished	335
73	On A Little Holiday	338
74	A Kid Made Alive By Storms	343
75	A Question Of Place	345
76	On The Sublime	350
77	The Women Half-Dressed In The Strong Light	354
78	A Dark Girl In A French Café	362
79	On Playing and Forgetting	369
80	Never To Be Lonely Again	375

BOOK ONE

THE HAPPY SPRING

Where shall a man find sweetness to surpass his own home and his parents? In far lands he shall not, though he find a house of gold.

Homer, *The Odyssey*

1

ON THE DISCOVERY OF FORGOTTEN PHOTOS, FROM WHICH COMES A QUESTION OF COLOR

There in the house I had buried them down in the dark of a drawer like the dead and she had brought them back out to the light as if to life, those black and white snapshots of who we once were and could never now be, lives caught and kept in an old desk drawer shut up and unseen for years. They were the young lives of her mother and me and she brought them out to the light of the yard to look at them and I let her look.

Through the kitchen window I could see her there a girl in the grass going through that beat-up cardboard box of photographs she'd claimed and carried out to the light. Her hair was fallen dark and uncut across her face. The grass was green and uncut and she lay down on her side in her dress in it. Her legs were stretched bared and browned into the long-bladed grass from beneath the yellow flowered dress she wore. It was that summer dress her mother had made her. The hem was frayed and she was young and barefoot in the green and she looked up into the light at an old black and white photo. She studied it in the light and I went out to her. She held a picture of her mother.

"Why is mother dark so? Why am I dark some?" my daughter she said that to me. She was young enough to say such things. I looked at her long dark hair in the light. I had forgotten they were dark.

"Your color's a color between your mother and me, girl," I said as simple fact and I was thinking on how to tell it to her good. I was seeing how the color couldn't matter to her and I found some of the old simple words and said them to myself. I stood there quieted in my looking to her all darkly lit in her yellow dress and I said nothing more about it but I was seeing a whole history to that question of color she can't ever see in that old picture of her mother let alone in her own look. I saw her. I saw her dark. I thought of how I hadn't seen her that way in so long while she lay there a girl in the grass struck dark in summer light looking on at those new-found pictures of them people we'd once been and could never again be.

2

LOST SCENES FROM A FAMILY ALBUM

And we lived on a little in her looking as she went through them snapshots laid out there in the grass. I didn't look at them, I lay down beside her in the green of the yard, as when you'll come at last to rest awhile home in the light with all the things of the world closed off. I lay there a time along her looking up to the far-hung blue behind the trees, and in looking to that summer sky, I saw old sights of us. I saw remembered sights. For a time I lay there fixed in nostalgic reverie, travelled off in a kind of waking sleep to a place or two of them pictures and the people in them, and she said, "Daddy?" and I was gone far off from her and home in those pictured-thoughts of mine looking to summer sky. I didn't speak. I was gone off in mute, ranging thought, and she got up from beside me in the green with those pictures put back away and shut up in that box, and I watched her rise and go from me. I lay on there a time in the grass without her, lost in returned sights, left to the recurrent images of people and places, to the remembered sight of her herself rising, to a residue of resemblances no matter all the real things I'd seen, and having gone nowhere in the world and seen nothing but in recollection, now left laid there in a sudden and great sense of the irrevocable loss of all people and places, I rose from the grass, I got up from the yard to go find her and those photos. I crossed to the house walking on barefoot in the uncut grass in the summer light feeling the substantial persisting fact of the earth beneath my feet. I stopped at the screened door, and looked out west to the great lake water stretched brilliantly lit beyond the tall trunks of trees, a great opened-out body, another world laid blued and deep to the far line of the sky. I heard a cupboard close, and I went in the back door to the kitchen, thinking to find her and take her from the house to the lake with me to swim, and her mother was making lunch there in the kitchen, and she herself was out front on the screened-in porch, sitting at the folded-out card table drawing from one of those old found photographs I'd let her have to keep and shouldn't have. She was seeing the people and places she'd never seen. I wanted to see what she was drawing from it and her mother told me to let her alone but I went out to look. She'd drawn a line or two in dark color on the blank sheet to begin on the bold outline of a body or a face and her picture was as yet unrecognizable. I stood in the doorway of the house looking out the porch screens to the green-leaved trees along the lake and she put down her pencil. She studied the photograph. She bent it one way and then another, as though wanting to find another way to look into the long fixed exposure, to see beyond the glossy surface of the paper past the opaque flatness of its static image, to find another scene set in it, even to unfix the time caught, composed in it, and there was none but that one unrepeatable instant, no other time or action to follow out in consequence but what she saw exposed at once in the mechanical click of the shutter and inalterably printed in ink before her, this inked paper representing the only evidence of that time and life left. I looked to the blank back of the snapshot where a couple names were scribbled in ink and there was a date written across it in my own hand and she studied the photo awhile no matter that in all her looking to the image of its fixed instant there was now nothing actual to be seen before or after the one set shot, there was no good way for her to get down past that papered surface of its printed frame into the significance of its spot in time, unless I told her of its lived-up time. And I was saying nothing.

"Daddy?" she said to me and she turned it round and showed me myself standing young with the boys smiling and alive and I was not unhappy to hear her and remember who I was to her and I looked to myself. "This is you?" she said, and she held up the old black and white snapshot with us boys all relaxed-looking out in the sun half-dressed in uniform green, holding rifles and helmets, smoking cigarettes in mock bravado, a posed shot beside sand bags, beer cans, a canvas tent. Ragged children stood looking into the camera behind us on one side. I looked to the children with their faces fixed forever young and sharp in deep focus. I felt the old loss come on in me and I shoved it away.

"Daddy, I look like him," she said in some simple self-recognition and she was a curious little girl pointing to a half-dressed boy in the background and I looked from her to him and then away back to the boys. There I was myself just a boy and I hardly recognized myself. I stood there beside them boys all alive held in her little girl's hand home in America. It was the end of a war. I looked at the picture of us boys held there in America in the house in her hand. I saw what came after out of it. There are no pictures of it. I looked out the porch screens to the lake. The fighting was finished and the fighting went on.

"Yes—that's me," I said.

"Daddy, are they dead?" she said to me.

"Let me see it," I said, and she gave me the picture and I wondered why I'd ever saved such pictures. I thought I had not. But you'll want to keep something of yourself. The pictures persist as the people cannot. I held the picture to the light coming in the porch screen and looked at it close as I could, seeing my young old self and looked away back to her across it, holding it, not giving it back to her, and she was all young looking at me waiting for me to speak and I kept holding it and kept quiet on her. She was at that age when daughters will want to know about the long done things of fathers, and you do want a daughter to love you knowing you. There are all the things left yet to tell those who would love you. I've hardly yet told it myself. I handed it back to her and she took it and she began again on the blank sheet, drawing the first outlines of a face and I found, and fit, a few words to the pictured scene, saying the one unsounded word to myself to find the other, as when starting on a story that has long been fixed mute in you but which comes up readily enough, and oddly whole, surprising you in the power of its spoken form once you begin to utter it from out of real feeling, remembered feeling, though you are now inventing it all to tell it true.

I said none of what I saw to her.

She'd begun for good on her picture and I was watching her drawing carefully, too exactly at first, from that old found and kept picture of mine from which to make hers, copying it close as she could, while I was seeing in my own unsaid words out beyond the glossy flatness of its surface in time to what lay in front of us, the brilliantly lit days yet to be lived, still freely unfixed in time. The done days came at me whole and she was drawing on and I was seeing the boys.

But fathers have to be careful with their words, and I have been.

"Daddy?" she said, and I was seeing what was to come and saying none of it. "I want to know about the boy," she said and she was waiting on me to tell her about him and I never got to the beginning of that for her in those days, although I do think I told her some good and even true things.

"I don't know anything about the boy," I said, and that was true. "I'll tell you a story about your mother," I said to her to stop the stark, strange vividness I saw coming up real in unwanted recollection, dimmed images of boys dead, living, appearing in a clarity of stronger light, all that which cannot pass irrevocably to dark, however long suppressed from sight. The brilliantly lit days emerged anew from dark, to be lit and lived again.

"I'll tell you something about your mother I never told you," I said to her and it was then in my words about her mother, that she looked up from her drawing to me and she stopped me, and as when solving a puzzle which one's worked over in the mind awhile, she said then in declaration of fact, "Daddy, you're right, that's why I'm dark some—like that boy—it's because mother's so dark, you're not dark like that," my daughter she said that to me happily in the pleasure of such discovery, and she looked down at the darkness of her own arm, at the in-between look of her color, and she looked back to me and mine, and she put down that picture of the boys and me, and she again picked up the one of her mother that she'd had out in the yard and she said to me, "But why is mother so dark?" as if now in her seeing that old, posed, picture of her it troubled her, and I was thinking on it myself, and she was all young-looking, waiting on me to begin it, and I looked at the odd juxtaposition of them two pictures she'd laid out there next to one another on the card table. There was that glossy snapshot of soldiers that showed me myself, placed next to the old posed picture of her mother dark and young, that'd been taken long ago off in another country, to be affixed to her official paperwork, a leftover cutout shot that she'd kept as a souvenir, and that she'd given to me, that I'd taken, that

I'd kept to see her in, and I hadn't seen it in years, and there she was before me, there I was beside her, and there was an unlikely logic to the juxtaposition of them two, to us, but the one did follow out from the other. In time, none of it is to be unlikely. I looked at her.

I looked out beyond the screened-in porch to the water of the great lake in America stretched big and blue off to the far line of the sky in summer light, and I said to her there in the nicely shaded screened light of the porch, "I'll tell you something true about your mother—," I said, and I saw her young in my talk, now in that talk of her mother, those stark sights of recollection passing a time out of view off into the pleasure of nostalgia. And I began to tell her of her mother and me there in America, and she stopped me.

"Daddy, but you never start at the beginning, start at the beginning—," she said and she wanted me to begin in the place and the time of those pictures she'd found, and not in America.

"The beginning is the middle," I said, playing.

"Tell it true, Daddy—you said you'd tell it *true*," she said to me as if I'd promised it to her and, in that, then she was the muse she'd be to me. And I went on telling her about her mother, holding to the middle of things and none of what I saw beginning, seeing the one thing and saying another, as in a life the one story irrevocably framed in another, and I began once more on her mother for her and not at the beginning.

3

WHEN A TELLING IS FORMED BY AN OLD FEAR, ONE BEGINNING NECESSARILY OCCLUDES ANOTHER

And she drew on making out her picture as she could in the leaf-shaded light of the porch. Now it was less an exacting copy than some visionary abstraction, an expressive sketch of the ethereal forms of children that she'd said looked like her, primitively stylized, drawn in bold lines, darkly haunted with overlarge eyes and thin limbs, to be hung on the wall of her room, where yet they hang in the angled light, so that for years I'd pass the door and look and look away down along the comfortable familiarity of a paneled hall in a house in America to keep myself there in that place in that time and no other. And I'll tell you right now, that like the origin of a childhood composition strongly drawn from the short study of a life caught and kept unseen for years in forgotten old photos, that you've got to assume a kind of godly ambition in your own voice, as she's doing in her drawing, if one day you'll want to say what you see of yourself, as if in some original song marking out some meaning in a life.

And I'm no singer, let alone a storyteller, but she was sitting there at that card table looking to those old lost and found pictures of our past, making out her drawing of those children from that shot of us boys on that screened-in porch in America, when I was seeing in my mind's eye all what came after out of it, came unfixed for us boys in the rising light, how we'd waked from short bad half-sleep to a fear tired-sick, roused and un-rested, to move out in dark afraid to move from the fresh dirt of shallow-dug fighting holes. We'd waked to come down out of the hills in a nice large light onto the field of big grass to walk it all so goddamned awake and deadened in good weather to cross to a village and she drew on in the summer light of the great lake. We came down from out of the hills in single file walking hard-worried in good light, strung out onto the field of grass pregnant with our packs in a little low plain in clear big sky so to cross to a village swearing seeing nothing new.

There was nothing new. There was the lateness of moving in the light. There was the wanting not ever to move in the light. There was all the strange familiar place come round us real. All was old and unreal, and there was the praying-swearing by habit believing none of it doing it.

We undid ourselves in our doing. We got half-way. Half-way across in big grass three of the boys went up in the mines and mortar fire and, as the record would say, another four boys at the edge of the tall grass fell to the green ground for good beneath a big-lit sky, and the boy they had made the lieutenant with his map and his radio had said in some hope that there was to be nothing so surprising as that in the field on the little low plain with the grass all a good green in the light. And in a good hard fear of his the boy-officer ordered everyone forward, with each one of them boys making their way in the grass swearing-shooting fighting something first in themselves and the one of them, the boy from the pretty little town in Texas, wild sick with the knowing of the place in him, shot the boy-lieutenant and looked to shoot anyone who had seen him shoot and shot a couple of boys from Missouri and Montana, with half of the rest of them from places like California and New York running back across the big grass to the high hills, with some boys now stuck from Ohio on the little plain past the mines and mortars with boys from Georgia gone too far to the edge of the field squatting in big grass seeing nothing shooting earth grass and sky along the path to the village, where I a boy from Michigan had made my way forward to be shot there beside a boy from Maine fallen dead I had drank with, where like that I came upon the sounds of the wounded boys from Minnesota and

North Dakota lying unbelieving in the first feeling of it.

And there in that nice light all very awake and finished fighting I lay myself down hard hurt in the place fallen to pray some in the sharp-edged grass put down for good with some few remembered, half-prayed words of no good use. The blood was come up out me across the dirt and sweat of my uniform, and I said some of those old worn words about god for no good reason gone down for good in the green, smelling the blood strong and wet, the muddy reddened color of a life spread thin and thickened up my side, seeped in darkening green through frayed cloth. I was shot up in the side, and I cut the ragged fabric of the uniform, opened it wide to the wound with my knife to stop up the bared open holes where it came on easily out of me without one thought of stopping, and found there was another one gone through the shoulder, and I'd seen it go bad with boys like that now gone and dead and I looked up from the earth to the sky and I remembered how we'd played at it. The funny thing was that once home in grass we'd played at it, we were kids, and I saw us kids and how we'd got up dead and unhurt and gone home happy to the house. We were kids young and alive, shooting-playing, killing one another laughing. I saw the old house and childhood rooms. There's always a war and the children playing. I saw the houses out beyond the tall grass set pastorally against the green fields as if in some idyllic country scene.

There the houses stood off burning beneath the sky. The blue was hung up above them. There far off from home was hung out the great blue of some happy childhood and I lay back bloodied to rest in the sharp-edged elephant grass beneath the great blue sky and heard them running through the green as I'd heard them kids long ago back home coming on hard with their arms and legs hitting on wild against the stalks through fields of corn in the Midwest of America. I smelled the dirt and sweat of the wet blooded cloth and they ran the big grass coming loudly unseen in it making a racket with their arms and legs hitting against the tall blades in their running giving themselves away. I lifted the rifle from the earth to the sky. The grass would always give you away.

They broke onto me from the green. There was the hard cracking shot. There was the smell of spent cartridges. The yellow casings came down round me emptied out into the green. I shot them sight unseen against the blue. They came down round me close. They came down bloodied in the grass in the light. I killed them like that without a thought.

Do not think that this is anything extraordinary. It is happening everywhere in this war. There lay a mother against me and there lay a girl. There we three lay gone down for good in the green. The three of us lay out there in the grass in the large light of idyllic afternoon in that strange green country. We lay there a time against one another as when once home you will come to rest awhile in the light. It is all of it a long time ago. You tell it on yourself as you can.

4

THIS IS THE BEGINNING

This is the beginning I never told her and hardly myself.

We lay there as two in love. We lay there alone. There we lay the mother and me in that great green field, and the daughter she lay there dead. The mother lay alive with me in a single simple quiet. I had not once heard that single quiet. I kept her close in it. I kept her held close to my green. She looked and looked to me with the reddened brilliance coming from out her laid long beside me in the green. I remember. It is all a way of remembering. She looked and looked to me seeing what I do not know. In all that looking there was the life of her opening up from out her as flowers I remembered opened brilliantly to the light after closing to the dark. There comes that vibrant opening without a thought to the light. She looked beautiful. I remember thinking that no matter she looked beautiful. We were laid out along one another like lovers with her looking beautiful in that strange greened place. Laid out long one another like that we might well have loved one another and she took my hand in some care as would a lover. I kept her close. I remember. I cannot picture all I remember. I remember these hands of ours.

What she wanted was the knife. She reached for it and I let the handle of it go to her hand. I had forgotten it in my looking to her. I'd done it to her. I'd killed her. In the last of her living she held the blade curiously in the light. If she wanted to I'd let her take it to me. The steel of the blade fell hardened along my ragged wound. The stink of blood was come all up me across my green. It is hard to believe it until you see it. You smell it. The redness was seeped on across my ragged green into hers and I could not tell if it were her blood or mine now all irrevocably mixed up the one gone run on in the other and I kept her good and hard to me in that wet smell laid out low one next to the other, a last time alive no matter a first time together, gone down in the brilliant big light in strange green country. There was the very high sky pulled clean across all the country, with the familiar commotion of artillery and machine coming on, all the confusion of gunfire and engine opening low and loud in the crowded light.

There is a way of remembering. I take her hand in my hand. There we lay already seen as if from a great distance, our blood come on in to one another brilliant and wet, feeling ourselves already other people to ourselves so soon laid low beneath the sky. It is too soon. We are too young to be laid like that. For years I cannot see it. I cannot picture her for the feeling. I see her clearly now. "Daddy?" she says. She's close

16

beside me. I cannot answer her.

She had the knife in hand, she kept hold of the knife, I kept her to me in some strange care, and she turned the blade from me to herself. She looked off from me to it. It was heavy and hidden beneath her in the green. She put it to herself down low where she was alive with it. She wanted me to see it. I saw it. She was all alive unshot down low and she looked off from me to her nakedness with the knife. She cut herself good. She ran the steel across her hard. I reached out to take the handle from her hand. I tried to take back the blade to stop her. She put my hand to the handle of it. She opened herself up in some last living act. She did not want to stop it. She ran the steel of it into her there where she was alive with it. She was not trying to kill it. It is some last good she wants. She wants to let a thing live no matter what is to come after out of it and she kept my hand held to hers in some care. She looked to me all alive with it. She looked to me to do it and I held the blade to her in the light. I remember these hands and looks of ours. She looked to me to get it done. She saw me. I have been once and truly seen. I think I have been once and truly seen and she looked to me and she saw who I was to be to her and her dead girl lay out bloodied and stilled in the light in the grass along her mother and me where she had come at last to lay herself down young and beautiful from my killing her.

We lay down long one another in the tall grass in the wet smell fallen for good down along the footpath that led from field to home with all the houses burning beneath the blue hung out above us and everywhere was blood come across hands and bodies in the light and she looked to me and what she saw I do not know if she saw one thing with my hand gone into her to let a thing live. I saw she saw nothing. Her hand had gone from mine for good and she lay there dead and one might well leave it all like that with nothing now to come from anything and she looked to me seeing nothing, all the life of her stopped

17

and undone but for what was left to go out of her to the world without her and the world did not give a goddamned thing about it or her and I know there are these things that should be stopped and that you yourself cannot ever stop in the actuality of your own life. And I lay on there with the knife gone into her in the unending stopped time of my own life, not able to go on gone too far to stop with her laid half-gutted along me, the knife gone hard and sharp in her with its unthinking wanting, wanting only out of her as all of us have wanted, and it is an inconceivable thing to think that it is to end like that with it all alive and living on in her. It cannot be so conceived. None of this is ever well-told. I've known a long time what is most lived cannot be.

I remember, now I remember she was young, looking almost a girl. I could not tell in looking if she herself were a woman or a girl. She is a mother no matter. They are all of them girls. She opens by my hand. I am covered over with it in the grass. It is wet-feeling. It is alive-feeling. It is a kind of butchery. I am a kind of father. It is done by my hand. No matter the knife it is naked and alive in the light. It comes clean out to the crowded light of coming choppers the oncoming blades lashing back the big grass in whirling concussion. It comes alive into the loud and brilliant light of men and machine wet naked a livid voice calling out for the whole world to hear against the burning sky. It is at last in the light for all the world to see and hear and no one does. I do. Once and for all we are awakened. We go from the quiet and happy dark into the loud surprising light to see and to say. It is years I cannot say what I see. I cannot picture her for the feeling. I see her. I see her. It is all remembering feeling. Let me tell you, all is remembering feeling. It is all remembering feeling a last time a first time.

5

THE TEMPORAL DISTANCE REMAINS BETWEEN WHAT IS REAL AND WHAT IS WRITTEN

And she said, "Tell it true about mother," making me see it, and I stood there on the porch seeing it beginning, and I did not tell her how I lay waked in the beginning in the light looking up to a high-fanned ceiling of an old French-looking room far off from home, how all was unrecognizable to me, how the killing was done, how in a fear I'd waked and named the place and who I was in it to send the fear out of me in the convention of that simple act of naming, as if in our time one could yet make one's world intelligible in the power of waking, naming, knowing who and where one is in a word or two, no matter it told nothing new or good. I lay there all stretched out in a nice clean bed of white linen, already old and cold to the new no matter yet young, laid out to rest along with all the shot up boys in a big clean room in one of those fresh made hospital beds.

I looked at her long dark hair in the light in America and I told her nothing of that weak wounded sickness and I saw myself from a great distance the boy I once was and could never now be and sometimes still missed, looking up in the brilliant light of the big French room in the city outskirts of what was once called, what had become called in those days in the convention of naming, Saigon, Vietnam, awakened to simply name the place that has now long been renamed and made more idea than actual place. I was wanting to make sense of it in the repetition of sound, feeling I'd left something undone and that I must go do it, with the name sounding already as if said in error, in those days the name of anyplace for any war to my ear, not yet mythic, an idealized notion of a place found most real in stories and books, but I couldn't move to go anywhere to do anything, let alone think of what it was I'd yet to do. We'd done the killing. We'd seen the dying. We'd waked once and for all wounded and quieted to the coming light missing this or that part of the body or mind. We'd done nothing good in the end and there was nowhere left to go and nothing good to do but to get ourselves on home the one way or the other whether dead or alive. Some of the boys they laid them long in bags to get back home. Then for those of us left with the living there was the official talk before you'd get shipped off for good and sent on healed up to home.

There was to be this official talk about all our killing. It's that they wanted it for the record. They wanted to get one of the boys for killing that Lieutenant. In those days and these no one really knew who did what to who where until you wrote it down. That's an old story we were to tell. Anyone could tell it. Knowing was telling. Telling was true. Well you try to get to the truth of a matter to put it down on paper and there are only more words.

I told my part laid out there looking up in the light. A Captain with shiny shoes came with a notebook and a pen early in the morning light. The old men they sent him to me with his polished shoes and his pistol and brass shoulders to make out his report and, just like in a simple book where you'll get the rote facts of the who what and where to start it off, the names came first to lend an appearance of substance to person, character, and mine was long undone and gone missing.

"You PFC John LeBlanc?" he said to me and he looked at his paperwork and he looked at me and the rank and the name sounded strange to me, but it told him exactly who I was. I was someone that the United States Army called *PFC John LeBlanc*.

The boys they'd never call you by your officially given name and rank, until one day you'd forget that you had one that told you who you were to the world. The boys they'd all

20

called me Geronimo as a joke, and I'd never taken it seriously myself, it was a simple caricature, if not absurd, but I'd still seen some of who I was in it, with some hope if not happiness, and he pulled up a stool to the side of the bed, and when I'd hardly felt the hope, the feeling went away in the irony of that old Indian joke. The sight of my mother came to me. He stood there before me naming me and I saw my mother dark along the water beneath the trees. Who she was seemed an apparition come from another life I'd never lived. I heard her call me home by name. *"John Little Wolf LeBlanc,"* she said the whole thing when she wanted me and I went on home happy to the house. I don't think it's ever been officially written. It's all a nickname otherwise.

"Could be anybody—who goes by that name," I said to him and my affection for the remembered feeling of who I was as a kid, the boy I once was, was lost, and I watched him sit down next to me without any invitation to and I've long known to be careful of such official associations.

He said, "Soldier, according to these papers I got, you're that *anybody.*" He held them up there in the light with the name and rank in proof of that fact. The lived lineage of my own name was nothing to that rote recorded fact. I was an American soldier. He shook his head feeling his clean-shaved face with a hand and he looked away. He watched a nurse walk by in her uniform. He looked her up and down like he was hungry and I looked off from him to her. She must have been just a kid like me. She went to a boy and bent over a bed in the light. The light hit on across the shine of chrome and sheeted beds. The boys' faces were cast in the sickly-paled dark-eyed visages of invalids. I looked to the sheet of paper to the name and the rank written out to designate a person of some substance, even of character, my own self, to be officially born by such records.

He was looking to the nurse. He turned.

21

He said, "Soldier let's get this straight, what's written here, *that is only who you are*," he said. He said, "LeBlanc, there are two ways of doing this—there's the hard way, and there's the easy way. Do not fuck me," he said, "And I will get you home." He said that in a kind of promise, like an un-struck bargain made with another. He sat there all easy and relaxed with the heels of his shiny dress shoes hung on a rung of the stool, his khaki knees spread in casual leisure, his pen and paper hung between them in hand like the picture of a living cliché.

The nurses walked along the white sheeted beds behind him.

"Begin with the Lieutenant," he said with his pen and paper ready to write out his report as though at last we understood one another. I didn't begin with the Lieutenant. I began with myself. I didn't hide a goddamned thing from him about what I'd done.

The talking hurt. The looking hurt. I looked up to the fancy fanned ceiling. I saw them wet in the grass. I saw myself a boy laid there in the grass. The knife was in my hand. Then the association came un-beckoned, and it fixed itself in me, and the sight of one killing came continuously put against another, imprinted in a doubled image. In the one act of killing I saw myself clearly in another. I saw myself a boy gutting deer young hungry and cold. I saw her a woman looking a girl laid opened up dead in the light. In that clear-coupled image of killing the boy I was was lost for good. I saw it. I didn't want to see it. I wanted to get it out of me for good all what I'd done. I thought I could rid myself of it in telling it to him. I went on telling it, seeing it beginning, now never-ending. In the words it didn't go. It came dire. It came indelible. The reddened life of them persisted in the green. The image would not go. It came heightened. It came sharpened. It came kept and clear in word.

It fixed itself in me all what I'd done.

The Captain said, "I know all about it, LeBlanc: now, the Lieutenant," he said as though I'd misunderstood the whole thing. He sat there on the metal stool beside the bed scribbling offhandedly and looking a couple times at his watch and at the passing nurses. In those too-casual acts of his I wanted to take his pistol from out of his holster and shoot him. It wasn't a good want. The want was real.

They wanted the story straight so. It was to be all official.

"Keep it simple," he said to me. I did. One must. What is simple is true, or so it is said. I wanted to tell it true. I went on telling it. I knew it was in the telling. I kept telling it. I told it in some few words, and the part I told about myself, he wrote that all out another way than it was on his yellow legal pad in a couple short notes in the side margin. He didn't tell it true, and I hadn't gotten it out of me.

In the pictured-words I'd said the sight only came stronger, and he got up looking at his watch, he shut up the legal pad, and he said, "There'll be an Inquiry, routine," he simply said to end it. "The Colonel wants corroboration on the Lieutenant, think about that, LeBlanc," he simply said to me and left. He went off away from me for good to them old men to make out his report to the Colonel. I lay there with it done and told as if a finished life. And we all of us had thought to get clean out of it knowing better. You couldn't get cleanly out of a goddamned thing. One can't get out of one's own self after all.

Then no matter I'd told it to him the telling did not stop it. It all kept coming on up in me to be relived in recollection. Years later you find a few apt words for it. I remember it came dire in its impression an actual non-existent thing none of it real in the world only persisting as a phenomenal fact in me. It became strange and badly overcoming to me. I tried to forget it. I shoved the sight of it off from in me. It lived on lividly in me. The recollection rose ever to be resurrected in the insufficient

23

act of its repression. It ran hard-lit through my head perfectly pictured except for the end. The end of it was oddly missing in my mind. I saw no child. I saw no life to come from it. The knife was in my hand. The woman was laid opened up into me dead never to rise again but in me. The rest was blank. It was fixed at the point of killing. There was no after to it. There was no end to it. I saw the boys all alive in the light. I saw it all beginning. It is all beginning. There is no end.

The boys wanted to shoot and the boys shot on into the big grass of the field each one of them motherfuckers a killer crouching-seeing nothing swearing-shooting wanting to shoot it over with and get away clean out of it. The boys they went on forward feeling themselves too young and alive in the light not wanting to lose that living feeling going forward toward all loss. The boys they went on sick-knowing. The boys went hard-worried knowing each fight was to be the last not knowing which fight was the last and every one of them boys was waked to it seeing nothing shooting everything looking to kill not to be killed. Every boy fighting was finished fighting and the finished fighting went on and every boy in dark or light waked a killer.

I was one of them.

That's the beginning. It went something like that and he wrote it all out otherwise for the old men in his jargon, the truth scribbled and rewritten offhandedly along the margin.

6

AN OLD WAR STORY

And she'd said to me while drawing, "Daddy, begin at the beginning," she said to me in some expectation of things to come as if I were to tell her a good and happy story as a father should, and I do remember how I began to tell her a pretty good story of her mother as I'd said I would, and will, to begin it. It isn't such a sad story after all. It's a simple story. It's a love story. It's a war story. By that time, too, I'd read some good books myself, both of high and low diction, and I saw how I could tell her an old war story about getting home like the ones you'll have heard since the time of Homer, and it's true that such adventures have all been told before but I think not quite in this way.

When the one day that Captain went off away from me for good to write out his report, I lay there waked in un-quieted hours laid out in that hospital bed all stretched out beside a nice row of the boys with nothing to do in them beginning days badly waked in bed but to heal up from the hurt to head on home, and that's when they had these young women come in to us and those girls they read stories to us from big books about people and places in far-off lands we'd never been to let alone heard of so to help us sleep some a little. There was this priest-chaplain who'd organized the whole thing and who they had around on hand in case anyone thought of dying. They didn't want you to go all alone. I didn't want any girl to read any thing to me. I told them to send me no one. I told them I did not want anyone at all to come to me. No one was to come to me. In those days in them girls coming across that room to me, I saw them come upon me in the grass. Under no circumstances was any one of them to come to me. That is when they all of them want to come to you the worst.

They came and they carried their books in hand, and I watched the girls walk on by in their white hospital aprons they made them wear, and I could hear their young voices rising off in the big room beside the beds telling strange stories of faraway places, and the one day with those girls going on by me to all the boys, the priest he came to me left at last alone waked to myself without one girl to come to me. He wanted to do good for everybody. He wanted to help me. He couldn't help me. The priest came over and I didn't believe in any of it, in none of that world of his. He sat down there beside me on the metal stool. We were to talk of what all was done and I said to him in rote remembered ritual and as if truly young, "*Forgive me Father*," for I would tell him some real things of a life and not the fake things of books as in a kind of confession, to get it out of me. I would if it got it out of me for good. I wanted to be rid of it once and for all in telling it, and he was a priest, and in some renewed hope of gaining my own good self, in profound weakness, I tried then to with him, and believing in none of it I said, "Forgive me Father, I have real things to tell you," I said flatly in such full lack of faith, and he looked at me in some wise care, and I told him some of them real things. He listened carefully.

But how can anyone ever be rid of such irrevocable acts in the simple telling of them to another I do not know, because when I started on telling it once more again to him, the words only made it worse, it all came once more sharpened, it came again strengthened and clear, it came dire, it came indelibly imprinted. It did not ever go. Its impression deepened. And now I never wanted again to say it to see the sight of it come stronger and ever stronger again and again. It came back badly livid and vividly unwanted in its un-weakened actuality, and just as it had with the Captain now it did so with the priest. I saw the futility of ever being freed from it. I felt the condemning impossibility of regaining some good sense of myself in saying that which should not ever be lived let alone brought back to life what all cannot ever become unseen in words and I was mute.

I stopped the words, and all speaking. I saw the old priest I'd once said such trivial easily said things of no consequence to as a kid in a confessional. This priest he looked too young to hear such real and unspeakable things.

He couldn't have been that young, but I began to laugh at my calling him *Father*, at the entire absurdity of absolution, and I couldn't stop it. I'd forgotten the rest of them fake words you say when you formally start to confess, and I didn't mean them words anyway. Then it was all a kind of joke. It was a joke on my own unfortunate self. I laughed, and for one so young, I laughed the unhappy and defeated laugh of the damned and condemned, and he looked at me strangely. He spoke to me gently. I stopped it some as I could. He did not understand me. He wanted to help me. He could not help me. He stayed put there on the stool. It wasn't that he was that young. It was that he had a face uncomplicated by his living. He had some generous look to him. I saw that he had some feeling of care in him. I did not want it. I wanted to make him forget me and the feeling in him.

So, no matter that I'd told him some of them real things that I've already talked about, none of it was real to him, and none of it went out of me. It was real to me. It was all words to him or to any one of them. I said real true things to him as I had to the Captain to make it all go away on out of me to finish it once and for all for good, and you'd think in the happy hope of some latent lingering belief, belief if not in a god, then in that of the authenticity of your own remorseful word, that a priest could help you if anyone could, but in my own utterance it all came alive again in its actuality, now was at last sprung whole and fully fixed in me in its deadened dark dreadfulness like the undone substance of a second self. The material irony of that, that in the spoken word I'd made the world in my own image, was nothing to the unfortunate fact of my unmaking, of haunting one's self in such wholly corrupted form in this deep unbroken continuity with the palpable and persisting past undertaken now for not one future good.

"Be quiet boy," he said. "There is nothing to be said," he said. He was really quite understanding. I needed to rest and get strong. I would live a long time well and good. It is all a way of speaking. I laughed and sent him away when he called me *son*. He went over and stood beside a big window and spoke to a doctor. I was laughing as they stood in their easy talk beneath a tall French window. I was laughing good and hard as they stood in their quiet and considered talk beneath the tall-glassed row of those rising old colonial windows. The sunlight was coming straight down onto the two of them dressed up in their white and black. The light hit on across all the cloth and chrome laid out in the room. I laughed and it hurt and I did not stop. I was a little happy in the hurt. After awhile I lay there quiet and tired but only quiet from tired and hated myself some for talking to the priest and got no sleep seeing it all come on in me hard-lit in the dark and thought of home not seeing any of it into the night no matter that I needed to rest to go on to some place, I do not know where. Call it what you want, home or what you will or want.

7

THE PRIEST SENDS FORTH THE DARK GIRL

That is when the next day a young woman came with her books and they sent her to me and I did not want her to come to me. She came to me. It was raining nicely. She came in out of the rain to me. I wanted to be left alone. You could not be left alone. We all of us faced a long tall section of high window opened to the overcast. I wanted to lay and to look up to the row of tall French glass and out to that rainlight stretched nicely long the length of the room. She walked on in the rainlight coming on in from the high-glassed window and I watched her come and she came on across the floor past the other boys to me. She came right up to me with no hesitation and she sat right down next to me on the metal stool where they'd each sat in their turn the Captain and the priest when I'd told them the hard real things I'd seen and put words to and I was done with speaking all them words and I hadn't ever seen this girl before. She looked straight at me and I looked at her. We took a good hard look at one another.

She was cut in the face. She was dark in color. She looked almost black. She wore this big blue shawl up over her head and hair and it came on down in a brilliant blued color draped across her bared black shoulders and arms and her yellow flowered dress she wore beneath it. The vibrant contrast of the blue and yellow and black those bright colors against her black that was what struck me. At first I thought they'd sent me some kind of nun like the ones I'd seen as a kid with that shawl the way she wore it up over her head looking all serene and shy like the figure of Mary in an old Catholic church. Then I saw how her fingernails were painted in red. I saw how her dark eyes were outlined in black making them look even blacker. I could not tell at all where she was from. She had that dark look which when first seen one cannot easily place. I lay there a little lost in my looking to her. I was lost awhile in the blackness and the cut. I stayed a time off in it. She was no American. I didn't want her to be American.

Anyway, that rainlight was nice and dim and gray coming against all the tall French-looking glass and it came on through the whole of the big room across that immaculate white of all the beds and the nice polished shine of the floor and she smelled wet from her coming in out of the rain to me and I was looking good and hard at her the way she was made up with red nails and black kohl eyes and the blued shawl and at the cut gone straight across her cheekbone clear down to the corner of her chin. It went from bone to bone and it wasn't an unbeautiful thing that had at all ruined her. I saw it was an old wound that she wore well. That was the thing about her

29

I began to think about. I thought someone had once tried to kill her and could not kill her. I thought how they'd sent me this girl who someone had once tried to kill and I was sure of that and I thought on that and I thought that she should have yet been in some school with those books held in hand sitting there like that all proper and young looking. I thought that she was yet too young for someone to have tried to kill her. But I know better.

She sat there a woman looking a girl with her hair half-hidden beneath the blue folds of that foreign-looking fabric. She took the blued shawl back up off her black hair. I looked up from her pretty cut up face to her black-black hair hung long and braided in the rainlight. Her hair came down nicely thick not too fine and straight to fall on down in those black braided strands on over her shoulders and bared arms and in the ends of her hair she had little colored beads that you'll see girls wear. I took my time looking. She stayed quiet letting me look and she was simply one by one taking up and drying the braided ends of her hair with the edge of the blued shawl and looking to me with that black cut face of hers. I saw she was not afraid of showing it. I saw that about her from the beginning. She looked right at me with it.

She said to me, "You are John LeBlanc. You are the American the priest told me about." She spoke very good English. She spoke it with a French sound to it. I had heard that kind of English spoken there.

"Yes," I said. It felt strange to hear her say it, to be named so by such a girl as her. I was John LeBlanc an American, and I have never yet known what it means.

"But you have a French name?" she said, and I heard how she was curious about it.

"I've never thought of the name as *French*," I said to her. "A lot of so-called Americans have names like that. Every good American name—it has to come from another country," I said as a clear fact.

She looked at me. She looked at me in some appraisal. She looked at me with those black-lined eyes of hers. She sat up proper and a little proud all dark against the polished and lit things of the old French room, a strange kind of beautiful black cut girl come from I do not know where, I could not tell from out of what country or why she would have come to the bedside of an American soldier to a French building not in France, looking all out of place against all that white of the bedding black and cut, serene in the light cast from those old colonial windows in Saigon, Vietnam. The smell of antiseptic was coming across the room.

She was a sight. She had dried her hair. She had the book in hand ready to read. She looked at me with the fine and delicate face of a girl. She had the full and easy body of a woman. I lingered in her look and she let me. I was gone off in her look lost a time in the whole picture of her, her arm laid dark in the light there along her yellow flowered dress on along the curve of her breast and the book in the light. The shawl was hung long and blued to the polished floor from off her shoulder. She looked all uncovered and serene. She was reposed and ready to read, and I saw new and unknown sights in her. I wanted to stay off there in them. Lost in her look I stayed travelled off a time in it. But to what land I'd went in her I could not tell. It was the lay of a land without one name. In her look was a land not to be seen or lent a sense of place in such a short-hand way by name. In them dark un-averted eyes I had no sense of known country or time. I was confounded by it. I was freed by it. I lay there stilled on the sheet in the bed gone off to as yet only imagined and unnamed places. In that look of hers which was as if without bottom or place I was taken from all what was known of myself in this time and place. She brought me back.

"You are the American soldier. You killed the woman

31

and the girl," she said straight out in her very good English. It was not an accusation.

"Did the priest tell you that?" I said looking to her cut-up face.

"Yes, the priest, he told me. He said I should know it," she said.

"Don't you have to read?" I said. "Read me a story."

"I am here to read, John LeBlanc," she said. "I will read you a story."

"That priest, he knows nothing about me," I said to her.

"He wants to help you, he sent me to you," she said. "He is a good man," she said. She lifted the cover of the book to read.

"Tell me your name," I said looking at her cut-up girl's face for I wanted to go off again from myself in this place to that one all unknown in her. I thought the name might tell me something of where she was from if not who she was.

"It's *Madeleine*," she said as though naming someone other than herself. "You see *John LeBlanc*, how we have French names," she said to me and then she laughed at that fact like a girl, the girl I'd first seen her as in her playing a little with the accidental fact of it. But her laughter was ironic. She was serious and intelligent in her look. Then I saw that her playing, her laughing didn't come from out of happiness. So, we saw something of one another then. Sometimes one is afraid of what one sees in another. But I think even then we saw the good to come. I wanted to think it. She laid a book on the edge of the bed. She opened a book. She began to read. She read me a story.

8

SCENES FROM AN ARABIAN STORY

It was one of those fancy old stories about love that was about something else she told me. It was an Arabian story she told me, and I'd never heard such a story told before in such a way by such a girl. She read from out of the French to the English, and I heard it was not ever her language, neither the English nor the French was hers and all came new and alive again as you can only hear in a voice that you've not ever yet once heard fit to what is familiar. In her telling voice she made it all sound strange and new all the old familiar-sounding words I'd long heard and knew. You'll want to believe there are yet these new stories to tell of people if you can only find a language for them so to sound them out. After all who knows how the world let alone a book should sound, and I kept quiet on her once she'd begun to speak in her strange and pleasant way. I lay there listening, I lay there forgetting.

She came back the next day and the next to tell me the story of her book and I hadn't wanted any girl to come to me and the priest he had sent her to me and she'd come and then I wanted her to and to never stop. I hadn't known I'd had that kind of want of such a girl yet to come to me. For days I listened to her sounding all pleasant and strange making it all new and unknown and I forgot all and myself in her. She came into the room to me. She came to the bed. She read on to me from out of that book in the big nicely lit old colonial room with the rows of chrome hospital beds set out on the polished stone floor the shine of that floor stretching on beneath the boys so many bodies set out on the chrome rails and the locked wheels that they'd sometimes unlock to wheel them on out across that well-kept shine to send them home in a bag.

She kept coming back to me in her telling making it

new. She came to the clean whiteness of the turned down bed sheet. She sat there beside me on the metal stool. I felt this large affection come on strong in me for her. It came up in me I do not know why, it came without my wanting it to, and it was the care of her, the life of her. She was all alive right there beside me real, she kept herself close there along me laid out in the light, and I felt myself once more come again alive and living on in her. In her reading to me all other dire sights went out of my life and she read on to me from out of the pages of the opened up book and I lived in it. I never knew that you could live in the story of a book. Then I never wanted her to stop it, I forgot everything and my own life in it, I wanted her only to come and to hear her tell of it without end, I only wanted such stories ever to go on inside the other stories without end laid out there in the louvered French light of the big ordered antiseptic room an American boy lost in the voice of a girl from a far off unknown country.

It was a good long story that need not ever end and I thought if only such telling would ever go on one could go on to live only in it forgetting one's self and all and it's really not that hard to fall in love in such times, for loving is a kind of livid forgetting, and I think I did begin to love her then for such forgetting. Then there came the one day, I couldn't remember when she'd not been there beside me, taking me off to all the times and the places of her book, and now we two went on from the one day to the next with her telling the one story framed in another, until I could no longer remember or tell, I could not remember how we'd got to where or what was told, and sometimes I thought that the way that she told it, that it was not to be found in the book but in her, but she said, "It is from the book. It is a famous book," she said to me. "You have never heard of this book?" she said to me. "It is a commonplace book."

"It is a book I have never heard of," I said. She was

surprised that I'd never heard of it. "I am a real American," I said. "I know nothing of such strange books." So she told me how they'd put a thousand nights and a night in that old Arabian story, to give me the proper title of it, when she was to go from the bed to leave me for the night once more alone and deadened without her in the dark.

"Everyone knows of this," she said to me.

"So, I want you to come to me and tell them all," I said then to her, "Won't you?" I said to her. "Come to me a thousand nights," I said, playing a little with the title of that book I'd never heard of and knew not one thing about.

And she said to me about the nights in that book then, "But it is a bad translation to the French. Much has been left out of the French, many nights. It is something that happens to books," she said in her serious and knowing way. She spoke to me of it in that kind of way, knowing these well-schooled things that I could never know without her telling me them. "I think we do not have the time for it, anyway," she said.

"We'll make the time," I said. "Find a book with them all," I said, "We can tell them all," I said to her, wanting us to go on like that in those told nights in that place together in a story. I didn't want her to tell the end, and I went on playing with it, and I saw then that she didn't mind me playing with it, for after hearing that she said to me, "Will you be happy then, will you live then again John LeBlanc, no you will only want me to read you more, you will only want me to come to you in the day and in the night and to read to you more and ever more, and to forget all, and to never stop," she said, but she did not say it in reproach, she said it in a kind of play, and I saw for the first time then that for an unhappy girl she herself still liked to play, in such a way, with her words, that there was a playfulness hidden in her, the kind you can uncover in kids, and she was no kid anymore, but she must have once been a happy girl I thought, and I wanted her to be, and I wanted us to keep on playing and forgetting, there was a happiness in her I had forgotten, and I wanted to hear all them strange nights told by her sounding like that girl I was sure she used to be.

9

ON FEELINGS OF SENTIMENT AND SENTIMENTALITY

Then the one day came too soon to us when a week or two was already gone and I saw all those nights yet off in front of us and, no matter it was still the beginning time, it was the end. As it is with most good books and even lives, too soon it was gone and done and the end was told.

I said to her, "Start in from the beginning. I don't want the end, even if it ends good," I said. But she was done with telling it and there were all the surprises of a good book and still the happy ending and a life should be so.

"There will be other books," she said.

"But do you believe in any of it?" I said to her. "Those people's lives—they aren't real," I said, and I know it's hard to make out a story of real people, to tell where the real life of living is, for books can be peopled-out with character-types, however recognizable, leaving the real life of living out, lived acts never written-out, to be passed over on a page to get on in a kind of shorthand with things and to what happens next.

"It is a story—it's true and not true—a kind of fable, a legend," she said. She was very matter of fact about it, as with children when such stories are simply told to pass the time until sleep as with a bedtime story.

"Well it's a good goddamned story," I said to her. I said that feeling something for her when I said it.

"It is an old moral story," she said to me in her serious

and knowing way of what has been written in books about our so-called lives. "It is real in that way," she said and I was glad it wasn't really real. It's easier on you when it isn't even if it's in a story. Life is hard enough.

And in that reality of our talk outside of any story left to be told, I reached out from the bed and I took up her dark and delicate hand in mine, to keep her beside me a little, and she let me take and hold her hand in mine. She let me touch her.

"Tell me a little of yourself," I said to her wanting to keep her beside me telling. She was to go and I wanted to make her stay beside me telling this or that, whatever, whether from a book or a life, it didn't matter to me. She had a lot to tell. She'd really told me nothing of herself, and I held her hand in mine to keep her there, and she let me. I was happy she let me. But she told me nothing.

She said instead, "You want to touch me? Why do you want to touch me?"

I said, "You are beautiful and alive and I know nothing about you," and I did not think about what I was saying in such a lyrical way, already loving her for no good reason. All the felt irony and absurdity of my life, the self-recrimination, sense of irresolvable damnation, it fell away from me with her, in the promise of her, and I think I was a little in love with her, no matter I was a sentimentalist in the thought, but the real feeling of it came on in me full of true sentiment. There are other things I could say, and they are all meaningless to the story.

So, she was not unhappy that I'd touched her and she let me keep her hand like that beside me, and then I wanted to think that she'd love me. I wanted to think that she'd love me if we could just keep ourselves close and quiet like that away from all the rest, off from the enclosing world, two people kept held to the feeling of a moment, which of course one cannot, and the priest then came in the big room to make the girls go and to end everything like that that was simple and real and of no consequence between two.

The priest, he'd tell the girls to go when he saw something like that going on with that kind of touch and talk. He stood there looking with his two pale hands clasped together before his black robe beneath the tall row of big louvered blinds opened up across them French hospital windows, he stood alone and cold, as aloof-looking as a statue cloaked in stone watching us boys with them girls, unmoved at it, and I thought that he did not know what to do with his own two hands, I thought that he needed to fill them with something of a life. He kept them clean and cold, and he was to make her go to keep her from me as he thought he must, for I think he knew even then that I would be bad for her, and so I called the priest on over to us and he came to us. I called *Father* to him in a happy voice and it surprised him. When I myself moved him to sensible life from his still life pose, he unclasped his two hands to come and he came, and I wanted him to know that she'd never go once and for all from me. I played a joke on him. As I had said he looked young for a priest, but I like to use *Father* on him, and when he came up to the bed and he stood beside her, I said to him, "Father I have good news."

"We are getting married," I said to him. I was very serious about it.

I said, "We want to do it right away Father. Right here, right now—you know the words. We do not have much time Father. She has stories to tell all the boys," I said that to him. But I was looking at her.

I looked at her. She let me go on with it. She was not afraid of the joke of it I think. Anyway, she went along with it, seeing what I would say. She didn't stop me. And even though we were just playing with it, I felt that we might have done it right then and there with her looking like that to me, seeing all what I would say. Sometimes the world changes for the good with what you say.

The priest said nothing looking at me. He had his unclasped hands buried in the dark of his robe. He stood there beside her looking to me. He was scrutinizing me. It was the whole un-likeliness and the simple joke of it, something so real and good, and all unlikely amidst this, and that was what made me want to do it. And, you know, I might have done it in the joke of it. Maybe we should have, but with that priest there, then with him in his wise and careful looking to me stood in his judgment, now all the fallen off absurdity and recrimination, all what I'd kept hard against, badly in my own self, the full sense of the loss of my own good self, what'd been pushed off in my want of her, came back to me to end my thinking that she'd love me, she couldn't love me, it was only my own bad want I had, and the meaning of what it all might have been, the happy hope of it was lost when the sense of loving her went out of me in my playing with it, but I kept her hand held in mine a little hard and tight just like this, knowing she would go from me not wanting her to. I didn't want to let her go for good.

"For better or for worse," I said a little seriously and I wanted the sentiment to return. I said some of the old remembered words that you'll have long heard said with little meaning but which are meant to effect the good for one's self and another in the world when spoken so. I held up our own two clasped hands in the light and I looked at the dark and the light of them put there one against the other, against the white-sheeted beds and laid out boys, and I wasn't playing, and I looked at my hand, and in the sight was stricken by what'd been done by it held there in the light against hers, and I lay there in paled repose like an invalid.

"Look. See. So if you please Father?" I said to him. I kept on with it as I could, and she kept hold of my hand, I do not know why.

"We'll make a happy couple," I said. "There'll be beautiful children," I said, and he looked at our two clasped hands held together before him in the light of the room. He looked all calmed and wise. He began to speak. He was conscientiously serious.

He said, "You do not know what you are doing—what you are saying. You are a little sick," he said and I had never been sick. "You must rest," he said like the good Father he was, and I couldn't rest.

"We want to live happily ever after till death do us part, Father," I said. I found some of the old worn words and I said them for no good reason.

"Get out your little black book," I said to him, and I kept on with it, I couldn't stop it. "Or you can use one of these if you want," and I looked over at her books. "One or the other will do. Whatever the book," I said. "You know the words."

Now, he said nothing to me. He was not even angry with me.

He simply said, "Rest, you must take care now in your own self, John LeBlanc," he said to me in some grave and serious way, in a kind of last command which was meant to comfort one's suffering once all had been said and done. And I think that people take it all too seriously even when it can mean nothing. I think in the end he was afraid to laugh at it, this sentimental and absurd life. He kept his two clean cold hands inside his black robe. He simply turned away. He went off from us in that black robe in the light.

Everyone had his little uniform.

He moved off officiously in his robe. He had his rounds to make. He sent the girls off. She stayed beside me. I lay there and felt nothing for him. He knelt himself at a bed with a boy hurt bad and laid out in the light to die far off from home beneath a nice clean sheet and the tall foreign windows. He knelt beside the boy to pray. He began to pray. I watched him pray. I felt something for him. I didn't want to feel it. I didn't want to feel anything. I was tired of seeing such loss in simple sights.

She let go my hand. But she did not get up from beside me to go.

She watched the priest. We stayed there like that. We stayed quiet on one another. We were kept close together in some simple quiet. We stayed a time like that with one another in the big room of boys and beds. I wanted to stay a long time kept like that with her. We were not uncomfortable in the quiet. There was a peace in it. There was a peace come in it to us no matter all what lay round us in us in ruin.

The priest went on to another boy to pray. She broke the quiet.

She said to me, "You are too hard on him. He has his belief," she said, "He must follow his belief."

"I am hard on myself," I said. "I have no belief—and I'm hard," I said.

"You have *none*?" she said to me wanting to know.

I took up her big storybook from beside me on the bed where it lay opened and unreadable to me and I handed the book to her. She took it.

"So, if you please? Tell me another story," I said. "Do you want to?" I said.

"Tomorrow," she said. "I will tell you another one tomorrow," she said.

"All right," I said.

"The priest," she said, and she then looked again to the priest, "He will help you," she said.

"I'm sorry," I said to her.

"You must rest," she said.

"I cannot," I said.

"You are hurt," she said.

She got up from me. She took her books up in her bared black arms. She crossed the big room going off in the light across the shine of that floor in her yellow flowered dress with the blued shawl hung on her black shoulder. At the far end of the room, she stopped in the light and she turned and looked back. She put the cloth up over her head and turned and went out to the street. I watched her go. I felt a loss. She was gone from me for good out into the lively street of Saigon to teach her schoolchildren. I lay there left to myself and the boys in the too close and abject light and I knew what I wanted from her. I wanted her always to return.

10

TWO PEOPLE GO ON TOGETHER IN A TELLING

The next day I waited for nothing but for her to come and when she came on into the big room of beds, in the sight of her all the loss was gone. I was reading from a book in English she'd left me. I looked up from the book. I closed the book. She stopped below the window in the light coming in across her dark and she looked across the boys to me. She saw me waiting out the afternoon light. She stood young and dark in the light. In her look I felt I'd regained, I'd been returned to my material life. I lived in her simple coming back. She came across the big shiny floor long and lit, walking past American boys living and dying in fresh sheeted beds with the smell of antiseptic rising in the stark light of French windows in Saigon, Vietnam, the name still strikes me strange in sound, comes as if wrongly put, no matter it has long been commonplace, and I say it to regain the full sense of it and still cannot, as now the convention of it continually erodes its actuality, it's hard to refigure it in its real when the convention carries so much attenuated sense in its shorthand image of the actual, yet I say it to myself so the time and place of us there in it may be somewhat seen, and she came right up to me and she sat right down next to me on the bed sheet beside the closed book to tell me a story just as she had said she would. She looked at that well-worn copy of Joseph Conrad's *Heart of Darkness*. I touched her arm. She let me touch her.

"Do you like that book?" she said. "Some do not."

"It's a hell of a good little book," I said. "I like it a lot," and the truth is I've always liked told stories ever since.

"I read it in school," she said. "We studied all the books in English. But you must be careful how you read books."

"You were a good student," I said.

"You were not a good student?" She said.

"I was never a good student. I only lived and read nothing."

I didn't want to talk about the book. I wanted to tell her that I felt something for her. That it was big. I said nothing wanting to say something to her that you'll want to put into words when you come back together again, are returned from a sheer sense of self-loss, persisting nothingness, to the intimation of everything to be, all that you want to be kept by at the beginning of things with someone, but you cannot too soon, and get it right, and I had no words for the extinguishment of loss I felt with her kept beside me and I know you've got to tell another something of what all is in you to begin, and I could not, I did not, I took up her hand and I put her hand in mine and I had her make up a story about two people like us.

I said, "I want to know how it can be with two people like us. I want to hear that kind of story told," I said.

"I will try. I do not know if it will be at all good," she said in her polite and good English and I held onto her hand, and her braided hair was very black in a brilliant light, and she smelled of some exotic perfume that I could not place, and I looked from her black arm laid there along her breast, I'd forgotten she was black, I looked to her fine and delicate cut girl's face, to the dark eyes that led me off again, I do not know to where, when I looked to her to try to see who she was in herself and she was quiet and I said to her, "It will be good."

"It might not be a happy story," she said.

"Tell it," I said. "Make it happy."

"I will tell you one, one happy story John LeBlanc."

And she did make up a pretty goddamned good story for me. She played a little with it and me, because I wanted all the surprises and still the happy ending that you'll find in a book, if not in a life, and we laughed a little there together over it, such a childish and good want.

She made up these two people who walked the little stone streets of a far foreign village. Their shoes hit down on the stone. She told me how they sat out awhile the two of them in a southern summer light all the afternoon at a little iron table. It was a nicely familiar and foreign light. They talked of all the things to come for them. There was much to come for them. It was a comfortable easy little story.

She told me there was a river running along a village, there was a mountain rising above the river, there were the old stone houses. They would return home to one. There was talk of a child to come and once the child came then everything they'd had to do in the world would be more than themselves only doing things and they got up from the table and they walked on along the little stone streets hand in hand with all before them.

They went on home to the house. Night came for them. They kept close together late in the dark. All was beginning for them. There was much to be done in their coming days. There was no end to what must be done. They would go on together in such days. She said some simple true things like that. All the time was kept off in front of them in a story like that.

44

11

THEN EVERAFTER EVERYTHING IS ALWAYS TO BE

"I want to hear about the child," she then said to me in my own telling. "Daddy, tell me about the child. It's me," my daughter she said. "I want to hear about that part now, about me." And I hadn't really forgotten about her, it's all founded on her, and what I was telling her. And I remembered her then again before all else, and felt the reality of us two in America and not in any story, and I said to her, "Be quiet girl, and let me tell it. I am getting to it, girl," I said in a kind of promise.

So, she was quiet once more and I went on to tell her that those two long ago imagined people upon their waking to the light of the old village along the river of that far foreign place that was told of long ago in the strange and pleasant voice of a girl herself living in her own far-off life in another land, I told her that I'd had that girl I already loved make it end good for them, with the day kept before them with the child coming, and she did.

"Mother's a good storyteller," she said and I'd never said it was her mother. But in the end she'd kept it good and happy for me like I'd wanted and I think she wanted to see it that way too after all what she'd seen in her own life.

Then I lay there along her thinking of them two people living far off in that story with all the time yet in front of them, and how they'd be happy. I saw how they'd live a good life long and well and because they were nowhere to be found but in a story, they'd stay forever young and happy in such a telling and I wanted it to end so for them if it cannot for us. And with all that telling of them happily-invented people ended, now we didn't really know what to say to one another of what we should in the actual passing time of our own lives. There with her beside me with the stories once and for all stopped in the brilliant light of the big French room with the light hitting on hard across us when I know we felt some real things for one another, we couldn't find the words for the true feelings that you'll have in a young life, and then we said nothing of what was before us in the coming days of our own time.

I lay there stilled in the bed. She was gone silent beside me. With her telling of them made up people in that imagined time finished, I felt again how one goes on with another in simply the telling of this or that, and we stayed shut up and wordless about what large and little things we felt that we might have put into words and we already had a lot to tell one another if we were to go on good with one another and we told nothing.

We didn't know how to tell about our own real things. We were too young. Too much had happened too young. I know I didn't want to say the real things wrong to her. I couldn't even say them right to myself laying there. I lay there afraid to say the real wrong things to her, but I didn't want everything to be left off in front of us, with it all left unsaid, and as if never now real, our regard, the felt sentiment for one another, when not one good true word had been put to the feeling between us. I didn't want her to go off for good from me, as one can from another in such times as these, without ever once knowing someone in the end no matter all that you've felt and felt true, to go off now from one another as if only these two accidental and passing acquaintances having met by some unhappy chance, without one real act begun between us of knowing one another, of coming to know another in the world you've begun to feel true if not lasting things for, and when I felt she might go and leave me there alone, lost to myself in that deadened and absolute quiet full of the possibilities of unspoken feeling, I said to her remembering how she was a dark cut girl come from out of an unknown country, "But Madeleine, tell me—how did you come, here, to this place?" I said to her to keep her there beside me telling something of her herself, and having said that I looked round in great and profound disbelief at all and us and that she'd herself come to this, and she didn't tell me that that I'd asked her. She didn't tell me anything then about herself, she wanted to know about me, she wanted me to tell her all them things I've already talked about, and there is no promise or possibility in telling them kinds of things. She wanted me to tell her the real things. And I know no acquaintance will ever want that from another.

She said, "Tell me what you did in that war, John LeBlanc," she said to me straight out instead of answering me. "The priest told me that you are sick from it," she said in some feeling of care she had in her.

"I can't talk about that," I said. "You know what it is. It is enough." I looked away from her to the beds rowed out in the light in the room.

"But you must say it," she said, "To get well, to go home, I think you must tell it," she said. I looked back at her from the boys.

"I have told it. The words make it worse, Madeleine. There's nothing to be done for it."

She wanted to help me and I wanted us to stay a boy and a girl to one another these two kids kept off from the world first in one another and we would have been but for hearing our own names said like that in such question by one another already heavy with the weight of history.

We couldn't be kids. She went on with it.

She said to me, "You must remember it John, you must say it to yourself—you must look to it in yourself, it is there in you. It is in you," she said, "The killing, the living. Hold it before you, look to it, then you will get well," she said. "You will go home. You will be happier for it."

"The sight will never go."

"You will be stronger than it," she said.

It was a pronouncement. She stopped.

"I'm all right," I said. "If that priest told you I'm sick, he's wrong. I really feel fine—I won't go home, now," I said, and I looked up to that high fancy ceiling and I tried to see what all that meant, to follow out the consequence of such words, to see what good could yet come in a life, and I couldn't but in her, I didn't see myself gone off from her, gone from her off happily to home, the good I saw was in her, I saw her.

She was before me.

I saw her all dark and unknown before me wanting me to be well and I saw how I'd go on good in her. I lay there with her herself become a kind of inexplicable center to myself and all the good to come, and in that strong feeling for her, in my badly wanting to go on off with her to all before us, I saw nothing more of what all was done and real. All other sights went. Again I was briefly freed. That must be love. There was only that strong feeling, want of her and not of home and in that wanting I'd cut off the weak sick feeling for what was done, for what couldn't ever be undone, but must be buried and forgotten in you as if it'd been done by another, all that that I couldn't put words to, to tell myself what it was, to say it to see it to hold it before me to look to it as she said I should, I'd closed it off in me in seeing her cut dark and alive before me. All the world was gone. She was the world. I was freed in a feeling of loving her, with all the hard-hitting loss gone in that one imagined moment of loving such a woman as her and no other and I was held transfixed as if in the center of my own life in the overcoming feeling of that want of her, and I said to her without thinking, "Could you love me?" and she looked at me blankly. I couldn't say anything real to her but that I loved her.

Then I felt like a fool once I'd said it, I felt this real self-shame for saying something so sentimental so straight out to her in such weakness and wished I hadn't said such a goddamned sentimental thing so openly to her, though I felt it true and that I loved her. I loved her more than a little when I said it, with all the persisting consuming want driving the one felt word on to the next un-thought one. In the feeling, the words made the words. So, I'd gone on with it no matter what, without once thinking it through, with the one spoken word leading on to another uttered all un-thought, "Could you love me?" I said to her, I said that, and I looked away from her in some weak shame and the strong feeling and its rightness passed, when in the act of saying it, whether it was wanting or words, I was afraid that she could not ever love me in return.

She took it seriously. The words were real to her.

"You are good, you are kind," she said. I saw her looking for and finding her own words. "You think you are bad, but you are not."

"We could try it," I said. But the feeling for it was gone and the words had then made it less than it was. I looked off to the beds and boys. "It can't be that bad. We'll keep telling stories with good and happy endings," I said and the feeling for it had now passed in the sight of that room. I saw the room.

"You will have only happy things to tell me, John LeBlanc?" she said not at all in question in her all along knowing better.

"Madeleine, I'll get out of here, and I'll come and tell you all good and happy things," I went on with it. I made it all less than it was.

She looked at me. It was a quiet and wise look for one so young. She took my hand. She held my hand in hers as would a good friend when visiting the sick. She stayed quiet and careful with her words.

She waited for me to speak. I did. In that touch of hers, then I broke the solitude between us.

"I'd tell you the bad things, if I could—I can't get the words right," I said. "Maybe you can teach me how to talk—

49

and still be happy."

"You want what's good," she said. "You have done bad things, but you are not bad," she said.

She was looking at my hand. She was studying it as though to see what good and bad things had been done by it. She said in her careful looking to it, "You are good," and in her words, in that touch of hers, I badly wanted to let her love me, and to tell her all, and felt that she might a little in time, and some of the feeling of the rightness I'd first felt in my feeling of loving her, returned in her words about the goodness. It returned in her regard.

I looked off to the chrome and light of the room.

"We'll go off together," I said, seeing it again, and us in another time, not now that room round us, and all how it would be. "What if we went off somewhere together?" I said to her and I was looking out to the boys laid out in the light and the words were real in the regained feeling however meaningless in their spoken fact.

"It is not possible, it is the end of a war, we must go home," she said. "You know that."

"Would you go with me?" I said looking out to the boys. "It must be possible—we're still young, we could go off someplace good, and fall in love." I said that to her. I said them kinds of easy earnest words to her and you've got to tell yourself it's possible, and in my act of speaking them now, them forward-looking words once more had their own motive power, and I wanted to get up from that bed and to walk right straight out of that room with her, to make a clean break of it and to start all over again and new, and to do that must be a feeling, to walk right out of one's past to all what is to be, as surely as you'd walk from out of one room to another, and I felt that if we just did that right then, if we went off together in the materiality of such a feeling, in the rightness of the regained feeling, if we left off from the one given world to arrive in another of our own making, I felt it would all go good.

We were yet young enough to begin again and would.

"But, tell me what you did in that war, John LeBlanc," she said wanting me to say the bad hard things to her even though she'd already heard them from that priest and she knew what they were, and I heard how she wanted to help me and that she knew I was fooling myself in them easy sentimental words about going on good, that I could only see and say the too simple, however true, things about what good two people could go off and do together having never yet gone and done one good thing together.

In her words the past came present. In her wanting to help me I looked to her in her care, cut before me, and I saw clear acts of killing. They were in me. She was looking at me, and she said, "What do you see?" and looking to her, I didn't say it. "Tell me, John," she said for me to put it into word, in her care she brought back up in me that which should not ever be lived, let alone seen once more in life in what words were to be put there in the room between us. "Tell me," she said and I saw her a woman looking a girl, a mother and a daughter the life of them laid in the light, her looking to me seeing nothing in her looking, the blade in the light, wet steel run in my hand, my hand fallen from her, my hand fell from her, her hand was gone, and there in the sight in that looking in that touch of her gone, I felt the condemning impossibility of regaining some good sense of myself. In what she'd said to help me, the forward-feeling of all the rightness went out from me. There was the room round us. The wounded and dying were round us. We were enclosed in it. In a life one cannot walk out of what is done to what must be done as one walks from out of one room into another, one must walk from out of one life into another and cannot even in love. In the depleted realization, I fell into a renewed sense of dire self-condemnation. It was material. She couldn't help me. I was caught and kept against myself. In the fallen feeling, I couldn't let myself be happy. I said to her in ruined feeling, with little care left for myself, even as though to damn myself and all hope of us in deep unhappiness, "How did you get cut—tell me who cut you," I said to her, seeing how she was this kind and caring girl looking like she should never have been hurt like that by anyone but who'd been badly cut up, wounded by someone who'd wanted to hurt her for good. I said that and looked out at the wounded boys. I wasn't careful with my words.

"That's not a happy story John LeBlanc," she said. "Don't you want a happy story?"

"You told me—to tell the bad things—have you ever told it?" I said to her.

"It is not a good story," she said. "You do not want to hear it."

"Tell me, if you want to. But, you don't have to."

"Tell me, why do you want to touch me? Tell me why you want to touch me. Tell me that, John LeBlanc," she said to me.

"I feel something for you, it is big, real—it feels like love, Madeleine," I said.

"You like me cut?" she said. She saw that. She said it.

"I like how you look." I saw life when I saw her.

"Why do you like how I look?"

"I told you, I feel alive with you. Don't you feel it?"

"I'll tell it to you then. If you want me to—do you want me to?" she said. She said, "Once upon a time there was a girl in a city by the sea," she began on it in her storybook voice, "There was a happy-beautiful girl," she went on in a voice of affected irony then she stopped.

"There was a soldier," she said. "It was a soldier in a war," she said flatly, and she did not begin it. She stopped it.

"All right—don't," I said. "You're right. I don't want to hear it."

She stopped at the soldier. That was the beginning. I saw what it was about. It was a soldier and I lay there and I couldn't hear it. I didn't want to see that, for her to put that into words, I didn't want to see that when I saw her. When I saw her I never wanted to see that. I turned from her. I looked across the laid out boys. I did not look at her.

"We're both hurt," she said as a fact.

We were shut up and wordless. We'd never said so much and we'd said nothing. She turned my hand in hers, in a last studying it if not reading it. The priest came into the big room and he stood there beneath a tall window along the wall looking at us two kept close and quiet on one another, and I couldn't tell what he thought of us together like that, these two kids telling their already too-long little histories to one another, holding on to one another's hands wanting to be happy at the end of a war. He did not look unkind. I know that he was not unkind. But when she looked at him, and she saw him, she took her hand away from mine as if she'd been seen doing something that shouldn't be so openly seen.

"I must go," she said and she stood from me to go.

"Stay with me a little—I want you to," I said laid out in the light.

"It doesn't matter what we want, John LeBlanc," she said.

"Stay a little beside me," I said to her, and I wanted to tell her some true things. I had some real things to tell her. I'd told her nothing, and I know that one must truly speak to keep those who would love you close. Or there is only the quiet to come. But the time was up.

The priest came to the bed.

"I want you to keep telling stories, Madeleine, I want you to tell the kind of stories you can't ever get to the end of," I said to her, and I was looking at him, to where he stood there waiting along us, and I was not playing now, and I wanted badly to keep her there beside me telling this or that no matter what was told, and she'd stood to go, and she stayed from my hand with him there. The priest spoke to her in French and I heard my own name sounding strange in the French the way he said it to her, and she was to go from me, and I simply said to her then, "Come tomorrow," and I could not remember now when she'd not come and been there beside me taking us off together to all the far off places in what she told.

"It's time. I must go," she said to me.

"I will see you tomorrow," I said. I let her go.

"You must rest, John LeBlanc. She must go to teach," the priest said to me, and he kept himself there beside her.

The time was up. She gathered up her books. The priest lifted the sleeve of his black robe and he looked at his watch as he went out. The priest walked off officiously in his robe. She turned to follow out after him. She went from me as she must to go teach her schoolchildren. At the end of the room with him gone out, she stopped and looked back across the boys to me. That picture of her standing there looking back struck me. She stood fixed in the light. She was strongly framed by the tall colonial windows. She was all dark in the light. She looked all out of place like a girl come from another age, from a time you could not put a clock to, to tell truly of its age, standing there in that so-called contemporary time to look out as if upon a kind of new world placed before her, darkly posed in great contrast as though by some famous long dead painter illustrating a girl of exotic origin in so many fine strokes of a brush as you will see in an old portrait painting hung in good light upon a high wall of a fancy building with tall antiquated ceilings. She followed the priest out and was gone. I was left with that picture of her not her. I wanted to get up out of that bed to go out to her in the street where we would walk along just a boy and a girl in the lively light and talk of this or that easy little thing in that place and time a little in love with one another for no good reason. I would have told her some true things that I'd never once told. I told myself, that when she came back again beside me, I'd tell her all what was in me. I'd tell her. I'd keep her beside me telling. Telling was keeping. You know that.

12

IN SEARCH OF A POETICS OF REVERIE, NOT DEAD RECOLLECTION

"Daddy, don't stop," she said to me and I'd stopped only to see what to say. I didn't want to, I wanted to tell it to her good to keep her close, all happy and home, and I'd stopped only to think on how to go on good, how I went on, wanting to find the real words for the rote facts. "Daddy, tell me about mother, now," my daughter she said that to me there in America when I went quiet on her, and I looked out from the porch of the house to the great lake water blue and immense stretching to the far line of the sky off behind the green-leaved trees of the bluff, with the white sails of far off sailboats appearing here and there between the black trunks of trees, the distant boats seeming to be not so much sailing that water as hauling on home, to far destinations, through the deep water of the great lake north to Traverse City or south to Chicago.

I wanted to tell it good, and now it's hard to tell of any real time like I've been doing, in a way, the actual lived days so long marked off in the convention of clocks, calendars, years, until you've remembered the feeling of being in them to get back beyond the so-called catalog of facts once more to the life, to tell how such days were undergone, not so much simply lived, as endured, as though you'd gone through them in a kind of brute travel, though you'd gone nowhere in them, nothing having yet been followed out from them, as all is now, and I told her that that is when she went off and she didn't come back. I always thought the priest had something to do with it. He'd come by my bed and take a good look at me in his going on to all the other boys. I let him go. He went on to the other boys with what he must. Some of them boys they'd lost their sense of humor and he had them with those little black books beside them that they never opened up to the light. I was afraid for some of them. He wanted to help them in his way. He'd help them in his way. He had a way about him. It's true that he was not at all that bad for a priest. He wanted to do good. He wanted to do good for me and for all them and everyone and he didn't know what was good for anyone.

  He came on along the beds and he looked, and I said to him in the look, "You sent her away," and it stopped him, the accusation of it, and stopped there beside me in the light he said, "Rest. Rest," he said gently, surely, somewhat imploringly like the good father he was.

  But I couldn't rest all laid out like that in the light only wanting to get to her, now to be with her more than any one thing else, anyone, anywhere else off in the world, forgetting all in love like that, like forgetting your own life. You can't and don't ever rest yourself wanting only to get on to another, and not to home, as if that is where your life must now be with them before the rest, and can be nowhere else, or you've lost yourself for good. I had lost myself gone far off in her from the beginning in being kept in all that forgetting. I felt it must be her from the beginning. I think she herself even loved me a little when she went at last not to return in having found some good soldier to touch her in some care and I was left at last only to that priest and he stood there at the foot of the bed stopped before me in his obligation to do good not going on. He could do nothing for me. I began to laugh in the light at his words.

  "You must take care in yourself," he said once more

to me, "You must quiet yourself. Or you will be unwell," he said. "I have told you," he said, "You will be happy one day," he said. "This will pass," he said. He said such meaningless things.

But I'd told him none of it all what it was in me. We spoke to one another as if in two other languages. I laughed unhappily in the light. He looked at me kindly in his gentle fatherly way. He thought he knew things. He didn't know a goddamned thing. He wanted to do good. He'd do good. He felt his obligations and he spoke of them.

"Quiet now. Do not make yourself sick—," he said to me in my laughing.

"I am not sick," I said.

He said to me to help me, "It is all a usual kind of thing this war."

"Do not tell me what is usual," I said to him laid there in the stark antiseptic light of the room left to him without her. The unhappily-felt laughing was gone, but rest did not come. Without her it would not come. Without her all good self-regard was gone. Without her there was the green of the field come the reddened life of them two come up my hands and arms the mother gutted and dead in the green the child come alive by my hand calling out wildly to no one in the world born against the burning sky. I was sickened in seeing them.

"Nothing is usual," I said and was undone.

"She is gone to another country," he said to quiet me.

"Go away from me, *Father*," I said to get rid of him.

He went away for good. That I thanked him for, if nothing else.

13

THE RECORDED SELF
IS THE AUTHORIZED EDITION OF THE SELF

She was gone. I was at the end of myself and deadened without her. The priest went on his way by me making his rounds to all the boys. She was gone for good and the doctor came dressed in his white. He looked at a chart. He took out a pen. He said I was healed. "You're going to live no matter yourself, John LeBlanc," he said and he signed a piece of paper and he handed it to a nurse to discharge me from his care. There was nothing he could do for me. The Captain with his shiny shoes and brass shoulders brought the official paperwork.

"Fill this out and sign it, boy."

"What for?" I wasn't signing anything for them.

"You're getting expedited," he said.

"You getting rid of *me*?" I said to get him to see the joke of that.

"You're going home," he said flatly with nothing left alive in him.

He dropped the paperwork on the bed and left. I filled it out in the afternoon light. I was to get clean out of the whole goddamned place. I was to get for good. It is always in the paperwork. Remember that it is always in the paperwork. One must remember that. More than the people it's the paperwork from place to place. The people are nothing to it. The nurse came and took it. I watched her cross the room and she put it in a manila envelope. A soldier came for it and left with it and all I had to do was to wait for my orders. But for the company of my own dire sights, I lay there in a day or two of stark and absolute nothingness. The day went and dark came. The light came. Nothing more happened until the paperwork came. Without the proper paperwork nothing could ever happen to you. Without paperwork you'd never get on with the rest of your life.

When the orders came there was to be a kind of court. It said "Inquiry." I was to appear before it. There was a time and date written on the inked paper. I was on what they called *in-country R&R*. There were all the authorized forms for it, and there wasn't even a real war anymore in those days, and that was kind of funny. I was off duty. I was on my own recognizance. I saw how I'd go get a room. I'd get out of sight from them for good. Maybe that's what they wanted. Everything I'd said would be filed away and shut up, buried in the dark of a drawer for good. I laid the paperwork on the manila folder on the metal stool there beside the bed where they'd all sat in their turn. I looked at the typed-out time of the official date. I had a week before I had to appear. I saw how I'd walk the wide open boulevards in the light. I'd get lost in the congregated little streets hung in shadow. I'd go off for good. They'd never find me. I'd be free. But in the happy thought of it I knew I couldn't be. I couldn't let it be shut up for good in the dark of a drawer. She'd told me all along to keep it in sight. I had to get it out of me. I saw how I could in telling it to them. I'd make it all official to get it out of me for good. I couldn't let it alone. I'd return. I'd return to them. I had real things to tell them. I'd tell them.

The dark came. I went into it. I was going early in morning. I lay there uneasy in sleep un-quieted in dark hours, and early in morning light she came to me real in dream. She came naked in the coming light and she came on into the bed and there she lay herself down to sleep beside me all black against me and the white of a clean sheet and I touched her. I touched all her body beneath my hand. All was gone in that touch of her. I touched the line of her breast and her dark girl's back down on along the length of her leg and she let me and she wanted to be touched like that by some soldier no matter what'd been done to her and that's what I couldn't get out of my head that she wanted to be touched so and was and with her own hand she touched the holes that went clean through she touched me there and I wanted her to and I let her in her own want and we were all in one another all alive in one another in our want in the coming light and it was to be all new and different as if waking once and for all all happy and lost.

I awakened alone lost to the old and same.

The nurse she shook me waking me from my want once more to the world and in my coming back to being without her, I was badly waked without her, and became afraid of who and where I was in my waking, and I named the place and who I was in it, not at all to know the nature of the world, but simply to try to fix the notion of myself as I'd been fixed in her, to send the fear of the continual loss of my own good sense of self out of me, to make myself whole once more in the repeated act of my own awakening, while, now I know, signifying nothing of fixed meaning or self in such sheer repetition of waking and naming itself, but the spoken facts of the material world and myself did then fit up to one another in some necessary accuracy, and did account for a real once more, like plotted coordinates intersecting on a map, a logistical designation of persons and places that was true, however sufficient to a larger sense of self, and the nurse she said to me, "Quiet," and I got myself up out of bed in early morning light quieted, and the nurse she found my few things, and she got my canvas bags, and she helped me pack up my bags, and she said not without care, "You know who you are. You know where you are, John LeBlanc," she said in that way that leaves everything settled and little in you and she left me to keep to herself, as though what life was left in her herself must now be kept close, and I looked round to the boys and there was nothing new to see.

The boys slept badly laid in dream beneath white sheets. Some lay starkly waked. I walked the row of beds across the polished shine of the floor. The nurse looked out an unlatched window she'd swung open to the air. I walked by her. She looked out in her own loss and she did not turn and I reached the far end of the room and I did not stop to turn back there myself to look. I walked the white and browned patterned tiles on out of the old hospital wing forward to cross the floor, and there at the end of the room, as though now to walk right out into another new life to come, I simply stepped with my packed bags through these tall green doors that looked like a set of louvered shutters, and walked right out of the old converted building that was once itself a school of all things before the war. I went out into a barbed wire courtyard leading to the street, with everything in the room behind me to become a long gone finished place and forgotten. The morning light was coming from the east down the street. A taxi came. I put the two green army bags in the trunk. The driver shut the trunk and I got in the taxi and shut the door.

14

A SENSE OF PLACE IS EXPRESSED IN A FACE

It's almost like the beginning of another new story, if not a life. You'll think you're at the end of things, if not now a life, and it's all there in front of you beginning. It's all beginning. I sat back in the taxi and we drove through the streets of the city. There was no end to the city. I looked for a time out a window in leisure. I might have been a tourist. The shop fronts passed. The people passed. We passed many people. There was no end to the people. I don't know where all we went. I remember going off from the front of the US Army 3rd Field Hospital set there in the city outskirts with its porticos and French louvered windows, I think on through what was once called John F. Kennedy Square, with the central Saigon Post Office and its grand-arched wrought-iron arcade filled with light, and there were the rising twin brick bell towers of Notre Dame Cathedral towering red in Marseilles brick set against the sky in their cross-topped spires on the Square with the stone statue of the Virgin Mary out front, then the fashionable iron-balconied Hotel Continental sitting in its pastel colors, named after the prestigious Hotel Continental in Paris, the Saigon Opera House, built after the Opera Garnier of Paris in the flamboyant quasi-gothic style of the Third French Republic the façade of the Opera a replica of the Petit Palais in Paris, where we came to the grand rising floors of the Hotel Majestic laid out in classical French Riviera style, and to the old Hotel Rex, where the American officers had rooms in the war, the most famous of the old French-built hotels, the one that'd housed the first American soldiers to come in-country with its rooftop garden and bar. I've looked the names of such landmarks up lately.

We passed by all that into the life of the place. The driver drove the little narrow streets and we came into a European-looking quarter full of commotion and I had him stop and I got out of the car lost beneath rising floors of iron balconies and shuttered windows and lost like that as if come to another country, I stood in a street called the *rue de l'Abondance* there beneath the city amongst the people of the city knowing none of them. You'll want the names to tell you where you are, and they'll often tell you nothing the way you want. The driver opened the trunk and I got up the green bags and smelled the traveled canvas. I sat the bags down on the street in the coming light along the façade of buildings rising with their little black iron balconies. He drove off and I was left standing there with the green army bags, to be enclosed by that vibrant ongoing life of passing people, things and voices, and being caught up in the congregation of that daily life, but for the bags and myself, it was hard to tell that there'd been a war.

    I stood there and saw how it would be to be lost in it. I looked across the street to two old women in black trousers who were sitting on the front step of a narrow shuttered building in the strong light cast down the street across them. They looked awhile at me. They looked at me as if knowing me and they knew nothing of me. They knew I was American. You could always see that. I looked at them women and the balconied building above them and felt I could have been somewhere like France but for the faces, and in them faces juxtaposed to that architecture, as in finding old disparate photos, incongruously placed images, I knew there'd been a war there a long time. The rue de l'Abondance was a market street, and up from them women and where they sat everything was for sale. The street was lined and filled with food, clothing, heaps of provisions, all the hardware of life was stacked, spread and piled out along tables in the light, heaped in bowls and on trays, hung in baskets, shaded from the rising sun in makeshift awnings, here and there, nicely casting the tables and the faces of the market sellers into shadow, where the young and the old of that old colonial quarter walked the street along them looking. The place was all alive in the light. A couple of girls came up the street along the opened-up shop fronts in the morning light, and the old women talked on, and I got up the army bags, and I walked on behind the girls. The old women laughed, watching me going on down the street after them girls, and the girls stopped and stood in a doorway. There a man was selling fish from out of large water-filled ceramic bowls painted in bright green and yellow colors. I could smell the water and the fish. I looked up from the cool water of the bowls to them girls. They stood there young and thin with their long black hair. I looked down at the fish in the clear shadowed water and I looked away and I went on. The girls stayed there in the doorway talking-laughing sounding young and I went on down the street off from them for good. I went down the street, on along the shops, and passed bent men carrying baskets hung heavy on strong backs, their stacked goods swaying on bent poles, and I was a boy carrying my own bags heavy in hand. I hadn't gone far, when I stopped under a sign and I looked into an open doorway and went in to a man at a counter. He was smoking a cigarette and reading a magazine. There was a radio playing jazz. He turned a page of the glossy magazine and I sat the bags down on the black and white patterned tiled floor and he looked up from the counter and saw me and that I was American. He put his cigarette down in an ashtray filled up with the heaped butts of cigarettes. There on the counter was a blue cigarette packet with a dark Gypsy woman on the cover. It said *Gitanes*. There was a layer of blued smoke hung in the air of the little lobby.

"Do you have dollars?" he said in his good English.

"I will give you dollars," I said to him in mine.

I gave him the dollars and they looked green and strange to me held in his hand and he took a key for the room off a wall and he gave me the key and he looked at the green bills as I went up the stairs to the door of the room and opened it.

I sat my bags down on the floor and shut the door. I dropped the key on the battered veneered dresser that had a silvered mirror. The room was painted a strange aquamarine color and the plaster walls were nicely cracked. I went over and sat down on the end of the made up bed and looked out across the cracked and dingy linoleum floor, to the slats of the green paint-flaked wooden blinds, to the black rails of the little iron balcony. The mattress was hard. I heard the voices of girls below in the street. I wanted to go to the balcony to see them.

I lay back on the bed and looked up. I looked round at the blue-green aquamarine color of the room and the room was hot and humid and that cool color reminded me of swimming pools in summer and I saw how it would be to get to water and to go out deep in it and I listened to voices coming in off the street and to cars going off in the city. In hearing them distant going sounds I felt free. I was freed in some vague sense of anonymity. I fell asleep on the bed with my clothes and boots on. I thought I heard French. I dreamt bad dreams. I was not yet free.

15

TO BE LAID ALONG A GIRL
ALIVE IN THE NIGHT, IS TO FORGET A GIRL

    I waked in the room in the night. I got up and went down the stairs. I walked with the people in the city. I walked in the day and in the night with all the people of the city of Saigon, saying the name to know the place if not the people. I walked. I did not sleep. I saw the familiar faces of girls. There were all the girls. I saw the beautiful bones of the faces. I saw them all as if always knowing them and I knew none of them.

    The days were indistinguishable.

    By chance I met a girl. I found a girl in a not unpleasant dark place. It is the only way to forget a girl. I touched her breast and her body, all her body in the close dingy dark, and we were all in one another and all alive in one another. Afterwards I lay there stretched along her naked in the night. It could have been any girl. It could have been any one of them at all and it was her. I'd paid for her and held her hand and she told me her name.

    "Phuong," she said to me.

    "Phuong?" I said to her and I tried to say it right. And I was happy hearing the sound of her name. It is a name I have seen used even in books. It meant *phoenix* in the language.

I said, "Phuong," to her and she thought it was very funny the way that I said it wrong and strangely and she laughed and I was not unhappy hearing her laugh. There was something of life in her girl's laughter at hearing her name said so unfamiliar like that though I'm sure that she'd heard it before like that from a boy. I said it to her naked in the night, feeling alive with her and all right with her there in the dark in feeling her beside me laid out young and alive.

"Phuong," I said. I said, "Phuong there are these times come upon you you cannot be alone," and I lit a cigarette and I lay there drunk and I gave her one and she smoked it elegantly, slowly, and she did not understand me and all what I said.

I looked to her naked in the night. She did not look away. I was all alive in the nights with her not ever now alone with her when I would think of her. Sometimes I saw her with her feeling her remembering her. Remembering feeling her I pictured her in the night and in the day not ever now alone. It was all of them in me now. I know it is not a simple thing to see or say. It is all an unreal lived thing. There is sky. There is grass. There is wetness. There is darkness.

I lay there with her in the night looking up and I remembered that story of the child that she'd told me, and I saw how it would be for two people like us to be like that. I told myself a happy little story. I set out an imagined scene. There I was laid along her and there the child was. There we the three of us were laid out in the long grass happy and home in the light. It was America. There in America her and I and the little girl we stayed happy and home in the light. I saw it like that, I saw how to be back home once again for good like that with that child and her in America, and in such thoughts of children, now come to me beyond all such imagined scene, I hear her, at such times I hear her say, "Daddy." "Daddy," she says to me in my own telling, her voice coming to me in America from the center of all things to unsettle everything, and of course I'd told her none of what I was telling myself. There was her, and the porch, and the lakewater through the trees. There was the grass. There was the room on the rue de l'Abondance. I lay there far off in a room in a foreign city, and it was her and it could have been any one of them at all. It was a girl named Phuong. Now it was her and none of the rest of them at all. It's like that when you're young. When you're young you'll want to find a way to be happy. You'll think you can. I was young and lay naked in her room in the night and thought of home and in her I was gone to home. I looked up in some peace come to me, and in the feeling of repose closed my eyes laid out along her. But in such unguarded respite, in my want of peace, the boys came back to me un-beckoned in the thin leisure of that dark, in their dim shapes they came these luminous resemblances all alive in uneasy unwanted reminiscence. Their faces came lit and livid in the dark. They took me from her to them in their talk, they were alive and dead talking on with an easy smile and a smoke telling you a happy little remembered story of what all they'd lived and done, would yet go do, how they'd get back home to be happy. In the sound of their sure and lived up talk they took me off with them, and I didn't want to go off from her to anywhere or home with them. Laid along her, I travelled on in their talk back to the acts and objects of actual places, I heard the casual metallic flip of the Zippo lighter and the now-dead and forever-young voice say in astonished wonderment, playful in the necessity of non-reflection, "Burned them to the bone—the whole fucking family roasted-up like marshmallows," after all such a story, it has to be a kind of joke to even tell it, and I saw the houses lit out beyond the grass burning against the idyllic sky, while there beside me he stood, and in a ragged grin he said, "Look, the fucking brains come out with a boot, just like a cracked-open coconut," and he took a full drag on his smoke, his head falling back, all alive, exhaling up into the happy blue not with displeasure, to hold his gaze on the white trails of

B-52s cutting north in geometric formation through the pristine sky. There the boys they talked on of home all alive in the greened field in the light. They saw all how they'd get to home. They'd be happy home like they'd never been, they were sure now like they'd never been. America was the place to get back to, to be in for no good reason, America's always the real place to get back to, to be in and it's just a word, a name said far off from home to feel some good come of a life lost between beers and a smoke, the name comes to tell you who, if not where you are, and lost like that as if in search of self or home, I found I was waked there with them laid out down in the green with the houses burning against the far sky, I was returned to my own old self not to home with her laid along me her hand on me her hand on the knife in the green, and with her hand on me my blood in hers the room came round me real, she had her hand on me there to wake me, and I found myself laid along her badly waked in the room travelled nowhere in troubled sleep, there she was naked and alive laid beside me real in the room in the night, and I said "Phuong," to keep myself there with her and none of them, knowing once more who and where I was in the night in the name. I said "Phuong," and I lay there quieted. I found myself there with her laid close along me in unsettled sights and with none of them boys.

"You sleep bad, boy," she said to me in her straightforward English.

"If I could—I'd stay awake forever," I said to her and she didn't understand me and I heard the French out a window and I followed it by ear in the street and I didn't understand it and I saw her dark and cut and it didn't matter whether in my waking or my sleeping the one sight was kept superimposed upon the other in my badly recollected self and she kept me there with her in her nakedness in the night with the bed sheet strewn to the floor in the indistinguishable dark.

"You go now," she said laid out there young and alive

along me.

"I won't go," I said.
"You have money?" she said.
"I have money," I said. She took it.

I lit a cigarette. I gave her one. I looked up in the dark. I looked to her laid out along me. I saw her. I couldn't see how to be back home good again without her. I saw her. I tell you, I could not see it at all, how to be back home once again for good without her. But you must tell yourself such things to return once more to yourself if not to home, and you will tell them.

16

A KIND OF COURT

So, I'd told myself a happy little story about America. Then it was America. There we were home in the light. And I'd told her nothing of it or anything of the boys. She was a girl, the girl I still see her as, drawing out her picture as she could while I went on with my own, remembering what'd been real, trying in my own way to tell what was true and telling her little. It's that I'd said her name out loud, "Phuong," I'd said and that's what'd broke the whole thing. I'd looked to her and I'd said "Phuong" and she'd said, "Daddy, what is it, Daddy?" and I don't know why I'd said her name to her like that spoken all of a sudden from inside the story but that it came out un-beckoned and kept me put with her there, there on that porch in America in what'd already been told and not in the days I saw coming. I was seeing everything to come. I'd been counting off the days. I'd counted off the days in my head to make sure it was the day, feeling it was too late, but it wasn't. The day had come. That was the day I had to go see those old men, to tell them what I had to tell them. I was waked alone in the room on the rue de l'Abondance and I turned from that shuttered light of the cracked-open blind and looked back into the thinly shadowed room. I saw how I lay there awake on the sheet of the bed without her in morning light. The day was low and gray and I'd slept badly and I didn't want to move from that bed to get up and to go anywhere again but to her, let alone to them men. I'd come to a stop. There was only her and that in the night. That is all. Stretched out there naked on that sheet looking up in the light I saw how I might've never now moved again to do one real thing in the world, and I thought then that it's better to do nothing, or as little as possible in the world, if not in a life, and I lay there awhile on the sheet in the coming light as if with this free choice before me, to go or not to go, to do or not to do what is demanded of one in the world, and the emptied insensible act of not doing was not free, for I felt the demand of the world and that I must act, that there was this self-imposed compulsion to act, to absolve one's self in the necessity of action and willful return. Though, one naturally hesitates, however briefly, at such turning points in a life, stopped before going on to such irrevocable things. And in the knowing that I'd go back to them, to tell them all what I had to tell them, yet I lay there, going nowhere, and I thought a moment how it'd be if I didn't, if I let go of all, of all myself, of all convention and conscience. I lay there and I imagined the freedom in never returning to them or to my own past. They'd never find me. It'd be hard to find me. Maybe they'd never look to find me. You'll think you have these free choices to make in a life and when you run them happily through your head, you can make out the logic as you want, tending toward the want, not the compulsion, or, one might say, duty to hold one's self accountable. But one must hold one's self accountable. I've always known that and that for people like me who can't get clean out of what they've done that there is only freedom in doing that. And I saw very clearly then that if I didn't go to them that I'd never be free. And when I saw myself not going to them like that, I saw how that deliberate lack of return would be forever hung on me, unhappily round me, as an immovable, persisting weight of self-condemnation. It's the kind of thing you carry in the body. The body remembers. And when I felt that direness come up real inside me once more, I found I wanted to get up right then and go to them as I must. So, in what you might call my simple moral deliberation, if one can these days yet use such earnest terms, I found, or rather concluded, mainly from feeling rather than thought, that I had to hold myself accountable, and I got up and got dressed in uniform. I'd go to the old men as I must.

Don't think of it as anything truly moral. I wanted to get out of it once and for all, to be rid of it as an insurmountable act, one that had stopped my own life and kept me bound to what was done and could not be undone, and I thought I could, by confessing to them what I could not to her let alone to myself, such a confession I now know never a true act of confrontation. I found I could only officially confess it, not confront it.

I got to the old colonial building. I got to the old men.

"You Private First Class John LeBlanc?" they said when I'd stood in the room before them. I said I was. It was almost like you see in a real war story. There were three of them. They sat me down, opposite them, with MPs at the door, and you got the feeling that it was all to be something serious and of some consequence. There were the official questions. There was the official paperwork laid out on the long table in the light in the fancy echoing room to be signed and sealed and filed away in an office drawer. It was a kind of court. It went on some for no good reason. It was all a formality. It was for the record. It would go good for me they said.

"You saved some of the boys," the Colonel said that and he looked at me with some significance. That was a good thing with the old men. The boy-officer had the radio buried all wet beneath himself in the big grass. I saw it wet in the green grass. I was to live no matter myself. It was almost official they said. I had done good things.

First there was the church-like talk. They sat somber and serious. Then I sat there in that too-large emptied-out room with the high fancy ceiling talking for a time with them too casually of killing and they wore their colorful medals and the one of them would cough absently and another would speak abstractedly. They were these plain-speaking kind of hometown men with their familiar ordinary faces talking on of killing as if talking of the weather or work. They were these lifeless and official men from places like Indiana and Iowa gone off in their ordinary and everyday talk of killing. The one in charge, the Colonel, said, "Answer the question, boy. Who killed the Lieutenant?" That's what they wanted to know for the record. The note taker put his blue ballpoint down to the paper. He held it to the yellow legal pad to get the words down for good on paper and there were none. They wanted to get one of the boys for it and that's what I couldn't help them with. They wanted the story straight so.

Now let me tell you this, it's not that bad to kill the people of the country and to leave them without a word dead in the grass. That's all a usual everyday thing. They didn't want to know anything about that. They would not let me talk about that. That's nothing out of the ordinary, and I looked to them old men and I saw them dead in the green grass, the reddened life of them come up my hands and arms. It had come all over me. You cannot ever get rid of the sight or smell of it. You will try to in telling. I began to talk about them. No words were ever written about them. They stopped me. I couldn't get it out of me. "Answer the question." I hadn't answered the question. The note taker lifted his pen. They wanted to know about how the Lieutenant got killed. They wanted to know how this or that boy got killed. They wanted it for the record, to dot their

'I's and cross their 'T's. They wanted to know none of the rest of it, the real of it. They would not let me speak of any of the rest of it to be written down to make it real in the record of it being inked out in blue ballpoint on the yellow legal pad, and right then, there in that room with them, I wanted to, to get it put down somewhere outside myself for good even if on paper, so to get it out of me that way in a kind of official accounting, even if one not to be a true accounting, a confrontation. I was weak.

Then the whole thing felt like farce.

"Do you want to go to jail?" the Colonel said. "Answer the question, LeBlanc. You're getting it easy, boy," he said and I was seeing them, and I heard how he wanted to go easy on me. He thought we had a rapport.

"I got to think it over, sir," I said and when I said that that irritated him, it hardened him. I saw it in his face. I wanted to say it for them to see it as I saw it or I had nothing to say to them. But he stayed easy with me because he wanted it right for the record.

"You got one hour, boy," he said, and he stood abruptly, and he looked at his watch, and I stood. "Let's get some lunch," he said to them other two, and they got up. I was dismissed.

"We know where to find you, LeBlanc," I heard that at my back. The MPs let me pass. I left the old men to their lunch in the abject and official light. The big door closed behind me shutting out their abstracted looks and absent talk. I walked on into the afternoon light into the commotion of the city on into the confusion of the people to get the sight of them to go from me.

17

ONE MUST ACT TO RELINQUISH THE PAST

From what I remember I went to her. I didn't go back to my room. But it doesn't matter, if it was then, or later, when I went to her. I went to her and I wasn't even thinking to hide out or even to try to. I know it's better to face the things you can and I wanted to, to free myself for good. What I wanted was to get her out of there. I went to get her out of there for good, to tell her that I wanted her to go away with me, to take her home. I was going to find Phuong to hold myself accountable in that way for her. I couldn't for the others. I found her sitting in the dark light beside a soldier. She was drinking a beer and she watched me come in the door to her as if she were watching a stranger. I walked up to her and sat down on the stool beside her up at the bar. She looked tired. It was in her eyes. I've seen it in the eyes. She looked away from me. Her hair was long and black fallen down the red silk back of her dress. She had her little beat-up black purse on the bar. She opened up her purse and she lit a cigarette looking away. She looked young.

"Phuong," I said to her.

She turned to look. She looked straight at me. She looked down to the end of the bar and lifted her head and blew out the cigarette smoke over the bar. I looked. There was the man. The cigarette smoke drifted out over the bar. There were a couple girls with soldiers along the bar between us and him. People were at tables. A jukebox was playing. That man at the end of the bar was watching us three. I didn't give a goddamned thing about him or the soldier with her. But maybe she didn't want a fight or she did care if I was hurt. She wouldn't let me talk to her or take her out of there with me.

"No talking," she said looking straight at me. She spoke a straight and simple English to American boys. "You go home, boy," she said. "You not want me," she said looking straight at me. She didn't sound hard. She turned away from me to the soldier. She wasn't a girl to be wanted in a good way. She'd decided. I'd decided nothing. Well, it's true that there're people who'd say that she wasn't a girl to be wanted in a good way. But what do people know. People they know nothing. People don't know a goddamned thing.

"Phuong," I said. "I will help you."

"No, I go—home," she said and turned to me.

"Where home?" I said. "To family—do you have family?" I said to her. She turned away. I couldn't tell if she was telling me a story to get rid of me. She was from the country. There are all these girls come from the country to the city. She cannot go to the country. There is no home in the country. There is nothing good in the country. She cannot go now there to the country.

"Don't go," I said. "We'll do something."

"What I do?" she turned to me and said sounding hard.

"We must do something," I said believing it was true.

"I do nothing. Nothing to do," she said.

Her voice roused the soldier. The soldier hung on her by the arm. He had her by her arm. I looked to the soldier. He was drunk hanging over her and the bar and his beer bottle with his hand on her arm. He hung on her. I wanted to take him off of her. The man at the end of the bar was looking. I don't think he could hear a damn thing of what we said over the air conditioning rattling over the bar. I didn't care if he did.

I wanted to take him off of her.

"Tonight, I will come," I said.

"You bring money—or nothing," she said and she stood up.

She got up from the bar stool. She took the soldier's beer bottle and her black purse from off the bar top and walked in her red dress with the soldier hung round her down to the end of the bar. She walked by the girls and boys smiling and drinking. At the end of the bar that man grabbed her by the arm and she put the soldier's empty beer bottle on the bar. He shoved her off from the bar by her arm toward a door. She went with the soldier to the darkened door and disappeared. She was gone. I didn't go after her. I wanted to get across that bar and get that man. There are these things that should be stopped after all. I got up from the bar stool. I had to go from the place to get back to the old men. I went out into the street. I looked up to the sky. The sky was overcast at the edges. These days there would be a brilliant big light in the morning and then for hours it would rain like hell.

18

RANK IS THE RITUAL OF AUTHORITY

I looked at the time. I still had time. When I'd got back to the old men I stood there at the corner of *Boulevard le Loi* where the white-pillared building with the alabaster-looking balconies and red tiled roof was long and shadowed in front of me. I stood there looking at it rising from off the boulevard and lit a cigarette and smoked it looking at it. They'd built them all to last and left them behind to rise for centuries off boulevards. Then I turned and went into it and the light and the sound and the color and commotion of the things in the street were shut out by the tight-shut doors. I walked down a hall in a simple quiet. I walked across a polished floor and listened to my shoes hit down on its shine.

I found the room. There were the tall doors and the high fancy ceiling. There were the four of us. We sat at the table that was too long for us. The three of them were opposite me. They sat quiet in their uniforms with medals everywhere and

I sat opposite them in mine with the paperwork sitting on the table. The Colonel was reading from a report and we sat in our uniforms at one of those long banquet tables you'll sometimes see set out for guests at a wedding or a funeral in a church hall in the middle of nowhere in America. The table was covered over in white paper from end to end looking like there'd been some kind of celebration in there but they'd only had their lunch in there and a Private from the cafeteria who was on kitchen duty came in with a steel tray and started taking up the scattered water glasses and silverware and sandwiches and plates from off that table and the white paper there in that place that was the thing that made me remember. I remembered those old church hall tables back home in America where the people would go sit down with one another after the promises and prayers were all said and done and the ceremony was finished. They'd get drunk there late and live a little with one another no matter the ceremony. Then sometimes at the end of things they'd be talking late about big things they'd forgotten no matter the living or the dead. Then in the light in the morning laid out in bed tired and too awake in a familiar room they'd think of how it was when everything was new and beginning.

    The four of us sat there quiet at the table covered over in white paper. What there was of ceremony was said and done. No one was getting drunk and all the talk was finished. The empty ends of the table went out on either side of us going toward the tall colonial windows. Around us the room was dim and empty of things and very clean with a tall fancy ceiling and a chopper fan above us that made no noise and a couple of wooden poles hung with American flags. The tall French windows were letting in a gray light down onto the table ends and against the hung flags. It was humid. The air was a weight sat down in the room upon us. The Colonel finished reading the report. The Colonel closed up the report in the manila folder on the table in front of him. He looked across the table to me with

77

his reading glasses on. He took off his reading glasses and he laid them down on the report.

"Now, why don't you tell us about the Lieutenant, LeBlanc, and we can stop all this," the Colonel said waving his hand at the report. He said it reasonably. They wanted it for the record. They had to get it officially recorded on paper to get one of the boys for it. I told them I hadn't expected a trial to be so simple. They said it was not a trial.

"You're going to get a medal boy," the Colonel said sitting there grinning, showing his teeth all yellowed from years of cigars and coffee, all colorful-looking, looking with a squared jaw and crew cut with his medals running down his chest like a cartoon character from a war, not a man who killed people for a living.

"Answer the question," he said casually. "Then you're done, boy. I don't want to see you in here again."

I saw it really was a gesture, an offer from him to wipe things clean and to get me on home. He was being magnanimous. I think he just wanted to get it over with too after he'd had his lunch in there, to get out of there to one of those air conditioned officers' clubs, to get a cold cocktail after all the day's work and heat hung in that place.

"Now tell us about the Lieutenant, LeBlanc."

"I'll tell you about the woman and the girl."

"Then you're going to jail, soldier."

The Colonel stopped talking. He stood up in the heat to go. I realized that I should stand up too, that it was over if I didn't talk. But I didn't move to get up. The Majors in their medals stood on each side of the Colonel. They all stood there tall and waiting and unmoved.

"Stand up boy," he said. "This is finished."

I didn't get up. He wanted it right for the record. I wanted the woman and the girl written down in the record. Then there was nothing to be done about it. For they couldn't have it. And I couldn't help them. I looked to the floor to the old French stone. I was wordless. It didn't matter what I said to any one of them about anyone or anything. All was frivolous, futile. I'd been a fool to think I could get it out of me that way with them anyway. There was no accounting for it with them. In looking to that stone I saw none for such a lived thing. I looked up from the stone to them. I'd decided. It was the principle of it. I got up from the paper-covered table and I stood there on the stone in front of them in the gray light. I looked at them. I said nothing to them. I tried to see them true once. They were ordinary lifeless men. You couldn't fight them. I waited for them to call the guards.

The big French doors opened up from behind me. But it wasn't the guards. There was the commotion of personnel coming into the room, and the Colonel looked off from me to an officer who came in with a Sergeant. It was the Captain who came in, and he saluted, and he said to the Colonel, "Sir, we got him, the Sergeant's bringing him in," and they didn't call the guards.

"Well, bring him in when we're done with LeBlanc," the Colonel said to the Captain.

The Captain said, "Yes Sir," and he left with a salute and went out.

The Colonel stood there looking at me in some appraisal, and he said to me, "LeBlanc, I want this to turn out for you, even if you don't," he said mulling it over and I stood there mute as though I still hadn't understood his bargain, his offer all along that he was giving me a way out of the whole mess if I gave them what they wanted. But in the end I didn't really want to get out of it their way.

The Colonel looked at his watch, as if reconsidering things, thinking on what he had on me, on what he wanted from me, on how to make it all work for him, and with the only movement in the room the chopper fan above us, the

Colonel spoke as if he were trying to be fair on my behalf. He said, "LeBlanc, I don't think you understand what this is all about," and he stopped at that, and then he went on in that magnanimity he'd had earlier. He said, "Noon tomorrow, you talk—you got a one day reprieve to consider the consequences for yourself," he said that to me, in some seriousness, sounding as though he were deliberating, making his final attempt for me to comprehend what it was all about, to give him what he wanted, but he was conning me, not convincing me, saying, "Tomorrow we're done, one way or the other. You talk, or you go to jail," he said. Then it seemed it'd all been a kind of bluff from the beginning, and once more, he returned to his tone of fairness, "Given the circumstances, I don't think you've had time to think it through." But I had. They wanted corroboration and I didn't really care. They were bringing in the boys to break them. I'd figured it out. They wanted a solid case and they'd take their own official time to do it until little was true or told. I stood there then and I saw how I could fight them. I wanted to fight them. They wanted it for the record. I saw how they wanted to break the boys, to cover their asses, in official acts to abrogate accounting for killing, to continue a career, call it what you want. They would go on in a continual kind of deferral of all but rote accounting.

I was dismissed.

If you were in the habit of saluting you wouldn't think about what it meant, but do it as you'd shine a shoe early in the morning, as you'd done when you were young and not yet awake. I'd shined a lot of shoes when young and not yet awake. I hadn't shined any shoes in a long time and I was young and I felt very awake standing there in front of them on that French stone in that fancy room knowing I'd never tell them anything they wanted, and I saluted them. I knew what I had to do and I thought when I did that there to them then, that it was a strange sign for people to make to one another. It felt funny to do it there like that to them the last time. It felt funny like when we were kids, and we'd used to do it to one another young and playing. It was just a different game we were playing. They'd waited for me to do it and I remembered that I should do it. I did it to get out of there and away from them once and for all and to have no more things to say to them. There was nothing more to be said to any one of them again. In the end, it's true that one must hold one's self accountable.

19

HOW ONE GOES HOME, AND GOES NOWHERE

I came all alive in her nakedness in the night. There was the alive and surprising night. I was all alive in her and I felt all right. I looked again at her girl's face, her browned body naked and thin, her long black hair fallen, nicely fallen against her nakedness, and I saw how her familiar strangeness got me out of all the ordinary badness. Maybe it was some thing like love that I had forgotten and it should not have been love. There was no good reason for it to be but that her body came round me real, and there was nothing, nothing but the seeing and the touching her and not one thing else but that, and all the deadness was gone, and I remembered, or rather felt once more all the goodness and the strangeness of a life to lose yourself in. I remembered that feeling of being alive. I remembered what it felt like to be living all alive. There is a great freedom in that feeling. I was lost in her and alive in the feeling and it was all a good wanting thing wanting her and I only wanted that. That is all one would ever want.

Then when we were done with it I felt deadened. She lay out along me. She took up the silver comb I'd brought for her and she liked it and she put it through her hair and laughed happily over it and held it close to her when she kissed me to thank me like a girl. She was a girl.

"Boy, why you bring me things?" she said but she was happy.

"Do you like it," I said to her, wanting to give her things and to make her happy. I'd brought it for her and she lay there naked and she ran its silver teeth down along through her long black hair and out the fine black ends. I watched her with the comb. I wanted to see her happy in her few simple things like that like a girl again and I lit a cigarette and offered her one and lit it for her. I lay back beside her and watched her smoke it naked, looking at her comb, wanting to stay quiet like that a time with her, thinking on how to get her out of there for good, trying to find the words that would make some sense to say, afraid to say them, feeling it was too soon to say them. The sound of drunken laughter came from down the hall to us. A door opened and closed in the hall. There was a fight going on in the street. The cigarettes were finished.

"You go now, boy," she said. The time was up.

I didn't get up. I lay there naked a moment in peace. I said nothing about getting her out of there. I didn't say anything to ruin it as I had in the day. She seemed to have forgotten it, like it had been a conversation between two other people. Then I thought I'd just do it. There was no talking for it. The words couldn't matter. One must act. There are all these things to be done in a life. It was some thing that had to be done if she were to live a good life. I almost did it right then. But I did nothing. The words did matter to the act as they had before. I had none to make sense of what must be done.

"Do you have family?" I said again to her.

"You have money?" she said to me.

She lay there young and alone in the sparse dingy room.

I dressed. She lay there looking to me. She was naked. Once I was dressed she covered herself in a kind of end to everything. I left her late without saying anything, without doing any one thing. I walked dark streets. I drank in dark places. There was no one for her. There were only these men for her. I lay drunk in bed in my room above the rue de l'Abondance alone late into the coming light thinking all along of her and not home. With her in the night in a room I'd be all alive and feel all right alive and I told myself right there and then drunk like that, that in the morning in the light I'd go get her. Laid alone drunk in dark, I told myself that. Two people together in a place could do good things no matter the people or the place. Laid out there very alone in bed I told myself some things in the coming light. The words came on in some logic. The words came then recollected in late tranquility. They came put to the act in a clear strong feeling full of sense and one without fear. In morning I'd go tell her. I'd go tell her all what must be done for good. I'd tell her that the what, the how, the why of it all, it couldn't matter to people like us. I'd go take her from it for good. One must act after all. I told myself that. I knew it was in the telling. When it was very late in the night I remembered the things that people used to say back home when they were drunk and everything was changed for the better against the worse. They'd say that in America you could have a bad start and end up good. They believed in it as when you become afraid of things that come about you and you can come to believe for no good reason in a ghost or a god.

20

THE FIGHTING IS FINISHED

In morning when I'd waked in the shuttered light, I lay there in that bed that must have been the bed of so many other boys and even some girls, maybe in this war and certainly in others, kids who'd long gone off to life, who knows to what as I would myself, and I didn't move. From where I lay stilled on the bed, I looked over at the few things of mine dimly lit in risen light where they lay on the beat-up dresser, a pair of sunglasses, a watch, an envelope of money, the paperwork of my orders. The silvered mirror rose behind them black-speckled in its age above the battered art deco dresser and showed them so-called personal objects in angled depth, illuminated them in elongated reflection, in odd interest, extending them and the room into the cracked green wall, like a window into another room that could never be opened or entered. I felt like I wanted to get up and walk into it. I looked off from it, up the nicely-cracked wall, to the ceiling the color of a swimming pool, and it was an old comforting color, and then down from it, to the slatted blinds of the cracked-open window, to the black rails of the iron balcony, down to the heaped folds of my uniform piled below the window ledge, strewn on the floor.

It stopped my little reverie.

I got up. I was due at noon. Maybe they'd send a guard or two after that if they didn't see me show on time. But then I didn't put my uniform on to go to the old men as I must. I stood over it looking at it and saw who it told me I was. I took it from off the floor of the room and got up the other Army things that told you you were a soldier, so I wouldn't see who I was anymore in them. I put them things in one of the army bags, and I dressed in shorts, a T-shirt, tennis shoes, and counted out my money, and put some dollars in an envelope, then folded that over and put it in my shorts pocket, then buried the rest back in the dresser drawer beneath a pistol, and took my knife and watch up off the dresser, and put my watch on and sunglasses on and turned in front of the dresser to go out of the room, and there I saw myself unrecognizable in the dilapidated mirror looking all out of place and dressed at last like a tourist. I left.

ABANDONED BY THE GODS

I went down out of the lobby to the street and round to the back of the place to the alley that ran behind it and emptied out the Army bag into the heaped crates of strewn garbage littered along a gutter and walked out of the alley with the emptied bag to the street into the light. I walked down the rue de l'Abondance to find Phuong to tell her what I had to tell her. I'd do what I had to do to take her out of there. I didn't know how I'd do it. I'd pack up her things. I'd get her out of there. We'd go get another room. I walked. And the strange thing was that in walking to her like that I felt more afraid of her than those old men. I was walking east and the sunlight came straight down the street at me off the walls and rooftops and that light was nice and warm. The iron bars were gone off all the store fronts and the shops were open for the day. Along the street cigarette smoke sat in the air and I always liked the smell of it there. People were out up and down along the crowded street to sell the things they had, to buy the things they needed. I stopped at a place and got a drink and drank. I went out and walked on in the street. Then the weather was changed up. Out in the street it was becoming the heavy wet weather that makes big storms. I remembered it was May. The brilliant light was gone. Back home the summer was almost beginning. I walked along the rue de l'Abondance under a low heavy sky. I stopped at a crowded little place in bad light to get a drink and I drank. It tasted good and cold. I went out of the place and into the obscured light. The light was all changed-up. I walked on and looked at the big purple rainheads built high in the sky above the city. I walked beneath it with all the other people crowded underneath it in the city. I stopped at a place and drank. I went out into the street and into everyone packed in the street under the obscured sky. The sky stretched low heavy diffuse. I stopped and drank and went out and walked and stopped and drank and walked on from place to place. There I walked along the waterfront near the river in small nicely dilapidated streets.

85

I walked on in streets cast in shadow looking into the faces of girls. I was getting to her. I wanted to get to her. I was afraid of getting to her. I was passed by rattling cyclos and streams of bicycles and loaded carts with no end to the people riding and walking and carrying every kind of thing there in that place where it seemed no matter what no person or thing would ever stop.

    I stopped. I found the place and went in remembering her in her red dress and how she'd looked in afternoon young and tired. The place was crowded with soldiers and girls and I sat down in the laughing crowd. She was not up at the bar. She was not over at a table. I didn't see her anywhere. She must have been with a boy. I thought of being there with her and all what it was with her and I wanted to sit there and to think of it and how it was good. It was good. I sat there and thought of it all as more than an empty act and I wanted a drink and I drank and I did not think it was a bad thing to feel all alive in such a way thinking of her and nothing else. But she did not appear. I drank at the bar. The girls came to the bar. I saw her in them girls. I sent them off. She did not come from out of the dark. The man came out. He went and sat at a table. He did not drink. He ate from a bowl. He was the one who'd held her by her young girl's arm when she'd first come out and told me her name. "Phuong," she'd said to me in the beginning and I'd paid him the money and he'd left her to me. He was the one who'd taught her her English and the things to be said and he sat there at the table eating from his bowl and I finished my beer and sat my bottle down on the wet bar top and got up from the bar stool and walked over through the crowd to him hungry at his table and sat down in front of him at the table. He ate from the bowl and he kept looking into the bowl. He ate. He didn't look up to me and I said, "Phuong," to him. He looked down and he ate without stopping. I saw how he was hungry. "Phuong," I said. He shook his head without looking up, and he said, "No

Phuong," and he ate from the bowl without stopping.

"Phuong," I said. I said, "*Phuong*," to him.

"No Phuong," he said and I reached across the table and his head came up by habit and fear and I put the dollars down on the table beside the bowl and he put his hand on the dollars and he looked up then to me and he saw who I was in the money no matter no uniform and he said, "OK, Phuong for you—for you, Phuong," he said and he laughed and he took the green dollars off the table and he ate from the bowl without stopping and I sat there across from him and he did not get up. He held his hand up to a boy standing over by the wall at the end of the bar. The boy knew what to do. The boy walked around behind the crowded tables. The boy was gone at the back of the bar where it was dark. He ate from the wooden bowl without one word and I watched the dark place back there. When a girl came from out of it I stood from the table to see her and she came on across the room to me as if knowing me as she came from out of the smoke and darkness and laughter of the drinking drunk-talking crowded little bottle-filled tables and I did not know that it was not her and she came straight up to me and she was a girl I did not know and she kissed me and she tasted of lipstick and opium and I began to walk to the back without the girl. I went through the happy laughing crowd to the dark covered door in the narrow corner and I opened the door and went down the darkened hall.

The light was nice and dim and low in the hall along the closed bottoms of doors and I was seeing her all alive in the dark light laid out in a bed with a boy, and I had to get to her to take her from it for good, remembering her and how it was good, all what it was with our bodies come on into one another with our arms and legs making us one, with our arms come all round us two kept all as one living thing in the dark, with the arms coming now on down all round me enclosed in the dark to take me back out of the hall to the happy laughing people of the lively crowded room, and I swung hard out in the dark, and it was funny how I hit one, then two, three of them wildly hard by hand remembering how good it was to lay there a time happy out along her in the night in that in peace as in nothing else, never wanting to go do one other thing ever again but that, and the fists came down on me hard in some unloosed fury gone out to the dark of the floor, thinking such happy thoughts, with the knife lost, gone at last from my hand, the blade gone out down for good beneath them boys to the stink of the floor. The knife was gone and lost at last. Once I thought I heard her whether I did or not I do not know but I do remember that I saw by the illuminated crack of one of them opened up doors, a girl quite like her herself looking on out at us, a girl in her own fear seeing the dim blank faces of the boys as they beat me bloody, in her seeing them beat me bloody not looking away with the blood come all over hands and bodies with the knife lost at last and, in her looking I let them beat me bloody in her looking, and take me from her for good out into the laughing room on across the stink of the wooden floor to the street into the rain where I lay looking up at the sky letting the rain wash me. I lay there in the rain. I looked up to the sky. The sky was big and heavy. The sky was made of many colors. The purple was on top. Then the sky was silvered along high wide edges and the sky was gray and the sky was black and low and heavy down underneath. I remembered the storms in America in the springtime when I was young when it made me alive to walk in it. I was young. I got up. I walked on in it. I walked on beneath the sky and the sky cracked open high in white lightning and the rain came heavy across the whole place and I walked on in the hard rain not knowing where to walk or to what and watched the faces of the people in the street going on in it with some of them stopping to try to find cover in it but most of them going on knowing that there was nothing to do but to go. Lost at last I did not know in what streets I walked and I stopped and drank and went out and walked and stopped and drank and walked on from place to place and stopped and drank in many places and lost the time and place and in the next place forgot the last and knew no one in any place.

21

A DARK GIRL COMES FORTH
WITH CHILDREN IN RAIN

One must go on and when I'd waked at last, I'd stopped for good, and felt at the end of myself. I found I was badly waked in the room on the rue de l'Abondance naked, beaten, strangely-sickened, left oddly-cold in the heat of the room not knowing how I'd got there, not remembering how I'd gone to get her. I felt deadened and didn't get up from the bed. I looked round at my few scattered things remembering who and where I was. I remembered the old men. I didn't care if the old men found me. I lay there. I looked to the dresser and saw the envelope with the money, and remembered, one by one, the things that'd happened as they came back in their own bad logic. I looked to my beat up self, laid elongated on the strewn bed sheet in the angled mirror, as if someone else, any boy, laid out in another room and realized how I hardly knew myself in that dim reflected sight and wondered if I ever did and never felt less myself in seeing the actual image of myself. The sunglasses and the watch were gone from the top of the dresser where they'd always sat in morning. You'll see yourself most clearly in discovering once more such ordinary objects put right where you'd left them as if only they will and can tell you who you are in that material way when you take them up once more. There were the curled-up papers of my orders in the heavy heat hung in the room, rolling up at their edges on the dresser top, looking like the scroll of some ancient document, denoting the duties of, or even delivering a sentence upon, someone I was supposed to be, would never be, now was not and never could be from the beginning. I lay there awakened and waited for them to come get me. I wanted them to come for me. No one came. They didn't come for me with the rains going on into the night and into the next day, and like the abandoned and soon to be dead, I lay there and listened to the rain waked, badly-sickened, beaten, living on in fact however as when mortally wounded, once and for all truly alone at last, and no one came for me in the new coming light.

She came, as an apparition.

I saw her, I saw her dark and cut come before me, and I looked up, reawakened in that secondary sight, on round the room to see only the reality of the room and not her, and saw her, and thought it was the fever that had fixed her image to my mind, making her more real to me than the actual sights of the strewn things of the room rising round me, and I closed my eyes so as not to see it, and saw her come brilliantly darkly lit, more powerful in her presence imagined than any one real thing I might reach out and touch in the light, and I couldn't get the sight of her to go from me, and I got up to go. I wanted her herself, not the sight of her to haunt me.

I dressed. I came up, close to the mirror. I saw myself all cut up looking in the face and beat up round the eyes. I was colored-up bad. I turned from that sight of myself, and looked here and there, on round the room for the sunglasses and the watch. They were gone and lost for good. I wanted the glasses to hide the eyes. I didn't know what time it was. It felt late. I left the room. I left it all. I went down out of the room and walked in the rain. The day was dark. I stopped a taxi and got in and gave the driver the address of the hospital.

On the drive over I saw her. She lingered on in my head as in a life. I saw her and none of it was real, the actual impression of this non-existent, persisting thing, pictured in a vibrant scene nowhere to be found in the world continued on, with the next scenario more fanciful than the last running vividly lit through my head, with only the phenomenal fact of such sightless seeing real. And in my seeing her like that, I told myself I'd go there and find that priest. I'd go find that priest to find where she'd gone. I'd go off to where she'd gone. I'd go to wherever she'd gone, however far, however unknown the place, the more unknown the better, the farther off and unfamiliar, the better. I'd find her. I'd tell her what I'd had to tell her. I told myself such things. I'd stop all such sights, I thought such farfetched things, feeling as if my own character had come unfixed, as if I'd waked fractured in my own life as in a story with no pre-determined plot for any one single action, thought, or judgment. I tried to sort out the logic of it. There seemed to be none at that moment heading over to that hospital in that taxi but for the lost and necessary sight of her, and of course I knew what it was all about in my going back like that again to find her, but I had to push it away, I couldn't look at it as I must, like I could look at her laid out all alive naked in the night along me. There was a larger logic. There always has been. Even this, now, undertaken in fear, I know makes perfect sense.

    The driver looked at me in the rear view mirror and I looked out to the rain. I told myself that, when I had got to that hospital, I'd go say goodbye to the boys. Maybe I'd go turn myself in. If I couldn't find where she'd gone, I told myself I'd go home that way, to stop it all and all sights of them, and in saying those unsounded words, then in some thin-felt promise of deliverance, in self-deception, brief respite, I looked out the window of the car to the rain, and there was nothing to see but rain. She and they were gone as though for good. There was only the wet dark vague street and the slowing taxi with the water sounding loud beneath the wheels. The car slowed to stop and stopped. The rain was coming hard against all the windows of the car, and I couldn't see a damn thing in the street when the taxi stopped. I paid the driver and got out in the hard rain. The lightning ran the high sky. The tall glassed windows of the hospital rose large and long lit before me hung with high florescent light. I looked at it. I didn't go in it. They'd arrest me if I went in it. I didn't step back in it right away. I wanted to find that priest first, to find her, and once I'd stepped out of the car to the street, I turned, I walked away from the French-looking building and crossed the street to a teahouse. The big room was cast in rain light rising behind me, brilliantly-lit, and I was seeing her, remembering her, how she'd come across the room past the boys to me. I saw all the boys laid out in the light. I saw her dark and cut walking the room, come up to sit beside me at the bed, and I looked down to the dark street before me to keep myself there where I was.

   I went out of the rain into the teahouse. I sat at a window and ordered hot tea. Maybe I'd see that priest. If I didn't see that priest, then I'd go on in to see the boys. Then they'd arrest me. I told myself some things like that. The porcelain of the tea cup was hot in my hand. I looked across the street to the big front doors of the hospital. The doors were closed up shut in the rain. I didn't see anyone go in or out. I drank my tea. No one came or went. I knew that time of day the priest would look at his watch and come on time each day in afternoon to make the girls go, and I drank my tea and thought through the time in some new found clarity, remembering how short a time it'd been since I'd gone off from the place. It was a week or two since I'd gone and forgot it, and it seemed a longer time in life than things I'd gone off from and forgot years ago. It hadn't been long at all. It's funny how the time passes and it's not the time at all, it's you yourself passing, and I looked out the window to the people caught in the hard rain making their way here and there along the street. The faces of the people in the street looked wet and blank and down and I saw her walking wet in a dress coming up the street with schoolchildren.

I put down my teacup. I stood up and I was weak. I felt stricken in seeing her. I didn't think it was her. I did not think it could be her. The priest had said she'd gone and the actuality of seeing her there like that seemed less real than the imagined vision of her. It was just another dark girl with children. The rain made everything you'd seen seem less likely to be true and she appeared from out of the rain as if she were yet an apparition of my own making looking all dark beneath one of those big white hats the people would wear there in the city. She was not of my making. She was walking up the street with school children in school uniforms and it looked like they'd got caught out in the rain.

The loud pour of rain was hitting everything hard and I went out of the teahouse and into the hard rain to walk down the street to get to her. She was several shop fronts away. She didn't see me. She was looking down to the wet street carrying something in her shawl. The rain was strong. It was bad weather. The rain beat everything and everybody beneath it. The rain struck the roofs and the walls of the street hard and I stopped in the street with the rain hitting into me hard. The lightning ran the high sky. It opened everything up. Everything opened up. There beneath the sky her and the children were lit up small in the street. You could see as in an old snapshot their hung faces and shoulders going on in the light of the strike. The sound of it hit down hard and loud onto the low dimmed shop walls and in the dark we were close and unknown. I might walk on unknown. But I would never be free of her and them and the whole goddamned place. I couldn't go on home and leave the rest unknown and forgotten. I couldn't forget.

She came by a metal-shuttered shop front. As I crossed the street to her, a child beside her looked to me. I reached past the child and took her by her bared arm. She looked up from her blued shawl held heavy and low against her. She saw how it was me. The lightning cut across the sky and broke upon the street. In the loud light of a strike we looked to one another knowing one another.

"John LeBlanc," she said matter-of-factly. She said it in some knowing familiarity, and the way she said it in seeing me was like a summing up, if not a reproach. I held her by the arm seeing how it was her.

There we two stood stopped in the street under the cracked up sky surprised by the light and ourselves. You might think that such things can only happen in books. Until they happen to you you might think that they're true only in told stories. But whole lives not to be found in books are made up so. For years now, I've known how things occur in a life. All is altered in the congregation of coincidence. Then you call it history.

"You are lost?" she said to me.

"No," I said standing there a little happily lost in my looking to her.

"The hospital—it is there," she said and she looked down along the street to it. There the hospital stood rising from the street not at all forgotten by either one of us.

"I know, I have seen it," I said. "I saw you in the street. But that priest—he said you went away. I saw you from the window, coming up the street."

"I have been here with the children. I have gone nowhere," she said. "I have been here each day, as before."

She turned and spoke in French to the children. She looked beyond the hospital to another building down along the street and the children began to walk to it. There was the little girl beside her who wouldn't go to it without her, and she kept hold of her hand and I looked to her, to them, I looked to her wet in her dress with the black from her eyes all run down her cut-up face. She held the girl's hand. She stood there in her yellow flowered dress, her bared black shoulders, her arms wet, her dark eyes run down in black like a mask making her look even blacker in the bad weather. The dress clung to her body with the blued shawl hung low and heavy against her wet in her dress and the little girl held onto her hand.

She said, "For a time, there wasn't rain. We went to a park, the rain came," she said to explain the facts of her looks to me and I stood there looking at her with the girl kept close against her. She kept the girl to herself and I looked to the sight of them two held into one another all alive before me real in the rain.

"Are you all right, John LeBlanc?" she said to me. She took a good look at me. "You are hurt," she said looking to me.

"I'm all right, Madeleine," I said and I'm sure I looked otherwise to her but she said nothing of what she saw. I think she'd seen worse.

"The children—where are they going?" I said about the children she'd sent off down the street.

"There—to the school," she said. She looked down the street to it and them, and the little girl kept hold of her one hand, and the edge of the shawl had come undone from her other, and was slipping to the street. I reached for it. I caught it.

"Let me carry it. You're going to drop it," I said, and I took the loosed edge of it, to hold it up for her. I held it. It was full of books.

"You will carry it?" she said. I took it from her all heavy and wet into my hands. It opened in my hands. I took the loosed edges of that shawl and I closed them up again carefully as I could to cover the books. The indigo die of the cloth had come off on their covers to stain them blue. My hands were black and blued from the fight. She looked to them and my face seeing something of me all colored-up like that, saying nothing of what she saw. Her dress was stained low in the indigo color where the shawl had hung against her heavy and wet. The lighting struck. She kept the little girl held afraid against her. She looked to the darkening sky.

"You will carry them there?"

"Of course, I will carry them—I was coming to see you," I said. "I have missed you, Madeleine," I said to her, and I felt a loss in saying it, and I hung the blued shawl of books over my shoulder.

"We must go, John LeBlanc," she said. She looked from that sky to me. She looked to me as though we'd always been together and the feeling between us had not been broken. The feeling had not been broken.

The rain had broken. The rain was coming.

We walked on together. There was the girl and her and I walking on in the wet street under the darkening sky. We three walked on beside one another without looking at one another. We went off the street into a set of old colonial buildings down along the street from the hospital. In the rain no one saw us pass by the hospital. It was the school and we went inside it with the children. We went down a dim hall with a worn floor. She let me carry the books down the hall. The girl went off from us with the other children. The children went off into a classroom where an old woman began to dry them off and we went into a little dormitory room down and across the hall with a sink and two chairs and a bed. It had these glass-paned French doors leading into a courtyard.

I stood there in the little dormitory room not knowing what to do with myself.

"Sit here," she said to me.

There was a straight-backed chair at the French doors. There was a book beside the chair where she must have been reading, looking into the courtyard. "I must dry myself," she said, and she had me sit down in that chair in front of shuttered French doors where you could look out onto a courtyard in good weather, and I had the books and the shawl, and she opened the shawl up and took the books from out of my hands, and she laid them down beside me on the floor to dry, and took the wet shawl from me as I held it up to her, and it was as if we had done such things all along in such rooms, and with her I felt that it could not be otherwise.

She went over and hung up her indigo shawl on a hook on the door of the room to dry. She opened the sheet of netting hung round her bed and she took up a towel laid folded up on the foot of the bed. She began to dry herself a little. She dried the ends of her black braided hair. I watched her with the towel standing at the sink wet in her yellow sundress in the little room and she was strange and she was serene-looking with the black from her eyes run all wild down her cheeks with the yellow front of her dress stained low in blue.

She washed the black off her face in the sink. The yellow dress clung to her. It held to the form of her and I looked away from her. I looked to the stone floor in front of me. I saw the form of her body before me. I put my head in my hands. I looked to the stone floor in the heat. The little room was warmed in the rain. The rain held the heat. The air was heavy in it. I was struck by the wet heat. It was a weight come upon me. All was going dark.

I lent forward to the floor. I felt like I were falling.

"Are you all right?" she said. She'd turned and she was looking at me.

"It's the heat," I said and felt strangely and oddly cold in it as I had in morning. She stopped drying herself. She came back over to me. She came to me wet in her dress. I lifted my head to her. She came right up to me and she put her hand on my forehead as might a nurse or a mother and she said, "You are sick. You have a fever, John LeBlanc," she said. "Don't you feel it?" she said to me and I felt it.

She took a towel off a shelf and she brought me the

towel to dry myself off. She went over to the sink and she put some water into a little pan and she put it on a hotplate. She took some tea off a shelf and she sat the tea box by the water and she went and got another little towel and ran it under cold water and came over to me to where I sat on the wooden chair and she held the cold towel there against my forehead. I reached up to get hold of it from her hand and I touched her hand.

"Keep it there," she said to me and left.

She went back to the hot water and she made a pot of tea and poured two cups of tea. She brought the tea. I took my cup from her and it was warm and felt good to hold in my hand. She brought a chair over from her writing desk to the courtyard doors. She sat beside me all wet in her dress with her tea. She smelled like flowers. She smelled like lilacs.

"The tea will help," she said.

We looked out through the slatted blinds of the French doors to the rain hitting the courtyard. I held the cool cloth there against my forehead and sipped the hot tea with her there next to me in that unfamiliar room with her smelling all wet like that in the dim rainlight and it was quiet there and we heard the rain outside and the lightning struck and we heard the children laughing off in other rooms and we drank our tea listening like that to all the things outside us and around us and stopped in the reality of that room right then with her I felt I never wanted to get up again to go off anywhere in the world.

"You are feeling better?" she said.

"I'm all right—I'm stronger," I said and I didn't feel too good, but I wanted her to know that I was really all right and not that sick.

She looked over the rim of her teacup at me. She looked me over as she had in the street in some appraisal. Then she said, "I must change, from out of this dress," and she looked down at the stain on the dress and she got up. She sat her teacup down on the chair and she went over to an Oriental screen that stood along the back wall of the room right behind the netted bed. The screen had one of those brightly stylized landscapes painted colorfully across it in broad and simple strokes that will make you imagine tranquil scenes of the East. There were the delicately-leaved dark-barked trees branched-out before the far rising mountains snowcapped white against the sky with a flock of birds going off in formation high across a clear wide sky. They might have been cranes or snow geese. There they forever flew off in that little room across a couple of those unfolded wood-framed panels.

She changed behind its stylized scene. I looked away from it out to the gray rainlight coming in the slatted wooden blinds from the courtyard being hit hard with the rain. I looked off from the sound of the rain to the tiled floor hard at my feet remembering the old stone in that fancy old French room with them old men that I'd never returned to right there with her gone behind the screen to change in her room in the old colonial school with the orphanage out back and she reappeared from behind that nicely unnatural-looking landscape dressed in one of those stark-looking white loose-fitting robes you'd see people in movies and magazines like *National Geographic* wear out in deserts. She came back there beside me a girl transformed and she was a very beautiful girl with the high line of her cheekbone framing her dark-lined eyes. She was a beautiful black cut girl in a pristine white robe. She was a pretty sight. I'd forgotten she was black and she filled our cups with tea from the pot.

She said to me, "I think you are feeling better. It is the tea?" and I didn't feel that good, it was only that I was with her, and though sick from the fight I was sick and happy with her.

"Yes," I said. "I really don't feel that bad at all."

I took up my tea. She watched me. I drank my tea. The children laughed. The lightning struck. She drank her tea very elegantly cut in that stark white immaculate robe with her eyes carefully lined out in the black kohl making them look even blacker and she said to me, "What were you doing, there, by that hospital today, out in the rain John LeBlanc?" she said. She was curious. She wanted to know.

"I was coming to see you, Madeleine," I said.

"Why didn't you come before?" she said. She sat her cup down.

"I thought you had gone home."

"You didn't come, John LeBlanc," she said as a fact. She looked at me with those eyes of hers, implacable and unplaceable, and I felt that it was a kind of judgment she was making, as though she were holding me accountable for something I'd said I wanted.

"I told you, that priest—he said you went away."

"I thought you did not want me," she said in a way that sounded like she was a girl playing a girl who'd been forgotten by a lover. "It is true for some boys. It is hard for some boys, to want such a girl." She said that straight out and not playing, and I felt that I'd failed at some unspoken expectation of hers, and I didn't know how serious she was, and then she laughed at what she'd said, and maybe we were just playing, she laughed somewhat tenderly now, as in realizing that whether or not I should have come was simply a thing of chance kept by a capricious world beyond what we wanted, and I heard her sweet and pleasant laugh. I saw some happiness that was hidden in her.

"I only wanted you," I said. I wasn't playing.

She said, "I thought of you."

"You came to me in the night," I said.

"I forgot you," she said.

"I dreamt you," I said.

She put down her teacup.

She said, "Are all Americans like you, John LeBlanc?"

she said.

"I really don't know anything about Americans," I said.

"But you *are American*," she said. She really was a very literal and intelligent girl.

"Yes, I am," I said.

"Then tell me a little what America is like," she said to me in her good and polite English, being all practical and logical as she was, and I drank my tea looking at her, and then looked into the teacup and said nothing.

Then I said, "*America*, it's a word. America, it's a big place full of little things," I said.

"What does that mean?" she said to me.

"I don't exactly know," I said.

"But you will tell me—why you say such words?" she said.

I put down my teacup. I looked round the room to her blue shawl hung drying out there on the door, to the standing wooden panels of the folded-out brightly painted screen, on across the stylized scene to the netted bed nicely veiled in its opaque film, already seeming a kind of sanctuary, where I saw how she'd lay shrouded in night, I looked to her few kept things off at the far wall, her school papers and the class books stacked up on the writing desk, then back to the stained blued-up covers of the books wet on the floor there at my feet, left beside my scuffed up boots, and I could smell their old ink rising from the floor in the wet heat, to where I sat on the creaking wooden chair beside her, a girl come from I do not know where or from out of what country, from an as yet only imagined place, and in my seeing those actual things of her and her room, in smelling them there in the heat and her close at hand, only that there was the realized world to me, I was there with her and the rest was unwanted recollection, and America was a far and distant abstraction hard to think real although the name constantly brings it into being as an idea.

"But tell me why you say such things about America," she said. "You will tell me?"

Then when she'd said the word again, the way she said it, I saw the land of it, the whole place coming on in another new image. I had another new feeling for it. The feeling went.

"I'll try to," I said. "If I have to, I'll make something up," I said. "Like in one of those books, there," I said, "I don't know if it'll be true at all," I said and I looked to them closed up at my feet stinking pleasantly of their old ink wet on the floor and felt I wanted to sit there and to have her read me one of them again. I only wanted to stay there in that room with her and to hear her tell me them strangely-intimated stories of books that would make the world new. I didn't want to recollect the world, I wanted to re-imagine it.

"But, you must tell it true some," she said then as if I'd promised her something in my saying I'd tell it.

"All right," I said. "I'll tell you a good long story about America," I said, drinking my tea feeling all at home with her there in that warm and pleasant place not wanting to go anywhere anymore again for anything.

"There are good things to tell of every place," she said knowingly.

"I'll tell you something true about America," I said to her feeling good knowing I could never get to the end of it. It was almost too big to begin it.

22

AN INTIMATION OF AMERICA

Then I said nothing to her to begin it.

I was to tell her of America. I didn't speak. I didn't want to go off with her in talk of America. I didn't want us to go from ourselves there in the room in talk of lived-up times. I wanted to be kept there with her in the actuality of that hour, and if we were taken off, I wanted it to be in her words, not mine. I felt all of myself there with her now and nowhere else. I wanted to stay fixed in the feeling. I felt present there with her as I rarely had. I was kept a moment in some un-fragmented integrity. I felt a time what was good and given in me with her there beside me. With her there beside me I wasn't left any longer off to the past.

I looked out to the rain. The room held the wet heat. I wanted to open up them courtyard doors to the air and rainlight and to look out into the open courtyard. I said to her, "Can I open up those doors?"

"You may open them, a little. The floor will get wet," she said.

I got up. I opened them. The lightning struck close by and hard. We sat there. She waited for me to begin. She was a patient and pleasant girl. You could see across the courtyard to the yellow stucco wall of the other side and other doors. I thought I saw the priest walk by them once going along a hall behind the glass panes in his black robe and the rain came hard and loud from the low sky to the courtyard stone, sounding on in through the opened doors across the tile floor of the room and I found no words for America. I was calmly quieted. The rain didn't let up.

We heard children's voices going off away in a hall.

"Where are they going?" I said. A child's laughter came down the hall to us. In their voices was the world coming once more to us.

"They must go to eat, it is time—they are going to the cafeteria," she said. She looked to a clock on the desk.

We sat listening to the rain drinking our tea. The children had gone off to eat. There was solitude. She broke the quietness come to us. She brought us back to all what I had

103

passed over.

"You are hurt, John LeBlanc," she said to me as a fact looking at my beat-up face. She looked closely to my colored-up face. "Tell me what has happened to you. Why were you coming to see me, today?" She sat there young and dark in that stark and immaculate robe. The rain hit down hard from the low broken sky. She did not wait for me to speak. She said, "You have been in a fight—why are you fighting—you are not well," she said. "You have done this to yourself?" she said, and it was not a question. It was a kind of reproach.

She brought me back to the bottom of myself, took me to what couldn't be passed over but in a rhetoric which continually represses one's ruinous acts, in play, while denying nothing.

"I always wanted to have an interesting life," I said.

"I think you are in trouble—and you do not take it too seriously."

"I'm tired of taking things seriously," I said.

"The priest, he told me—about the child," she said and she sipped her tea. She said things straight out like that that one must pass over. She was interested in that. She had concern for that. She said, "The child is here." I looked at her.

"I can't talk about that. You know it. It is enough," I said. I could smell the rain come in from the courtyard. "Never trust a priest," I said.

"He was good to you, he wanted to help you. He wanted you to get well, to go home. He tried to help you. You must look to yourself, you must look to what is done—if you are to be well, trust yourself, John," she said outright. "I have told you that," she said and she was looking right at me. I looked off from her.

"He lied to me," I said. "He said you went away."

"You are too hard on him. He sent me to you," she said. "But I think, he does not believe so much in love," she said. "It is only that."

"He's a damn good priest—he could've married us," I said.

Then again we were wordless. She saw I couldn't tell anything true of it. I could not look to it the way she said I should. It was too soon to in any truth, to see what such things are in the world, let alone in words. She let me be.

"You are hurt. You must rest," she said.

She was kind. She was tender, she was this kind and caring girl, and she took my hand in the quiet, she held that hand to hers that had done such things, and her touching me changed me.

I said, "Why are you good to me?" in her touch of my hand.

"You are good," she said, being all young and wise as she was. "You are like a kind hurt boy, but you are not. You have done something bad like a man, but you want to be happy like a boy. You are a man, and you are not a man."

"Why do you like that?" I said.

"You yet feel things."

"You don't?"

"Not like you."

"Someone hurt you. Tell me who hurt you."

"Don't you want a happy story, John LeBlanc?"

"You're a good storyteller, tell me about it," I said.

"No—you really don't want to know it."

"I do, I do want to know."

"I told you—there was a war, like this one—a soldier in a war," she said.

She did not go on.

"All right, you're right. I don't want to know about it," I said. I didn't want to hear too soon about that, any of that, that was too unhappy and hard to hear too soon like that, in that way, from her, I didn't want to see that when I saw her when we'd just met once more, and she knew it, and didn't say it, and I said, "But you can tell it, if you want to," I said. She sounded like she wanted to, I don't know in her mind whether for herself, or for me to hear.

"I told you, it is not a happy story."

I didn't want to hear it, but I think she wanted to tell it.

"So, tell me a happy story," I said.

"I don't know any happy stories."

I think she wanted to tell me that one.

"You told me some pretty good ones. Tell me another one."

"They were really not so good," she said sounding young and shy again like a girl, and not so knowingly wise, as she was. I saw again how she was a girl. She had seemed otherwise. There were the dark and worldly eyes, but she was just a girl. "Once, I told you what you wanted to hear, John LeBlanc—I shouldn't now," she said.

"Tell me another one of them with a happy end—we'll tell the bad things later," I said to get her to go on telling what wasn't unhappy and hard. I saw how we'd go on right there and then good in that room in the rain as we'd had before when we were making it all up. We'd forget the bad in people and ourselves.

The lightning strikes hit and the rain came hard to the courtyard.

"Tell me a good, long, happy story to pass the storm," I said to her in some fun and I was not simply playing. "Make it happy," I said.

"But you didn't tell me about America," she said. "Tell me—there are good things to tell? Tell me one good thing," she said.

"All right," I said. I finished my tea. "I'll tell you something—one good thing."

She waited for me to say what it was. Nothing came to

me, and I only saw her before me, and I said, "There are good things." I wanted her to know that.

"Tell me one true thing about America," she said.

"Say 'America' again," I said to her.

"America?" she said. But it was a question.

"Say it again—say 'America'," I said. She said the word, *America*. The way she said it some of the land appeared to me in big and burnished light like some far off majestic idea when she said it. It was her voice. There was this boundlessness in her way of saying it, as when one believes in the greatness of what is said. She made it another place in her saying it.

"When you say it," I said, "I see it good. Say it," I said.

"America," she said, "America," and a sight or two of it came again good in her voice. I felt something new for it in her voice. Then she was gone quiet. Then the feeling was gone. The sights went. There was the room and us in it.

"What did you see?" she said.

"I saw a great lake," I said and stopped. It was the water that came.

"Tell me each thing you saw," she said as when instructing a student.

"It's all gone," I said.

"Close your eyes," she said.

I closed my eyes.

She said, "*America, America,*" strongly, slowly, strangely and we were like two kids making up a new little game to play if not a whole new land to discover.

"Tell me what you see," she said.

So, keeping my eyes closed I said, "There's the big water of the lake, white-capped to the sky—I see the big bluff, with the tall trees, black-barked against the sky—there's the old house, sitting back from it—the windows dark, rattling in the wind—there's browned leaves blown across the green of the yard—like a storm blown through off the lake—," and I opened one eye a little to look at her, now making it up as I went, wanting to tell her good things about America, seeing only those few stock images of the land along the lake and she was listening to me quietly, contentedly, as though approving of a student's recital, and so I said, "there's golden light hitting the water, the light slanting down far, out across water that goes to the sky—the light's breaking, cutting down to water through high overcast sky—everything's brilliantly lit to the far line of the sky—the water's lit like fire," that came to me with little effort, and as much as I was making it up, I was seeing it real as I was saying it, and I stopped saying it before I said and saw things I didn't want to see, with her own voice now gone quiet too long on me. I opened both eyes and she was sitting there quieted looking at me.

She said, "It is a kind of vision, John LeBlanc. It is good. You will go there. You will get home." It was a pronouncement.

"I don't want to go there."

"Did you see anyone there?"

"I didn't see anyone."

"You didn't see yourself?" she said. "You didn't look."

"You don't believe in it, do you?" I said.

"But, I think you must believe it," she said to me.

She looked at me. She was thinking it through. What it all was and what it might mean. I looked down to the old books sitting there on the floor wet at my feet. I picked up a book. It was heavy and wet. I didn't want it to be ruined. But I couldn't read it anyway. I opened it up. It was that big book of those old Arabian stories that'd been put into the French and that she'd read in the school to the children and to the soldiers in the hospital. I remembered how she'd read the English from out of the French, and I saw the boys laid out in the big room of beds. I sat there with that big old book of hers I couldn't read opened up on my lap looking at the pages of its undecipherable text with her there beside me, and having gone not one place in the world but in her words that'd led me on to mine, whether to home or not, with all that far off only imagined travel done, I found no matter all where we'd went I was kept put there in that place with her all happy and home. I wanted to stay there feeling how everything had stopped with her. I did not want to go too soon off anywhere without her, feeling now I mustn't be taken by them old men, and I said, "Read me one of those old stories you read."

I had the book in hand. But she didn't take the book from me.

"You've already heard them. They're all still the same," she said.

"But I like how you tell a story," I said.

"How do I tell it?"

"Like it's all a world I've never seen."

"That makes you happy?"

"Happier than I've ever been."

"Will you be happy, if I read you a page?"

"Read any page—forget about America," I said.

"But you will go home there," she said.

"I've never thought of it as home," I said.

She looked at me. She took the book from me. She opened it up. She began to read. She read aloud to me from the pages of that old Arabian story to make me happy. She was a good reader. She brought it all to life. I travelled on in her strange and pleasant voice hearing in it all the far off imagined places, seeing us two ourselves gone off a time like that, I don't know to where or what, and when she'd turned the one page, having taken me off for good out of that room with her not to return as long as she turned another, after the one page she stopped with the book, and the life of that world was gone, and without her words we'd returned to the room having gone nowhere. I looked up at her. There was the blued shawl hung up behind her. All the things and us sat right there left unmoved in their actual places.

"You don't want to read?"

"You didn't tell me about America. Tell me something true about America. Tell me about the people—you didn't really tell me anything of the place or the people." She said, "Tell me of your home."

"Tell me that story of those two people you once told me."

"I've already told it."

"What happened to those two people you told of?"

"They went home—nothing happened." There was the house along the river.

"Were they happy?" I saw the village.

"They were home." She said no more of them.

She was done with all the books and the stories for good and I was seeing once more them made up people, remembering how in that hospital I'd had her tell that happily-imagined story of those only invented people that weren't anywhere to be found in a book. I remember when she'd left off with them there, in those days everything was in front of them still to be in what she'd told, and I remembered how they'd gone on together home. I remembered their talk of a child. They'd sat out at a little iron table in the light. They'd gone on home together to the house. She'd told a pretty good story of them. She'd told me a good story of them people in a place. And I was thinking then that, just like in that vision of America she'd made for me in her own girl's voice, for me to believe in to get home, that all what she'd made up when we'd first met in such a good way to tell me in that hospital about them two people, about how it could be between two people, that that could be a true story never to be found in a book if we ourselves just went on with it long enough wherever we went.

23

THE TRUE STORY OF A NAME

And wanting to stay held in her words for the world with her in the room in that feeling of home I inexplicably had in her, and felt true, I said at the sight of her shawl, seeing the blue of it draped in its dark folds hung up in the little room off the door to dry, in seeing how she'd kept it close, how she covered herself with it far from home, I said, "Why do you wear it here—?"

She said, "Do you want to hear a story of Africa?"

"I want to hear a story of Africa."

"Do you want me to tell it true?"

"I have never heard a true story of Africa," I said.

"I will tell you what cannot be found in them books, I will tell you about the people in the place," she said.

"Tell me about the land and the light," I said, and in her voice, I saw a whole continent coming.

So there in that room that day in the old colonial school she began to tell me about the people and the place. She told me a true story of herself that day in that room in the old colonial school.

"Do you know what a *Tuareg* is?" she said.

"Tuareg? No—I have never heard of the word."

She said, "*Tua-reg*," to me and I couldn't say it the way she said it.

"I am a 'dark Tuareg,'" she said as a fact.

"*Tua*-reg—it's a strange-sounding name," I said, in my sounding it out to her as I could.

"There are these people, and that is how they are called, how they are known, even though it is not their true name," she told me.

"And you are one of them?" I said.

"I am one of them. They are desert people," she said.

"They wear those blue cloths—like yours?" I said, and I'd never seen anyone wear one but her and in those few words of hers about the place I saw the blue color of it brilliantly worn by the people in striking outline against a great desert sky.

"The men wear them, to cover their faces," she said.

"Not the women?" I said.

"No. The women wear it up, like you've seen me do."

"But, why do you wear it here like that?"

"It is a custom, a kind of protection," she said.

"You never hide the face with it?" I said, looking at her face, and then felt I should not have said it.

"No, I never cover it," she said. "But once—I did it once," she said to correct herself, to tell it true. She did not look away from me in her saying it, and in that talk of that shawl she began on the story of herself. She told me a true story of herself and her people.

I sat there in the old French school with them old French books closed up quieted in their covers at my feet, listening, not looking to them any longer. I looked to her. I looked from her to the shawl. In the sight of it, I traversed a continent, in her voice were pictured desert scenes, I looked back from the dark blue of it hung on a door, to her all darkened in look sitting tranquil, composed, elegantly-cut in that easy flowing white of her robe telling me of her people. Her people were the people who wore the indigo blue, dark desert people riding with rifles, hung strapped with swords, fiercely coming from out of the continent of Africa from vast unsettled land, for centuries crossing the desert land, attacking and trading, from the far southern mountains of Ahaggar to the heart of the Sahara, traversing the continent in caravans across sheer sand and sky, some of them now gone in years of revolt against the French as far as the northern cities of the sea. Her people they had no official land. Her people they lived in, on, across this unbounded unmapped land with nothing having been put down once and for all by them for good on the land to claim it, nothing put on paper to properly name it, ever built to defend it, nothing left to last across the lay and look of the land to change it, possess it, to make it appear their own in the style of an architecture, and all round us the rain hit the stucco walls of the French courtyard hard and her blued shawl hung out there on the door hook to dry in the dim light of the little room in the old colonial school and, in that walled space in her words for the world, there was the immense crossing of land and light, the emptied-out expanse and barren brilliance of the land-light, the deep blue riding up high against the unending sand and sky across vast and vacant land-light.

"*Tuareg*," I said the name trying to see the people real in that land as she brought them before me and I'd never heard of the word or the people, and I saw them clearly, saw the look of them in the look of her, in what I saw of her, in how she'd told of them, this dark girl come in her sharp contrast to the stylized look of this old colonial land from that limitless and undefined light. There I saw her before me free, then as if another girl. I think I saw her herself for the first time. I forgot who and where we were. I forgot the fact of the city called Saigon, and the old French school surrounding us seemed an insignificant thing. I wanted to forget. She made me forget. I forgot what was done and what all could not be undone. I forgot what I wanted from her. I think I saw her herself for the first real time there when I saw who she was once outside my wanting. I saw her outside my wanting her. I saw her in her own history.

She said that they called her people the Tuareg in the French in loose translation from out of the Arabic. She said she was not an Arab. She said in France she was called *black* as all dark people from Africa are. She said that her people they were called 'Tuareg' but they were named the *Imashagen* in their own language.

"*The Free*," she said. That's what it meant in the original *Tamahak*. And all the words came strange-sounding and new in her saying the word 'Imashagen' and now I saw us gone off and lost to the boundlessness and brilliance of that as yet only imagined land never to return. There we two were out in an unending, purely invented land in that French courtyard, and I saw how we might go off together good to such an imagined and immeasurable long unsettled land. It was a sight.

"The Imashagen," I said. I sounded it out. And in the act of my own saying it, it sounded familiar. I heard it then by ear as when one recognizes some old song, and I said to her, "It sounds like an old Indian name," I said and I saw all those old Indian names like that that you'd find set out all over a map of America that you'd found in an old desk drawer and folded out over a kitchen table, thinking of where to go off to for good, or you'd discovered printed in the pages of a history book you'd read in a schoolroom written on how the land was named, lately, in a multitude of places, for the people who'd first long ago lived on it and never named it and, in my seeing all that in the simple saying of the sounded-out word, I looked to her in uncanny realization, recognition, and I saw some of that old Indian look in her. I saw it for the first time. I was happy seeing her look so. There was the look of home in her. In that looking I saw my own mother dark. I looked off. I hadn't seen her that way before or just hadn't known it, maybe I hadn't wanted to see it, and when I did, though I was unsettled by the association, I was not unhappy to see some of who she herself was, in that way, as when reading one of those old books she'd given me when I'd come across a character, to see them appear at last in some few passing images, if not to appear in given name, then come alive in a world when, to form an apt picture, some true words were at last fitted to them in time, when richer associations were congregated to people-out a stretch of pages. And just as if having myself turned, in the pursuit of such peopled-images, from the one page to another of a book, I turned from such recollected sights of home, and looked back to her herself from the yellow stucco walls of that French courtyard struck with rain, and I said to her about her people, in seeing some of my own:

"But why are your people called the 'Tuareg,' if that's not their name? Tell me what it means," I said to her wanting to know what it meant in the language.

She said to me, "It means *abandoned by the gods.*" She said that it came from out of the Arabic into the French to be put against the people. For they were seen as godless wandering tribes.

She said it slowly, in some hardness, in a kind of staccato enunciation, so I could hear the designation of the phrase, as if she were not so much naming the people, but translating the enigmatic title of a treatise or a history book from school to me and then she said to me, "I'll tell you something about my own name, too, John LeBlanc," she said. "The *Madeleine* was never my name."

Then we began to talk too seriously of names.

She said that that name *Madeleine* that she now had, and that I called her by, that that name it was not her true name, that although now it was her real name, that it was not ever her given name. That name was just the name officially given to her on her paperwork. It was an officially given name.

"*Madeleine*—it's not your name?" I said to her and I'd seen her in it all along, and now it seemed I'd seen in my saying it someone else, and I felt the familiarity of her go, no matter that she was right there before me as she'd always been.

"It is not a true given name," she said, and I'd only ever called her that.

"But you call yourself that. Why call yourself that, if it's not your name?" I said. "Madeleine," I said to her and now it felt funny saying it, like I was saying her own name, her name from the beginning to me, now to another person.

"The world must know who you are, John LeBlanc."

"Well, what is your name then, girl? Madeleine, tell me your real name," and I saw her in the Madeleine.

Now, I've long known that there's everything and nothing in all these names, and even in my own. But I'll tell you, that when she told me she had another name, I wanted to know that name, I wanted to know what her true name was. I wanted to see her in it. I wanted to know that name, to call her by it. That would be her name then for me to call her, I wanted to know her in her name.

"Tell me your true given name, girl," I said.

"I will tell you," she said. "I was first called *Tintifawin*—," she said. "It means 'of the light' in the Tamahak," she told me, remembering. She said, "No one knows me by that name."

"I like that name," I said. "Tintifawin," I said to her, and I saw her a dark girl lit against a desert sky, and she told me the *Tintifawin* was lost for good when she'd gone north. It was never written down.

"The 'Madeleine' comes from another," she said. "When I was older, I went by another given name." And she said that when she was a girl in North Africa she'd been given an Arabic name that she was called by. She said that the French they'd then written that Arabic name out another way on her official paperwork so that they could read it. When she'd come to France, they'd put it down that way on paper for her in another alphabet so to read it. Then that name was her real name. The one day when she'd got her official paperwork, she was called *Madeleine*. There was the whole bureaucratic genealogy to how it'd become her real name though it'd never been given to her from out of a lived lineage. It wasn't true-given.

"So, tell me that name, girl, the name it comes from," I said. "I'll call you by it," I said, "I'll call you by your Arabic name—isn't it more your name than the French one girl," and I'd called her *girl* then again and then when I had, I liked the sound of it, calling her girl, and she didn't tell me, she was thinking back on them names of hers, as though seeing other girls, and then she'd no name but that of *girl* for me while there we sat in the little room in the school in the storm having traversed all those far off times and places in those some few spoken names, interchangeable names, ones that in their bureaucratic etymology told really nothing of the actual individual girl right there now before me, whatever the name, but did tell of the history of her, of the general history of people in places, and I saw her herself right there before me who she was and would be to me in my simply calling her girl outside all the rest of it, the whole history of it. I saw how I'd only ever call her girl and I'd be happy in my calling her that without knowing any one other name or the history of how names had been given, taken, written, and unwritten, and she began to tell me of the history of her name.

She said to me, "The *Madeleine*, it comes from *Mahdiyah*," she said.

"Mahdiyah," I said the name, sounding out the separate syllables as though a child, as when one is learning to speak a new language. I said it to her as I could in my trying to see her in the name and I didn't and I had the Madeleine in my head for her because it'd been the first thing I'd called her however wrongly. "But what does it mean, girl? Tell me what it means in the language," I said to her. I wanted it to mean something. It is meaning one ever wants in people, places, and things. I wanted to see her in it, as in one of them old Indian names you'd be given to tell you something of the person, of the living person, who they were in themselves, to let you see someone in the saying of the name.

"It means *rightly guided* in the Arabic," she said. And she said it was taken in translation from the original *Tintifawin*, and she said she was not an Arab. She was a Berber. She was from an ancient Berber tribe of noble lineage. She spoke a language older than Arabic, *Tamahak*. She'd only been given the name in the North. She'd gone by the name in the North, and I said, "But why did you take the name in the North." She said to me, "There was a war," and we passed over that part in the genealogy of the name, and then I said it to her as I could. And she said then, "No, don't say it. You know it. That's enough—call me *girl*," she said. "I like it when you call me girl," she said.

"But isn't it more your name, than the French one? Shouldn't I call you by it?" I said to her, so that she'd have a proper name for me to call her by, though I did want to call her girl.

She said, "No, I'm no longer that girl. That girl is gone. I'm someone else. I'm another girl now. I don't want to hear it said anymore now, when I'm someone else." She said she was someone else. She was neither the *Tintifawin* nor the *Mahdiyah*. Those girls were gone.

"All right, girl," I said. "It's all right—. We'll get rid of the names, I've never liked names anyway," I said to her. I said, "You'll want to see someone in them, and they'll never give you anyone as you'd want them anyway."

"So, you've learned something about names, John LeBlanc?" she said to me.

"But, I do like the name *Madeleine* for you," I said.

"Why do you like it, 'John LeBlanc'?" she said.

"When I say it, it feels familiar for you," I said. "Maybe I shouldn't, but I see you in it—it was the first thing I called you," and I know if you repeat such a thing, calling another by it long enough, it sounds right and of proper origin, originally said and as though first said, no matter how lately taken up, in arbitrary, official attribution, and she knew that. She'd long known that.

"Then, you can use it for me," she said.

"All right, girl," I said to be funny about it.

"And yours—tell me about *John LeBlanc*," she said.

"It's any name—it comes from nothing truly given. I've never seen myself in it," I said. "Do you see me in it?"

"'John-The-White'—it is a father's name?"

"Yours," I said. "Tintifawin—is it a mother's name?"

"It is a kind of mother's name, given to girls—it's an old Amazigh name from the Tamahak, given to Tuareg girls."

"Then, I'll say it to you sometime, girl—I'll call you by it, and you'll see yourself young again. You'll just be this girl again—before all the rest of it," I said to her, and in our playing, in such a way like that with all the names, I reached out and I took her hand, I held her hand in mine, she held on, and we forgot the names.

They were gone in that touch.

"Yes—all right," she said in some simple relinquishment, she said in tenderness, and I felt young and close to her, and in that feeling, not thinking any longer of who we were, how we were now called, no longer gone off in the names to old selves from our actual selves, I lay my head there down on her, in brief regained respite, I lay my head there, right on the stark white of her robe, there in the center of her herself, and she lay her hand in care upon my head, "You are hurt," she said and there she held me to the entirety of herself, to the full form of her, the dark-felt curve of her, she took me into her and she let me be like that held against the whole of her.

"Are you all right, John LeBlanc?" she said.

"You are not afraid when I touch you?" I said to her.

"Tell me why you want to touch me," she said in her care.

"I told you, I'm alive with you, I don't feel deadened,"

and I'd touched her and she'd touched me, neither one of us knowing if or how we should touch one another in our want and whether it was wanting or love, but touching one another in quiet care.

"I am not afraid, I want you to touch me," she said.

"Tell me why you want me to touch you," I said. I lay in her lap, "Tell me, why do you want me to?" I said.

The rain struck on into the courtyard stone hitting it hard.

"No—you must rest. You will stay here, tonight," she said. I looked up to her. She looked to me as though it were a settled thing because she'd said it. She sounded all practical about it. We weren't playing anymore.

"I don't want trouble for you," I said.

"We are not children anymore, John LeBlanc," she said.

"Sometimes, I wish we were," I said and I lay there kept like a child into her in real repose and stayed that way awhile.

24

WHAT IS TO COME

I was waked naked beside her dark in the light and I saw her, I saw her laid out all alive and naked along me in the coming light and I remembered how I'd gone to her in the rain. I found myself waked there without the deadness of waking and looked round the room at her few familiar things and at my clothes strewn on across the floor as if awakened to another unknown place and time, if not a life. I lay there. I could smell the morning air coming across the tiled floor. The French doors to the courtyard were left opened and the whole room was filled with that damp cool smell of morning and being waked there like that with her I felt all young and alive and as if I'd waked without a past with everything in front of me. I felt at the beginning of myself. I lay there in that bed with the mosquito netting closed round us, shrouding us nicely in the slatted light, with the books scattered on the floor about the two chairs, with all we'd said to pass the storm having passed the day into the night, having said little to nothing in the night, but come all alive in one another in it, and as the world came back returned on into the room I heard the boots of running soldiers in the street and the passing jeeps honking, echoing up over into the courtyard walls and I remembered who and where I was and what I must do. I must return to them men or flee.

  I remembered my own life.

  "I should go," I said.

  "Don't," she said.

  We lay there quiet.

  "I don't want to," I said.

  "You're hurt. You haven't rested," she said.

  "Why do you want me?" I said.

  "Don't you know, John LeBlanc?"

  "I've got to go to my room—change," I said.

  "You will come back?"

  "Of course, I'll come back."

  "John LeBlanc."

  "Yes?"

  "Be careful."

  I got up. I took my pants off the floor and put them on. I did not know if the old men would find me or not if I went back there to the room. I did not want to go back there. I did not want them to find me. I felt I must be free of them for her if not myself. But I'd left the rest of the money there, my clothes were there, the bags, my shoes, the pistol. I had to get the money, get my things out of there. I'd go get them things that told of me out of there, I'd go get another room. I'd come back to her and we'd talk as we'd talked. We'd tell the rest of what we'd had to tell. We'd keep together in telling all what we should have told before.

I took my shirt off the back of the chair and put my shirt on. I sat on the chair and looked out to the courtyard and put my boots on. The light was hitting the courtyard walls. It was brilliantly lit. The weather was clear. The priest went along the other side of the courtyard behind the glassed doors in his black robe. I don't think he could see into the room to me. I didn't give a damn if he did.

"I've got to teach, French to the children—but there is time for tea," she said from behind me. "You can stay here. You don't have to go. I'm making some tea." I heard her with the pot and putting water into the pan. I stopped and looked over at her. It was almost like we'd waked up at home and as though we were going off from one another to work. She said nothing about the night. I didn't either.

"I'll come back this afternoon," I said.

I tied my boot and stood up. I was dressed and I turned from the light of the courtyard. She stood there black in her robe in the light. I came up to her. She looked shy. I held her. She held her robe shut against her. I put my arms round her. I held her lightly. I held her to me. She leaned into me. I held her harder. I held her close to me. We held then to one another. Her hair was against me. I rested my head gently there against hers. She smelled good. She turned her face up to me.

I felt how I loved her.

"You want me cut like this?" she said. She was young.

"More than I ever wanted anyone," I said and I was young and that was true.

"John?" she said.

"Yes?" I said.

"Are you coming back?"

"Yes, I am coming back."

I went out into the street. I walked down the street in the light. Every thing was changed. All was the same. The street was the same close-crowded street. The room was the same unremarkable and anonymous room. The room was all untouched.

When I'd got back to my room on the rue de l'Abondance it was all untouched. I saw no one. No one had come. I took the envelope of money out of the drawer. There was the pistol laid along it. I looked at it. I left it there laid on a shirt. I went back down the stairs to the little lobby. The man at the counter said he'd seen no one. No one at all had come looking for me. No one had come for me.

"This is for you," I said. "Take it. You have never seen me," I said to him. It was a hundred dollars. He took it without a word. He gave me another key. He said, "I have never seen you." I went up the stairs. I moved my few things to the room next door to the one I'd been in. If they came, I'd hear them come. If anyone came, I'd know they were looking for me. I changed my shirt. I looked into the mirror. I got a razor. My face was blackened and blued and yellowed-up from the fight. I shaved. It hurt to shave. I left. I went down the stairs into the light to get to her. I was finished fighting.

25

THE WOMEN WERE STORYTELLERS, THE MEN WERE WARRIORS

I found her having tea in the courtyard. We sat out in the courtyard. It was afternoon. She was done with her teaching for the day. She made me tea and brought it and we drank a time in the afternoon solitude awhile before I said to her, "But how did you get here, to this place, to this school?" and I drank from the cup and she told me about France. She'd been a student in France. She'd lived in a city by the sea called Montpellier. She'd walked the beaches there in Montpellier whenever she could and she said she'd been close to the sea there in the South of France as she'd been as a child in the North of Africa. She'd look across the water. Across the water was Africa, and she said it and I saw it. The long coast of it came in the name to that courtyard to illustrate the actuality of the water and land as if clearly pictured on paper before me and it's not even the ink and print of a map or book it's just her voice I hear. There I saw her a girl living in a place she called in the English *Oran, Algeria*. She was living in a city by the sea. Sitting there in that courtyard I was off with her in the streets of that far city seeing her there in it hearing it living all about us. She was a girl again and she wanted to talk about the sea and in what she said it came round us real in that place once called Saigon, Vietnam, I use the name now so that it, and us in it, may be somewhat seen.

  I sat there beside her in the courtyard in the French school in the old colonial city of that far Eastern country travelling off gone in what she'd said to the pictured images of another far off unknown country and I tell you that that Mediterranean Sea going out from the North African city of Oran, Algeria that I'd never once seen, I saw that water as clearly as you'll see in the Middle-West of America in what is now a place called Michigan a great lake going out to the far line of the high sky. In the elemental affinity of such images all is remembered. The water is always to be something real. She said she hadn't seen the sea enough though it'd been right there before her. She'd been too close to it. She saw it easily now that it was gone.

    She said, "Now I see it clearly, and it is gone."
    "I see it—it isn't gone," I said.

She felt she'd read too many big books too young and not seen enough things in the world though she'd seen some things. She said she did no real reading now. She was finished with books for a time and after her studying in Montpellier she had gone off from France to see and to know some things in the world and she did not have a real country to go back home to in North Africa. In those days there was not even a name in the French for the land she had left. In those days when she was a girl in the North of Africa there was a war with no name in a country with no name. She said if you look in a French history book of the time you will see that that is true. No matter the names and the country, there were no names and no country. Nothing was official. Not even the war, and I had not thought of her coming from a land like that. I had not thought of her herself coming from such an unofficial, actual place.

And I saw some of America once more in what she'd said, and I reached out and I took her hand in my hand as you know I have often done and there in that French courtyard I was seeing how it was to be going off like that once and for all for good from an unofficial actual place. I saw her long dark hair in the light and I remembered that America was once such a place. America was once such an unnamed place long before I'd gone off from it where everything, however named, lay unrecorded, unofficial, the land and the people, who they were, what they did, was only to be ever known in the telling of them, never to be recorded in name only repeated, the people who they were, never to be known once and for all in their being officially written out on this or that piece of paper to end as a named fact. It was all a lived lineage. Though it's true even today that it's not the name itself, but who does the naming that matters.

We talked on of people and places and how they were to be known in names.

"It's funny," I said. "They put you down on paper—

who you are—and no one really knows anyone that way," I said to her and I wanted to know her and her people, who they were beyond all names and official things, what they'd done, where they'd gone, how they'd lived, and I said, "Tell me what happened to your people. Where are they now?" I said and I saw them dark and distant. I tried to see them. I saw my own. "What became of your people?" I said that to her then and I saw her seeing them come before her in her remembering them. Her look changed. She was younger in it.

"Were they good people?" I said.

She said, "In Africa they were free. We were never poor." She said, "The women were poets and storytellers. The men were warriors," and I saw them riding once more strapped with swords, riding with rifles from out of the great desert of the south to the unnamed north to fight the French.

"There was a war. You were a girl," I said. "You left Africa."

"Yes," she said. "I was young, and I was not even unhappy. It is a usual kind of story."

"Tell me about the war."

"It is ended," she said. "We went to France. In France everyone becomes old and poor."

She said no more of Africa. She said no more of France. I tried to see the land she had come from and I saw a doubled kind of land. I saw the North of Africa and I saw the South of France. I saw a contradictory unlikely land and we heard the gunfire and looked up to the sky. There were the heavy concussions of the far artillery strikes and we heard the impact come close across the city to the open air of the courtyard to the yellow stucco walls going up to the red tiled roof to the clear blue sky. The window panes in the courtyard doors rattled. The priest came out to the hall along the opened French doors on the other side of the courtyard to look up. He'd heard it. He stopped. He looked out. He saw us. He went on.

We were sitting out on these aluminum lounge chairs on the stone of the courtyard and we got up from the chairs not so much from the concussions but from his look and went into the room of the school and lay down in our clothes on her bed close to one another and she told me about how she had gone off from France. After Montpellier she said she'd gone off to teach French because she didn't want to go back to things but away to things. She said, "I wanted to make my own life. Perhaps it is a French idea."

"A very American one," I said.

Then when her studying was finished she had had no money and she had not wanted to go back to live in the south in the poor rocky mountain land of a place called the Ardeche.

"The *Ardeche*," I said it and I couldn't see it in the name.

"It is not easy in the South," she said. Then I saw some of it.

Nothing was easy in the South. That was where her people were now. What was left of her people, they were living there in the South where her parents were living and she told me how all the young people like her they had left the place as soon as they could leave it, if they could leave it. She told me how after the last war in France and long before she herself had come from out of Africa, there was a time when some of the French themselves had left off from the land of France for Africa. She said that in that time between the wars even the old people had left from that poor place in the South of France and gone off to the North of Africa. In those days there was land in Africa for the French. In that time between the wars when after the end of the one and the beginning of the other there was then all the transient and migratory travel off from home to find a home. The people they went to Africa. The people they came from out of Africa.

So it was. There her parents they lived in that poor

place in France where there was no good work for a long time in those days after the wars in the land of the Ardeche. Her parents they were not now any longer young. Her parents they had had no money and she had not wanted to make it hard on them now that she should have been gone off on her own and she said that then when there was no good work in those days there in the South of France when there was nothing in those days for her in France she said that that was when she'd left. She'd gone off on her own. She'd left the place and the people. That is a little of her history. And I wanted to hear more of it.

You know I've always been bad at telling my own.

So, laid out along her I said to her, "But tell me how you got here, to this place, girl. Tell me that—how is it possible," I said and I looked round the little room in the coming night with her naked and dark along me wondering how we two had really got here to this. What happens to you in time you will wonder on. There is all that that you do not ever think will happen to you. In time all happens. But even when it is happened to you, you will think it is all unreal at times, your own life, and there in the little room in the colonial school she said that when her studying was finished she'd wanted to stay on there in Montpellier and to live by big water so to be able to look out into it and to think back on things. There in Montpellier she was to make sense of the things that had happened to her. The bad had already happened to her. There are in time all these things in a life to recollect. She'd look to the water to see some of those things. She wanted to live by big water so to simply look out into it and to think some. She was young. She would walk the sea. She remembered her things. That is how she remembered her things.

When that was not possible she wanted to go off away to an unknown place to be where something new might happen. She wanted to live an interesting life. She was still young enough to. She had read in an old French book about the big beaches on the China Sea. It was a place you did not need money to get to. There were all the children to teach. She knew about them children and she could teach. She said, "It is possible to do it with the Catholics." She said, "There are all these people like the priest to help you." She was not afraid of it. She would go to the sea. There was the sea. It was the water for her. I understood it. After some few people in a life it is always some real remembered thing like that in a life. It is something too familiar of a place put into you. It is to be remembered in all others. If it is water or if it is mountain or if it is land or even if it is city you cannot stop it inside you no matter the place and it will take you away like that to a new and familiar place where you feel at home and happy but not at home.

26

ONE SEES IN SIGNIFICANCES

The mornings passed in some new and unknown sense of home. We waked shrouded in the sheer netting of the bed and I looked over at her uncovered in morning light to find myself, all of myself, always there beside her in them happy first few days. We were happy some as we had not ever once been in those first days. Her unbraided hair hung long and black across her breast. The morning light was coming nicely across us and all the things of the room. I looked at the cut gone straight across her dark and pretty girl's face. It is true I wanted to know about it but I would not ask her anything about it. I was shut up about it. I wanted it to all have been done by some bad-chance. It looked too deeply-done to have been by chance.

I looked to her laid naked out along me young and

alive in the morning light and I wanted to think that she had been lucky in her life. I had never seen such a thing done to someone in such an un-ruined way. That is why I looked. It set off her look. It was the whole look. It was no simple beauty. It was beauty transformed. It was the sight and the feeling of her having overcome it. The light was coming across it.

She looked at me. She looked away. She turned it away. She turned herself from me. She said, "It must be more than looking—," she said. It was how I had looked to it waked in the light. She thought I was looking at her for it. I wasn't looking at her for it. I was studying it. She wasn't self-conscious about it. She only looked at you like that, if you'd looked at her for it. I'd openly looked to it. She'd seen me do it in that unguarded and as if too casual way as when one turns to look at an oddity. But it was not that looking when I'd waked to it in the light. In her, I was looking to myself, as she said I should.

"It is more than looking," I said, and she had wanted me to look, but not without self-significance to the look. It was that insensible looking she could not stand. It must be more than simple looking. It cannot ever now be some sheer and curious looking. It wasn't. Even in the familiarity of awakening, one must have the real regard for another, and we did. We did have that.

We were waking to one another.

"Do you want to know *what it is*, or only to look," she said. She was facing away from me. I looked to the dark untouched skin of her girl's back going on down along the felt curve of the whole of her. I reached out and touched her there along that unmarked curving darkness, seeing, feeling the color and form of an entire world laid before me.

I felt very awakened to the given world in the touch of her.

"I'm not looking at you for it," I said touching her in

true affection. "I am studying you with it, girl—and myself." I told her I was studying her and how she was with it. "It is not some simple looking—I am seeing some of myself." It was more than a look much more than simple seeing.

"You are studying me—and yourself? I will let you look then," she said as though in instruction but she sounded a little hard in her saying it and I had forgot in all her wisdom that she was still a girl who had been hurt bad and she turned back to face me. "What do you see?" she said. "Tell me what you see—do you see some of yourself?" She looked at me. She looked me right in the face. I felt naked in the look.

"There is something I cannot see," she said looking to me. "You do not wear it. It's not those holes. But I know it is there. I see it in you. It is a darkness. It came to you young. And I am studying you with it, John." Then she said, as in some regret, "It is in me too."

She said she could not see what it was in looking though she knew it was there and she said she had studied me and how I was with it. And I did not have a goddamn scratch on me you could see in the broad light of day. You could not see a goddamn thing of what it was. I had a hole or two. You do not wear that like she did. You cover it. You hide it. You continue on in a kind of too easy concealment to the world as she could not. She had seen that. She had touched that. Anyone looking to me they couldn't see a goddamned thing of it. She saw some of it. She saw the rest of it.

"I'm sorry," I said to her.

"Don't be—it is done," she said, and she got up naked.

"Don't go," I said. I felt bad. I wanted her in bed beside me.

"I have to go teach," she said. "That is all."

We got up and dressed. I looked to her, "I'm sorry," I said.

"You should look," she said. "I want you to look," she

131

said. "You know that," she said.

"It is more than looking," I said.

"I know—it must be," she said. "It must be, I'm sorry," she said.

"It is," I said. I was dressed. "I should go out, walk awhile."

"No, don't." She stopped me by hand. "Wait for me."

"I'll wait for you—I'll make tea," I said, and she let go my hand.

I looked off to her things in the room. There I'd pleasantly pass the time waiting there amongst her things for her return. I'd nowhere good to go. There were only the close-crowded streets. There was the dilapidated room, my discarded things. She was fixing her hair, getting ready to go. Now, I'd nothing to do but to wait for her return amongst her things and I looked round her room to them as she dressed amongst them. I saw her in them. One only sees in significances.

She was dressed and turned to me and said, "Do you want to read?" She wanted me to occupy myself. "I could read," I said. She said, "There is a classroom, full of English books—down the hall. The priest, he has been teaching English to the children—he says these days, the French is not enough."

She took me down the hall.

"Isn't it strange that they still teach French, here—to these children?" I said in the hall passing the doors of classrooms.

"It is not strange—it is history," she said.

I held her at the door. We looked off away from one another. Then her hand fell from mine. She went off to teach her children. I went and sat in the empty classroom. It had long rows of ink-stained wooden desks. It was in a part of the building that sat along the street. There was a row of huge sycamore trees running along the classroom windows at the edge of the street. The trees were old and tall. I looked at their spotted bark where the big trunks of mottled green and white and brown were mixed and patterned indiscriminately looking as though a kind of natural camouflage and I heard the coming of engine and the shifting gears and looked past them trees out into the street to a line of coming trucks beyond the line of trees and saw the green helmets passing in the dark canvas covered ends of the army trucks beneath the tree canopy. I watched them go. Bicycles came down along the street. There were boys and girls with long black hair on bicycles.

    I left the window and took a book out of a walled bookcase and opened it. It was the title that caught my eye. It was an English translation of Bergson's *Time and Free Will*. I smoked cigarettes at a school desk by an open window and read it. I understood none of it. I turned the pages. The traffic passed in the street. The time passed. I lost the time. Once I'd been lost in that book in time the door opened and when she came back into the room the priest was with her and they were in the middle of a conversation in French. I looked up from the book. He saw me. He looked to the cover of the book. He didn't talk to me. He looked to her. I don't think we even disliked one another. I read the book I didn't understand at the student's desk at the window of the classroom while they stood along the far wall talking in French. I looked up from the book. I looked out the window. Some blue-hooded nuns in black loafers were walking up the street along the trees into the place. The whole place had the institutional and official feel of regulation and order no matter what went on round it and outside it. The school was in one of those big French colonial style sets of buildings spread out, laid out like a kind of self-enclosed compound with courtyards and red tile roofs and dormitories and a cafeteria and there were always these more or less official people coming and going from the place. There were the nuns with the children in school uniforms coming up the street while the two of them quietly talked. It took a lot of people to run the whole place with them children there like that priest and them nuns and the girls and I looked back from the street over at the priest talking to her. He'd left us alone to our own little life. He hadn't tried to stop us. Maybe he knew he couldn't stop what it was that late in a war.

Then they were finished. He went out the classroom door. She shut the door behind him. She came over to me. She took a cigarette from me. She lit a cigarette. We looked into the street. The priest walked out of the school down the street along the sycamore trees. He disappeared down the street along the trees. She was beside me. There were the bicycles passing in the street.

"What is it?" I said to her. The priest was gone. She was looking out the window smoking.

"They must close the school," she said.

"Then we'll be left here alone," I said.

"They are sending me back to France," she said.

"We'll go together," I said.

"You don't have the paperwork—you must have the proper paperwork for France."

"We'll stay here together."

"It is no longer safe here, for the children, for us," she said.

"It is never safe," I said.

She looked at me. She put out her cigarette.

"Put the book back—are you going to read it?" she said.

"I'm going to read it," I said. I had it in hand.

"Then take it," she said. She turned from the window.

We two were to talk. We were to talk about the going away. We left the classroom. I took the book. We walked down the hall. We went in her room. She made tea. We went out and sat on those plastic-slatted aluminum lounge chairs in the courtyard and drank tea. It felt like the place was finished for us.

"It is to end badly, here," she said about the place. "The priest, he said that."

"It has been ending that way all along," I said.

Then we said a couple easy little things like lovers would.

I said, "I just want to tell you, you've made me good, girl."

"But you are good, John," she said, and I'd never really thought of myself as good, but with her.

"No, you've made me good—you can't go away now."

"You were always good."

She poured out the tea. She had got out these fine flower-painted cups and saucers for it. For tea she was proper like that. I liked how she was proper and a little proud in her things. I watched her with the tea and the teacups. There was a nobility in the things she did. She did them small things in her careful and considered way no matter the rest. She made and poured tea in a kind of reverence. I watched her do it and it was a thing I had not really ever seen so much of such care taken in simple things. She made drinking tea beautiful even there in that place in that time when everything was to be finished. I felt the fine and delicate teacup warmed in my hand. I couldn't see myself there without her. I saw none of myself without her. We drank the tea.

The going was before us. We felt it.

I said, "These are very fine tea cups. Where did you get them, girl?"

"There is a girl on the rue des Amis, she sells them from a stall," she said.

"I haven't seen her," I said.

"I'll take you there to her, if you'd like."

"If you want," I said.

"Would you like that?" she said.

"Pour me some tea," I said to her.

She took the pot and poured again some tea. We drank tea. We simply drank tea and there was then the passing feeling of one another. We sat there a time fixed in the present and passing feeling of us. It was the significance of us. The place was finished for us and I had that cup in my hand and felt the great and fragile significance of this simple and quiet care we had for one another in that courtyard. The place and us in it was soon to pass and its presence was not felt like that until it was to pass. It felt like the passing of a life. I had not felt it so present as it was now in the unexpected act of its power and passing. It was the life of us.

We drank our tea in the courtyard and the place was nice and close-quiet about us with the greened leaves of the courtyard trees come about us in the afternoon light and the birds came down to our feet from the low branches of little trees and our fine teacups clinked on the fine saucers she had got out for it. She had to go to France. We sat there in the stucco-walled French courtyard watching the little birds. They would shut the school she did not know when.

"Soon," she said.

"Did the priest say when?"

"He went to talk to the Americans."

"He will tell them, that I'm here?"

"He will not," she said.

"You are so sure."

"He promised me. He doesn't like Americans."

"I forgot. He's a man of God, a man one can trust," I said.

"He will help you—when I'm gone, John," she said.

"But, we're going together," I said.

She stayed quiet. But in her look I saw her thinking. We kept drinking the tea and she said nothing. You could stay happy that way. We should not talk or tell one thing anything to stay that way, let alone talk about going from one another and I put down my teacup. She sat there this strange dark cut girl on a lounge chair in a treed colonial courtyard and I felt how badly and largely I loved her. In the simple feeling of it, such love it was like life. In her I was all alive, happy to be in such life. In such love, I was happier than I had ever been and she was to go and it hit me hard the feeling of it. I couldn't fit any words to the real feeling I had for her. There was only that word love for it and for all the idea of it but not for the feeling. I felt a little afraid in the feeling. I'd never felt happy and afraid like that before.

"What is it?" she said, looking to me across her cup.

"I don't know. I love you," I said.

Then I felt a loss and I'd lost nothing. She was there beside me.

"Are you sure?" she said.

I was struck by how I loved her.

"Yes—I'm afraid."

"It's a kind of love, then."

"I'm happy," I said. "And I don't feel that good about it."

"That must be love," she said. She was serious about it.

"Why don't we just stay here, like this—we'll just keep together in telling about going off and go nowhere," I said. "Let the whole place go to hell round us—we'll still be together in it."

"It is not possible. You know that, John," she said. "I have to go—you have to go, if there is to be anything. There is no life here for us—there is no good life. It is all to be ending badly here."

"We'll never feel these things again with one another, like this," I said. "It will all be over, if we go from here," and I was stricken by the feeling. I told her that.

137

"It is to be hard, I think," she said. "But it is not over, it is not the end for us. It will not be the end," she said. She told me that. She sounded sure of it.

She took up her cup from the courtyard stone.

"How is it not the end? If you go—it is the end," I said and I saw how them men they would arrest me. I would go to the room. One day they would come. Without her I would let them come. Then it would be over. That is the end. I felt some strange respite in the thought of all being finished without her. It was the return of my ruined self. She saw some of it in me.

Then she told me. She told me about the priest.

"No," she said, "The priest went to find a way," she said outright to me. "John, listen," she said looking right at me.

She put down her cup on the courtyard stone beside the pot.

Then she told me about what the priest and her had said for me to know, what he'd promised, where he'd gone, what they'd said in the schoolroom when I'd been reading the book, "I must go to France. You will go to France—if it is possible," she said, "That is what I was talking to the priest about, what I had to tell you," she said, "The priest will find a way. The priest, he went to find out if it is possible—how it is possible," she said. "He must talk to the Americans, to the French," she said explaining it all.

"Is it possible?" I said. "Why didn't you tell me?"

"I am telling you, I don't know if it is possible—that is why I did not yet tell you, the priest must find out," she said. "The priest will find out, the priest will help you, us," she said. "If it is possible, if there is a way, the priest will find it."

She sounded sure of it and that it would be possible.

"It is only paperwork—there must be a way," I said.

"Yes, I think," she said, "But you must have the proper paperwork for France," and all the possibility of it, of us came back to me as a real thing to be before us in the courtyard light and I felt then awhile freer than I had ever been in my life. It was the sheer feeling of possibility.

We'd begin again. We'd become other people. We were yet young enough to. It is all possible. The feeling of it is enough. In the feeling you can go on anywhere to anything.

We drank the tea. The priest would come and tell her, we would wait on word from the priest. These official things took their own time. We sat there in the feeling of going but now seeing and saying some things about the good and bad of places and of the people in them seeing them come before us in knowing how we might go off good. We were sitting there with the place finished for us seeing a little of how we might go off good together to a place like France.

"France, is it a beautiful place?" I said.

"It is a beautiful place," she said.

"Is it a good place?"

"It is not always good."

"What is the bad in it?"

"It is the bad of every place. Is America a good place?"

"Tell me about the city by the sea—was it good there?" I said.

"You never told me about America," she said.

There were good things to tell. We told some of them. We told some of them from that time before when we were a boy and a girl.

She remembered the sea from that time when she was a girl. She told me some of it.

"What was it like along the water?" I said to her seeing it, "You were a girl there," I said wanting to see her happy there in that time when she was a girl. She was once a happy girl. I saw how she would be again.

"The water—it is vast, unending," she said. "The city, it is nothing."

"Tell me about the land," I said to her. I wanted to see

the sight of that land again where she'd once been a girl, maybe one day we'd go off to it from a place like France. She'd been a girl in a great unending land.

So, the whole place and us in it was to be finished, and in that talk of our going we kept close together in the courtyard gone travelled off nicely to nowhere at all a time but in our casual and pleasant talk to far-off lands, and she told me of the brilliance of the light and the land along the sea, and there was the striking and unbounded image of the illimitable desert, and she told once more about the unimpeded immensity of the light of that vast and vacant land kept close beside one another constrained in the dim tree-shaded light closed-off from the city between the cool stucco walls of the French school on them aluminum lounge chairs drinking tea in our little contemporary time.

"It was not all bad?"

"It was not all bad, John," she said.

There was often a happy quiet in the city along the sea.

"But it was not all quiet—like this one is, now?" I said.

"No, it is not the end yet, here—not like that," she said in her knowing of such places. "There, it ends badly—and everyone goes away. Do you want me to tell you the end?"

She put her cup down. She looked at me in question. She would tell it.

"No, I don't want the end," I said, "Not yet."

"All right," she said.

She didn't tell the end. She poured more tea. The light was lowering along the stucco walls. All was kept before us to begin again in this or that word about to be spoken in the courtyard quiet. The birds were at our feet. She took up her cup. I didn't want the end, so she began on America.

She said, "Tell me about America—when you were a boy," and I think she saw all this great and unexpected openness come before her in the word *America* and I did too then when she'd said it in her curious way, strangely, strongly, and she took us back to America, brought the look of it before us and she'd never seen it, and I said to her, "I'll tell you something about the land," and she said, "America—is it *beautiful* land?" she said to me, and I saw the place good again in her naming it, I saw such limitlessness in it, and I began on it for her, and I told her about the beautiful beaches that go for hundreds of miles all along the great lake in America where I was once a boy, for her to see me there young, and told how I was happy, and told her that though it was not a sea like hers was, that still it was just like a sea with its big water and that it had these big sand dunes risen up too like a great desert come from off the water onto land, and when I'd said that, that'd kept the image of it big and boundless, opened-up and unending for her, and in the natural history of that elemental image of the land, the time again came large and limitless to the land, all was at a beginning again in the wild and unsettled sight of it, and I knew then even again in myself, in a kind of happy hope come to me in such an ideal telling of it, that it was all still too early and hard to tell in the short history of the place, what the place was to the people living right there at home on it even today in our own contemporary time, no matter all what'd long been built and put, risen as though in permanence across the lay of the land, to change the look of it, as if to define it once and for all, one couldn't no matter even if it was named everywhere in signs and all laid out easily before you in printed maps and books, because the history of it hadn't ever been fixed long enough in time to be stopped in any categorical or inalterable sense of place once and for all as with some long discovered lands.

"Tell me more about *America*," she said. "I like it when you tell me about America, John," she said. "But tell me about *the people*," she said looking to me. "Tell me of your home," she said.

We were looking to one another in the light having forgotten the going, drinking our tea from out of those fine French teacups in our remembering the good of places. We were simply looking to one another in the courtyard light and I did have more in my head to say about it, but I wanted to keep it good for her, opened-up and boundless for her like I'd seen it when she'd said it, she'd conceived it in a kind of majestic immeasurableness when she'd named it, and I'd seen all this unclaimed land come pictured all unsettled without the people, and I didn't want to ruin it in any too detailed particularity with the people to have it all go, as I was seeing in the irreducible affinity of such natural images, in the long-familiar sight of all that water and land of home, the sea she'd told me of now laid across the generality of what I'd said about the natural aspect of America, and had then the idea of *Africa* in my head, as firstly an elemental place of great sights and grand landscape, and in the juxtaposed sight, I said to her instead of telling her anything of the people in America, "But what does Africa look like? Tell me what Africa looks like, girl. What does the land look like, there where you were a girl?" I said that to her in my wanting to see Africa in the land when she wanted to see America in the people.

We all want to know of other worlds if not selves.

She said, "What does Africa look like? I will tell you something about the look of Africa—I will tell you about the people. Do you want me to?" she said.

"If you want to—tell me. Don't, if you don't want to," I said.

"If you want to know about the land, the people will tell you all about the land," she said looking to me across that teacup in her hand. For her it was not now another little game we were playing with words to see the simple good of places or how we would go happily off to them. That was all an aversion. That was all an ideally pleasant conversation about our going, a convention of going, and she said, "You know John, that it is the people in a place—that is what a *land* is," and I had stopped her before each time when she had wanted to tell me of the people, and I remembered then even when I had asked her once of her people, to see who she was in them, that it was true it was only in some simple curiosity that I had asked her about from where they had come, and I saw I had only wanted a kind of too-simple little, cursory, generality told of 'the people,' of history, of names, and not a complicating-implicating picture of the particularity of the people, told in what lives had been lived and lost and ended.

"All right," I said. "Tell me the end."

"I will tell you about that girl that was cut," she said straight out to me about herself. "Do you want me to?" she said then and not too hard but almost in some regret that it must be said.

I looked in the courtyard light to the cut there long gone across her, fixed on her face in the lowed and walled-in light. When she'd told me about that soldier, I hadn't wanted to have it and its history come too soon round us in a kind of end to who we were now, when beginning on all what was to be new and good before us. But now I felt like I'd been a fool, a child, about it all along. It was in her. It was in me. It was in us all along. It was almost us, and why we were sitting there now together.

"Tell it," I said to her. I meant them words. You cannot go on stopping the people you love from telling the truth of their own lives because you are afraid of confronting your own.

"It is better for us, to know one another—if we are to be together," she said as a fact. It was to be about that soldier. She was all along to tell me. She was to confront what it was in her with me. I saw that. I saw that now. It was not finished for her. I realized she had never told it.

"But, you didn't ever tell it—what it was?" I said to

her.

"No—there was no one to tell, not like this, with us," she said. There had never been a time before like us. There had only been herself in it. She had been alone in it. She did not want to be alone in it. I did not want her to be.

I wanted her to tell it. I was sorry I had ever stopped it.

"I love you, John," she said. "Do you know that?" She sounded young. She did not say such things.

"Do you know how I love you, like I have never loved anyone," I said to her. I wanted to love her knowing her.

"But, do you know I love you?" she said seriously to me. "I want you to know that," she said. "I would not tell you otherwise, it is for you too," she said.

"But why love me? I don't know why you should," I said, "You really should not," I said to her.

"You know why," she said. "You are good," she said. "You have made me feel," she said. "You have made me feel," she said. "I want to feel. I do not want to be dead," she said.

When she said that I only wanted to hear how she was not at all ever ruined with it. In her wearing it she was more beautiful than it. I knew it that she was. No matter if she herself did not in those days. I wanted her sitting there with me all dark and cut sipping her tea telling me how she was happily all unruined with it in the end when it was said and done. After all the rest, it is true that it had ended well and good. There we two were sitting together not unhappily out in that courtyard light. We were nowhere else in the world but in our words.

"*What it was*—as you say, no I have never told it, John," she said. "But we are together for it, it is not simply chance—we cannot now be afraid of such things in one another," she said.

I knew that that was true. I had first looked to her and I had seen the cut. I had seen that first. Then I had seen her blackness. I had seen how she was marked in another way. I saw it in the lowering light. She was not at all ruined with it. It was not at all an unbeautiful thing. It was the thing of her I had happily first seen and loved her for for this loving look she had had no matter her wearing it.

We sat drinking tea in the courtyard light.

"Do you want more tea?" she said.

"I'll have more tea," I said.

She poured out more tea.

This is what it is to love.

She sipped her tea. "So, I will tell you," she said, and she began it. The light was cast nicely across all things and us. We drank our tea from the fine French tea cups. Drinking tea it is such a good quiet simple thing to do with another in such a going light. Drinking tea was the first good thing that we had ever done. To do such a thing in such a place that is the thing. In the midst of all one does not give up on the beauty of things. In such simple things you are sure of the beauty of all things.

27

A QUESTION OF CONVENTION AND WHAT-HAPPENS-NEXT

The birds came to our feet from beneath the trees in the courtyard. The yellow stucco walls stood pleasantly cool round us. The city moved on round us. She was twelve years old. She was a girl. It was in a city by the sea. She lived in a great city by the sea. In those days in that city it was no longer quiet. She went to the water to go swimming and to live a little in the light. She said everything real happened to her along the water in the light. There the streets of the city went on along the white stone walls nicely on out to the cliffs stood tall above the sea. The streets of the city went on out as if to sky from the stone of buildings. I've never once seen the place and yet I see it so clearly. There the long ago sights came recollected clearly in what she said of what she remembered in her telling of them. In her telling there was all the brilliant water and the light of the city by the sea. I remember in my own telling how they came in their simple picture and I told her about the city. I told her about the sea. She liked hearing that. I liked hearing her happy.

She was a girl travelling far-off from home and happy and when I found I'd gone from the generality of the place to the particularity of the people, it's then that I'd stopped the story on her, and I looked at my daughter in the light and she was just a girl in America and I had not forgotten how we were alive in our own lives outside the story and I looked at her long dark hair in the light. And as if now at last returned home from long reverie, we stood once more there without one word on the bluff that I'd been telling about, we looked out to the water I'd told about, there were the beaches I'd seen in the story far from home that went for hundreds, for thousands of miles all along the great lake in the Middle-West of America, with the water cast before us stretching north along the big sand dunes come up off the water risen onto land like a desert dune, where it was still too early and hard to tell all what the place was to the people who lived there on it in our time because the history of it was not yet ever fixed enough to be once and for all written, let alone definitively told to such a girl. But it'll always be too soon to tell of your own life and, when you do, hard to remember the reality of your own life the more you fit it to the convention of a story.

But she was happy hearing me tell the pleasant little parsed-out story of them far-off places and people in a little love story that had taken her off from home awhile to a new and unknown world and she said once I'd gone quiet on her, "Daddy, tell what happened next," my daughter she said that to me, but I was stopped and everything I'd said and seen that'd appeared before us as if it were yet to be lived fell away, and I wasn't unhappy to find myself there with her and not ever in any story of us and wanted to stay stopped.

It's an old game we play. Her mother and I, we had long played it. It is hard to know what you can and cannot tell another you love.

"Daddy," she said. And the particularity can't be told.
"All right," I said. "I'll tell you some of it."

I said that to her to keep her close and I will tell her something of what happened next for in my passing over what the life of it was, holding to a rote form of detail, as in the travelogue of a tourist who's kept a catalogue of destinations in order to give a kind of book report of persons and places, as I must in this part, it doesn't really matter what we tell only that we're kept together telling, it is that all along after all, and she said, "But, tell it true some," a girl grown older beside me there in America when none of it was for years now any longer real and if I told her anything true what I wanted to tell her was only about this land and this light along this great lake in this place now and nothing of any people from another time and place even if those people they are us. But she's always there to put them and my old self before me.

There we two stood a father and a daughter on the bluff above the great lake at the limit of the land in America, and she said, "Mother won't tell it. She said you must tell it," and I couldn't tell if she was a woman or a girl and the birds in the courtyard trees came down to our feet and she was a girl, and there in her words, out beyond, between the stucco walls stood the stone of the city made against the sea and we came to the sand along the sea. There was the unexpected openness. There stretched all the far-off blue-green water of the sea. The openness stretched without end to the flat blued sky in the high light along the sea. There the people they went happy in the high light along the sea. There was a great and unending good weather in the strong light along the sea. In that good unending weather the people they swam in the sea. They lay in the light. It was a high heavy light and everyone moved carefully in it. There were times everyone moved happily in it. It was a good strong light and the people must move carefully in it. It was a weight on you and you went to the water to get out from under it and there she left her indigo shawl on the sand and she went to the water. There I saw the blued cloth laid in the light on the sand in the North of Africa that she'd dried herself with in the little room of the French school in Saigon, Vietnam hearing the children laughing off in other rooms. It hung there dried on the door. I looked at it and listened to her. There are these some few things that you'll keep from place to place for no good reason but that when you look to them and touch them you'll know who you are in them and one day you cannot even know yourself without your touching or your looking to them or without your telling of them.

28

THE FRENCH SOLDIER

"It is history—there are reasons for it," she said in her studied and knowing way, bringing him back to life in her own voice, now her remaking him, and that soldier had returned as if alive and risen Lazarus-like from the dead to come once more on to her by some unhappy chance. She herself brought him back to life and told it as simple fact as if she were telling about another girl, how he came on down along the sea a wandering mirage in the blue of his uniform, appearing from out of the light and heat as if a kind of apparition. His pistol hung black in the light. His sleeve ran with blood. His blood ran reddened in sand. The razor was bloodied in his hand in his want to kill himself. There he came all undone along the sea in his young life to her. There she herself came brilliantly lit wet from the sea as if to save him. He went down with her in his want. There he lay beside her. He called her a girl's name. He spoke to her in his French as if to a lover. She saw how he was sick. He was not the boy he once was. She knew how he was sick. She knew all about these people in these places. There are these beautiful places that one must go from and he could not ever go from it. He could not go to get to her. He wanted only to get to her and home and he could not get to her or home and she came on brilliantly wet from the sea and he held her and there he held another girl. It is always to be so and she was to tell him little loving things in French. She said nothing to him in French and everything was brightness.

He held the blade to the brightness. The sky was up all round him. The light hit down hard on him. The water closed in round him. He hated the light the light it made him sick. He wanted the darkness. He wanted the sharpness of it in the light. He eyed the blade in the light. It is a simple thing. He wanted to feel what it was. He wanted to feel. He put it against himself. He came all alive against it. He called her her name. It is a kind of question. It is always a question. There is no answer. There is the land and the light. There is him heavy and hard across her in the light.

There she lay. She lay there beneath him as if the dead. There she lay not ever now to go from him. She could not go from him with it held high in the light. She lay there like the dead and he was not wanting to kill her. He wanted her alive in it and there it came to her as it had to him and everywhere was blood come across hands and bodies in the light and she lay there with him at last deadened and done with her and he rested like that and she was awakened in it. She was awakened as she'd never been.

She felt the deadened nothingness direly awakened.

She felt the hardness of the holster against her. She felt him. Her hand roused him. She lifted it from him in the light. He let her take it up. Its black barrel shone against the blue. She was surprised by the feel of it. He watched her with it a girl being all careful. He himself cocked it in her girl's hand to show her how to do it. She held it all heavy wet and cocked. She turned it to herself. She held it there into her. She held it to the whole of her. He watched her. She was alive in it. She turned it beneath the high wide sky. She put the barrel to him against the blue. It was all a new and surprising thing for her all hard-cocked in her hand. It was good weather. The white breakers were cracking into themselves all along the land a thousand miles east and west on along the sea beneath the high wide blue. That is how it is done. It is done in the broad light of day. I have seen it done. He waited for it unbuttoned in his uniform. He wanted it done. He was done with himself. He waited for it in the light. It did not come. He suffered it. She watched him suffering it. She saw him suffering it. He waited on it suffering it. She kept the barrel to him low at his loosed belt. She did not shoot him. She kept the barrel put to him unbuttoned in his uniform more alive now against the hardness of that one thing for wanting it more than he had ever wanted any one thing in the high light of the North of Africa or any other place one might want to name in a life.

"Shoot him, shoot him, goddamn it shoot him," and she did not shoot him in the pleasant and lively light along the sea. She would not shoot him with his want more real now than the light itself with her watching him waiting on all what must be done and was not done. He looked off to the sea. All other sights were crowded out of his life. He looked out happily to all that water. He listened on for it. He remembered himself once a boy along the sea. The shot did not come. It was her voice that came to him. She spoke to him in his French. It surprised him to hear her. He thought it was a sister or a mother calling out to him as a boy. He felt himself young and alive. He remembered his life. He saw old happy sights. She spoke to him in the French. She wanted him to know her by her name. She said, "Mahdiyah," and she kept the pistol put to him there in the broad and pleasant light of day along the sea, and she said, "Mahdiyah," and he turned from the old happy sights of his to look to her and he saw her herself then another girl. He saw her another girl. He saw her outside his want. He saw what was done and what could not be undone. He forgot his own life looking to her. The place came real. All came round him real.

"Do it, Mahdiyah. I am waiting on you, Mahdiyah. I am not afraid of that, Mahdiyah," he said to her in his French. He called her by her name. "It is not that Mahdiyah," he said to her. "It is this," he said. "It is all this," he said, and he stood from her and he tried to understand it and he could not understand it and she did not shoot him and he fell on unbuttoned before her in his black boots to the edge of the coming water along the sea raising his arms to the light with the pistol pointed to him in the high wide light hitting hard blank and down on him looking to the light turning himself round and round beneath it saying, "It is all this," he said to her, "The sky, the sea, the sand," and he laughed unhappily in the light and she did not shoot him in her looking to him watching him suffer it turning himself on round and round falling on forward along the sea to turn himself again and again round and round on forward in the high light hitting down round along the sea until he was gone from her suffering it unhappily in the light.

29

IN THE TUAREG STYLE
SHE FOLLOWS HIM TO KILL HIM

"It is done. There is no forgetting it—you must confront it—the badly lived things are in us, John," she said looking right straight at me.

"Did you kill him?" I said to her. That's what I wanted to know. That's what I said to her in the courtyard light. I wanted to know that he was dead and that she was a long time alive and all right alive and she was. She kept the pistol and she went out to the water of the sea. She put the indigo shawl in the water of the sea. She wetted the blue edge in the sea. She washed herself in the sea. She took up the shawl all heavy and wet to her face. She closed it up round her face. She did it in the light in the Tuareg style. She covered her face with that blued cloth for the first time in her girl's life. It was a thing she had never done. It was not done. It was not a thing done by Tuareg girls. Only the men did it like that round the face.

She must do it. She did it. She was a strong girl. I have not yet said how strong a girl she was. There was the cut of it gone right straight across her cheek from bone to bone. I looked at it in the light of Saigon, Vietnam and she felt the newness of it along the sea. She covered herself as she must. She felt the cut of it as she had not with only her eyes to be seen in the brilliant light of the sea going on in the high light along the sea following on after him the sight of him kept before her. The sight of him was kept before her and he was gone and the sight of him did not go and she saw what she must do feeling now that first she was to kill him.

She went on out to the water. She washed the reddened indigo. It stained her blue in wet darkened indigo. She put it once more round her face as she had not ever once done in her young girl's life feeling first that she must find him and kill him that she was right to kill him. She'd seen it done. She knew how it was to be done. She wetted the blued shawl. She rested some in the light. She looked up in the light. She saw him come before her as if real in the room. We were there close in the room in the school. She looked away to the city by the sea. She saw him a blue-colored boy climbing the stone stair to the white walls of the city. She crossed the sand with him in his blue kept at a distance. She followed on after him wearing that brilliant indigo her father himself had once worn from out of the great desert of the south crossing the far continent to kill the French as if a warrior riding with only the eyes to be seen a girl going on in the high light along the sea she did not know to where or what in her following on after the blue uniform from afar. She was a girl wandering bloody in the light. There was a big quietness in the city along the sea. She went on up through the old French quarter in that pretty part of the city where on along the stone streets always she was seeing him and it was not him but another. It was another and another. There were all the blue uniforms come close to her and kept afar. There were the red tiled roofs hung nicely rowed atop the black-ironed balconies of boulevards of rising French stone the buildings white-pillared in alabaster colonnade and she saw him there following on after another. There was the blue-greened sea stretched wide and white-capped to the sky another world laid off from old colonial boulevards to the black line of the far circumferenced sky and there she followed on after another along facades of stone following blue uniforms from afar beneath them high-rowed black-ironed balconies of the long-lit boulevards red-roofed above the blue-green sea. There she went on along the far-curving and unending coast of the sea in that pretty part of the city gone to kill him with the white breakers cracking on a thousand miles east and west along the sea the unbounded land laid off from the ended city inland to the immense South running in rock and sand bleak vast and solitary to the far dark mountains rising up into the big brilliant land-light of the great illimitable desert stretching on into the North of Africa into the whole of the green of the continent.

30

SHE WAS LOVING A SOLDIER

There she stopped. We were enclosed and kept off in all she had said. It was come hard round us two in the evening light in the walled-in stucco. We were caught in it. The stucco walls rose up cool about us. I sat mute in the courtyard. I said nothing seeing it. I kept quiet to keep us there in that time and place. No matter that I must say something I'd not have said it right. I didn't want to say it wrong. I was not to speak. She was cut like that by a soldier and she was loving a soldier who had cut and killed and I must speak. Then I did. I myself broke the quiet.

"Tell me if you found him. I want to know that," I said that to her.

"I found you," she said. "I have found you."

When she said that I loved her the more for it and she turned her face to me and she said, "Touch it," she said to me. "I want you to—do it." She wanted it done once and as if without a thought by me. She wanted to feel it done. She did not want to be afraid of it absently or senselessly done. "It is for you, too," she said to me, "Nothing bad will happen," she said to me.

She wanted the casual everyday act.

"You didn't want me to, like that—I don't want to do it like that to you," I said. I did it. I put my hand to her. There was just a soldier's hand put to her face. She let me. Then she took my hand.

"I'm afraid too, John—but you must remember it."

"But why remember it? I forget everything in you," I said.

"Do you?" She said. "I don't think you do."

"That's why we want one another?" I said. "It can't be—it can't be that."

"It isn't only that—but does that frighten you?" she said.

"Is it love?" I said.

"Isn't it a kind of love, to see everything in another, John, and yet to love?" To see everything in another and yet to love that is a love.

"I can't look at it, like that, like you do—I'm not that strong."

"You must look, I think."

"But, doesn't it go away?"

"No," she said. "It is always before you." She knew. She knew a long time now how it was. Then I saw how it'd always be before us in one another in that way and I was afraid as I had not been and I loved her as I never had.

"Forget him," I said.

"I do—with you, that way."

"Why can't we just forget it all, go be left alone and happy?"

"Have you ever yet forgotten it?"

"I want to—I do with you."

"You will not—you will only make yourself littler and littler to it," she said, "You must be larger than it, make yourself strong in it, John."

Then I thought she was done with it. But she broke the quiet before us again with it. And we returned in one or two more simple words to what all she had said. For some reason she must yet speak of it.

She said, "I felt nothing then in those days afterwards. Now, it is always later," she said. She felt real true things later. Later she felt many hard things well and good. Not in those days did she feel the things that she had had to feel she said. She was young. Much later she felt it inside her. She felt it when it was a badly lived thing in her. She felt it inside her and she saw it outside her when it was long done as a thing and never-ending as a feeling and a face she could not not look to to know the things that had been that were that would be.

She brought it all up out of her. She told me the real things. She said much later she felt it when in times she was living behind it in her badly wanting to forget it and she should have been happy. Then she felt nothing in them days. She did not want it to live in her. Then she would not feel. In time she could not feel.

"There was a time I did not care to live with it," she said.

"Did you hurt yourself?" I said, afraid of what she'd done then.

Now it was still and always later she said but now in her feeling it and knowing it she would be happy. She would be happy no matter her wearing it. She turned in her talk to me. She turned it to me. I was looking to the beautiful uncut side of her face. She turned off from the beautiful uncut side of her face. She showed me only it. It was not that pretty a thing. "We must be happy," she said and I was happy she would be happy. She should have been good and happy by now. She was yet young enough to be happy, and I said, "Goddamit girl," and I held her to me hard.

31

A TIME OF CONFESSION
IS A TIME OF AVERSION

Once there was a time you would go off to confession as a kid to say some words to get rid of the things you had done as if you could make the bad things in the world good again from worse to better in words, and I tell you we must be careful with our words. There are all the things we are to stay a little longer together telling about. There is too much to tell. There are tellings that are to take years, and she said in some tenderness to me, looking to me with that loving face of hers, "It is your life, you will decide when to live in it—or not," and it was that I myself had done it, that it was a thing that I myself had done. It wasn't a thing done to me but a thing that I had done. That was the difference.

"But I have done it, I have done it," I said to her, "It is too soon, it is all too soon," I said to her and I was too much and hard against myself to get the words right.

"I know," she said.

But she waited for me to speak. She waited for something to come. She wanted me not to be ruined in it. It was as if she and I both would be made whole in it.

From what I remember I told her nothing. I was tired of telling. Of course one wants to bare one's self to another one loves. It is a kind of pleasing act of the self to see such regard in what you tell. But when you are too hard against yourself and too careful in your words in fear of the ruined feeling you become quiet and shut up in things. You have got too much to say and you say nothing. You are too much against the authenticity of your own word. It is that you have felt too much too soon and you cannot get your words round it right. It is that you should be shut up to live a little. No matter that you cannot help yourself in your quiet. No matter that you must be careful to be too shut up in too large a feeling. No matter that for one who truly feels nothing must ever be too felt.

She said in some patience, "John—let it come," she saw it right there now risen in me and she wanted to help me. She wanted me to be happy and whole in the end.

"There is no talking for it," I said to her. "There is no talking, to cure one's doing. There's only more doing to be done," I said.

She said, "I am studying you, John, and how you are with it," and I kept quiet on her while she studied me a bit.

She studied the look of my face in our quiet. She looked a little hard at me awhile in the coming light of evening in that little French courtyard. She looked at me as she had looked at me in the rain in the street with her books held in my hands with her arm kept held round the girl. I didn't want her to look to me to study me so closely to see me so well and good like that. I felt too bared and naked to her look.

"Goddamit," I said in heavy and realized regret.

I leaned forward in my lounge chair and put my head into my hands. I tell you I did not want to hide from her. I have never wanted to hide. It is too goddamned hard to hide. I just did not want anything like that to live in me. It was simply that. I was weakened in it littled in it.

I looked down to the French stone of the courtyard and the sounds of the city going on outside us and around us came to us and I kept myself there in the actuality of that hour and I didn't lift my head to see her. She was looking to me from where she lay on that lounge chair. I heard the city moving out beyond the yellow stucco courtyard walls. The sound of traffic came and went. I heard the heavy trucks hauling artillery and I thought of the things done and the things to do.

She let me stay like that. She let me be awhile. The

trucks rattled on and there came the shifting gears and there was the sound of engine and there was the diesel layered on the courtyard air and in my resistance to all what was done, lived up, in my wanting only to go do, to live forward into things, into myself, her, the old sights came on once more unsummoned in their own loosed logic, confounding to the present, to the sense of everyday life, congregated in some unthought sense, all the more vivid in their clarity of being no longer seen in the world but only in mind, the unsettled mind making its own recollected, material place as ever, and I saw the green country come to the courtyard stone, I saw all the country come, I saw them there, strewn there once and for all fallen, there laid down like that, I laid them down there like that without a thought and left them abandoned, there they lay, a mother and a daughter, the last killing in a lineage of killing, the life of them lost in the grass, and there was no sense or sacredness to it. It is that. I let it come before me. I took some care looking at it. I tried to see it as she said I should. They are the proliferation of all thought, the persistence of picture in aversion in irresolvable repetition, amplified, aestheticized sight, in it I saw the child come all alive livid into the world by my own hand no matter the knife alive and wildly naked beneath the burning sky, risen to the light from reddened grass, then nothing, darkness, forgetting, nothing to be new in resolution, and there were people and there were things and there was nothing to be done for done things and I heard her name, *Phuong*, it came to me in the dim light of the hall in the bloodied fight, and the knife was lost at last and gone for good to the dirtied floor, and in her looking I let them beat me bloody, to be washed in rain, and her teacup clinked against her fine French saucer and the birds came and went at our feet in the light and I saw her there an uncut girl along the sea, and she sipped her tea, and I said her name out loud, "Madeleine," I said to her to bring myself back, I only wanted to live in those last days, to feel the material actuality of those happy hours of her, to go off to all the unrealized promise of what lay before us two, freed, unbounded from our acts, and, once more in an acute sense, powerful feeling of the necessity of fleeing, though one cannot flee, I saw how it would be to get up and to go off from that courtyard stone with her out to the water of the sea, it is the water that unbounds you from all the limit of the land a time in a life, from a life, I remembered that, and it was hot and humid weather now always in those days, and I saw us gone off in the morning from that little courtyard to the sea to go swimming in the light, to go a time from all what she had brought before us in herself, and up in me, in what she had told, in what I had had to tell, she had kept it held before us as if it were yet to be lived, and she was right to, I didn't know how right she was in those days, and I saw the sea, saw how we'd lie on a beach side by side close all alive in one another, lovers in the light laid stretched out on that curving whiteness late into the dark not ever now alone in any of the night with all the rest of it, of all what is to be good kept before us.

We'd swim out in the dark water.

Or if not the sea, I saw us getting to a swimming pool somewhere in the city as I'd done sometimes when young in America in the summertime in that kind of weather when you felt you had to get out of rooms and closed up places and get yourself to water. It's always the water you'll want to get to. After all that swimming in the light, no matter what, you were always comfortably tired and clean. It's an old want, and when she'd stood up, at my saying her name with my head held in my hands, her lounge chair scraped the stone of the courtyard. It was one of those familiar old sounds you'll hear as a kid that make you happy for no good reason. I was happy hearing it. I heard that scrape on the courtyard stone in the heat that way with my head down in my hands and I saw how it was to be young and home back in America with everything in front of you. There is a time everything is in front of you. You are young enough in it. There is a time you're not at all ever kept held behind a thing and don't see how you can be. Once upon a time we were all of us young-alive I said to myself as if starting on a story that I didn't know how yet to tell let alone to begin and I remembered how we used to get up in the light from those old aluminum lounge chairs in the summertime to dive into clear water not wanting to come up for a long time from water we wanted that time to last coming up from under the weight of the water into the light to rest. Broken up from that water you will feel once more born into the world.

    She came to me. There she stood before me in the light. She took my head into her hands. She put me against the whole of her. She held me kept into the whole of herself. She held me hard into the whole of her. That is a feeling. You'll go places in it you can never get to in the world. You go forward a little time in your life in some big unnamed feeling and I was taken in it all of me was taken with my head kept rested right there in her black bared arms against her yellow flowered dress and I began to cry and I couldn't stop it. It was a thing come up in me held to her like that and it was heavy in me and I was not even unhappy and I couldn't stop it and I felt young for doing it and for her seeing it and hearing it like that. There was nothing to be done about it. There was not a thing to be done about it. I was too young a boy held right there like that with her and she let it be that way.

    She let it come a time as it must. She let me do it awhile.

    Then she said, "Quiet." "Quiet," she consoled me as if a child. If only it could be so. She stood there before me and she kept me held hard in her arms and I was lost in her. That is a way of losing yourself. That is the way to lose yourself.

32

THERE WE LAY ALONG BIG WATER

We lay naked in the night out on one of those great white beaches along the China Sea. We lay naked in the wet sand awakened to the night. The water came and broke upon us. The sky stood tall and black and clear with millions of stars. We lay on into that lit night in the coming water, the water breaking white beneath the blackness. I wanted to lay there with her until the light came to us in morning across the dark water.

She looked at me with those dark eyes of hers.

"I want to go swim with you, girl" I said.

"We must be careful," she said.

We looked to the loud breaking water wanting to go to it. We went to it. We swam in the dark illumination. We came back from it wet and alive. We were made alive by it. We went down naked on the whiteness lit from the high blackness. We lay there in livid contrast along the sea.

The wet sand cut into us. We felt it and we felt alive in the coming on water. We two lay as if one with the sand cutting into us and it felt good to be awake and alive like that and when we were done we got up to go wash it away. We swam into the dark. We washed it away. We came back in. We went down in it again. It cut into us again and again and we were alive in it all over again.

We went to the water. We came from the water. We were all in one another and when we were done at last with one another we fell off to sleep. We rested in that loud quiet that such water is. You would want nothing else. We awakened naked and surprised. The water broke over us as if two children waked to the world. There was the livid sea, the earth itself as if alive was all about us. I think it did something to us, it seemed all the things of the earth themselves were waked and alive and it did something to us naked in the night waked to one another there along the sea. We said things in the dark that we would not say in the day.

"What if we have a child?" I said to her.

"We have one another," she said.

"You're not afraid?" I said.

"No, I am not afraid," she said.

"We'll be together in it, without the rest," I said.

"We are together in it," she said.

We said such things. We talked of little nothings.

There was the long line of our bodies, the length of our legs gone down along one another in the night. The water broke upon us without one thought of stopping. We talked of mostly nothing. We lay out there as if washed ashore in night with no before or after to any little thing and every little history you could make of things was nothing to us laid out there along the sea. There we lay a time simply a boy and a girl. There was us and there was nothing to tell. There are some few times come in life like that. There is a grateful peace. I want you to know that.

The water roused us from that peace. There was the big sound of the breaking water we went on into crashing white against us. We were gone past the breakers. We were gone in dark water. We went out in it. It could take you away. We let it a little. We were not gone long in it. You could not be. We swam out in from it and lay there nicely tired-out. We looked back to it waked by it.

"It is dangerous," she said.

"It's alive," I said and that water there in that night was strong and alive as if this great wild river come along the shore in the night and I looked to it and I wanted to get back in it. I looked back off from it to her dark marked face.

"It is dangerous, John," she said and I did not look off

from her and we did not go to it. We went into one another. We came all alive in one another in the night along the sea again alive livid like that as we must be and whether it was love or wanting we let it be what it was. We were all alive in one another again and again as we were not in all else and there she laid herself hard across me. Her whole bared body was laid there against me. She put herself hard there on against me all black in the black lit night with her long dark hair come on down along me and she moved hard against me. She made me forget. Then there was only this forgetting. We forgot the rest in it. All was little, gone unremembered. It was this one living in which to last. It was the largest kind of living left.

  She lifted her head all alive in it to look to me. She looked to me alive all of her awakened and alive. She looked to me cut livid and alive along the sea in it. I would have that look last. I would have that look last if nothing else and the sand cut into us and hurt us to the end. When we were done with it and one another we were quieted and lay strewn in sand as if deadened.

33

ON THE PHILOSOPHER-PRIEST

  They closed the school and the teaching was finished for her. She was to go back to France. The priest he came and told her that. He looked at me and he talked to her. We stood in the classroom of the old French school building with the little brown wooden desks empty and stained with ink and they spoke in French and I went to the window and looked out into the street. The priest he was French French. I don't remember if I'd said he was French. I turned the latch that held the window closed and opened the window and lit a cigarette.

I stood there and smoked. I understood none of it the way they talked all politely and practically, seriously to one another, sounding all official. I heard my name in the French. I smoked. I listened awhile. It was not uncomforting to listen to someone talk like they knew what they were talking about.

They stopped it, the room went quiet. I turned to them.

She said from across the room, "The priest must talk to you," and she went to go.

"Stay here with me," I said to her. She'd put the blue shawl up over her head to go out and that picture of her reminded me of the time she'd gone and not come back.

"Let her go," he said. "She must put her things together."

"All right," I said and she left us. She went out the door and closed it and was gone. I stood there by the window. He came over to the desk.

"You are reading Bergson?" he said.

I looked to the opened up book on the ink-stained desk.

"I don't know if I'd call it reading," I said.

"But you are reading it?" He sounded interested.

"It's like another language," I said.

"You know, I am a Jesuit—not just a priest," he said. He laughed. I'd never heard him laugh. "Once I was a philosopher, I sometimes think of that—I taught philosophy—then this life made me a priest," he said and looked round the schoolroom at the books and desk and back down to the open book. "That is my book. You may keep it," he said.

"I shouldn't take it from you."

"I want you to have it—I translated it to the English."

"That is your name?" I said, and I looked at it, to that name on the cover of the book, as though it referred to someone who must exist far off in another world not the actual man standing right in front of me in this one.

"Yes—I taught at the University, in Paris—it is another

165

life."

"But, how did you come here?" I said and I was grateful for the book and I opened it up looking again at the pages.

"My brother—he was killed at Dien Bien Phu," he said. Then he said looking at me, "He was wounded, and died in hospital. I came to take him home. I didn't go home."

I closed the book. I turned from him and looked out the window to the street. The bicycles passed. The soldiers passed. The trees stood tall and spotted with their trunks rowed in the bright light along the windows.

"Why did you tell me—in that hospital—that she'd left?"

"It is not so easy to help people, and I did not know that she loved you," he simply said. Then he said, "The Americans are looking for you—they are asking of you."

"Well, let them look. Do you think they will find me?" I said to him. It wasn't an accusation. I remembered how he'd bent himself to kneel beside an American boy shot up and dying in a bed. And there were all the French boys from the war, his own brother, there was his own brother.

I turned from the window. I looked at him.

"I don't think they'll find you. I don't know. That is up to you," he said. "But you must leave here. The Americans are coming, retreating, from the country in to the city outskirts, some will occupy here a building—off from the school." The soldiers were to fill one of the dormitories, waiting in transit to ship out home.

"You will go to France? To her?" he said.

"I'll go with her," I said and he came up and stood beside me. We stood there looking out. The light was hitting down through the leaves on the trees. They were lit up all golden and green.

"Do you have a cigarette?" he said.

"Of course," I said. I offered him a cigarette and he

took it. He bent his head and I lit it for him. He stood straight and he blew out the smoke.

"Is it possible—that we go together?" I said and I looked to him.

"It would be nice to think you could," he said. "But, you cannot go with her. You do not have the proper paperwork—and you cannot get that paperwork for France in time. She is leaving in a matter of days—now you must wait—there is the risk the Americans will find you out, perhaps they will arrest you. Then they will put you in jail because you did not tell them what they wanted. You should have told them what they wanted," he said. He saw it as a predicament.

The street was full of light. We stood looking into it.

"They want too much," I said looking out.

"Tell them what they want, it will go easy on you," he said. "I know these Americans. You have made it too hard on yourself. You must think of yourself first," he said. "Tell them now. You will go free."

"You know, it's the principle of the thing," I said and I knew it sounded funny to talk like that about such a thing to him. I saw how it'd be to be happy and free. I said, "I can't tell them what they want."

"So, it is the principle of things with you?" he said. "But you must think of yourself, and you think of principles? The principle does not matter, now," he said. "You must know that."

"You're a hell of a philosopher-priest," I said to him.

He put out the end of his cigarette on the iron frame of the window sill and threw the butt to the street. "May I?" he said.

"Of course," I said.

He took another one. I lit it for him. He smoked it. He was thinking on things. I think in the end he didn't want her to be alone, and he said, "There is a way. They will not find you in France. You will go to France—she loves you," he said in some loneliness of his own. "John, I will help you," he said in his fatherly way, and all along I was wrong about the priest. I didn't ask for his help but I think he wanted to do it for her in the hope that she'd go off and at last be happy.

"Things can be arranged, with the French," he said. "It is only paper. Children are being sent to Bangkok—you will cross the border with them. It is an official envoy. You will have French paperwork, a visa from the Consulate." He turned to me at the window, "She is leaving in three days, for France, alone. You will go to her there, once your paperwork comes through from the Consulate." He was to go. He stopped and said, "That child. I will tell you about it? Do you want to know?" he said.

"No," I said, "As long as it is not alone," I said.

"I understand," he said. "It is not alone," he said. "It is alive and well," he said. He turned from me after he said that and walked across the room to the door and went out. He left me there alone in the light of the emptied schoolroom where I stood at the window looking out to the well-lit street at the bicycles coming down it. I watched him walk down the street along the trees in the light.

34

AN ODD JUXTAPOSITION
OF BLACK AND WHITE PHOTOS

I picked up that book of the priest's that I didn't understand and on my way out of the room I let my hand run across the wooden top of an empty ink-stained desk thinking of all the children that had studied right there in the room, where they'd gone off to, what'd come of them, feeling that I had to get out of that schoolroom and away from them thoughts of children and back to her. I left it and walked down the hall to the courtyard doors. I heard the voices of unseen children coming to me from up the far end of the hall. I went into the courtyard and looked up to the sky. There was nothing in it. I heard the children. I heard the birds in the trees along the yellow stucco walls. I crossed the courtyard stone. I went in to her in her room and she was writing at her desk. I put my arms around her from behind her. She had an address book open on the desk. She was writing out the names of people and places in it. She kept writing in it.

"The priest will get you the paperwork," she said. She knew.

"Yes, I'll give you the address of the room," I said and I saw the many people and places in her book that'd been blackened out in pen. She turned to a blank page of the book. Her pen was ready on the paper.

"Tell me your name?" she said being funny sounding serious.

"John LeBlanc," I said.

"Is that your real name?"

"I've never thought of it as my real name—but I guess it is."

So, she wrote the name down in the book. She wrote the address of the room on the opposite page. I went and lay on the bed and looked at her blued shawl hung on the door while she wrote in the little book. She was writing out all the names in her book. She put it all, everyone and me, down in her book, and she put down her pen on the desk and she closed the book. Then she turned around and looked at me, "If you tell them Americans what they want, then you will be free from them men?" she said. "Free for good?" she said. She sounded hopeful.

"I could tell them what they want. But, I can't let them

make me who I am," I said. "They've made me enough. It's really too late to tell them anything," I said. "The priest, he doesn't understand that."

"He does—he will help you," she said. "He knows you are good."

"I know—he's good—you were right," I said.

She was still thinking about them men, and she said, "If you tell them what they want, then you will be free but not free," she said in her understanding it. She understood it. She knew if I told them what they wanted I would have been wrong and unmade in it and that it never would have been right for us even if I could have gone with her. She accepted it. She wasn't unsettled by it. She was someone who'd long seen such goodbyes. She was resolved to the risk of such goodbyes. She'd thought her things through in her own way sitting at that desk writing out those addresses on her way to home and had made up her mind about our going and how it would be hard.

"They want to give me a medal for killing people, Madeleine," I said as she wrote the note for the priest.

"You were a soldier in a war," she said.

"The people weren't—you know what it's about," I said.

"I know," she said. "You can't talk about it, not now."

"I can't let them make me worse than I am."

"I will give the priest your address when I go," she said. "The priest, he told me that he will come to you—," she said, "If he can't, then another will come. You will be free of them men in France," she said. She said, "John—."

"What?"

"Be careful."

"Yes, give it to him then," I said. "I will wait for him to come."

I saw myself alone there waiting to go to her. I was afraid of it. But it wasn't them men. I wasn't afraid of them.

It was me.

She was sitting there turned round in the chair from her desk to face me looking at me with the address book closed up and I lay on the bed with her things laid all round me. She was going. She'd be gone with all her things. There was her little hand mirror on the dresser. There was her blued shawl. She had a couple pairs of shoes lined up at the door. It'd all be gone. Then in seeing them things of hers, I missed her and she was right there. But they told me of her. They told of her in a simple everyday way. There was a whole other world in them. There was this sense of her private and domestic life. There was her in them in that simple ordinary daily life. She had nothing of mine to see me in in that way. I wanted to give her something that'd tell of me in a simple and real everyday way. I wanted to give her some real thing that told her something good about me in my own ordinary life for her to see me in to remember me by in a good way. I wanted her to see who I was to her beyond all this round us. I didn't have one good thing to give her.

I'd nothing to give her. I had a picture in my wallet. I remembered it. I turned in the bed and I took my wallet out from the back pocket of my khaki cutoffs. I took the snapshot out of the worn leather from where you'd keep a driver's license. It was folded over. I unfolded it. It was a thing I could give her. I looked at it. There I was a boy standing in uniform beside a canvas tent with some of the boys all alive lounged-about half-dressed in the light. There were ragged children stood behind us on one side. My hair was shaved short. I hardly recognized myself. I looked to the children. I looked away to her. I saw her. She was sitting at the desk.

She'd been watching me while I looked at the snapshot.

"What is it?" she said. I'd been looking closely at it.

"Just an old snapshot, of the boys, and me," I said to her.

"Let me see it," she said.

I got up from the bed with it. I went over to her at the desk. I put it face down on the desk, to write a date on the back of it to give it to her.

"It's just a picture of me," I said. "I want you to have it, to keep it with you." I took up her pen. I wrote down the date across the blank back of it in the blue ink of her pen. I signed my name on the back of it. I think I put her name on it beside mine, and I'd have to look to tell.

She took it up off the desk and she looked at me standing in it. She looked to the children. I left the desk and went back to the bed.

"You look young," she said. "You don't look afraid," she said, and I was gone back to the bed and laid out there on it. I watched her with it. She kept looking a time at it. She left it unfolded. She put it carefully away. She opened up her address book. She pressed it flat and unfolded in her address book, and I said, "Come here girl. I am afraid."

She got up from the desk. She came over and she lay down there beside me. I held her hard to me and we were a little afraid in our going off from one another like that after all them things we'd felt and felt true and it was still all a fragile thing.

"I will take it out when I am alone," she said.

"Will you look at it?"

"I will look at it. I will see you," she said.

In her words I felt how we'd be so goddamned alone and there we were kept together held to one another hard and close. She was against me, and I said to her, "Don't you have a picture I could have?" and then she said, "I do have a picture of myself. But it's not so good. It's the one on my paperwork," she said, "I don't have any other to give you." There had been an extra set of official shots taken. She had never had any others taken. She was not that fond of photos. There are all

172

these pictures people will have taken of themselves and she had none but that official one of her.

"I'm sorry I have nothing to give you, but that," she said.

"There is nothing you can give me. Don't give me anything girl. I do not want one thing from you—but I'd like to have your picture to keep," I said, "To see you in it, let me see the picture," I said. I only wanted her and not one thing of hers. I wanted her herself not a thing of hers.

"No, I will give you something."

"I don't want anything," I said. "I only want you," I said.

"I will give you something to see me in," she said.

She got up from the bed. She went to the door. She took it down from off the hook. She brought it to the bed. She handed it to me. I took the blued shawl from her into my hands. I held it in hand. I'd never held it like that before, dark, dry, lightened out and emptied, and she lay down there again beside me with it laid fallen alongside us on the bed.

"You must keep it," I said. "Give me the picture of you."

"Don't you want it? You will see me in it."

"Yes, I want it—I do see you in it."

"So, take it then. I'm giving it to you."

"I want you to keep it. I want to know you have it."

She must have it herself.

"You want the picture? It's bad."

"I want the picture. Show me it."

It seemed there would be less loss in the image of her. In having a real thing of hers but not her I would badly miss her. I couldn't bear the significance of such objects as that shawl seen kept close about me in her sheer absence. I knew that about them things of hers.

She got up. She went to her desk. She opened up

the desk drawer. She took out the picture. She came back to the bed looking at it. She lay herself back down there with it alongside the shawl and me. She showed me the picture of her. I held it to the light with her laid there along me. It was a black and white shot of her. She looked all dark in it against the frame of the white screen backdrop. She looked young. She was turned to show the cut. She was posed. She was pretty. She was all dark and cut.

"I'll keep it. It's not so bad," I said.

"If you want," she said. "But, I'm not that girl now," she said to me. "Do you see me in it?" she said. She didn't like that official shot of herself. We were both looking to it. "I like it," I said to her, "I do see you in it," I said. "You may keep it then," she simply said. She let me have it. We talked no more about it or her going. I put it away in my wallet. She got up. She began to pack her things. She packed up her things. She put them away in her old suitcases.

"Do you want any help with it?" I said to her.

"No, it is nothing." I watched her. She did it carefully and slowly.

When her things were gone from sight the room was bare. The clear light came in from the courtyard across her snapped shut suitcases and the cleaned out room. It was two black beat-up cases sitting side by side on the stone of the floor. There were a couple things left on the dresser. Other than that it could have been any room anywhere but for us.

35

A GIRL AND A BOY IN THE NIGHT

We lay there the last night close along one another late into the night. She was going in morning. We left the courtyard doors open. When it was late there was wind in the leaves of the little trees. We heard the trees and the room was dark about us and if you wanted to hear a thing laid out in the night to know where you were in that late darkness there was the wind in the trees that told you almost nothing about where you were. There was us close next to one another naked in the dark in the room. A voice came now and then from off the street to the courtyard. There was gunfire. There were the far artillery strikes. There came across the city the close heavy concussions in the dark that told you where you were. In them we knew where we were in the night and when it was very late in the night we knew how it was the last night and she lay there next to me gone a time in sleep and I was waked badly alone in early morning. I thought of how I would wake without her. I was with her. I would wake with her. I did not want to wake ever once without her. The light was coming. I would. It was real. I lay next to her and looked up in coming light. I never wanted to sleep again.

She was awakened beside me in the early light.

"Tell me how it will be, that life," I said to her, "Our life."

"You must sleep," she said to me. "It is early."

"I won't sleep now, I want to know it will be good," I said.

She told it half waked of how it would be. It was the South of France. We would go live there a time in the poor country of the South in that place called the Ardeche. That was where she had lived and left off from that land then to live a little in the world. She would return to it. Everything she knew was in the South. She said she'd waked thinking she was already there. She'd gone to it in sleep. She'd walked a road or two. She told it half waked how she'd seen it and gone to it. Then she'd seen me and she knew it couldn't be, that she was in bed beside me, and she was not unhappy to be, and I lay there with her in the room seeing that country walking with her out along a road or two in the light. One returns as though to home a time in such sights.

"We can be happy there," I said seeing it.

"We can be," she said.

"Will we be happy?" I said.

"I want to be," she said. She said she wouldn't be as she'd been before when she was alone in it and left it to go live again a little in the world. It was a world too.

"What does the land look like in that country?" I said looking up in coming light. In going to it you will want to see it.

It is always that. Then she was telling about it and telling what was beautiful and good about it. It had many wild rivers and great wide valleys with fruit trees and mountains with oak trees and a big clean sky full of good light. She was not unhappy telling it. It was a pretty sight to see. I saw it all and I saw us there in it and I was happy. I was happy in a way I do not think I have ever been in any one actual place. It was kept before us a place of good promise full of great sights.

"We'll be happy," I said. "No matter what—no matter the place," I said to her, and now it was France. That's where we would and will be happy. We must be happy. There in France we would be.

"You will be happy, girl?" I said to her. She was all awake. "It is a nice, pleasant, beautiful-sounding land," I said to her in seeing it. "But you will be happy?" I said to her and she'd never been happy in France.

"I will be, I must be, now it is different," she said.

Now all is to be different.

The coming light showed the suitcases on the stone and us naked in bed holding one another close. It was getting very light. We were awakened seeing that land before us now how it was. We were letting the land live before us a little all

176

new and different not sleeping the rest of it beside one another to forget the going.

She said, "But you will not see your family—go home."
"There is only my mother. She has her life," I said.
"Not your father?"
"No."
"No brothers, sisters?"
There were none.

"And the others?" she asked, in her wanting to hear of the close relations of known family.

Dead or gone off never to be heard of again.

"Do you think of her?" she said of my mother. "Is she in front of you?" she said. "Does it seem another life?" she said. She said then some things like that. She was seeing her own old things and I saw mine. She wanted to talk to the end. She didn't want to sleep the rest of it.

We were awakened to the beginning of the going. I saw her seeing her people and I saw mine and I asked her of her mother and her father wanting to know as one will a little of them living there off in that life in that far Southern land.

"Tell me what they are like, girl," I said to her asking her of her parents. "What kind of people are they?" I wanted to see them as she saw them.

"You will see them," she said. "They are practical people," she said, "I will tell you a good long story of them when you come. And your mother?" she said again to me asking me of mine. "Tell me something of your mother, tell me about her—you've never told me of her," she said and she waited for me. "But do you think of her?" she said again. "I have kept you from her," she said. "Is she happy in America?" she said in her wanting to know of her and a little of who she herself was in America.

I think she was thinking of her and her own parents.
Then I saw America in seeing my mother. I saw her.

"Who is happy?" I said seeing my mother.

"There are happy things for her in her life?"

"Yes—not all happy things," I said.

"What things?"

"The things that mean nothing, that must mean nothing to anyone anywhere."

"Yes, all right," she said.

Then we stopped that talk. We told nothing of our parents. That would wait. We didn't want them before us and all to tell of them.

It was getting very light in the bare little room.

"Were you in love once?" she said to me.

"I'm in love now," I said.

We had never said such words so openly. We'd never said such words so easily.

"We're in love, girl" I said to her.

"But from before," she said.

"Once I was. I was young. I don't think it was love—it wasn't this," I said.

"Was it long ago?" she said.

"It is all long ago," I said and I took up her hair from off her face.

She was a girl and I a boy. We two lay there the last time in our going saying such leisurely and sentimental things as that laid into one another in the cleared-out room. In our going we were a boy and a girl again like we'd never been. It seemed we'd only be that way from now on in the end and keep it easy and good and not too hard on one another. So we said one or two things like that of no consequence to one another.

We must say them then or lose them and the time to talk of them all easily and openly like that. We could then in going. We lay there a time in the ease of such talk. The light came across her dark hair long and brilliant and unbraided where it lay strewn and fallen a little wild down the line of her girl's face down on along her breast and the whole curve of her in the light.

I lay there looking at her. That is a look of love.

"You are a goddamned beautiful girl," I said. "Did I ever tell you that, girl? Do you know that, girl?" I said. "I want you to know that, girl," I said.

"It is only you who think so," she said. "Do you think so?" she said.

We talked all easy and rested like that waked in the coming light. We might well have long been home by now waking up off somewhere once more all peaceful in morning light long gone to home with it all over and done with all our going done for good in our talking like that in our being a boy and a girl in the end to one another.

"Was she a pretty girl?" she said.

"Was who?" I said.

"The girl you were in love with," she said.

"It's all finished, pretty or not," I said.

"You do not love her? She does not love you?"

"What is it anyway? We were too young—it's nothing. It's young love. That, it's nothing."

"You cannot have it apart," she said. "That is true—it is not possible. Is it possible?"

"But it must be possible," I said. "It is possible."

She said, "You will tell yourself it is possible."

"Too young it's never possible," I said. "I know that. But luckily we're not young anymore."

36

NOTHING IS TOLD IN GOODBYE

There was the vague shuttered light of coming rain. I looked at the grey slatted light coming across her suitcases. She was all packed up. The room was all cleaned out. We'd lived in it. It looked now as if it'd not ever been lived in. We'd never see it again. Now I cannot forget it. We sat on the two chairs waiting for the taxi. We were simply sitting on two chairs waiting for a taxi to come to take her to the airport. We sat as we had that first day when I'd come in out of the rain with her to the room and I said to her, "Tell me a story to pass the time."

"I'll tell you a story when you come, boy," she said.

"You will tell me a good story?" I said.

"I will tell you a good long story," she said.

Her hair was black and long and uncovered. She was wearing a dark blue dress. She didn't look like a girl. She no longer looked like a girl. She looked like a woman going off. The old woman came and knocked on the door and the taxi was there. It was waiting out front in the street.

"I've got something to tell you," I said to her when I knew we must get up from those chairs and go. I was to tell her something and I could not get the words for the feeling to be simply sounded out. It was too large, and too late.

"What is it?" she said.

She sat there dark and serene in that royal blue dress.

"It is just that I will not see you tomorrow, girl," I said.

"Are you being funny, boy?" she said.

"No—I am not being funny. I am not being funny at all," I said.

"All right, John—I understand you," she said. It was too late to talk.

"I must go," she said. "It is time." She got up and she stood from her chair in that room that we would never see again. She walked over to pick up a suitcase. I did not go over to her. I sat on that chair where I'd first sat with her there in her room.

"Come here, John," she said. I did not. I knew she would then go.

She came to me. She came to me and held me. I felt her up against me this good and lovely girl in my arms going off. She felt good to hold. I felt all of her and only wanted to keep her there. We held on to one another saying nothing in the shuttered light. You cannot know what it all is to you until such a time is come to you. We said none of what it was. We'd write it out. We'd write big letters.

The car was waiting out front. We broke off. We picked up the luggage. We went out of the room and down the hall and out of the school and we did not look at one another. There are times looking tells too much. That looking tells too much. We walked to the car parked in the street beneath the big spotted sycamore trees. The driver got out and opened the trunk. We put her things in the trunk. There we then stood as if two strangers to one another beside the car. I think it must be so in such times. Or one cannot leave another and go on all right.

The driver shut the trunk and came and opened the car door for her and she got in. He closed the door. I stood beside the closed car door. The window was rolled up. The sky was all overcast. She looked to me through the glass of the rolled up window. She did not roll it down. The school and the trees and all the things of the place were reflected across the grayed glass and her face dark in the window. We were looking to one another through the flat-glassed reflections of the obscured sky. The driver put the car in gear. She put her hand up to the window. I put my hand on the window. The car started.

181

She dropped her hand. Mine fell from the glass. She looked straight ahead. She knew how to go. The taxi drove off with her looking straight ahead. I watched the car go down the street along the row of trees beneath the canopy of green leaves. The car disappeared in the far traffic. I walked down the street away from the school. It was going to rain. I felt it would soon rain very hard. That tells nothing of what it was. It is only a little picture to keep things by as you will find in simple books.

37

THE FRENCH PRIEST, HER LETTER, THE OFFICIAL PAPERWORK

It is true that there is such life in books. Then it was I lived in the books. I was left with them in the end. I lived a time in books. I never knew how well you could live in a book. I sat in my room drinking tea in the afternoon reading them books from the school she and the priest had left me and drinking gin at night. The first book I read was that Bergson book. I found marked pages. I put the book down. I closed it up. I opened it up. I went on in it. Once when I was very drunk I smelled spent shell casings in the air and it was the old ink and paper in the heat and humidity from them books I had all opened up on the bed because now I was reading them all at once. To go on only reading that is a thing. I thought that. I didn't want to see anyone. I did not want anyone at all to come to me. No one was to come to me. I read. I drank. I lived little. I lived little in the room and large in the books.

I thought the old men would come get me. There were times I lay there badly waked and I thought I heard them coming for me but they did not come to the door of the room. They did not come to the door of the next room. I listened to all the footsteps coming up the stairs and down the hall. I listened for the sound of boots. There were none. There were never hard steps. There were always light footsteps. I would read on. I read on.

But I know when you stay put long enough that sooner or later you will get tracked down by people whether you want them or not to come, you just hope in time the ones you want will come before the ones you do not want, and the one day came when I was lying on the bed looking up to the cracked painted plaster of the ceiling reading and I heard the steps and listened to them on the stairs. It was different. I lay there on the bed and listened. I put the book down. At the top of the stairs the footsteps stopped in question. I knew whoever it was the way they walked that they had never been in that hall before and I got up from the bed. I went over to that art deco dresser and opened the drawer and took out the pistol. I had the pistol in hand. I held it up in the shuttered light. Its blued barrel was pointed out at me from the dim image in that decorative oval mirror. I dropped it from sight to the drawer. I put it down back away beneath a shirt. I closed the drawer and the footsteps came down the hall to the door and stopped in front of it. They did not go to the other door. They knew I was in there in the room. I went and stood in the room before the door. I opened it. It was the priest. He stood there looking all out of place. He wasn't wearing his robe. He had a hat on like you'd see someone in an office or train station wear and he was wearing a light-colored dress shirt and pants and black shoes. He looked uncomfortable in clothes. He looked like another man.

"There's a letter for you," he said. "She left it with me, to give you when I came." He handed it to me. I took it. I looked at the handwriting. It was from her. He took off his hat and stepped in from the hall and I shut the door behind him. We stood in the strange color of the aquamarine room. The light

183

was coming off the street through the shutters of the cracked-open window and across the length of the floor. I had the letter in my hand. The light was hitting the blue envelope. The paper was very thin and it said *par avion* across the envelope though it had not been mailed.

"I'm going to the French consulate—on another matter," he said about his clothes. He looked into the dresser mirror at himself.

"Thanks for the letter," I said. I put it on the bed.

I picked up a packet of cigarettes from the dresser.

"Do you want a cigarette?" I said.

"No," he said. "I need a photograph of you."

"I don't think I have one," I said.

"Is it safe, here?" he said.

"Nothing is safe." He looked at me.

"But one must be careful," he said.

"Down the street is a cigarette shop, with one of those photo booths." He knew what I was talking about. In a casual little aside, he said they were from old French metro stations.

"That will do," he said. "A resemblance of you is good enough."

We went out of the room and down the stairs to the street. We walked the narrow shadowed street of little rising balconies. We walked along the opened up shop fronts that had the iron bars and corrugated steel shutters. They were all lifted in the light.

"The Americans are asking after you, they have been again to see me at the hospital," he said.

"She is in France?" I said.

"Yes—she is home. You will go to her there," he looked over to me in confirmation not in question.

"Yes, I will go there to her," I said to him. I looked back over at him.

We went in a shop and at a counter there was a girl. I

sat in one of those old French photo booths that the priest in his own little reminiscence of home had told me was saved from an old French metro station and I pulled the curtain. I took the pictures. My hair was little by little longer. I was beginning to look like someone else now with the uncut hair. The girl cut a couple pictures out from a sheet of shots and I paid her for them. We turned from the counter and went to the door of the shop. I gave them to him at the door. He put them in his pocket. We walked out.

"It's no trouble for you—to do this?" I said. I didn't want to make trouble for him.

"It has been done a long time now," he said.

"When will you come back?" I said.

"Someone else will come," he said. "I cannot."

We walked back along the shops in the shade of the buildings. With that hat and shirt and shoes he looked like a newspaper man. I was in my cutoffs and t-shirt. We looked like two people who knew nothing about the place. We kept walking on past the room.

"I will not see you again," he said. "I think it is better that way."

"You are going to France?" I said.

"No," he said. "You know, the children are here—there are many children," he said seriously. There was something lonely in his voice. I took out my cigarettes.

"Have one," I said. I felt something for him. I felt some things for him. He looked at me. He took one. I lit it for him. We smoked and walked. I was wrong all along about the priest.

"I can do nothing to thank you," I said to him.

"There is nothing to do," he said. "Do what is right. You know what is right. It is hard to do what is right, the more you live," he said.

"All right," I said. "I will."

"You must make her happy," he said. It was the last thing he said.

"I want to make her happy," I said. I said to him, "I will."

We walked and smoked. We kept on walking down the street smoking. When we were done smoking he kept on walking.

38

THE REMAINS OF REVERIE

I saw her. I saw her come in me. I kept her close in mind. Then they came. When most in rest or leisure, to be then at the beginning of respite, there in the room they were risen in me. They were material in me. I lay in bed back there again in the green looking up fallen in the ruined feeling badly deadened in the dark and I tried to make it all up over again like she'd made it up for me, to see not that, feel ever that, but only us out in the light of the country. We walked a road or two to home. I saw some things that were to come. I saw the things that were to be. What it was was gone a time. I was a little all alive in the things between us that were to be. I felt the good that was not yet come in feeling a little of how it would feel. I tried to feel it all not knowing how it would feel. I wanted to get the ruined fallen feeling to go from out me. I thought I could do it that way. I did it. I did it awhile. It all went the scenes of them and that in the grass it went off awhile from me. But between every new sight I'd made out in my mind, the real picture of them two, they came back badly in the good story I'd made up of myself, they came more vivid and alive in their re-imagined return than anything new I could materially make. Then they had returned to stay. They stayed on there before me fully rooted in me. She had made it all go. She was gone. They came. They would not go. I felt a time that I would never be free. I was defeated in the feeling. I was defeating myself. I knew that. It is all a kind of way of badly hurting yourself. It is a hard way of hurting yourself.

There are things one must just outlast.

I took refuge in reading. The recollected life came real. I lay there afraid of my own recurrent life and in renewed effort, in refocused force I remembered all the feeling I had had about the good to come. I retold myself all the happy little stories. Then it didn't work at all. The harder I tried to get free of it the more vivid and real it came. It came again and again with less and less effort. I had to shove it away harder and harder each time and each time I did it clarified and heightened the vision. It went badly round and round like that stronger and stronger in impression larger and larger to my littleness all unrelenting in the repetition of its return.

I got up. I went as though in going, in simply moving off, I'd get all to go out from me. I knew better. I opened the door. I went out of the room. I walked the streets of the city. I felt like I was not really there in the light. I was dead living. The days were indistinguishable. She had made me all alive. It was hard to move and all I did was move. I went everywhere and nowhere. I saw every one and no one. I walked with all the people in the city seeing all the familiar faces of the girls knowing none of them. I looked away from them. I saw them. I looked into the faces of girls. In looking into them faces that now would not change no matter that the girls had changed, in this continual fearful aversion to the pictures of my own making, not confronting one thing in me so as to be able to change it, I remembered what she had told me. She had told me to look at it. She had told me to hold it before me. She had told me not to look away. She had told me to study *what it was*. She had told me it would never go away, and to look directly at it, to know all what it was, and not to look away, and I did, I did awhile, and I went on, and didn't look away and walked on. I looked into the faces of the girls. I looked at them all alive. I studied them and that what I had done. They were dead and them girls were all around me alive and I walked on in the streets of the city with the sounds of the city with the people of the city and that was real, that was what was real, and nothing of the rest of it was any longer real, and nothing bad would happen. All the bad had already happened. I was freed in the thought.

I had to remember that, that I must look and know that the bad had already happened, and could not happen, and I returned to the room remembering, and for awhile in reading lost myself once more in new and unknown sights and scenes of imagined life, until when I'd left off from the book, and let it lay wordless a time down on me unread, they were right there risen in the room, and then when to read I took it up again, I took it up and them. I kept them close, I must not first forget. I remembered not to forget. I must remember, I kept them all alive right there now risen in the room as they were, and I then lived awhile with them and the book. I became larger to it letting it live awhile at its leisure before me. I became a little larger and unafraid of it letting it live as it would. It would no matter. I studied it and who I was. I was remembering who and what I was and nothing bad happened.

I got a little over the dead living feeling letting it have its free reign in me seeing myself getting on to her. I saw her and some happy sights to come. I kept happy sights in mind along with keeping it. I got a little larger and stronger than the badly lived time seeing us happy off in another time no matter I could not ever get out of that past one. Little by little I began to get round it. I told myself what I had done. I found true words. I found hard true words. I told that story and it was real and not a story. You will leave off a little from all what is done in telling it true. I know that now. In telling yourself what it is and what you have done in your own life you wake to your new days. You get on to what must be done in a life.

I was a little young and alive some. I was sure I would go do many new and good things. I was a little happy in the light. I was young and alive some in the light. You cannot be afraid to be sure some and a little alive in the light.

39

THE BOYS IN THE BAR

That is when one day badly alive in the light and sure of nothing, Jack Jackson came to my door to get me and I'd thought the old men would come get me for good. They never did. It was the priest who'd sent him to get me out of there. I thought Jack was long gone for good and when I heard hard-boot steps at the door, I put the book down on the bed and there he stood with a big fucking mock-smile at the door when I opened it, and I was thinking to see the MPs and to go off with them without one fight.

Jack stood there looking in smoking a cigarette, and he said, "Shit," and drew the word out as a greeting, looking me up and down in the grinning-look summing me up and he started laughing like hell in the sight of me there before him as though all was a joke to him, in his facetious look, in his false-mocking voice bringing the boys back before me, "*John-Le-Fucking-Blanc*," he said. The faces of the boys came back there all alive to me. The faces of them old men came with nothing left alive in them.

"Motherfucker," he said and stepped in. "I thought you were gone. I mean *gone*," he said and pointed to his head and he laughed a big crazy fucking laugh. I looked down the hall and then shut the door behind him.

"Jack—How the fuck are you, man?" I said to him and I was happy to see him, and said, "No, haven't gone anywhere in a long while," I said and stood at the door and heard no one coming in the hall and looked at him and he was dressed in one of them Hawaiian shirts and he was wearing mirrored sunglasses in the dim shadowed room and he said he was all right. He was right enough he said. He wasn't gone himself like he'd been before. He felt all right now sometimes for awhile. He even felt, often, as if he was himself once more, and he bent his head to the one side saying to me, "Sometimes, I'm all here," he said, as though he could not believe it, and pointed with a fingered-pistoled hand to his head, "But then *bang*, I'm *gone*," he said, smiling a big fucking smile laughing sounding all happy saying it.

Then he grabbed for my hand and he held up the little black book he'd carried in with him and he put it in my hand, "The priest thought it'd be good for the soul, if you did a little reading," he said and laughed all crazy again. "Look inside for the Good Word, motherfucker," he said.

I opened it. It was inside the back cover. There in the flap was the paperwork from the priest. It had the French Consulate seal on it. There were the signatures in blue ink. It looked all official. For all I knew it was.

"The priest told me, I was to help you pack up your shit, and get you out of this room pronto," Jack said. "He said, '*Tell him, go to the schoolroom—it's safe tonight*,' that you're goin' tonight. He said tell him that. He said, '*The old woman will be there*,' the old woman, she'll wait for you, '*the old woman will take him*.' He said you'd know what that shit meant. Where the fuck are you goin,' man?" Jack said as if it was all mysterious.

"To France," I said, and that sounded funny to him.

"France? Well, don't look like it in here, motherfucker,"

he said and he looked round the unpacked and strewn things scattered in the room. He clicked a Zippo lighter, lit a cigarette from a packet of Kools. "You got shit everywhere, man," he said and looked on round the room at the opened books and bottles and bags. His head stopped at the bag. He picked up the canvas bag at the foot of the bed. "We got to get this shit cleaned up, man," he said and he closed up the book I'd left laid on the bed, and looked at its cover, and said, "Why you readin' this crap, JLB?" and threw it in the bag. We started. We packed up what there was into the two duffle bags. It didn't take long. We just shoved it all in. Jack wanted to get the hell out of the room.

"This place gives me the creeps, motherfucker," he said. "What you doin' in here, anyway—and the boys, they's asking for you—nobody heard one word from you," he said, going on with another conversation, "Wondering what the fuck's happened to you, and all. Wondered if you was in the clink and all, and *all that fucked-up shit, man*—," and there he stopped. He stopped talking. He said no more. He looked off.

He reached for the canvas bag and touched it.

"*Shit*," he said in the sound of some heavy long-realized regret. He took up the bag to go.

"No, nothing's happened—I'm too much of a fuck-up to be locked up, Jack," I said to humor him up. "I'm in love," I said.

"Love?" he said as if attempting to recall the concept.

"Yeah—love."

"Shit man, we's supposed to kill them—not save them and love them." He smiled, "You're a fucking humanitarian," he said. "All right, JLB," he said. "Love," he said, letting himself understand it.

I didn't answer him. He understood it.

I took up the pistol from where it lay on the bed and I put it in the back of my pants in the waist with my shirt over it.

191

He watched me do it. He nodded at it.

"We got to get the fuck out of here, man. Go for a drink," he said. "You're not going anywhere, motherfucker, until I buy you a drink," he said all seriously.

He had the bags up off the floor ready to go in his hands. I looked at him. I laughed. I wasn't going anywhere for a drink.

For him it was not an option.

"I won't take no for an answer, motherfucker," he said solemnly. "We got time—a-plenty," he said, looking at his watch. "There's a taxi waiting," and that was that for him. Jack had kept the taxi he'd taken over waiting in the street.

We stood in the cleared-out room. I looked round the room with nothing left in it. Jack stood there before me holding my packed up bags in front of the silvered oval of the dresser mirror. A voice came up off the street in through the shutters to the room. "Give me a bag, Jack-O," I said, and I took one of the bags off him, and turned from the shutters, the bed, and looked in that veneer-framed mirror the last time and left.

We left the room and went down the stairs into the lobby and out to the street to the taxi. The man in the lobby did not look up from his magazine. The taxi was waiting in the street. We got in the taxi with the bags and drove through the city. Jack talked. He lit cigarettes. He handed me cigarettes. Things had happened to him. He didn't always know when not to talk but I liked him and I knew why he had to talk. Then the drink was the one thing on his mind.

"I know a good place—near the school, not too close to them head-shrinkers," he said about the hospital. He looked over to me. "You got to wait anyway," he said. I didn't want to go. "Gets the shit out the mind," he said pointing to his head, "Good for what's left of the soul," he said pointing to his heart like a mime. The car went along balconied buildings.

I went out with Jack Jackson for a drink because

he would not take no for an answer, "You saved my life, motherfucker," he said to me in that taxi as we drove through the last dilapidated streets, and I was thinking of how I had met her with the children in the rain in the street. Jack said, "Just returning the favor, Geronimo," and I looked over at him and he was always so full of shit to cover and keep off the rest. There was a time we both were. We were both from Michigan, but Jack Jackson was from Detroit. I looked out the window, and I remembered there were the days he used to say to me when he was drunk and stoned and so shit-scared that it hurt that he knew his goddamned shit and that I should just shut the fuck up because I didn't know a goddamned thing let alone my own shit. Then when he'd got fucked up pretty bad for awhile himself in the head he didn't say that to me or to anyone anymore and for a time he had even lost his sense of humor.

When we were down past where the hospital was, Jack had the taxi stop in a narrow side street. We got out in the street. The school was at the other end of it, and we walked on into the people going on in the street. I looked back behind us down the street. There was no one we would have known. There was no one in the street we would ever know. We went on with the bags against the people coming up into us in the street. It was all close-crowed. The life went on in it.

We turned down a dark side street. It was a dark little place that had good music. Jack knew the place well and we went in it. Some boys he knew were in there. The tables were crowded. The place was filled with drinking. There were the girls. I looked at the girls. What was left of the war was good for business. We sat down with what was left of them boys he knew. Some of them boys were waiting for their orders home to come through. None of our boys were there. They were in there drinking-forgetting. Then I was sitting there with a drink not unhappily in hand thinking that the old men would come in and get me. Or that someone had seen me in the street. They probably all knew where I was by now. But I stayed there with them boys. I stayed put with them boys drinking. They started to smoke. They wanted me to smoke too. They were not unpleasant company. I couldn't refuse it because it was a point of hospitality. They were smoking-drinking with me and I took it and I smoked with them and everything came clear to me. I was freed a time.

The band was playing something you could dance to. All the people were out on the dark floor their bodies moving to the music. A man and a woman were dancing as if asleep in one another's arms while their hands moved everywhere as though they were awake. Jack ordered whiskey. Whiskey bottles banged down hard onto the table.

"Jack Daniels Jackson, you motherfucker," one of the boys said.

We began to drink whiskey. The music did not stop. Many men and women were dancing. Their hands went everywhere and the people at the tables watched it all. There was the black-on-yellow-yellow-on-white-white-on-black and you saw none of it that way. We were all away.

When we were nicely stoned and drunk someone started to talk about home. We were pleasantly stoned and drunk and someone started to talk about getting back home, like it was the place everyone had always had to get back to, to be in for good as they always do. They talk it up. They talked it up. There came the leisurely clicking of Zippo lighters. There was the chain smoking of cigarettes. They began to talk about getting back home like it was a place everyone needed to get back to, to be in for some good reason. That is the talk in such times.

"Geronimo, he ain't going back to the States," Jack said.

"Where the fuck you goin' man?"
"He's goin' to France," Jack said.
"He's going to France?"

"*Fancy* France," someone said.
"What the fuck for?" another said.
"He's crazy."
"He's gone in the head, fucked for good."
"No, Geronimo *he's smart*."
"Fuck the States," was said matter-of-factly.
"Fuck you all," was the un-thought answer.
"You got the chance to go home, man."
"Do not fuck it up, *man*," that was said with genuine feeling.
"*Home*?" someone said, "Ain't no fucking home."
"There's mashed potatoes, and pie, and hot dogs, man."
"There's roast beef, and turkey, and corn on the cob, motherfucker."
"There's chicken and gravy and stuffing—there's ham and eggs and toast and bacon every fucking morning."
"Don't you want to eat some real fucking food man?"
"He don't give a shit."
"Why should he give a shit?"
"Where the fuck you *goin'*?" was said again.
"He's going to France, man," Jack said diplomatically.
"Fuck France—That ain't no place."
"Everywhere's a place man."
"Not anymore. This place ain't no place no more."
"Get your shit together," Jack said.
"What's he goin' to do there?"
"It's a *woman*, man," Jack said politely.
"What?"
"He said it's a fucking woman."
"It's always a fucking woman."
"He's goin' there to *fuck*, man?"
"That's all there's left to do, man."
"Fucking's all that's left."
"Shit, you can do that *here* man—you do not know

fucking shit."
"You don't need to go no fancy place to do that man."
"No, he's in *love*, man," Jack said softly.
"Love? Fuck love."
"What the fuck is love? You got family man?"
"You got to see *family* man. Straighten your ass out."
"What do family know?"
"Family don't know shit," someone said.
"Family know shit you'll never know, motherfucker."
"They ain't nothing like family."
"They ain't nothing like the States."
"Fuck you all up."
"Fuck you right up."

They argued it out amongst themselves. They went on with it. They had their reason. Then they were all of them laughing with it and none of them were afraid now believing in nothing, no god no country, nothing but their own laughing and none of us were afraid. That laughing that was what was real. Then in my laughing the priest he came to me. I felt the little black book against me. I saw the priest in my laughing there with them for no good reason. He had always been afraid to laugh. I had him in my head for no good reason but that I'd wished he'd been there with us laughing once and to see it. I saw him knelt down to pray beside a bed with a boy. I wished he'd heard them all laughing so. Had he ever heard any one of us laugh so? He'd have been happy. He'd have been happy hearing it. That's what I kept thinking. He'd have been happy to know it. I wanted him to be once.

We were none of us afraid now. None of us were left afraid and alone in that laughing. The priest he was there in my head and I saw how he was alone in it. He would always be alone in his living. There are these people who will always be so. They choose it for themselves for no good reason. He was to be alone in his living. He was to be alone in his living

I kept thinking that and that he'd have been happy to know such laughing come on in them boys all alive and living and the music played on and the whiskey was poured out and all went on and I was getting truly drunk so to think and we were all of us laughing now none of us ever alone in our laughing. If loving could only be so. If that were so that we were not ever alone in our loving. We were never to be alone in our loving. We were goddamned alive in our laughing. We were goddamned alive never alone laughing. If that were only so in our loving. The thoughts came hard onto one another. The music played. The people danced.

Then came the quiet. The real quiet then was come. The quiet was come on amidst all that loudness. It came on in us. We were all shut up once more in ourselves. We sat there in the din of dance and music in the dark-crowded drunk-talking tables left a little badly alone in the real quiet come. We must not be so. We must not be so now. We must not be deadened again. We were living. We were living sat shut up in our old selves deadened again. We looked to one another and away. It was that wanting not to be alone. It was that wanting not to be alone in living. It was that wanting. It came clear to me there with them and I knew it true there with them a clear knowledge come in the cacophonic din of wordless dumbfounded drunk-hearing with all become ill-sensed listening in the hard congregated sound of the language put to the music at the crowded bottle-filled tables with all sense dispersed into sound in our hearing how the words and the songs sounded like they were all of them saying the same things until all logic was lost and I could not understand any of it anymore. I wanted to understand it. I would never understand it. There was music in it no matter.

197

40

THE END OF THE HAPPY SPRING

Then the old woman was there. The children were there. Then in late dark I rode with them children west. In rising light I looked into them children's faces going to her.

They were sending them children out from the country. They were sending them all where they could send them to whoever would take them. I saw their faces in shadow in the canvas covered truck heading west. I looked into them young faces. I hoped they would find a home. Sometimes they sang in some happiness to pass the time. Then they lay fallen off to sleep.

I rode with them children awakened to sing in rising light fallen off in sleep to silence in going light getting to her. I was getting to her. The country fell behind. We came into new country. They lay on in sleep along one another crossing in such brief oblivion into new country. There was all the new and unknown country.

That is the end of the happy spring.

BOOK TWO

HOLIDAY IN THE COUNTRY

For WAR consisteth not in battle only, or the act of fighting, but in a tract of time wherein the will to contend by battle is sufficiently known. And therefore, the notion of *time* is to be considered in the nature of war, as it is in the nature of weather. For as the nature of foul weather lieth not in a shower or two of rain, but in an inclination thereto of many days together, so the nature of war consisteth not in actual fighting, but in the known disposition thereto during all the time there is no assurance to the contrary. All other time is PEACE.

Hobbes, *Leviathan*

41

ON THE ADVANTAGE AND DISADVANTAGE
OF HISTORY FOR LIFE

We were out on the porch looking at her half-done drawing in the summer light. Her mother had made lunch and called us to it and we went off from the porch into the house to the kitchen table and ate in quiet. We sat quiet at the table. It was no simple quiet. She had those pictures now and her mother and I took a look at one another and we looked away. We were seeing some of our own old selves that day. Then after lunch with the table cleared and with the coffee and the afternoon begun she went back out from her mother and me to the porch to look at the old pictures. I watched her go. I wanted to go out to her.

"Let her do it, John," her mother said. "Let her look."

So she went out. But then she got that old cardboard box full of pictures and she brought the box back in to me to the table from off the porch. She was done with her drawing and left it. She took the top off that dilapidated box she'd set out on the kitchen table and she sat there across the table from me looking through it. Her mother was opening and closing cupboards. She stood at the sink. She looked over to the two of us. It was a Saturday and she was making her grocery list to go to town. Her mother left the two of us there alone at the kitchen table and went to town. I heard the car door shut and start. I heard her in the car go off down the drive. Out through the kitchen window the afternoon light was coming down in the back yard onto the greened leaves and black branches of a big oak. It was mid-summer and hot and the leaves shone green from all the trees there along the lake with the leaves lit bright against the branches and bark. There were spots of blue lake water behind them.

"You don't want to look at those old pictures. Why don't we go out, and walk along the lake?" I said to her. That would be a pleasant way to pass the time.

"I want to look at them. Mother kept them for me, and I want to," she said and that was that.

And she took out one of those old black and white pictures from that beat-up cardboard office box and she looked at it and looked at me and I was looking at her long dark hair in the summer light across the cover of a book I was trying to read. Then she got another picture out. She laid it on the table next to the first one. It was a picture of France with the hills rising along the river to the sky. "Daddy, where is this?" she said. I told her. She found an old postcard. She found many pictures of France. Then she had the blued cover of an old passport in her hand. It'd all been kept put away in that box. She opened the passport and she'd found the old visa the priest had gotten for me. She looked at the printed date on it. I could see the signatures in ink across its official consulate paper. The official French seal was stamped on it. She felt the embossed paper of the French seal with her finger. She looked at the affixed picture of me that I'd taken in the cigarette shop and given to the priest.

"Daddy, are we French?" she said to me seeing all those things.

"No, we're not French," I said to her. "You know that."

"But we have French names?" she said in some logic.

Then she held the paperwork up to me as would a kind of official when making an inquiry into one's identity, and she

204

looked across the table to me to see who I was before her in relation to that boy, and she said out loud to me reading off the name on the paperwork, "*John LeBlanc*," and I was sitting there drinking a cup of coffee, trying to read that book of mine looking to her and away out to the strong light coming down brightly across the trees and yard wishing her mother had been there beside me to face her, together the two of us, because she was better at it, but in those days she already had a way of leaving us to it, and that day she did, she went off to do her shopping, and with all them old times and places laid out before her and that paperwork held in her one hand she picked up the soldier picture of me in her other and she said in simple, serious, curiosity, "Daddy, did you kill people?" and I'd told her very little of that war and I wasn't telling that I was seeing in my own unsaid words how I'd gotten here to home and she was serious about it for a girl her age and she waited for an answer from me and I put the book down on the table and took up my cup of coffee and drank some coffee from the cup looking at her over the rim and the summer light was hitting down hard in America outside the kitchen window.

"That part doesn't matter to the story," I said. It's not a war story anyway, it's never been a war story, not in that way. I know that's true. It's about a homecoming. It is how one gets to home. That is the story, and in my thinking that, I put my coffee cup down on the tablecloth, and I thought then that all what I had told her in morning could be about any two people in any war. I hadn't really told her about the two of us her mother and me as particular people in a particular war. What I'd told her could be about this war now and any two people in it and how, the thought's come to me lately, they'd got there not by some chance but by being so-called social types constrained in history, and it's always too soon to tell about that at the time it's lived even if you'd been in it and it'd all just happened in your life to you. It takes years. It returns in a kind of parsed-out renaissance born of extended self-critique.

And I looked out to the summer light in America and she held the paperwork from the priest and she wanted to know about the actual particular things of our lived life and why she had a French name and why her mother had kept pictures of France and why we weren't French and whether her father who she had in a picture in her hand had killed people. She wanted to know the singular defining and however unlikely things of a life and to do that in telling you have to continually break down the distance between you and your own self, and keep yourself now from an easy absurdity and irony which wants to come to you in the distance of telling, keep yourself from the rhetorical shorthand of it, in reverting, however in play, to a formal stance and language which can easily eclipse the actual life of it, which is to escape the earnestness and sentiment of it in an act of rhetoric you find refuge in in a kind of continual repression when telling such a girl such a story, for it extends, or rather attenuates and delays the affect of the story, in aesthetic effect it holds off all confrontation and resolution. And there are whole late histories of literature written so from such a distance which in formal acts of composition mimetically turn away from scenes of simple feeling-pictured to pass over the lived sense of life perceived and persisting in some duration on a page to illuminate first and foremost a stylistic way of seeing and speaking within which to lose one's self in sheer language and I myself have always loved such books. I aver with them. And she wants the particular life of it, and it can't be told to her, not without censure, but once you've begun on it at length you find you want the clarity of it for yourself, and so in her want, and your need, for you've lived years in such a rhetoric of play which avers, there comes to your mind's eye a kind of scenic realism, more a poetics of reverie, or perhaps a kind of hyper-realism, an actuality of being, there is no simple form for it, where you do see at times clearly what it was you lived, you see how you stayed off from home, how you came to home, a whole history of homecoming, where people, places, and things are pictured in their sentiment not sentimentality, where acts and objects come into view and reverberate in their persistent moral significance, at last collapsing, for your own good, no matter what you've told her, the distance between regret and absolution and where, in the end, your life meets its meaning. This happens years later.

So she sat there with them pictures of France put before her and all along that day I did want to find the words for the life of it to tell her. I do want the life of it for her. I want her to know who I am as an individual and not a character type, for I know there were all the little unlikely things of a life we'd lived, without constraint, no matter the large disadvantage of history for life. And in our quiet she said, "Daddy, tell me about France, you never told me," she said to me wanting the place and time of those pictures she had laid on the kitchen table before her, and I said to her, "I'll tell you about France," and she was listening and she put down that soldier picture, and I looked to the rising hills in France laid down there on the table in that house along the great lake in America, and I was seeing myself getting on to France to get to her. I saw some of those old gone places in France. I saw the red roofs of a village along a river. I saw the far rooms I'd lived in. There are all these rote facts. I saw how I could tell her about France, how there were these good times and beautiful places we'd lived in in France. But you'll want some well-put words for them to find the life of what it was. Or it is only the dead recollection of detail. But like anything lived up it's hard to rediscover let alone resurrect the life of it to get on good with it. You'd think it'd be easy to keep beginning on your own life. After all you've done the living of it. But it's not that easy to keep beginning on your own life now, when it's made up out of large, unseen, left-out times stretched blankly between a few fixed pictures that'll come to you clear once in a while like the ones she'd laid out before her. But I know I went from East to West, and I said the names first to myself then out loud and the places came strange-sounding from far across the years and continents to that kitchen table to her: Bangkok—Luxembourg—France. I went on to Bangkok to get on into Luxembourg to get into France to get to her. Saying it I see it.

  I said, "I took a train south into France, to a city called Valence," and I saw the river, and I said, "Valence, it's a French city on a famous river where they make linen—it's an old French city famous for its fine linen," I said to her and I touched the tablecloth laid there beneath them pictures and that paperwork, and remembered that that worn linen tablecloth put right there on that table in America by her mother, that it'd been made there and brought here and I saw the wide embanked river running south along the city to the sea. Sitting there with her in that house, I looked out the kitchen window past the trunks of trees to the blued horizon of the great lake in America and I saw the water of the Rhone River running wide and gray. I looked back from the water to her long dark hair in the summer light. She was just a girl in America. She was young beside me in America and I have never invented that. I do want to tell a true story. The funny thing is that to tell it at all, you've got to make it up as you can, and then you find it's not even that untrue in the telling it.

42

A TOURIST IN A TRAIN STATION

  We forget I'm telling it. It's as if in a book that I landed in Luxembourg in the light and it was a place that I'd never been and I would leave on a train south before I'd seen any of it. I rode a bus that ran a route from the airport to the train station and getting off the bus with my bags, I saw myself in one of those long-glassed storefront windows stretched blankly along a strange street in the gritty light of an unknown city. It was by accident I saw myself. I saw a lost-looking boy carrying two bags down a strange street. It'd surprised me looking in the light the one way and feeling another going on along at last to get to her. I was not lost and I turned from the misrepresentation of that reflection of mine and went off from the sight of myself. I went on down the street to the train station with my head kept down looking to the grayed pavement before me. The place was all strange and I wanted it that way and I crossed the street to the station and went in it.

I was to cross the border into France by train as just one more American tourist, and I felt I might've even been one as I walked into the train station, feeling a forgotten old feeling, like when you were a kid and you'd feel the coming of good weather after bad once one season gets on good at last into another and you can't any longer remember the days of the one as they were for the new feeling of being in the other all around you as it is. It was that feeling. It was a hell of a happy new feeling. It was a long gone goddamned good feeling going on in a morning light getting to her not yet got to her knowing none of it yet to come. Feeling that feeling I didn't wander about the train station. I didn't go anywhere or do anything to lose it. I felt a time at the beginning of myself in another new life. All the past was pushed off in travel. I was early and in that feeling of self-renewal I sat my bags down on the platform. I looked off from the army bags and I sat quiet against my two canvas bags that lay fully packed on the platform to feel it and I felt it. I didn't want to lose it and in the thin leisure of that waiting time I lost it. In the solitude and stillness of waiting too long a time in that train station come travelled and tired to rest in such sheer leisure without any one new act but

209

my own far-ranging reverie, I came back too close to myself and didn't know how to get the feeling back. The old dark feeling returned to me there in the daylight, not seen by eye as the station light is seen, but a material darkness, visible first in mind and, after that generative feeling of having come into the light of the station as when arrived and gone for good into the days of another new changed-up season, wherein you will no longer go on round badly in the old lived-up days of the last, but fall forward into all to be, I saw them dire sights coming, I felt them familiar scenes to come, ones now unexpected there in such soon return, and I had no resolve to confront them, I was hard-tired and too travelled-out to and, in that dark feeling risen and come on in me, before I saw anything re-formed in it, I looked off, into the light of the station to see the congregation of the surface detail of the station, to lose myself in such a scene of so much anonymous insignificant description which will have nothing to do with a self.

I looked dimly round and even as though in an act of reconnaissance. I looked out along the grayed cement of the quay. I looked back from the rowed and numbered quays to the station café. I looked to the little black iron tables sat out under the high-arched iron roof where there in quaint sky light come down from the high glass you'd go over to sit awhile for a nice easy drink at the station café. I wanted a drink and I was tired of drinking. I looked to the time marked out before me, measured out by the minute on a station clock hung up on an iron pole rising to the roof from the platform, to lose myself awhile in the watching its incremental turn of the huge black hand traversing as if imperceptibly to the eye across the numbered face making the time, the feeling of time lengthening in the looking to it, the entire span of the turned face of the earth to reside there in time in the glass-cased turn of the clock face, and I looked away to shorten it in forgetting, however unchanging it, the train time of all arrivals and departures remaining exactly measured out, to look to the people there in the station in their private time looking to their watches, strolling in on along the platform, and someone on the quay lit a cigarette, and no one knew anyone waiting like that, and the cigarette smoke mixed nicely with the tar and the stink of grit in the morning air in that sky-lit train station.

The affliction I'd felt was weakened, in the cosmopolitan look of architecture, in the look of destinations before one, and I looked to the train before me which I was to take, and a conductor walked through it. The train looked long-travelled, like one I'd seen in old movies with actors travelling on in it speaking in strange accents, with the side of the train streaked with diesel and grayed with the dirt of foreign cities and countries on down along its windows and doors. This was the train I was to take into France to get to her, which in another time must have carried many people many places into the beginnings and the ends of many things. The dispersed sky light of the station, high, luminous light, hit across its dim gray roof. I would be out on it in the country under the far sky, and in such scenic diversion, I had looked along the parked train in some duration, as when a camera pans a set scene, to find and focus on something of visible interest and, so to hold myself kept in them sights, I looked out past the cars of that parked train, up the tracks, off to where we would depart out of the station. Out the far open station end there was an enormous shadow cast out across the rails of half the train yard. There, the high iron of the station roof was cutting off the coming light. I watched the light. The long shadow of the roof fell out west across the rows of tracks curving southward. The light was coming in time across the iron station roof. The fixed roof edge was cutting off less and less of the light cast across the train yard. I looked to the lengthening light. The shadow shortened into the station. Out beyond the grayed edge of it stretched the shining rows of steel laid into light. The time passed with the light making the feeling of time. I smelled the dank fresh stink of the concrete platform. I smelled the tar and oil of wooden ties put down half-buried in the ground, evenly laid out lit at a distance one after the other, the ties set out nicely as far as you could see into the brightening distance, with the worn clean rails spiked down and bent out brightly upon their leveled backs laid in dirt along the dim shuttered buildings in morning light. I looked to that gleaming-railed lit steel running side by side going on out of the station, out of the city, cutting on out across country, across countries, and in all that going never getting to the end of a country. There was always more country to cross.

Out the station end the pigeons flew in the light and shadow, and three men in blue uniforms and caps appeared. They walked officially down the dank platform. A whistle blew. There, the birds flew. The doors to the train were opened. The people were loaded up into the train car by the directive authority of the uniformed men and I got in with my two green army bags and went down the aisle and put the bags up on the luggage rack and sat beside a good wide window in one of those red-covered bench seats like ones I had sat in in booths in old diners in America in old train cars sat up on concrete blocks going nowhere in a small town serving simple food that tasted good when you were hungry and tired. Another whistle blew and the doors to the train were shut for good and the one conductor on the platform signaled to another conductor on the train and the heavy sound of the steel on steel came on and the clock got by and the iron poles of the station roof came by and the sound of the going got strong and straight. Along the blocks of shuttered buildings the train gained speed into the light.

It was the beginning of July.

43

A KIND OF TRAVELOGUE

It's almost like the beginning of another new life, if not a story. You'll feel at such times of travel that you're going off into another new life. You'll even feel in such times of travel that you'll have many such regenerative if not reclaimed, restored lives in a life not just be living in this one that you are living in. It is all at a beginning again before you in the sheer travel of a train, and I sat back in the old train car on that bench seat, and the world was again all new and unknown to me. The good feeling little by little was returned to me. There was the wide-opened feeling of coming into new country. There was no end to the country. In the long unceasing travel of that train southward toward her I was sure at times that the rest of my life was gone behind me and as if it had been lived by another person who now could not ever possibly be me. One must start anew and can.

Out of Luxembourg the summer light was strong and there was a far mist that hung up high in the hills the train followed into France. The daylight burned off that impressionistic mist and the far sky was clear. The train came away down from the high hills with grass meadow going on up into lines of trees to rising forest and in that lulling travel south I began to feel a little like a tourist. I pleasantly followed the lay of the land by eye. There was the long and beautiful order of it, in the look of how the land was all laid out for generations, in its being cultivated by the people for centuries, tended a millennia, and we were coming down south onto a wide plain and the sun burned strong on the flat field land of wheat and grain planted golden to the feet of far hills. We were going south slowly across the Moselle River to Metz, into the Lorraine to Burgundy, to Dijon to Lyon to Valènce far in the south and the sun burned down on us in the good weather and all the people in the train got hot under the metal roof of the old train car.

Out of Luxembourg the conductors came by and asked you for your ticket and looked at your ticket and then punched it efficiently with a metal hand punch and then gave you your ticket back to prove that you'd paid. Then going into France there were blue-uniformed men with guns and they asked you for your paperwork that told you who you were, told what you were named and showed how you looked, and you gave it to them crossing the border and they looked at you seriously and as if you'd done something, and then they looked back at the paperwork, and then they handed your paperwork back to you. And when they'd got to me and I'd given them mine, they'd looked at it and then they'd looked at me, and then they'd handed it back to me with the look and said to me, "*John LeBlanc*? So, you are *American*, *eh*?" they'd said in that English that I'd heard before from the priest and her and I'd said, "Yes," and they'd said nothing more then than that, and they'd left me with the official look of authority and went off on down the aisle of the speeding train and on into the next car as if there was nothing out of the ordinary in that. But it was when they'd come to me, that I'd then looked right away from them in the old fear and out the window at the passing landscape in the light to the far horizon of hills and thought that they'd arrest me. But it was all just a formality. I had the paperwork to get to France. It had the French consulate seal on it. It had the official signatures in blue ink that the priest had got put on it, I do not know how, and I put the paperwork back away carefully in with my ticket and I saw the priest.

When I put the paperwork away, I felt her letter, her picture was in it. I took out her letter. We would never write letters like that again. I looked at the colorful French stamps, the thin blue envelope, at the black-inked postmark date telling me the place it came from. In them inked marks it all looked like it had come from a far off and interesting place. In looking to it you got the hopeful feeling that it was even a place where you could become at last who you were to be and I felt I could with her. I took her picture out from the envelope. I looked at the pretty posed shot. She looked dark and young and even as though a girl from another time. I put the shot away. I read over the letter again looking at her carefully schooled penmanship to pass the time pleasantly. I put it carefully away in my pocket with the train ticket and the official paperwork. It was all a nice little reverie and, in it, then for a time there was this persistent real sense of coming freedom travelling south into new country to her. I did not think it was just the insensible motion of that train. I do think travelling does change you. Travelling to another you love changes you. In stretches of respite you'll think it must and hope it does. It did in getting on to her, and the little picturesque villages passed, and I lingered in the little thoughts of how we'd go live an ordinary and simple life and be happy to. We would never be in big things again and know what it was like to live in them and we wouldn't miss them. We were in something big being in our own ordinary given lives. It is enough to be born after all. The most interesting life can be a simple life.

  Out the window were long tall tree lines running up rises of ploughed land where the trees were planted between the passing fields to break the wind so to hold the earth. There were solitary stone houses made of rock the color of the earth. There were all the little named villages. The train stopped off in them all the way south. In time, the pretty looking towns and the village houses and the land it was all the same kind of country. It was all beautiful country. I shut my eyes to sleep the rest of it. I did not sleep. The train kept stopping off at the stone stations of villages. The people kept getting on and off. I kept looking to the people travelling the country.

They carried children and luggage up and down the too narrow aisle. Sometimes getting on there were then young couples and groups of kids with canvas packs on summer vacation some of them not much younger than me. They went to sleep soundly against their canvas packs with their tanned faces all peaceful when they slept in the crowded and rocking train.

I did not sleep. I looked to people travelling all the way south getting on and off. It passed the waking time. The people were not uninteresting. Sometimes when I would see someone who looked a little out of sorts, I would think of what all they were coming from or going to there on that train, I would think of where they were getting to on a hot summer day like this, think that maybe they were going off even so that they were not after today coming from or going to the same places and things they'd been to yesterday and maybe there was nothing for them to get to or out of and I did not sleep and I passed the time in such thinking not sleeping kept too awake in that absent kind of reverie that leads nowhere in the world no matter how far in thought when what I wanted was to have long been sleeping.

44

THE GIRLS ON THE TRAIN

That is when these girls came on at a little French town. I was kept awakened on that train heading south in the little travelogue I had kept up for myself, told myself of all them people, to pass the waking time, to fill that time without her, to fill it without myself all the way south. In its diversion, it became an extended little travelogue in its small dramatic interest, visual continuity, comprised of simply looking to all the people as I told myself unfamiliar stories of such anonymous and unknown lives, invented but not improbable lives, and it was peopled-out with even some brief character-pictures, and one of the last scenes I remember from that travel south before I got to her, was when we were coming into one of those French villages I've long since forgotten the name of and three girls got on, and they came down the aisle, and they put their packs up on the rack above me and sat down on the long bench seat in front of me to face me, and the train pulled out of the station.

It turned out they were Belgian girls on vacation in France and were going south on their holiday, that's what they called it, and on their way south they'd stopped to visit a friend from school in the small French town. They had cans of warm beer and opened the cans, and were drinking the warm beer. I bought a beer from them for a dollar. I made them take the American dollar. They looked at the color and the feel of it, and the touch and the look of it was strange to them. I cracked the can open and I drank the warm beer and the very tanned blonde girl said in good English, "You are American?"

"Yes," I said, hearing the word the unusual way she said it, not now in that French sound I'd long heard in the English as she was Flemish, while I was wondering what the word meant to her. They spoke very good English. They asked me some things about America. They were very friendly girls. They wanted to know about America. They asked if it was true that you could get rich in America. I told them that you could get a lot of things in America you could get rich in America I told them. I told them you could get all what you wanted in America. I told them. I told them some things. I told them everything and nothing. The list of what all you could get was too long and I kept it short. They told me the three of them they were going to the South of France to camp and to swim along a famous and beautiful river. They said all the Belgians went south in summer to the beautiful rivers in France or Spain to swim and to live a little in the light.

217

Then they were gone to sleep against one another in the rocking car. The three of them then were all young and quiet and peaceful. I looked to the three of them there, then all young and quiet and peaceful. I looked at their girl's faces and they slept on fallen one against the other. They kept me awake in my looking. In looking to them fallen girls in France, I saw how they'd awake to rise once more and go on in life. For all I know, they could all be mothers with grown girls of their own by now, and the last thing I remember travelling south was when we were coming into a place called Chalon-sûr-Saône, when an old man got on with his wife, and he was very thin, and though it was very hot in the train car, he wore a blue spring jacket and he looked very ill. His paled skin was thin across the bones of his face and he moved himself very slowly with his wife as if otherwise he would break himself. His wife sat him down beside a window. She sat herself beside him. She herself was alive in a kind of appraisal of people. He stared out the window at the passing landscape. His eyes were all watery. He kept wiping his nose with a blue checked handkerchief and he kept up a little cough over the clicking of the tracks. The whole thing looked hard on him. She took it well. She was alive to the traveling. She wore a summer dress. She had her hair done up. She looked happy to be out in the day. She was in the midst of her life no matter him. They got off at a little village. He held her sturdy arm all the way out and down to the ground. They walked off to a darkened stone building set off from the tracks. The train pulled out. They walked off in the hot bright weather to the stone of the building. They were gone from sight. I was sure he was happy to be alive in that summer light. He must be now long dead.

  She had written me that it would get bright and hot in the summer in that part of France and that it was the kind of weather that made the people there healthy and happy and I was not unhappy to be in that part of France that now in the brilliant landscape and the light became the South. The sunlight had stayed heavy on the roof of the old train car all the way south and when night came the heat stayed on and hung close to everything in the darkness and no lights had been turned on when it turned dark and I had stayed awake too long looking to them girls' dim slumberous shapes feeling at times that no amount of travel would ever overtake who I was no matter how far I went and the girls slept on in France in the dark fallen one against the other in simple peace and in time I myself fell off to an uneasy sleep lulled by the unceasing travel of that train south hitting on across the tracks and slept in short bad half-sleep the rest of the way south and waked coming into the train station at Valence.

45

THE UNREAL ACTUALITY OF ARRIVAL

This was the South and the night heat was hung dark in the trees and heavy along the stone houses and city streets along the tracks as we came into the city outskirts and the train slowed and shifted across the sets of tracks. We went by the shuttered backs of buildings and houses into Valence with the train slowing and hauling the line of cars to a stop into the dark and badly lit station where the people were standing in long shadow on the dim lit station platform waiting under the clocks. The train stopped four or five tracks away from the station in the July night and the people got up and got their things down from the rack. I got my bags. The girls slept on in the dark. I went down the aisle with my two duffle bags and stepped off the train following the others out across the tracks to the station.

The train moved out south behind us. I came across

the tracks and had the feeling that she wouldn't be there. It felt too late and that the train had taken too long to get to where it was going and that if she'd come she'd gone back home because she had thought I hadn't come. But the time passes oddly when you're arriving after such long travel and even when early you can feel and think in a kind of lateness. She had told me the train to take and the city with the arrival times and dates of trains. She'd told me she would wait at the train station at those times on those days for the trains. The priest said he would write her when I had left, so that she would know which days to wait. I hoped he had. I was sure he had, and I looked to the faces along the dark wall of the station to see her there and I didn't see her as I came across the last set of tracks to the station. There under the wide slanted roof I couldn't see any of the waiting faces clearly in the bad light and thought then she might even look right at me and not know it was me and I didn't know what we'd do then if something like that happened to us in a place like that, and I walked on with no sight of her when I crossed the platform, she was not there on it and, crossing it, stepping into the high open door of the station out of the night heat, and into the coolness of the stone, I didn't think to see her, and there she was.

   She was sitting on one of those long wooden train station benches looking to the people coming in off that train, waiting there reading a book, looking to me and knowing me as I came into the coolness of the high stone. She looked right at me with all them people coming and going in and out of the station. She'd been reading a book to pass the waiting. She stood and laid the book down on the bench. She looked dark. I was happy seeing her so dark. I stood there on the stone with the bags in hand and didn't walk across the stone to get to her. I looked at her waiting for me like that there in that train station and she looked almost like another girl. Her hair was cut short. She wore a blue and white bright-striped short-sleeve shirt. She wore Capri pants. She had black sandals. She looked like a dark French girl. I was struck by the look of her and she started to walk from the bench to me as if she'd thought I'd looked right at her and not seen her. I'd seen her. I put the bags down on the stone. I crossed the stone to get to her. We two crossed that stone and came into one another. I had her in my arms. She was there against me and it felt unreal. It was real. I held her into me. She kept me close to her. I felt her held up against me and that was the only real. Her hair smelled good, I felt her body all her body up against me, all of her came to me, "*John*," she said. That was all she said. I didn't speak. We held one another as if we didn't know how it should be done. We didn't know how it should be done and they were announcing the departure of a train. The train times and names of cities came unintelligible over the loudspeaker crackling metallically on through the station. She let herself go into me and we were doing it carefully and not too hard. We were holding one another good and hard. We held one another not at all letting go. It's not a thing you can say. We held to one another saying nothing. The feeling went on. It is some great going off. The announcements of arrivals and departures echoed over the station stone. It's a thing you'll want to come to again and again in a life and it's a thing you're lucky to have come to once with another. We held on there in that feeling of one another. We held on to one another beneath the high clocks. That is all. The big station clocks in their great glass cases marked off time high above us with the people passing in front of us and behind us and all around about us going on in the station across the stone of the station floor and we two stood there stopped like that outside of all time and place gone far off to a place you can never get to in the world arrived at last after long travel to be stopped only in the actuality of one another.

  In front of the coming and going people we kissed one another on the cheek, and then the clocks were striking above us and, in the striking hour, we broke off, having gotten it done, and we took a good look at one another and I said, "You cut your hair short, girl," I said to her and I looked at her black short cut hair the way it came down dark and straitened all unbraided on down along the line of her face in one of those fashionable French cuts with her dark eyes outlined in the black and she looked less strange and somehow more French to me in a way that she had not ever looked before but she was still the same unplaceable girl in those dark eyes of hers and none of the feeling for her had gone and in the look of her I felt how I loved her. I knew how I loved her.

"Yours is grown longer, John," she said and she touched my hair with her hand, "It looks darker, longer," she said touching it by hand, and she kissed me once more with care on the cheek, and I held her hard to me again, I felt her close against me, I felt all of her, and it wasn't done, the whole unbounded feeling of it was there in her, we were yet in the big things we could've said right there, when held to one another close and hard again in that kind of unfinished arrival to a place when what was felt was more real than the fact of reaching one's actual destination, and we didn't say them things, and they were passing from us, to be gone little by little, in each new touch and look that we took they went, and we looked and looked away, there are times looking tells too much, and she was crying against me, and I said, "Don't cry," and she said, "I am happy," and I let her cry, and it was real, and then I simply kept her held into me to quiet her in the stone of the station after we'd said those couple simple things that didn't really matter to either of us. Then it was passed.

Then in our ordinary voices all the overcoming feeling was passed. It was come and gone. It was all the more real to us in our simple everyday talk. The big things to be said were gone from out of us. I can't tell you what they would've been now in words once the time was gone and done to say them.

We'd already said them. We'd written it out. We'd written it out in letters that people didn't ever write one another. We'd written it out in words we'd never write one another again. We'd written that we hadn't known how we'd be together in any place but that we must be together in some place. We'd written that we didn't know how our being alone would be once and for all finished but that it must be finished. I had the bags in hand and she had her book. The taxis were out front. We were walking out of the station beside one another out front to the taxis on across the stone floor going on out of the train station beside a great glass window where they sold tickets and took luggage and going past it into the night I looked to it and saw us in the big glass sheet two faces among the coming and going faces of the people with the two of us framed-out in the dim light as in the style of an old black and white photograph you might find one day left in a desk drawer of an old house taken many years before of a place visited long ago by people heard of or even once known.

46

ONE IS EVER AND PERPETUALLY ARRIVING

We walked into the night. The night was warm and pleasant. We took a taxi out of the city up over the big bridge over the Rhone River with the water running wide and black beneath the stone and turned south into the night. We were holding one another by the hand. We went on south. We went on down the road in the dark between the river and the rising mountain. We were close together in the back seat of the taxi and I could smell her beside me and I could smell the cigarettes from the taxi ashtray and no matter being amidst the solidity of those things I felt like I was still arriving and I know people can never arrive like their letters arrive. One has the feeling one is always arriving whereas a letter simply arrives and I pulled her to me and she sat up against me on the back seat next to the window and I was there in her and I lay my head against the window.

"John, you are tired?" she said.

"No, I'm awake—I don't want to sleep," I said. I looked to her. I saw her young beside me dark in the night there in France and felt I could've been anywhere in the world once more in that car and that I was but for her. That I was lost in the whole of her. I was lost but for her.

"I want to keep this feeling," I said. "It's large, and I'm alive in it."

"It is still the same?" she said.

"Yes," I said and she was there close against me.

"There is nothing to say, then," she said and she stayed against me.

"We should say nothing then," I said, and we went on in that taxi held close into one another on the back seat not talking of any one large or little thing, kept first in the feeling of one another, in the significance of such love, life, of us, and we didn't talk of this or that little or large thing as people will do in some purpose, to pass the time when arriving to another like that. It's true you don't want too much quiet too soon but we weren't ever that good at such small talk. We knew that.

We went south between the running river and the rising rock and now with all the overcoming feeling of the train station gone yet the large feeling of arriving was kept alive in our holding one another and wasn't made littler in words. I wanted to keep the feeling of such large life in me as long as I could. I kept my arm put round her pulled close and she kept her hand closed hard in mine and that kept it and we looked out the windows of the taxi. We went on in that taxi alive in arriving, and we didn't lose all the regained power of the feeling to have it pass in too easy looks and talk, and even when we'd said then one or two of them little everyday things to one another as people will and must do, even then in that small talk that came to us, all the feeling of arriving was kept alive and large.

"How far is it, now?" I said to her.

"Not far," she said. "Twenty kilometers."

"Will we see your parents—are your parents waiting?" I said.

"No, it's late," she said. "They will be sleeping. They will see you in the morning."

I looked at her. She saw me looking.

"What is it?" she said and we went along a curve in the night with her leaned into me and the taxi headlights hit up on the trunks of the trees. On the straight-aways the bright lights went up into the canopy of leaves branched over the highway with the wind hitting the high illuminated leaves. The wind was coming hard into the trees. It bent the high branches lit in the headlights.

"Nothing, I just wanted to see you good again," I said.

"Do I—look good?" she said and she actually wondered.

"Of course," I said. "But, you drove off in that taxi, and I didn't know if I'd ever see you again," I said.

"You didn't know, John?"

"How could I?"

"I knew," she said. "I knew it would be."

"But Madeleine, you've always known much more, many things so much better than me," I said and I took some careful little looks at her as we went along the many curves of the foot of the mountain going south in that taxi the first night between the rock and the river, wanting to see her good again. But one is careful how one looks to another in the beginning again. I didn't want her to feel that I was looking too long. I took some little looks at her. I looked away out the window. I had forgotten how it felt. I felt all that life in her I had forgot and there really was nothing to say then and it was good when we didn't say anything. We've often been quiet all along and it is not anything bad.

47

IN A FRENCH HOUSE IN A FRENCH VILLAGE

And there on the river plain the taxi came out from beneath the trees in the night along the stone houses and streets and, just as she'd once told in the little room of the school in Saigon, we came to the little French village of Beauchastel to the house along the river in the South of France. It is the village out of them all that has remained the clearest in my mind. Even now I see how it was laid out. I have not seen it in years, the others are long gone from sight. She'd told of it and, there arrived in it, we drove in dark along scattered houses at the foot of the mountain, past the old stone shop fronts lit golden-orange from a few streetlamps to the center of the deserted village, and there at a dark shop front turned off from the highway, going from the foot of the mountain toward the flat of the river, following a narrow little road out from the old medieval village of Beauchastel, its houses rising in stone behind us unseen in dark, the ancient-like ascending village run up a steep rocky foothill to a fortification lying a thousand years in ruin.

The yellow taxi headlights hit up across the grayed pillars of a narrow concrete railroad bridge. We went beneath the bridge and there was an unreadable alphabet painted in graffiti on the illuminated columns. Beyond the bridge she told the driver to turn into the street with the house. The street was called Castel-Pavillons and if you are ever to go to the south of France to the village of Beauchastel though I do not know why you would ever go to such a place you will find the house there just after the railroad bridge on the river side of the village beneath the mountain in a little circular street with the cropped sycamore trees and stucco houses with their red tile roofs where one house is built up right next against the other house.

The house was number 16. That is where I had sent the blue envelopes of mine to her addressed *Castel-Pavillons No. 16*. They had been delivered right there into the metal mailbox hung on a stucco post not so long ago and it now already felt long ago with her beside me, when, waiting in that bleak time apart, she'd taken them to her room to read them, and I was imagining her in her room reading them, and the taxi slowed and we stopped in the street in front of the house arrived as those letters had arrived, and I held her there beside me, and it is none of it now long ago.

The taxi headlights hit the gate of the house the yellow light going on in across a garden. We got out and got the bags out. The headlights hit across the canvas on the ground before the gate and the taxi pulled out. The car went down the street its lights illuminating the rowed houses. The trees were blown and bent at their tops along the houses.

The wind came hard into the houses from the north in the night.

"Listen," I said to her. "Do you hear it?"

It came on strong toward us two in the street.

"I hear it," she said. "I think you have an ear for it," she said listening to it. The wind came hard and loud to the tops of the trees, "What is it?" I said. The wind came on to the whole place, and I couldn't tell where it was coming from. There was no storm. The night was clear. When I'd heard it approaching, first I thought it sounded like a train coming hard on the tracks across that railroad bridge we'd just crossed. But it was the wind in the tops of the trees in the far end of the street coming strong in the clear night sky from the north down the river valley. It came into the trees as though it would break them. The iron gate to the house banged on in its metal hinges. The treetops were come all alive in the street loudly bent in a wild noise of leaves.

"It is the Mistral," she said.

We stood at the gate in the sharp lashing sound of leaves.

"It is strong—it doesn't break the trees?" I said.

"They have grown up in it," she said.

The houses in the street were shuttered up against it. In the dark you could see no light or life at that hour in the street.

"How long does it last?" I said.

"Sometimes, the people stay inside for days," she said and the ripping was hard and there was no lull to it and in that kind of wind the land felt wild and unsettled in its country aspect where those village houses had long been built and we'd turned to the house with it alive in the trees, and gone through the gate.

We were walking a stone path through a flower garden green with dark stalks, bent heavy under flower tops swaying down in the night into our way, and I followed her into the flowers blown wildly in the night, up to the front of the house shuttered against it. She unlocked the big wooden door to the house. It had a square stained-glass window with iron bars. She swung it open heavy on its hinges. She shut the door. The wind was shut out behind us from the house. We stood in the little dimly lit foyer. There were stairs going off it to the second floor. There was a muddied pair of boots sitting there on the foyer floor beneath a rack of hung coats. We crossed the tile to her bedroom door and went in her room. She shut the door behind us. We stood there with the rest of the house closed off from us. She'd left on a low shaded lamp. The walls were papered over in a flowered rose wallpaper going up to a yellowed ceiling. It was all lit up a nice golden red. The light went up easy from the lamp shade cast onto the faded red-flowered walls to the yellowed-up ceiling.

I stood there in the low easy light of the room with her I'd imagined many times before in many unusual ways and never once seen the way it was. It was an ordinary lived-in room. I sat the bags down on the floor beside the bed. She said, "Do you want water?" and before I answered she went over to a sink and filled a glass with water. The room had a sink as they'll have on the first-floor bedrooms of such French houses where the bath is upstairs. After she ran the water, she brought it. I took it, and drank it, looking to a wooden chair, and a writing desk off from the sink. There were her books along a wall. The bed was opposite the books. Before the desk, the room had one of those big picture windows too looking out front onto the flower garden that we'd just come through, and I'd never seen a window that big in a bedroom, with a wide metal shutter made of unfolded panels locked across the outside of the window against the wind and dark. When you opened it up in the morning light, it would let in all the air from off the garden into the room.

"Do you want more?" she said. I'd finished the water. I didn't want any more. She took the glass from my hand, and put it on the sink and she said, "You must wash yourself, I will get you a towel," and she crossed the room in the lamplight to a wall of closets opposite the big window and opened up one of the closet doors.

"I don't want to wake anyone," I said to her.

"We must be quiet, if we can," she said and then looked up above to where her parents were sleeping.

"Is it all right?" I said quietly to her. I said nothing more. I didn't want to wake her parents to have them find me coming like that into their house in the middle of the night without them ever having once met me.

"Don't worry, if we do wake them—they wanted very much to see you," she said then not at all that worried about it.

She slid back a panel door to open up a closet and she reached up in the nice low light of her room and she got me a big clean towel from off a shelf and she got one for herself too. The closet was lined in cedar and I smelled the cedar when I took the towel from her hand holding its cotton cloth to my face in the low light of the lamp unfolding it smelling it in that kind of light in that room with her and all her things once more laid out about us. There, in the touch and feel of that towel, I had the feeling I'd gone nowhere, and that we were somehow still in that first far-off room, and that nothing was new and unknown. It was all new and not at all unfamiliar with her and her things of the room laid out there in the late easy light. In the feeling, I looked to her little address book on the writing desk, opened to a marked page beside her pen, there was her hair brush up at the room's sink, and it all struck me in its familiarity, there with her sitting on the end of the bed beside her blued indigo shawl that I'd not kept and knew that she must have to keep, laid there at the foot of the bed, her looking to me, taking off her shoes and, in her look and them things, I felt that no matter after arriving from such long travel to such an unknown place that I was once more in the center of my life with her in that room in that house in that country that I had never once been in in my life.

"Take off your shoes, we must wear slippers," she said to me.

"All right, girl," I said and I hadn't called her girl in that private little affectionate way in a long time and she took off her shoes and made me take off mine and she got up from the end of the bed and crossed the smooth stone floor in her bare feet in the low-cast light of the lamp and she put our shoes down on the floor of the cedar closet and she put on her house slippers. She did it in her measured and elegant way and she was in no hurry no matter the lateness of the hour there in her parents' house. I'd never seen house slippers worn as a habit and she got a pair out of the closet for me and they were to be mine and she came over and handed them to me and she made me put them on to wear them out of the room. It was a custom in a French house.

"I have to wear them?" I'd never worn them and I did.

"The bathroom is upstairs," she said. "You must wash yourself."

We had our towels. She led me by hand. I followed her in her house slippers in the faint light cast from her bedroom door to the foot of the stairs. We went up steep white-stone stairs. I ran my hand along the cool railing. We went up in a tight turn to the top. I felt the littleness of the house. At the top was a bathroom on the second floor right above the foyer below. There was a white claw-foot bathtub and a porcelain sink and mirror with a cabinet and one of those aluminum radiators you don't see in many houses anymore. Above the radiator was a window opened to the night sky. Beyond the window you could hear the Mistral come down the whole of the valley to the sea.

Our faces were shadowed in the vague light of a far streetlamp from the village, and she said, "It's dark." She turned on the light. Our faces were lit in the light of the bared bulb swung from the ceiling on a chain hung before the sink.

"Stay with me while I wash," I said.

The wind came at the window and it was a wild sound come to the houses in that country village.

She went and shut the door. She turned on the water in the tub. The pipes rattled in the wall. The wind was at the window. She ran the water over her hand. When the water was hot she plugged the tub to let it fill. She turned to me in the light. She took her shirt up from out of her pants. She loosed her belt. She didn't leave me there alone in the light to wash. I was to do nothing but wash myself and go to bed and she stood there in her loosed shirt. I held her to me. I held her to me in that late light. I had my hand up beneath her loosed shirt. She wanted to be touched. I touched her. I felt her in her loosed-up shirt. That smell and touch of her was all one would want.

"You need to wash," she said. The tub was filled.

We broke off. She turned the water off. She sat on the tub in her loosed shirt and pants. I came to her. I took back her hair from off her face. I felt her short cut hair fall off beneath my hand. She turned the side of her face into my hand. I touched her face there. She said to me, "We must not hurt one another," when I touched her there like that, and I had no thought of it, and I said, "We won't," I said, "We can't. We've already been hurt enough," I said, and I did not know what she was seeing saying that, and I lifted her face, to see her, I looked into them dark-lined eyes of hers to see her with my hand kept to the line of her face, and I saw her, and in her dark and bottomless look, she took my hand from off her cut-up face. She put my hand down on her low there between her legs to her. She kept my hand there on her low in her loosed pants. I looked into her un-averted eyes with my hand put to her. She unbuttoned her loosed-up shirt. She took it off. She took up my shirt. She took it off. She touched the holes that went clean through. She felt them there along me with my hand put to her. She had her Capri pants kicked off to the floor and mine were dropped and gone to the floor. We were laid out there on the floor gone down across our strewn clothes. We lay there fallen on the scattered clothes and kissed. I brought my hand back from in her there to her face. I touched her face. She took my hand back from off her face. She caught and kept my hand in hers. She broke it off and came across me. We went into one another. We were all in one another. We two were lost then one in the other in our want gone out on a bathroom floor naked and alive amidst the strewn and dirtied clothes. We felt the hardness of the floor. We were lost in it and it hurt us. It was not a bad hurt. We did it hard and it hurt. There is a good hurt. We were bared in the light to one another and ourselves in that hurt. It is not anything bad to be lost awhile in one another like that fallen strewn across a floor. You live in it. You forget everything in it. It is a thing done without one other want or thought of wanting or ever stopping and laid down there against that hardness and one another we were most ourselves in it and one should only live so. One cannot long. We made it last lost as long as we could. One lives most lividly in it. It is the largest kind of living left. We only wanted that and to make that again and again and we lasted as long as we could with one another. We had that with one another. Then we were done with one another.

48

REBORN TO LIFE

It is like being born from out of one another and we held ourselves in the last of it one to the other laid out on our strewn and dirtied clothes on that bathroom floor in France naked and bared in the light to one another feeling all what we'd once felt in the little room of the far-off French school hurt a little good and came at last apart to clean ourselves up. I pulled her up from off the floor. We went to the tub and got in it to wash it all off us, and she said, "I will wash you, I will wash you clean," she said to me, and she took up one of them big lavender-perfumed blocks of French soap to my skin and she started to wash me clean.

"Wash it all off me, girl," I said to her.

I felt young-alive in it.

She washed me good. She washed me good and clean. It felt goddamned good. I hadn't ever felt anything like her washing me clean like that by hand. I had not ever felt anything like that feeling and she got my arms and my legs and my whole body wet and washed and nice and clean and she did it slowly and carefully feeling me and all what it was like to do it beneath her hand seeing me now or another time I do not know and she made me put my head down under water and she brought my head back up in her hands from the water to wash out my hair with the hard block soap before lowering me to water once more and she rinsed it all off me and I felt good and clean and as if from that washing of hers somehow reborn to life.

In that clean feeling I took the soap to wash her.
"Do you want me to?"
"Yes," she said to me, "Do it."

She wanted to feel it and I had the hard block soap from her hand put into mine. She wanted to feel what it was with my hand to her. I put it all to her. The smell of lavender was everywhere. I put it all across her body by hand and there was the smell of the lavender come all over her and I felt all of her beneath my hand and she let me. I washed the dark curve of her all of her up her legs black in the smell and in the touch I took my time with her and she wanted me to and to be touched like that a time in care and it felt a thing that you did not ever want to stop. I didn't stop. I hadn't ever felt anything like that washing her all over wet and alive smelling her beneath my hand and everything was wet-smelling and clean and she was alive in it and one lives in such goddamned simple things.

We stood up washed and clean. We got out of the tub cold. We dried ourselves off with those big cedar-smelling towels. They were big white towels and she stood there naked and dark before me and she put hers round her like a robe when she was done and dry with it tucked up over her breast and in under the arms and she was barefoot with her bared legs standing shining black before me beneath its soft whiteness.

"You must shave," she said.

"I don't have a razor," I said and I put my towel round my waist.

She got out a razor for me. Her father had an extra one and she took it out of the cabinet and she set it out on the sink and she picked up our strewn clothes from off the floor putting them one by one over her arm in the yellowed light to leave me there alone to shave. She went out the door with our clothes and I stood there with the towel wrapped round my waist with the razor held in hand looking into the mirror. I lifted the blade in the light of the bared bulb. I put the steel to my face and heard her going down the stairs in her slippers to her room. I smelled the lavender of the block soap drying on the edge of the bathtub. I heard the door to her room close softly behind her. My face was all wet and soapy in the mirror with the razor held to it. I shaved and I saw her laid out in bed. I saw myself getting to her and I shaved as if right at home there with all her father's things laid out in the light. I turned the water on and off to rinse the steel blade good so I could shave quick and close. I looked into the mirror. I saw her laid there naked and clean in comfort on the sheet of her bed and I happily saw nothing else. The pipes rattled in the wall from turning the water on and off and so then I lathered up good to shave all at once and not to rinse too much. I wanted to get it done and to get to her and didn't want to wake anyone up in the house to have them find me like that looking all comfortably settled in amongst their things already as if at home but like a kind of intruder come in the night.

I tried to be careful and quick. I cut myself once. It didn't hurt. I didn't think there'd be blood. When the blood came I didn't really feel it. But when it came I felt a little sick. I wiped it off on the end of the towel without thinking. I looked at the reddened cloth hung round my waist. I'd cut myself and I was trying not to and I'd done it. The sick feeling came on in me. I hung my head on the edge of the sink. The sick feeling came to me real and cold as the porcelain sink. It was in me. I shut my eyes to let it pass. I felt strange to be alive. I saw her below in her bed and stayed bent to the sink. The sickness went little by little. I felt the hardness of the sink. There was the cool hard whiteness of the sink against my head. I was knelt on the floor in the light of the bare bulb looking to the porcelain lit cold and hard against my head. The whiteness of that sink is all what I saw. The feeling was gone and passed. I lifted my head from the sink to get to her.

  I saw myself in the mirror. I was hardly cut. I carefully put away her father's things. I stood there looking to myself in some self-strangeness. I shut out the light. I left. I went down the darkened hall quiet as I could with the blooded towel hung round my waist stepping on down the little marble stairs in my house slippers half-dressed in the night not really feeling at that late hour as if belonging but nevertheless not simply out of place not yet got to her not knowing if she were waiting in the darkness awake or fallen off to sleep in the night.

49

AT LAST ARRIVED IN A NAME IN THE NIGHT

  She was naked and awake in bed laid out on the clean-smelling sheets and I loosened and dropped the towel to the floor and lay myself down there next to her in the night and she lay her arm lightly round my side and she said, "*John*," and when she'd said it in the darkness of the room I felt myself there with her, all of who I was came familiar in her voice, and the strangeness I'd felt was gone, and I lay there in the dark on the sheet clean and comfortable in the shuttered room in the night in the south of France as if I had at last materially arrived in the act of her speaking my own name, and she said, "We will sleep."

We were laid there at last to sleep. We did not sleep. We lay on there in that bed of hers awakened in the night in a late easy peace. An easy sleep could then come to you late and we felt one another awake. We held hands.

There was solitude. We were awakened in the lateness.

"Sleep," she said, "It is time." She wanted me to be well.

"All right," I said, "I will." She felt this care for me.

Then off in the village there was a train come on in the night hard along the tracks going south along the river to the sea. The dank traveled canvas of the army bags lay packed up on the floor in the dark. The train rattled by hard on the tracks sounding close to the house. It broke by in the clear quiet. The train was gone past. The wind was down and died out a time. The gate stopped its long rattling in the lock.

In the simple late quiet I was awake.

"You are getting to sleep?" she said, "You must sleep."

"No—I'm too awake," I said, "I'm too tired-out to sleep," I said and she lay herself up along me to hold me.

We lay there on the sheets in that late peace that can come to you after long travel, laid in one of those very late quiets when you can begin to think at such an hour awakened in such a way that you've come to some true realization, come to know something truly true you'll not in morning when you waked rested. That was what I felt waked there with her. I did not know what it was that I felt was true at that hour which I wouldn't in morning in waking. I could not name it. I wanted to name it to keep it. It is just some feeling of being found in your life which comes strongly after such long travel once you've stopped and got to such another you love, and the bags they sat there on the stone floor in the dark of her room in the South of France. I know that is true. The bags they lay there all packed up beside her bed left right where I'd dropped them to the floor and they'd be sitting there in morning. The canvas smell was mixed up with the lavender. The lavender soap smell from our bath was mixed up nicely in the night with the dank canvas of the traveled bags. There was that smell. There was the touch of her beside me. There in that bed in that room in morning I'd be beside her in the light. That is true. I was with her. I'd wake with her. I felt that and it felt very real. I'd stopped for good in her. That was true. It was only that that I felt true. I thought then that that is a goddamned feeling. To get to another and to know it true that is a good goddamned feeling to know to wake to. I lay there and I thought that and felt that. That is a feeling and she lifted her head from my arm, and she said, "You're not sleeping?" she said to me. "You must sleep," she said to me, and I held her to me awakened-alive in all such thinking-feeling.

"Do your parents know how we are to be together?" I said to her.

"They know," she said. "I have told them," she said to me, "Go to sleep," she said to me, and I'd wondered on it because she'd really told me nothing of what all they thought about it and it was late and we should've long been sleeping but I wanted to know, too, if they understood it.

"Do they understand it," I said to her, wanting to sleep knowing it was all right.

"No," she said. "They do not understand it," she said.

"They do not see how it is?" I said and I felt a little afraid.

And she said, "No, they see how it is—it is just a thing that they would never do themselves. Don't worry, they want you to come," she said. "They wonder about you," she said. "You have made them curious about you. You have made them curious, in your coming to me," she said to me.

"But, what do they know about me?" I said.

"They know nothing of you. They know you are American—they know some things. They were young once, too," she said.

"But they don't mind me coming like this?" I said and we should've long been sleeping, but I wanted to know that it was all right. Then you rest. "As long as they don't mind," I said to her. "You said that, that they didn't mind, girl. That it's all right," I said.

"They do not mind," she said. "It is all right. They want you to come," she said. "You asked if they understood," she said. "It doesn't matter if they understand or not," she said and she wasn't worried about it.

"All right," I said. "They do not understand. But they do not mind," I said. "As long as they do not mind—I don't want that coming to you."

"They are practical people," she said. "Practical people do not do such things. That is all."

"Well, we'll have to be practical then," I said to her.

"You cannot ever be practical like that, I think," she said.

"I will be practical in my coming to you," I said. "I will be practical in everything I do," I said. "So, they'll understand that I'm being practical in my coming. We'll be practical in all our coming, girl," I said and it all sounded funny and I was tired in it and playing with it to forget it, but said, "The real things have to be right," I said, and I felt everything was then and lay at peace beside her.

"I have not ever been easy on them," she said then awakened in thought.

"We are not to be hard on them," I said. "We'll be easy on them," I said. "I'll be hard on myself—I'll behave myself," I said to her.

239

"They will like you," she said.

"I don't want them to be against us," I said.

"They are not against us," she said.

"As long as they are not against us—."

"They have wanted things a long time for me," she said.

"We will give them what they want," I said.

"They never saw me with anyone," she said.

"They will see you with someone," I said.

"They never saw me like that," she said.

"They will see you like that," I said.

"You understand that?" she said. "What *that* is—what you are to be with me, what we are here? The people will look at us—you understand what it is to be dark in the South, to be seen as Arab—to be Black?" she said, "To be dark—in look?" She said, "The people will look." She did not sound hard in her saying it.

"Let them look," I said.

She said, "I look Black—and I am not even *une femme Noire*—. She said, "I am from North Africa, and not even an Arab," she said as if to understand it. "You understand that?"

"No, I understand nothing of it," I said. "Nothing of it at all—I'm an American," I said. "I don't even understand that. I understand nothing of it all," and I shut up, and she lay there away from me, and we were awakened.

"It is not so easy," she said. "It is only that," she said, and she came over me, and she lay herself down there against me.

"Don't make it hard—harder than it all is," I said, and I held her to me.

"Don't talk," she said and we shut up about understanding it. We shut up awakened in it come alive in one another beyond all people and place. Then there was nothing but that in the night. There was no color in it there was no naming one another this or that in it there was nothing then in it but us two made one with no looks or names left.

50

AN ACT OF WAKING
IS AN ACT OF REMEMBERING

Then in morning when I'd waked from a far-off hard sleep I thought I had not yet gone and got to her, and that I was waking up again having gone nowhere, and as I came back once more to the room, came to find myself there in it, came to myself in it, I looked off from the bed, over to the closed-up shutters folded flat, shut there across the big window of the bedroom, where they were locked to block the light, and looking to them laid there in that bed of hers, I remembered all the night and her and knew that it was true that I'd gone and got to her.

She had left the shutters closed up for me to sleep and I had slept on in morning and waked late to the shuttered light. I had needed to sleep and slept. The summer light was hitting hard on the closed-up metal and the room was hot. The canvas lay there packed up on the floor where I'd left it in the night. I could smell it in the heat. The shuttered air in the room was heavy. I looked from the bags and stone floor on round her room real in its things. Her hairbrush was up at the sink. The glass I had drunk from was sitting at the sink. There was a blue-glassed perfume bottle. There was her blued shawl hung in the shuttered light over the back of the wooden chair at the writing desk. Her address book was left opened with the pen on the desk in the dim light beside a couple schoolbooks. The lavender scent from the bath soap was beneath me in the bed sheets. In the sheet smell I remembered us in the night. I had slept hard. It was hard to get good and awake. I was not yet awake. I was waking remembering.

I lay on in the bed looking across the strewn sheet to the foot of the bed to where the rose wallpaper in its intricately structured pattern rose in its flowered print, coming from off the floor up across the wall, climbing on behind the bookcase, remembering in waking how it had been lit up all golden red from the low-cast lamplight in the night, when I'd come late into the room with her, and remembered the rows of schoolbooks stacked on shelves, lit before the delicately flowered pattern in their colorful covers and printed titles, and how they'd looked all deeply lit with intimated interest rising in the late light of the lamp, where now in morning they were shadowed and all unreadable as if receding into the roses on the bookshelves against the papered wall in the shuttered light.

In seeing them remembered things I remembered my slippers and my eye fell from the wall of books to the door to where I had left my house slippers in the night. There at the closed bedroom door were my house slippers. Hers were gone. At the sight of them I felt her gone and that I shouldn't have slept so late and I had had to sleep.

I got up from the strewn bed sheet. I went naked to the sink and the stone floor was cool beneath my feet. In the summer heat I stood at the sink and I ran the water cold from the faucet. I ran it across my hand. I wanted to get good and awake. I ran it cold to the touch. I waked some in feeling it. I filled a glass with water. I drank the cold glass of water. The water tasted good. I hadn't looked at myself in the mirror. I looked in the mirror and drank the water. I saw I was cut. I remembered the cut. I remembered it and that I'd cut myself in the night and I drank the glass of cold water looking at the cut. I was waked. I remembered that I hung my head on the porcelain of the sink. I looked at the porcelain of her sink. I remembered the hardness of it. I sat the glass down on the sink. I was waked. I went back to the bed. I lay there on the bed sheet waked in the lavender smell laid in the strewn sheets to wait for her to come get me. I wanted to get up and go see her to find her for her to know that I was waked but I didn't want to wander about there in her parents' house without even having met them first. I still felt that, that I should wait for her to come get me. I lay my head back against the flowered wallpaper to wait and waiting heard the pipes rattling off and on in the wall above my head. I looked up. Someone up there was running water. I heard voices above. There was a kind of conversation going back and forth. They must've been in the kitchen. I caught the rhythm and the sound of the voices. I tried to understand them in the sound of them. I couldn't understand them. I tried to understand what was said in how it was said. In listening to them voices that I couldn't understand they didn't sound unhappy or hard. I listened awhile to their way of speaking and in that talk I tried to see her parents and who they were in the sound of them. I heard them. You can often hear who someone is. It's something in the voice. How one says things is something after all, and I lay there on that bed listening laid up against the rose-papered wall hard against my head wanting them to like me and not to be against us and, never once having met them, I pictured them as I'd often pictured her. I saw how they were dark. I heard how they were good.

51

IT IS NOT A QUESTION OF COLOR, IT IS A HISTORY OF COLOR

"Daddy were they dark so or dark some?" she said that and that question of hers about color stopped me when I was telling her about that first day in France. She could say such things. She was young. She was curious. I was telling her the beginning, feeling myself arriving. France was in front of us as if yet to be lived. In telling it can always be so, and so I'd stopped when she said that, to think of what to say to her next about them people that I hadn't even met yet that first day myself and she said when I stopped, and didn't go on, "Daddy, tell me about mother's parents—did she look like them?" She wanted to see them and who they were. She'd looked for a picture of them and found none that could be them. She'd found no kept picture of them in that old box and she wanted me to get to them for her and I myself have not yet got to them in my seeing what to say to her next to keep it all in good order, and I said, "I'm getting to them, girl." There's a way of getting to them good to see them true and I'd said nothing to her about the color of them and she had that dark picture of her mother I'd taken to France with me, where it lay left there that first day in my pack on the floor in France, she'd laid that picture out there on the kitchen table and she picked it up and she looked off from the color of it to herself and she looked back to me and she wanted to know whether the people there in that place that they called France were dark so or dark some, and there are people and there are people, and that is the funny thing about any people in a place. You can never truly tell of them in their look, and I said to her, "It doesn't matter if they're dark so or dark some," I said that to her. That's what I wanted her to know. She'd looked to herself and she'd seen she was different and I wanted her to know she wasn't in her look and I said to her, "You can only tell of people—who they are—in what they've done, or maybe in what they say. Sometimes—you see someone in what they've said, but it's really what one does." I told her that. That is who one is. To tell about any people truly you have to tell all what they have done to one another and themselves, and I'm trying to, and that tells you everything beyond a look or a color.

But there is such significance to color.

It lingers everywhere in the light.

Then I said to her, "If there's a coloredness that matters, it's not a color. It's a history of color," I told her. "The color of them is nothing to the people as they are," I said to her. "I've told you that, girl." That's a thing I've always told her. That's a thing I tell myself, and she looked with some scrutiny to herself, and she looked to me, and she looked to the color of that picture there of her mother, thinking on all what looking couldn't tell you, and there was the one real thing I did want to tell her about her parents and her when I met them that first day in France, and I'll tell it next. I told her, "It's not about color, girl. It's about history." I told her that. Her mother had long told me that.

Now as you might imagine, and as she'd not yet once heard about her own grandparents until I'd got to them that day, she wanted to know all about them as girls will at that age when you'll first learn that there're these new people to meet that one should've long met and now will even if for the first time in a story, and never will otherwise, and she said to me, "Daddy, stop playing with the story—you're always only playing—you're not telling it right, tell what happened next—," she wanted me to stop leaving things out for her, she said some things like that to me as if she'd learned a thing or two about my telling, and I know you've got to leave some things out to get on to anything good, let alone true, and she'd learned a thing or two about my telling.

"I'm telling you girl," I said and I was. It's not that easy to tell it at all well after such a time to such a girl, for unlike life one wants a good and happy order now for what happens next, and I turned back to the story for her, and I tried to forget her to tell it well and good for her. But it's not that easy to forget her and who we are to one another in the actuality of our own lives, sitting there in that house beyond the framed convention of such a telling. It's hard to forget her. I don't want to. I was looking right at her. She was a girl right there in the light real beside me. That is true. I saw her herself again and who she was as I hadn't for a long time in the telling. After all there is no story that we've been all along in but only in our own lives. All along we have only been in our own lives. There are these lived moments you want to keep. This is one of them. That is what I do not want to pass. It is that real feeling of being with her in the light. I think what a wondrous thing it is to sit there with her home in the house in the light along the lake in America and not in any story. That is the world. There in that world I see her, I see her as I have not for a long time in the telling, and she says, "Daddy, Daddy?" she says to me to make me go on from her with it and I do.

52

SHE CAME ALL DARK IN HER DRESS

So then I told her how I'd come too late in the night from the train station to see her parents until morning and that's why it's taken me so long to get to them and I told her that waiting now laid out in that bedroom to see them in the morning that I myself wanted to see them as badly as she did, and I lay there out on the bed and I didn't want to wait any longer to meet her mother or her father but it's true I was a little afraid of meeting them for the first time and perhaps that's why it's taken me so long to get to them now too as if a story itself in how it's told whether to another or to one's self in its being extended and attenuated in the continuity of its content could be a narrative structure formed by an old fear. I've thought that lately.

I had wanted to do it right away, to meet them when I'd arrived in the night, and then it would've been good and done with. It would have been over and done with in that act of arriving and now it felt the good time to do it had come and gone when I'd waked late to lay there in her bed feeling I had left some little thing undone I shouldn't have in coming into their house. But there has always been that feeling of undone things about me, and I lay there out on the sheet of her bed naked in the dark of her room listening to the voices above and they'd stopped.

There were footsteps on the stairs coming down to the foyer and I heard them at the door, and the door opened into the room and there she stood dark in her dress.

"You are awake, John?" she said looking to the bed to see if I slept.

"I'm awake," I said. "I was waiting for you, to come get me."

She came from the door to the bed, and sat down on the side of the bed beside me in the shuttered light. I held her to me, her face came against mine, her hair, she kissed me in the hot dim room. I wanted to keep her there beside me. Then in that closeness of her, I felt the private little life of that room, her life, and I felt I wanted to say all these things to her, things I hadn't said and felt I could say right then, waked like that to myself, and to her. I started to say some of them things. I wanted to tell her, I do not know all what I would've told her, I would have told her some of them true things from before, all what I'd once wanted to in that hospital, and hadn't, and before I could tell her anything, she said to me, "My father is sick."

"What is it?" I said. "Is he all right?"

"Yes, he must only rest," she said. "He is too hard on himself."

She sat there looking to me in the hot dark light.

"Then he doesn't want to see anyone?" I said, and I

247

was happy that I'd waited in the room and gone nowhere to find her in the house.

"No, he wants to see you," she said. "He's waiting for you," she said. "He doesn't want to talk about being sick," she said.

"I don't want to bother him," I said.

"I came to get you," she said.

She took my hand. She got me up from the bed. I stood naked before her.

"Get dressed," she said looking at me.

She went to the shuttered window. She unlatched the metal shutters. She shoved them back out of the way of the big window. They made a clacking noise as she folded them up to the side. The light came strong and hard into the room and hurt the eyes. She had the unlatched window opened wide into the room. The flowers were brilliant in the strong light. The summer heat came off the garden into the room and I stood there naked in the light in the smell and heat of the garden come into the room. It was the smell of the earth.

"You will not wake up in such dark," she said to me and she turned back to look into the room. She looked at me dressing in the light.

I was getting clean clothes out of a bag and looked up. She stood there in front of the big window in that yellow flowered dress of hers. She stood there lit black in the light. I felt how I loved her. She stood there all dark in that yellow dress she'd once worn in the street with the children in the rain. The light came all across the red walls of rose wallpaper hitting on across the green canvas bags sitting there on the far floor of the room. The light hit on into the room and all across the walls and bed and books and desk and I looked up from my dressing seeing it cast strongly across all things and her.

53

THE FIRST LOOK OF HER PARENTS

We went past the hung summer coats and hats of the foyer. The air was nice and cool across the stone floor of the foyer. She led me by hand up the short steep stair with its little metal rail and I ran my hand along its coolness going up. There at the top of the stairs the noon heat of the South was hung stilled in the hall of the house.

We walked down the little narrow hall of the house past an opaque-glassed kitchen door opened to the kitchen with a couple pots and pans on the stove cooking with the smell of something good going out into the whole house. There at the end of the hall we went through a set of clear-paned French doors into the living room. There in the living room her father was laid out in the heat of midday sitting leaned half-up with his feet on a couch looking out west to the mountain rock rising against the sky above the plain of the river. The sky was big. There was a big view of things from the second floor of the house looking out a row of tall glassed doors that ran the front of the house. They were all opened up to the strong Southern light. There was no wind. The Mistral had gone in the night off down the valley of the river. You could see the mountain rock struck with summer light risen against the high blue from the green treed foothills. There were the bleached-looking stone houses of Beauchastel scattered up the foot of the rock their far roofs set red against the blue. There was the village built right into the rock ascending steeply against the sky to a medieval fortification rising in ruin its fallen stone laid scattered against the sky.

Her father looked out the opened-up doors of the house to that mountain rock set against the sky in good weather and her mother looked to us two come down the hall of the house to the living room door, and when we'd come to the end of the hall to the opened doors, her mother she'd put her hand on his hand and her father he then turned at her touch to look back to the French doors from the big lit sky. They looked at us two and our own held hands, and she led me through the French doors into that well-arranged living room. We walked into the living room, and they took their hands from one another. We stood there before them and before I could think of what to say to either one of them I took my hand from hers and I shook each of their hands as was the custom of the country.

They had a couple wooden chairs in there from the kitchen for us to sit on so we could face her father and I sat down on a chair next to her mother and she sat down next to me. We all sat there looking at one another in the light. I looked at them. They took a good look at me. We looked from face to face. We took a good look at one another. We looked and looked away from one another. They were not dark. They were not dark these parents who were and were not her parents. But they didn't look unhappy to see me. I'd been worried about meeting them the first time and I saw that they were not that unhappy to see me. It's a feeling you get sometimes seeing people. It's the way they look at you no matter you know nothing of them. They'd seen me. They were happy some.

They'd brought the chairs from the kitchen into the living room and I was sitting there stiff and straight upright on one of those hard wooden kitchen chairs with the tall straight back facing the couch with her father laid out on it in the heat. He wiped the sweat on his face with a handkerchief. He was dressed in one of those blue workman's uniforms. He looked like he'd been outside working in the strong light and then he'd felt the heat. Her mother had on a good dress and shoes and her hair put back elegantly off her face and had gotten out a tray of liqueurs and I sat there in my khaki cut offs and a t-shirt and I think we were all a little surprised to see one another. I don't know who they'd thought to see. I don't know who we'd each thought to see. I'd seen them many times. I'd seen them dark. I'd never seen them. She'd told me nothing of the color of them. She'd told me really nothing of them in that way I don't know why but for the fact that their color was nothing out of the ordinary to her. I don't know who they'd thought to see. They were to see an American soldier. They were to see nothing but an American soldier. Then they'd seen me. They'd seen us. She sat there dark in her yellow dress. I was paled beside her. I saw their color was nothing out of the ordinary to her and just like that I'd met her parents before I could think of anything about what they thought about me and it was over and done with right away in the handshake and in the look and the look away and it wasn't so bad.

54

A NEW LITTLE STORY OF HER PARENTS

In France it's a marked occasion when someone travels from far to visit and it's a point of hospitality to have a kind of formal drink after arriving from long travel. We were all to have a drink right there in the living room looking out the big opened up doors to the summer sky in the noon heat. In front of the couch there was the tray of colored liqueur bottles and glasses for the drinks sitting on a coffee table within the reach of her father. The bottles were filled with all these fancy things to drink that I'd never heard of. It was hot in the house. It was very bright outside. The light hit the white stucco walls of the houses along the far end of the street. They were brilliantly lit in the heat. Her father wiped his face and forehead and eyed the bottles and glasses he'd had her mother get out on the big tray of liqueurs. I think he wanted a drink. I felt like I wanted one. We were both looking to the tray. The tray had one of those fancy golden metal rims for an edge going round a glass silvered mirror. There were the many colored bottles sitting on the silvered mirror reflecting their glass bottoms off the lit glass of the mirror. They'd bring it out on special occasions, like holidays or anniversaries, and when you bent over it to get yourself a drink you could see your face strangely lit in the mirror along the metal rim. Her father wanted me to pour myself a drink. I bent over the mirrored tray and took up a green bottle. It said *Pastis*. My face looked strange in the mirror. I poured the Pastis into a glass. Her mother reached for the little water pitcher. I drank down my drink straight and they were telling me to put the water in it when I did it. They wanted me to do it right and cutting it with water was the custom. It was good and strong. I'd wanted a good strong drink.

      Her parents they had the Pastis too. They showed me how to do it with the water and it turned milky white in the glass. She poured out a glass of beer for herself and she drank a glass of beer. We all had our drinks in hand. We drank a drink in the living room. We held our glasses in our hands. There was a grandfather clock marking out the time against a shadowed wall. There was one of those big wooden veneered cabinets where you keep your good dishes with all the fancy plates and glasses stacked on shelves shut up behind nice glass-paned doors. There was the big browned comfortable-looking couch her father was laid out on against the blued wall of the room across from the clock. There was a television set on a console next to the clock. The clock sounded out the time. The time felt to have stopped no matter that continual clicking and the chimes. We were having the customary drink and there were the long cream-colored drapes pulled to the one side of the wide-opened doors of the living room. The drapes hung straight and stilled to the smooth stone floor. The whole house was very properly arranged and practical-looking and her parents they were very polite and practical-looking people and no one said too much. They were very polite these parents who were and were not her parents, and we were well into the drink and no one had said anything awhile and she didn't seem worried about it, but I felt it. Someone must say something after all. I felt I should speak. I was in their house, and I should speak, and they spoke no English, and I spoke no French, and I looked back from that stilled and emptied clear unchanging sky fixed and framed across all that rising rock, to her and them and we were all sitting wordless with our drinks in hand in the hot half-shaded living room of midday in the South of France, and I said without thinking, "In America there is sky like that," I said, and I pointed out the doors of the house to the far immobile blue cast against the bleached ridges of rising rock. Her father, he looked out at it. "There is a great lake," I said, and went on. They were listening to me. I found there were these simple things that I could say to them about what I knew of places and they are true in the most simplistic way of all places. They were the things I found I could say right there to them arrived like that with no language no country in common but for the sense of the land and light, and I had her tell them then what I'd said, and she'd already heard me tell them kinds of things, so it was not that hard for her to find her words, and in that way with her, I began to talk to her parents a little about the land and the light of that place where they lived, in my knowing nothing of it but what I'd seen out the living room window there in waking in France, remembering all what I'd once seen of home in America. I looked to that immoveable rock of the mountain fixed against the sky framed-out by the big glassed doors of the house with it all looking like a long painted landscape, and I said a couple of those simple easy little things of the land struck in all that light, I told some of those good remembered things of places you'll know when young that I'd long told to her about America so to see it, and it was not so bad. Her parents they were very matter of fact people, and polite to listen so carefully to a stranger. "You can stand on a bluff, and see the water go to the sky," I said, and I waited for her to tell it. She told it. "There, the trees rise up tall, high on the bluff, all along the land of the lake," I said, and she said it. I went on with it like that about the land and the light along the water.

Then her father, he spoke, "The water, it is like a sea?" her father said to me. She told it.

"Yes, but there is no salt," I said to him. She told it.

"It is big fresh water?" he said.

"Yes—and there are the great beaches, that go for hundreds of miles," I said to him. "But there is no tide, like a sea," I said.

"This sand, it is like the North of Africa," her mother said to her. "This bluff, like the cliff of a city by the sea," she said to me. She told it.

"But, there is no tide in such water?" her father said.

"No, but there are big storms—in winter there is ice," I said.

"It is so cold as that?" her father said and he was thinking on places.

"Some years, the water freezes to the west, all across the lake, and five hundred miles to the north," I said to him, and he looked out the window in France to the rock of the mountain in the heat of midday, and he said, "It is like a desert of ice. It is another world," he said, and no one said anything awhile.

So it wasn't so bad, and once I'd told them a little of where I was from and what the land was like, I think they saw what I was saying seeing it all come like that in relation no matter I'd had to do it in my English in order for her to tell it to them in their French. But we really didn't have that much trouble talking like that that way about them certain simple things, though I don't know if her parents they understood the things I said to them the way I did, the way I meant them in how I'd said them, because she had a too careful way of speaking to them I thought. She was very polite with them. They were all very polite with one another. That was the way the three of them talked with one another and I'd never heard such polite conversation spoken like that between close family. But they'd seen what I was saying about the affinity of places in what she'd said to them when they'd listened to me talk a little of that water and sky in looking to all that rock and sky. They saw how the water went to the sky and there was all that barren rock stretching to the sky. They'd listened closely. They were generous people. I saw that in them. They didn't even know me and they were generous with me. They were generous with someone they'd never met and didn't even know at all in a way that is rare with people, and I was happy at that, and felt that she was lucky to have had such parents as that, and when I'd stopped in the relation, that analogy of them seemingly disparate images for such apparently dissimilar places, if not for people's lives, her father he then ran the handkerchief across his face and forehead and he pointed with a hand to the bottle on the mirrored tray for me to pour myself another drink and her mother she got up to go to the kitchen. And the funny thing that I'd said I'd wanted to tell about her parents and her that was about history and not about color, was that when her father had stuck out his hand to the tray pointing to the bottle to offer me another drink, then her mother and her and I, we all looked to his opened-up hand, stretched out to the bottle, showing the old wound he had in his hand. He had an old hole gone through his hand. It was exposed in the act of his hospitality, and he closed his hand then so we wouldn't see it. There was one thing I knew that made those holes like that. I'd seen it. I'd seen it done. Some of the boys they had done it to themselves with a pistol. In the sight of her father's hand I was returned to that and them, and I began to think a little about him and her mother, I began to think a little about her parents and her, I began to tell myself a new little story about them.

55

PIEDS-NOIRS

Her mother left the two of us there in that living room with her father laid out on the couch in his blue uniform with his drink and handkerchief in hand. Her mother had to go tend to the cooking. She was very preoccupied with the cooking that time of day. Her father was finishing his drink. We stayed beside him finishing ours. Her father bent his head to me and looked to the bottle. I took the Pastis. I poured myself another. I had another to be polite. I put some water in it from the little water jug and he nodded as if he were satisfied that I'd done it right. He lay there with his drink in hand and I had mine. We were done talking.

She finished her drink and she said, "I will help my mother." She stood up to go from us. She said goodbye in French to her father. He lay there looking to her in his blue uniform. He looked at me then back to her then out the house.

"I'll come with you," I said. I didn't know what to say to him. I didn't want to stay kept in that quiet there with him drinking saying nothing to him.

We two got up from him and left him with his drink in hand looking out the window of the house to the sky. He stopped us with a hand at the door to the hall. "You will walk into the village, with him?" her father said that to her. He told her she should show me around. We should see things. He'd take me but he couldn't see people as he was. When she told me what he'd said, I went and shook his hand again, and his hand was darkly lined and deep-cracked from weather and work. He had big scraped knuckles and a strong grip and when I let go his hand I liked him. I felt something for him. I didn't even know him. He was her father and I felt something for him. He looked like a man who'd done some things. In those days he was no longer a young man. He must have been about sixty then. But he looked like a man who'd once done some things in another time. He must have done some real things once and we left him lying there like that. He lay there looking to the rock. He didn't look sick. In the end I think he was just sick of seeing people and I know what that's like.

    She took me from him down the hall and when we came into the kitchen her mother was standing right there at the stove, and it's strange to say, but when I saw her standing like that I saw how it was to be home and young again. The smells and sounds of such women, of mothers doing such things are all the same. She had the stovetop filled with all these pots and pans cooking all these things. It looked complicated. It smelled good. She'd gotten a rabbit from the butcher. The rabbit was cooking and smelled good. We stood in the kitchen leaned up against a cupboard counter across from her watching her cook at the stove. She took a lid off a pot. She stirred the pot. She turned the flame down. She turned another one up. She had her blonde hair put back up off her face. She wore a well-ironed flower-print cooking apron tied up over her good housedress. She wore that nice dress in there even when cooking. I'd never seen anyone cook in a kitchen all elegant-looking like that. I looked at the dress. The dress looked old but was well taken care of in that way that people without real money can take care of their few good things. I'd seen that about her parents in that house. I looked at her hair and I saw the real thing about her mother that made you look to her was her hair. Her mother she had a nice blonde kind of hair that you didn't usually see there in the French in the South.

    She saw me looking to her mother. We stood there

leaned against the kitchen counter looking at this well-dressed blonde-haired Frenchwoman who was her mother, and she said to me in her very good English which her mother did not understand, "She was once beautiful when young," and I knew that she'd never told her mother that, there are children who never say that to mothers, and I thought she should've once, I don't know why, and I saw her how she would have looked beautiful young. She was beautiful. She was serious. She was hard at work. She was bent to the stove in her good house dress. She tasted something and she added something. She brushed back the blond strands of her loosed hair from off her face. She had a way of doing things. There was a way of doing things. She knew how to do her things. I liked her in the way that she did her things and I didn't even know her. She was sure in the way that she did this or that little thing in this or that particular way of hers and she had a very stylish way of doing things as if there were some significance in the very act of stirring a pot with the act not ever separate from who she was in the way that she did it as though one must take some care even in one's most casual acts and pay attention to them and how they tell you who you are by how you do them for they make up your life, that is what makes up your life and she looked then back over at us when she'd spoke about her mother's beauty and she was very busy making a big lunch and it seemed a serious thing and she said then something in her French to her and it was then that she took the empty Pastis glass from out of my hand and she sat it down on the kitchen counter behind us and we left her to it. Her mother she knew all what was to be done and she wanted us to leave her to it.

"She wants us to go outside, to let her work," she said.
So we went out the balcony door of the kitchen.
We went along the front balcony that ran the second floor of the house where it went the whole width of the house front from the kitchen over to the big glassed doors of the

living room. We went along big terracotta flower boxes hung off a black iron balcony rail, where we stopped at a flower box and leaned on the black iron rail and looked out to the line of village houses down along the street. That's where the taxi had gone off in the night. The light was big. It hit hard off the white stucco of all the houses lined along the street.

We stood in the strong light. The iron of the balcony was hot to the touch. The mountain rose in rock and tree, scattered with houses before us. There below us, past the flower garden down along the one side of the house was the big garden. There were bed-sheets hung out on a clothesline in the light to dry along the green of the garden.

"Your father was working that garden?" I said looking down to it.

"Yes, the heat it made him sick," she said.

"What do they grow there?" I said. I looked to it from the balcony, to all the green grown up in it there along them sheets.

She told me some of the things planted there in the garden. Some of the words for what was grown in it she couldn't find in her English. "*Aubergine*," that was a hard one, and made no real sense in English. "*Pomme de terre*," that was an easy one, and that made some sense. So, then I'd tell her the word for it when I found it, if she didn't know it and I could find it, and we named the things like that in the garden in what words we found. It passed the time pleasantly awhile in that little leisurely time before lunch. It was nice to talk of easy comfortable things.

Her mother came out of the house below us, and she went along the stone path through the flowers to the big garden, where she bent to cut fresh green lettuce for lunch. The lettuce grew in rich black plots of boxed-in earth. Her mother bent to the black earth. The bed-sheets hung out along her washed white in a row.

I said, "They are good people."

"They are kind," she said.

"What is it?" I said. "You don't want to talk about them?"

"No, I do—I will."

"Aren't you happy here with them?"

"No, I am happy," she said.

"You are happy with them?"

"I am happy with them."

"Then, tell me the good things about this place," I said. "There are good things about it. You once told me some pretty good things about it," I said.

"There are good things," she said.

"Not all good things?" I said.

"Not all good things," she said.

"Tell me what things," I said.

"The things that cannot matter—you know what they are—the things that can mean nothing to us," she said, "The things that must mean nothing."

"Tell me what things must mean nothing," I said. "You know you can say things to me," I said. We were looking at her mother with her basket in the light of the garden.

"I know," she said and she looked over at me. I was looking at her mother. "I know I may tell you."

"But you don't have to tell me. It's easier that way, I know that," I said to her.

Her mother cut the lettuce. The sheets hung out brilliant.

"Things cannot be so easy for us," she said. "Nothing is to be so easy for us, here. That is all," she said to me then.

"Well, we'll make it easy—this time," I said. "It doesn't have to always be hard," and we stood there looking off from the garden up in the light.

The strong light was hitting everything, every seen

thing was sharp and clear to the eye, the landscape strongly lit, everything very real in the light, the pleasant-looking faded red tiled roofs up at the top end of the village softly paled and picturesque in their actuality against the stark blue, and I followed a little road by eye going up above the village the road changing from black asphalt to red gravel to bleached rock running up the side of the mountain going on in-between stands of pine and oak trees until it broke out of the trees to rise bare and rutted on into the high blue. In looking out west to it I wanted to get up there on it all that lit land and to look back down to see the river behind us and all to the east to see where we really were there in that house.

  The sky was very tall and wide and clear, and I said to her, "Has it been so hard for them here?" I said that to her in the lit quiet of midday with her mother bent below in the good weather to the green of the garden in that strong summer light bent to the black boxed-in earth that was good for growing and she began to tell me of how it was hard.

  We looked out from the house to that beautiful land called France before us and she told me how she'd been brought across the sea to Montpellier from Oran and then sent North into the country of the Ardeche to the Southern village of La Voulte-sur-Rhone into this beautiful land before us. She told me how she'd come from the North of Africa to the South of France. There was a Catholic orphanage there in La Voulte. It was four kilometers away and we would go there to see it one day. She was thirteen years old and they gave her a cross to wear around her neck. She wore the cross around her neck and she didn't believe in any of it. Her mother and her father they took her away from there back home here to the house. Her mother had the basket filled up with the cut lettuce. We heard her shut the old wooden door below us heavy against the house. Her mother came up into the kitchen and she put the basket of fresh-cut lettuce down on the kitchen table. The pans rattled.

The cupboards opened and closed. We were quiet in the light looking up. There in front of us stood the steep foothills of the Vivarais Mountains where the peach and apricot orchards of the *Pieds-Noirs* who'd come from North Africa grew their fruit trees far up back on the plateau that led into the high country of the Ardèche into the Cevennes Mountains where there was snow in winter.

That is where her father himself had once had land of his father's and lost it.

"They are not French?" I said and I turned from looking to that land. I looked to her. She was looking off to the garden.

"They are not French from France," she said looking there to that garden where her mother had been bent to the black earth. She said, "They came from out of Africa."

"They are North African French?" I said and I saw how her father had looked out from the house to all that rock and light.

"There was a war," she said.

"They never went back home?" I said.

"There is no home," she said and we looked out to that beautiful land before us.

56

A KIND OF HOMECOMING

That day she told me some things about her parents and her. We two had really told nothing in our going off from one another. She told me a good long story as she'd said she would when I came. In afternoon we were returned in some few words of hers there in her little room in Beauchastel, to where she'd stopped her story of the city by the sea in the North of Africa in that old room in the Catholic school in Saigon,

Vietnam, when she was just a girl following on after a French soldier in Oran, Algeria, going on there along the sea, and I saw her there again a girl wandering cut in the light who could've never known, at that time in that place, how she'd come home here to this place and time.

"But you didn't come with them, to France?" I said to her of her parents.

"No, they came before me."

"They came without you?"

"They must come," she said. "They must leave the land, to live."

So she began on the story of her parents and her but when she began she didn't start with them and her. She started with the soldier and the sea. That was the beginning again for her.

"But, did you find him?" I said to her when she began that again.

"I went to kill him," she said outright, and there came the land. There was the light. There stood the city by the sea. There was the great and good weather in the high light along the sea. There the people they went to the water to live a little in the lively light along the sea. There once more in her words she went off from the water a girl going on to follow after a French soldier to kill him, a girl in her following after him feeling the cut as she had not with the blued cloth closed up round her face. She covered herself for the first time in her life knowing she must not feel too much too soon in her following on after him to kill him. It is all to be felt later. Later it is always felt.

That's where she'd stopped before. She'd told all that part before.

She'd never told about a killing. She took a little care then in her telling of the following on after him to kill him. She lay there along me in the little room in France finding her words as she went on, with her shawl laid there in the light

263

across the back of the chair, her gone off from all that far opened-out expanse of the water of the sea on into the walled city, where the boundlessness of the sky and the sea was then left off behind her with the coast gone below her, with the city closed in round her to come before her so much stone laid mute and immobile in brilliantly lit boulevards lined with blocks of rising buildings hung with black iron balconies in that pretty part of the city full of alabaster façades fashionably rowed in colonnade beneath red-tiled roofs stretching to the far sky. There she went a young girl wandering bloody in the light her face covered in the blued shawl in the Tuareg style for the first time in her life as if a warrior with only the eyes to be seen going on in the city by the sea the badly kept sight of him in his blue uniform held before her in her following on after him to kill him as she knew she must.

"Tell me if you found him," I said again to her.

"I was to kill him," she said.

She told it outright. It is nothing so bad. It is to be ended for good. Then she laughed once at how she looked. It was not a happy laugh. She broke the vision of the place. I saw the bookcases rising in the light across the wall of her room in France. In looking to them books all along I'd been seeing the city and the sea. Then in that sight of seeing only them books the telling was stopped. We lay there returned to that time and place first to the actuality of France. The light hit the books brilliantly lit along the wall. The light came to us from off the flower garden in across the delicately-patterned red papered walls of roses to illuminate the books rowed all unopened and closed up in their covers, in our looking only now in that light to the books fully un-receded from the papered wall where they'd been obscured, recessed in shadow in morning in the shuttered light, to be lit and rowed however all unreadable until once more reopened again and, just as in them shut up books, it's true that once one uncovers some few told facts of a life, that there are then in all simple lives the large lived scenes to find and follow out, for a lived life itself, as in a book, in time contains a kind of necessary plot to be retold to another, if not first to one's own self, in order for it to be fully understood. Though it seems one cannot ever go on simply from scene to scene in such a telling, even to one's own self, let alone when told to another you love without the right words. Nothing real is to be told without the right words. She was re-finding her words.

The house was stilled. There were footsteps coming down the stairs to the foyer. There were her parents' voices. They went out the front door of the house. There was the real quiet of the house. We were left there alone in the house to go on with it to tell the rest of it what was real and ruinous and I saw him dead and wanted it so and she saw all what she could say and she went on with it and she told it. She began on it again for good as much for me as herself.

57

INTERLUDE OF AN OLD INDIAN TALE

Well there are all the times you'll see what you can't say. There I had to stop when I myself saw all what I couldn't say, and stopped there, without the right words, nothing of it was anymore real, and I heard her say, "Daddy, don't stop," and I'd stopped, and the story came again undone for her, for when I found I'd gone from the telling of the land of France to my telling of the people, to tell her all about the land in telling her a little something true of the people, I found I was stopped as I must be there in such a lived particularity of them people, in that place.

I found no words for her which could be said.

We stood a father and a daughter in the light and the whole story of us two, her mother and I and who we were, was finished there in that relation by the fact of her and I, who we two were there in the light in America outside of all telling. She was a girl in America that was a fact and I was only wanting to tell her another happy little picturesque scene of such a good and beautiful place as France there before us, when she spoke, and she came to me from the very center, the entire frame of everything yet to be told, when she came from inside the story out to me and we remembered our own lives.

She said, "Daddy don't stop—don't stop it, there," and she broke it all, all the continuity and convention of it, it went away all unseen, and I saw her. I saw the land along the lake laid out real in the summer light outside us and all our telling just as I'd seen the actuality of the bookcases rising in the light in the room in France outside hers, when she herself had turned to look to me and stopped it what it all was in France, I stopped the telling of it and all what it was in America, in that turning from my telling to look to her herself. There were the green-leaved trees tall in their black bark high on the bluff above us. Below us was the long curve of white sand beach lining the edge of the blue. There the house with its familiar rooms stood behind us struck with summer light and the shade of trees. We would return to its familiar rooms as we'd always returned, and stopped in the story like that turned first there to look at my daughter along the great lake in the so-called Middle-West of America, we saw ourselves again as we were in that great North American light and none other. That was what was real, it has been all along. I looked at my daughter in the light. I told her none of what she'd once told me. I was with her in America. I looked to my daughter and to her long black hair. I saw her dark-colored skin. She was a brown-skinned girl in a great North American light. I was struck by the long black color of her girl's hair. There was the sun-dark look of her golden-colored skin in her yellow dress. There was the particular look of her girl's face. She said to me, "What is it Daddy?"

"You could be an Indian, girl," I said to her. "Maybe you are an Indian Girl," I said.

"That's why I am dark some?" she said.

"That is why you are dark some."

"I am not an Indian, Daddy," she said to correct me.

"You might be an *Indian Girl*," I said to her and there in that land and light I saw how it would be for her to be such a girl.

"Daddy, stop playing," she said. "Tell what happened to Mother now—she won't tell me. I want to know what happened to her in France," she said to me sounding older than she was. She was done with the playing. But I liked the idea of her being an Indian Girl.

"We could all be Indians, girl," I said to her in the great lakelight along that water lost awhile thinking that, in seeing her there along the water stretching to the far line of the sky in the Middle-West of America. And I felt then there with her, that it could've been anyplace anywhere we were in. The time, it could've been any time. Without the names, the clocks and calendars it was, it is. That old kind of unknowing came upon me with clarity, and feeling that true kind of knowing come upon me again, I wanted to tell her a couple of those good old Indian stories, while she wanted me to go on with her mother and not America, to hear all about France as a far-off place.

I saw how I could tell her one of those old Indian tales that you'll hear told of in remembered stories as a kid in America in a place like Michigan and all across the land. My own mother she had once told me such fantastically-imagined fables when I myself had wanted to know of her own life lived there on the land. They were all the long-spoken remembered and retold myths of tricksters and shamans all what she told. She was that kind of teller. I was a boy. I wanted to hear

267

them. She herself did not tell me the particularity of her own life. She would not. But such stories do tell of lives. Just as in them books I've read that are held to be true-to-life wherein realism becomes moral allegory. As in them books, I know such legends of the land are a part of the people and the place, and that they do tell of lives, if not the hours of them, then the spirit of them, and in that way they are true-to-life, however fable-like, and I was thinking hard on how to tell her one of them good long legends of that land all round us and of us two there in America and not now in any story of France.

I know you need only look to a map or to a book to begin to tell one of them, even in some cursory way, for beyond those for the most part forgotten fables, printed there in them pages of books and maps you'll see that the people are a part of the place, should you find none of them left living on the land these days to see that it's so, there they remain recorded in place-names, left written in the official lists of archives if not any longer in a life, and I know it's hard to conceive that there are all of these people who have truly been in such a place in the lived time of their own lives once you are to tell a little of them, and who remain and who will remain only on paper in compiled and printed names, preserved in documented record, in inked-out ledger pages, filed by name and year, reams of them catalogued by war, laid in wooden, in metal drawers, in imprinted books stacked in unopened covers, so much life left off from, congregated across the dusted metal shelves of barely-visited libraries, where to live at all they must be taken up and retold, or left all these closed lives ended with no narrative. So, I told her one of those never-written only remembered legends of a long gone place that is yet all round you that you've lived in all your life that you can never get to but in telling.

Then once I'd begun it, she wanted it to go on, and she said, "Daddy, make it like a story in a book." She wanted it to last. She was a girl. For a time I did. She forgot about France.

I even put her herself in it young-dark in her dress there on the land along the lake. I remade her life into legend. Then sometimes it was just as in books I myself had read. I told her a good and happy story. I made it last that way for her. I made it that way for her if not myself.

58

A KIND OF HOMECOMING, CONTINUED

For myself there were the stone streets of the old city. The streets went on along the old stonewalls nicely. There she went a young girl bloodied in the light following on after him through the French Quarter of that old colonial city. He led her in his boyish wandering way off to the quieted parts of the city. There were the little shaded squares. There were the nice cool streets of shadowed stone. She said then in some contradiction, "There was a peace in such streets," she said as an easy aside to me in her recollection of the good of the place, amidst all that was ruinous in it, and in hearing that while seeing them closed-up books of hers mute in their covers brilliantly lit before us in France, I had it once more again in my head, and I couldn't get it out of my head, that a life and each thing it contains must be told as in a book to become real to another if not to one's self, that a life is just such a shut up thing as them books once lived until retold, even if no person can ever be read or perceived in such intact form, as some invented characters are held to be in books, when consistent and non-contradictory as persons set out in such pages, and I was not unhappy to hear her tell such an easy little aside as that, to see some of the good of it as it was lived, for it was her life however badly or richly lived, it was her girl's life where she went on following after him where he went on along the pretty quieted streets lined in nicely shaded stone set heavy in block beneath the spotted bark of sycamores.

Then he was disappeared. She saw him no more. Then no one reappeared. She walked them peaceful quieted streets. She followed the well-lit streets of rising stone. There was no one. She saw the remembered sight of him. She followed the stones of the next street seeing him and he was gone. He appeared real to her in her own head. There was no one. There were the stones and the street. He was disappeared and lost to her for good. Years later she sometimes still wondered whether he'd ever been, "Sometimes I do wonder," she said and she lay there in repose beside me in her bedroom seeing her herself there another girl, and said, "I can't even remember what he looked like now." But she'd only to look to herself to know that he'd been and I looked and saw that he had.

"It is another life, it is years," she said.

"When was it—the year?" I said to her to place the time of it.

"It was summer—1962," she said in her looking back to that time from this with me laid easy there beside her in bed with everything now kept before us, who we were in this place and what'd happened in that one, and she said, "They were killing the Frenchmen—these Pieds-Noirs. It is already years," she said in her seeing it, the remembered streets coming on to her in her following on after him down along the closed doors of the houses of them emptied streets to kill him but he was gone for good from sight and there was only the stone of the houses. There were the doors of the houses shut up against the street in the light. There was the far sky. All the Frenchmen who were not French were locked up in their houses in summer 1962. The Arabs were killing them. They kept to themselves. They kept close to home. They kept themselves from off them pretty streets of the Quarter where she herself walked on in the solitude of such pleasantly-deserted streets, where when she'd turned from the end of one on into the hard lit stone of another, to go on following after the image of him held in her head, on along the shut up doors of the French houses of them Pieds-Noirs thinking never now to see him again in her life but in recollection, she said that that is when he stood there in the far end of the street in the plain light of day walking back to her in his blue.

He walked on beneath the sycamores and up the lit street across the nicely shaded stone as he came to her from the far end of it without any hesitation in his walking to her. The sight of him appearing as he did, it surprised her with the pistol cocked in her hand, looking to him in his careless way of walking on to her as he closed the distance between them, and as if he'd no fear in him of such a girl as her in his walking like that on to her. She wanted him to know her as he had not. She wanted him to know that it was her herself come to him to kill him there in the Quarter in the broad light of day. She wanted him to see what it was with the pistol cocked in her hand when she came directly into his way, there to stand before him in the closed distance, to block his way with her slight form, where then he looked up, and he saw her, and that she was a girl. He hadn't seen her and who she was. He hadn't seen that she was a girl. He saw her then as she'd wanted him to, surprising him in his looking to her herself, in his seeing the pistol in her girl's hand held to him himself. He looked to her a girl with a gun and he didn't look away. He was struck by his seeing her and she was happy he'd seen her so. She'd stopped him that way in her look. The sight of her herself had stopped him.

But what had stopped him was her looking as she was. That was what stopped him. It was her strangely covered face. It was that she wore the dark blue robe of an old warrior and worn there about her face was the indigo-dyed *tagelmoust* to cover up the face but for the eyes. He'd seen such indigo worn by such people. He knew The Blue People. It was not at all an unfamiliar or strange sight to him. It was her covered girl's

271

face that was unfamiliar and strange to him. There against the white of the stone she herself looked to him like she'd appeared fully sprung from the brilliant sandscape of some far southern desert. He thought of his own old desert dream. He saw the widened-out expanse of the brilliant land-light there with the pistol pointed at him the barrel hard-lit from the long fold of the blue she wore. It was a French pistol. He recognized the make. He looked off from the pistol to her. She was a dark girl with a gun. It was that she was a girl. That's what he couldn't get out of his head. She was a girl and he'd not been sure at first, but he saw it in her dark-lined eyes. He looked to her for the first real time and he thought she was sick. He said to himself, "She is a Tuareg girl from the South," as if that fact would tell him something about her and her holding that pistol to him in such a way that he'd not ever seen from a girl in the North in the city by the sea, for he knew all about the people of the South. He knew there were Tuareg girls now a long time exiled up in the North. Some of them they were gone years now in the North. But he'd never seen one of them covered up as she was. Tuareg girls never covered the face. It was the men who covered the face. The women and the girls they never covered the face as did the men. They had these beautiful faces. That he couldn't see her face was more strange to him than the fact of the pistol. He understood the pistol. He knew the people and he knew the place. He knew the direness of North Africa. He was a man who knew many things about the land and the light and the people and the place. He knew who'd come from where and why and he knew who'd gone and done what to whom when and why. He knew who was dangerous and who was not as one does when living in such times in such places whether in the South or in the North.

  He was a man who'd long known guns in his life, and he simply stood there in the street in the North of Africa with the canvas sack hefted and heavy on his back hauling it to home from market when she came into his way, and in his looking up to her he stepped to the side of her to let her go, to get himself on to home, and he wasn't afraid of her, when he'd stepped to the side of her. He was to let her pass without incident and she followed him in his step with the black barrel of the gun and he looked from it to her wild young girl's look and he saw that she was afraid. He saw the seeped blood run dark in the blue and in her fear he became a little afraid. He saw the reddened indigo and what it was all about and that she was a cut girl and he saw he was standing too close beside her in her fear with that pistol barrel pointed to him in the closed-in street, seeing then that he shouldn't ever be stood there with her now in that bright lit street like that that he should let her pass without one word on to what life he didn't know what life it would be with that cut with that pistol pointed at him for he saw that she meant to kill him that she was to shoot him. That is how it would happen to him in the end after all the rest, he thought, and then in the absurdity of it, a simple feeling of futility, he spoke to her in his French, "You are lost?" he said to her in his French, as he reached for the pistol to take it from her in his speaking and in her hearing his French and in his hand come to her as if once more to come across her, she shot him in the hand sickened by the cut and the sight of him in his blue with him come once more across her to hold her to him in the high heavy light.

    All was dark. She was fallen faint to the stone of the street. He caught her and held her there in the sick feeling. She was gone out in his arms. The pistol hit the stone of the street. The sound scattered along the houses of the street. He simply swore and he said to himself, "It's the bad luck that's with me," and he held her leaned up against the high façade of a stone house wall. The blooded cloth was fallen from off her face. He saw the uncovered cut. He'd seen such cuts in the South. He'd never seen them in the North like that but done by those few who themselves knew the knife. Her blood was on him on his bared hand on his arm seeped along his blued sleeve come up across his blue workman's uniform with her head hung on his arm. He held her kept up from the stone close to him bent to her with the hefted sack on his back. He was a strong man of fifty in those days. He held the weight of her by the strength of his good hand and he looked to the blued and blooded tagelmoust fallen wet to the white barren stone before him thinking first to take it up so to put it back on round her wound. She told me that many years later when she'd asked him to tell it to her, as I know a daughter will ask such things of a father, for she could not clearly remember the act of her shooting him, that day or in others to come, she remembered little of it then but for her waking in fear laid out sickened, weak and wounded, in the bed in the house with her mother bent in some care to the bed before her, that he'd simply told her in his factual way all what she'd told me there in afternoon in France, how he'd reached for the tagelmoust, how he'd took it up from off the stone with one of his big knuckled hands, told her he let the sack fall from his back bent to the stone, with her out as though in sleep across his knee, and when he had the tagelmoust in hand to put it to her face her blood was dried, so he wound the indigo cloth round his shot-up hand, and he rose from his knee.

  He took her up to him. She weighed nothing. She was a girl. Her black braided hair was stiffened dark in dried blood. He looked to her cut girl's face. He took a good look at her. He didn't look away from her. He knew all about it. He'd seen it. He'd once seen such strangely beautiful girls. He saw them once more in her. He left the canvas sack there behind him on the stone in the street. He did not leave the pistol to the stone in the street. He took it up and put it in his jacket pocket. He carried her down along the closed-up doors of the houses of the street. He carried her already as when a father will carry one's child to home when fallen off hard in sleep after too-long travel, and as he came to the door of the house she was out in his arms, and he opened it with a bloodied hand, then a boot, and went in through the wide swung door to the pretty blonde Frenchwoman where she stood in her nice housedress come out to the little living room to the front of the house in having heard the shot in the street in the city by the sea, and that pretty blonde Frenchwoman, in her seeing him and in her feeling some old fear that they themselves had never yet got out of, already she knew then what needed to be done with him come to home like that into the house with her with her blooded cloth come undone from his hand his blood gone in hers in the blued cloth fallen wet and dark to the French stone of the little living room floor in that pretty little house in them days. That Frenchwoman she already knew what all needed to be done in them days in those ordinary rooms of that well-ordered house in that pretty part of the city by the sea when already in those days there were now no usual little days left for any of them in that time in the North of Africa.

There she ended it and we were returned to the room in the South of France to the strong summer light hitting on brilliant across the rose-papered walls and books.

"There was a war," she said in her studied and knowing way. In that summing up we lay back there on the bed in her parents' house in that southern French light looking out to the flower garden and to the mountain rising in rock above us, and I thought, but it is all by chance. It is all made out of happy and unhappy chance. I thought that of a life. And I thought then, in my thinking that, that there really is no ordinary and likely life, if you are to think about it. I thought about it. It's all extraordinary, and we lay back there on the bed in the room with it all done and told for the better, and I looked back on my own life. All one's life is unlikely I said to myself, and I felt a little free lying there then with her on that bed in her parents' house in France, and it must be all unlikely, or I cannot be here where I am now with her.

275

"Madeleine," I said. "But, it's all by chance, one's life," I said. "There is some freedom in that," I said that to her, seeing the good in it.

"But, it is not by chance," she said. "Do you think *who* you are, what you and I have done, is simply by chance, John?—even *how* we are called, your name, my name, not even our own names are simply by chance. *John*, you are not so free as you think you are—you want to think you are, and you are not," she said.

"But everything lived—is lived forward," I said to her thinking it through as hard as I could, and I said then, "Nothing lived is fully fixed, it cannot be—all one's life is unlikely," I said feeling free in the thought.

"Do not think that it is *all* unlikely, John," she said.

"Nothing is that likely," I said.

I was seeing the good of it, for her if not myself.

"What you think of as unlikely, is only unlikely, later—once it is lived, when it is told—when what seems so unlikely, in telling, never was in a life when it was lived," she said that, and I lay there when she'd told me that, and I thought about that, I thought about how she'd told me all what was so unlikely to happen in a life and had there in the North of Africa, and too many people think that if you are to tell a true story you must tell what seems not at all unlikely. But if you're to tell of a life you can't do that. Living doesn't hold to such simple convention.

59

ON LEARNING A LANGUAGE

Then she taught me some French in morning, and the mornings after. In them first mornings in France, she began to teach me the language from out of one of her schoolbooks she'd used for the children, for I had to learn the language to live in the land, and when I had asked her too many questions about the language, while we were looking out to the flower garden with the student schoolbooks opened up there on her desk, she said to me, "You must start thinking in French. That's the way to learn a language. You cannot think it in the English," and I said to her, "I think it like that when I want to speak it—when I'm finding my words," and it's hard to give up a way of thinking about the world, and yourself, when one's own words feel as real as the world, as another's cannot, until you learn that the world, if not yourself, is always a lot larger than your own language or anyone else's. It's not a bad thing to learn, if you want to learn anything new about the world and yourself, and there that morning in France she was teaching me some things like that about the way to learn to properly speak of the things of the world.

She said, "You cannot think about what it means to you in your English. You must think the words—all the things—in the French when you say them," she said. "You must see it new, to know it," she said, and I sat there at the desk with her instructing me, she wanted me to be a good student, and I thought about how to see things new. I wanted to see the world new and the world was the same. However likely or not a life is to be, nothing was new. It was a funny thing to think it through when you thought about it. But she was right. And when I began that day to think in that way she said I should, in only the one language not in the other, when I didn't try to fit the one sense and syntax into my translation of the other, to them words I seemingly naturally knew, when I didn't paraphrase the perception of myself and the world in a transcription of the French from out of the English, to be converted from the one utterance to the other in some too loose fake semantic sense however denotatively correct, superimposing the significance

277

and the order of the world as words, in my speaking the one language ever attenuated and fixed in the other, so always to get to the sense of things secondarily, then I knew all the same old things new. I saw the world a little different and as though originally known, though nothing was different or originally known. In her instruction, I looked out the window to the flower garden to all before me, framed-out anew, and the workbook and my pen lay down on the desk, and I saw the same old things renewed in another form in the French as in reinventing the actuality of what they were, if not now myself, and I had invented nothing, changed nothing round but the words, and everything, all was different, if not myself.

  She taught me to think that way in them mornings in France and she was a good teacher. She was very serious about it and I began to see France in the French. From the beginning, she wanted me to learn the French right and proper no matter it was not ever her own language, and I did want to know the language that way that she said I should, I wanted to learn it as unthinkingly as she knew it, with all the sense known by spoken sound, there is a pleasure in that, as in the freed-up playing of music, in how a song arrives beyond its notation, without ever once thinking through the apt placement of a note in a scale, a word in a syntax. From the beginning I did want to see France that way first in the French, and in our studying in them summer mornings she was teaching me to and to be a good student, but I don't think I ever was yet in those first few days in France such a student, as I wasn't yet arrived there to the life of the place long enough to learn to see only France in the French, but in time, sitting side by side with her at her desk, looking out from the French books to the window, I felt the land come a little in its language, and we'd looked up to the garden, and she told me to name to her the things I saw in the garden. I was her student. I looked up from the book. I looked out the window to the flowers in the light. There out in the village street beyond the garden and the gate to the house a car started. There were far voices. There was the rattling sound of diesel in the far off engine, the metal sound of a car door closing, and the English came back some in such sounds, there were old sights in them, long known lands, other worlds, and she said, "Tell me how each thing is called," she said. It was a kind of exam.

So, looking out to them long-named and known things, I renamed the things I saw for her to again know them. She made me repeat them each time when I said them. Then all the known world was once more realized in that repetition as though in the rediscovery of a land. I made errors. She made me re-repeat what all I had misnamed. I was to internalize all what I could not name. I was to put it in me beyond the consciousness of remembering as a rote act, to possess it without a continual act of retrieval, one of searching for words in me for the real. But I'd lost the words and I was remembering. I was looking again for my words in the too conscious recollection of them as when one looks to a filed note-card for a fact.

Then, I had to look down to the book to read it off right. Then, there was the sound of it. But, I'd lost all the sense of it. There was all the senselessness to the signifying sound. I spoke. But I named nothing. The things of the world came all arbitrary in whatever given name to me in my saying them, in my losing them in sheer sound, what they themselves were, and they were right there given in the world before me out the window as they'd always been, the things in themselves, whatever the names, and with her beside me waiting on my word, she said, "John," for me to go on, to proceed in the simple lesson, and, in losing them words, the world, I'd felt the sense of myself had been lost a little, in such insignificant un-corresponding sound between world and word, there was some self-strangeness come on in me in the sheer abject sound, there was a senselessness of self, come briefly in the whole

279

recognition of the arbitrariness of all, until then in her little summons to me, in her speaking to name me as I could not name the things, the sense of all came back on in the *John*, I was once more held there to the world of signified things, to myself, but then as in an accounting to her in her act of naming me, and then in the act of her naming me the strangeness was gone, and I looked to her looking to me, I was present to myself in that look of her, in her spoken, directive voice which was not ever to me senseless sound, in her look, her regard, her recognition, her demand for me to act, as in a kind of accounting for myself and my own acts, for what she required in the simple lessons of learning a language.

There were the schoolbooks all opened up on the desk in the summer light containing the whole of the language. It was all to be found that world of things in the lessons of a textbook there in the determining and formal logic of a language. There was the hardcover student reader with its illustrative and cropped little vignettes and there was the soft-covered workbook with its repetitive exercises of the grammar of person and conjugation of selves and things. I looked to the French textbook reader she'd got out for me that was one of those they'd used in the old French school and, looking down across the central text of its lined and columned print, to go on for her with the lesson, in some good comprehension, I saw in the margin in French the hand written notes of a schoolchild, and in the unordered congregation of places held in that book, I remembered them old rooms of the school, heard them happy classroom voices of schoolchildren, and she was beside me waiting for me to speak in some meaningful sound and syntax, and I did then a time, in a couple uneasy utterances, and afterward I had my ink pen ready then in hand to do the repetitive exercises of the workbook, for in repeating one learns all what one must internalize about the significance, sense, and order of things.

She worked me through the beginning chapter of the French reader with its formalized phrases and caricatured pictures of French cultural types, all well-defined for instruction and often comedic with little ambiguity or contradiction to their utterances and actions, wherein the so-called verisimilitude, the continuity of person, character, there in the world of the planned lessons of the schoolbook, is most properly, if not profoundly, formed by those briefly, clearly drawn persons living out their everyday hours in such predictably fixed and contiguous everyday habit, in thought, in emotion, in action, all this rote, practical instruction a necessary reduction of individual reality, so to see the supposed persisting sense of someone, the constancy of a cultural type, self, as a pedagogical aide, nothing now seen as unlikely in a life, however to be new in a language, and I had the workbook open for the grammar and syntax to write out my simple little sentences for her, to put down correctly on paper what I'd learned about the logic of the language, the convention and consistency of people in repetition, and she got up from beside me at the desk.

"You must practice your French," she said to me.

She was to leave me to it.

"Don't go—," I said.

"You must work on your French—are you going to work on your French?" she said.

"Stay—you're a good teacher," I said.

I had my arm around her. She felt good to hold.

"But, you are not a very good student—you must work harder," she said.

"I never was good at books—school," I said. "You know that. I was never a good schoolboy," and she took my hand from her when I said that. She left me at the desk and got her slippers. She went and opened the bedroom door to go. She stood at it putting on her slippers, "You will study until lunch," she said looking to me at the desk left to the books. It was not a question. I was to work to lunch. She was going up to help her mother with lunch.

She was to make me into a good student.

She stood there at the door in her slippers and she said gently in instruction as to a child at a desk in school, "You must take it seriously, John. You must do it alone, now. Then, you will learn—if you work, you will be good," she said.

"All right, girl," I said, "I always wanted to be good at something—even school."

"You will take it seriously?" she said. She stood there all dark.

"Yes, I will—I will take it seriously," I said, I wanted to, and I was sick of taking things seriously.

She turned and left the room.

She left me to them books to write out the French sentences. I started to correctly complete the written exercises. I wrote them out like she said I should. I lit a cigarette. I watched the smoke go blued into the light. I looked into the garden light thinking through the words. The words made the words. I worked on them words. I worked on them words awhile. But in that working on them words in the French I came upon my own. In finding them right expressions to be formed in French, I came upon some things I myself wanted to say. The work of them words led me on to my own. Then it was not an exercise. I followed out the proliferating sound and the sense of things came in extended form. I hadn't expected it to all come on in written word. I stopped the studying of the French. What was lived started all to come sounded-out in the English. I got a piece of stationary out of her desk drawer.

I heard all this sound come on in my head and it was all the sound come for things I had seen. It sounded true. I started to put down half-formed images as I could on the stationary. I started writing. I took the work of the writing seriously. I wrote with some seriousness awhile. I'd left off for good from the exercise of the French. I put down some things that she and I had seen and said. I saw the good things we'd lived. I saw them come on in the sound for them I had in my head. I wanted to say them to save them that way on paper. I wanted to put them down the way they were lived. It's too bad that you can't ever get it all down on paper the way it was lived. I saw whole livid scenes of life come before me that I didn't know how to write out so to picture them on a page in apt form. I couldn't fully re-form them. The good things were passing in picture as I heard them. They would not persist in picture as did the bad. They were passing. I had no ready good form for them. But I thought I should keep them. They were things that struck me true-to-life. They were true to us and passing. Maybe someday someone might read them again and see what it was once like to have lived some few good things in a life even if badly formed. Maybe even you yourself would come to them again one day to see what it was once like to have lived your own life.

I made out crude little pictures of richly lived things. They were like forgotten old photographs found about a house. You want to save something of a life. It's the thinking that you're saving something. It's the feeling that you have. There without her I made pictures out of words awhile. Then I stopped to read them over to see what I'd said. I read in some discovery then what I myself had just made of the world. I read as in a first discovery of the passing world and myself on a page. There I'd set out a half-formed scene of some remembered feeling. Maybe that's all it was if you wrote it true to life. It was the remembering feeling. There, it seemed I found my own life and the sense of things in it most profoundly on a page in reading over what I'd just written. There on the imaged page I read, in that half-formed, unset scene, which wasn't ever fixed as a feeling on a page, stopped in time as in the surface of a found photograph, until a printed photograph itself is recalled as an object made into an image in an act of memory, a passing picture of feeling, perceived and placed in its passing time, and in my reading, then in recalling that feeling, retrieved from all the objects of my own little written-out scene, I now found that the words for things were arranged in repetition, the words, things becoming in repetition, in rereading, reverberating images, not signs, but symbols giving sense to the sheer perception of things, where in the sight of one street, you saw another, in one house, another, in trees, gates, gardens, you saw all other gardens, gates, trees, in an accrual of meaning, amplification of sight, sense signified in congregated place, time, or there was nothing in the material sight of the world but the sheer surface of an inert scene, and I wasn't looking to the world, I was looking to the page of written-over ink before me to know the realized world and the richness of things in relation, in circulation, in duration, not now in the correct calling of any one repeated thing by name to know it, whatever the language, now not knowing anything in naming but in narrative. But to begin I know that one must start with the words and rote repetition, first the simple signs for things, then, in time, the life of symbols.

In the realized thought, I looked up, out the bedroom window from the page to the world, to the flowers of the garden before me, I looked out beyond the house-front, past the gate, off to the village street, then to the parked cars immobile in their steel and glass glanced in midday light, on to a line of cropped plane trees, leafed, greened in diminishing perspective and picturesque in aspect to the eye, not ever now in the perceived world simply trees in such a looking, where they stood strung out and rowed in their mottled trunks planted in line along the white stucco-walled French houses roofed in their red tile diminutively set at a distance, the congregation of houses rising on into the village, the village rising in its roofed stone strung up on along the mountain rock set in strong light against the blued sky to a fortification fallen in ruin and, in the panoramic composition of that picture, I heard their voices in lively talk above me in the kitchen, and I lost the whole continuous thought of it, of how to give life to the objects of a life, and the logic of following out the proliferating words was gone and lost. I sat there left in sudden solitude and without one new word. Then, I wanted to get up there to them two in the kitchen. Now I felt I'd lost my time in misspent rumination, was missing everything with them up there in the kitchen, that life of them, and I looked over to those books of hers at the rose-papered wall. I was to go, and I went and stood before the books. She'd never taken one out off a shelf. I read a couple titles on my way to the door, to my slippers, thinking yet of written pages. I took out a big blue-covered book. It was in English. English poetry was one of her subjects in school. I opened it to a marked page. I turned the fine-papered pages randomly which were marked in black and blue ink here and there in her hand. The book was the "Collected Works" of an English poet now long dead, *Complete Poems and Major Prose*. There was a piece in it called "Areopagitica," a speech for the liberty of unlicensed printing, it said, and looking to her inked marks I read a page on Parliamentary censorship I did not understand, and with the book opened in my hands, in reading the rhetoric of the argument, I found I was following the sense out then in the sound, just as I had in what I myself had made, written out on a page, and the pipes rattled above my head, and I looked up, I shut up the book, I put it back in its place on the shelf, and I only wanted to be up there with them and missing nothing, not left any longer off to parsing the words of that long dead poet. But it is a book that I have looked at much lately.

60

A SERIOUS LUNCH

    Sometimes her mother had half a beer there with her in the kitchen before lunch in all the steam from her pressure cookers and when she drank her beer the glass was beaded and the beer looked cold in the glass and good to drink. Her mother would cook the potatoes and carrots and beets and green beans and all the vegetables fresh from the garden that way in them cookers and she would never boil them. The pressure cooked them quick and kept the flavor. She cooked everything for lunch straight from the garden and nothing came out of cans.
    I went up to them. When I came into the kitchen the two of them were there at the table talking and the steam from them pressure cookers was going up from the whistling valves onto the ceiling and I stood there just inside the door and looked up to the peeling yellow paint where the steam hung in clear drops from the kitchen ceiling and was slowly peeling off the high paint with all that cooking. They were drinking their beer. There was a big brown bottle of the French beer sitting on the table. The beer was cold and beaded in their glasses. I looked to them. It was good to be there in the kitchen in the steam with them where it was warm and everything smelled good, and I went from the door to the table and sat down at the kitchen table covered over with its blue and yellow checkered tablecloth. I forgot about what I had written, and all I had read, I was there with them in the coziness of that kitchen, and she said to me, "You have finished your French?"
    She wanted to know that I'd completed the exercises in the school workbook, and I said, "Yes, I'm done thinking for the day."
    "You must do, not think," she said but she wasn't too serious with me there with her mother. She was playing

a little with me with that beer in her and with the work done for lunch. She pushed the big beer bottle over to me and I poured myself out a full glass. We stayed there sitting at the kitchen table feeling that passing time right before lunch and coming afternoon when you're hungry and drinking and you feel the short opened out time of late morning lingering on a little between waking and working with the rest of the day held off before you and, in that brief passing time, we then talked easily of this and that with her mother awhile in the kitchen until, in time, we were talking a little seriously about work and what work there was round there and if we could get it.

Her mother she told us there at that table what the work was and where the work was in the city and in the country.

"There is work in Valence," her mother said. "It is a big city. There is work advertised. It is in offices. It is in shops in the city," and her mother she looked at her when she said that, "Sometimes, there is work in the country," she said and she looked at me, "There is the harvest season," she said. "There is work then, in the country."

"Where in the country?" I said to her. I had done that kind of work. I could do that kind of work. "We will go to the country—work in the country."

"It is hard and according to the season," she said, "But it is good work, and well paid."

She told then about the many orchards and the harvesting of fruit and the many local vineyards and *la vendange* in the fall when there are the autumn weeks of cutting the grapes off the vines in all the vineyards. Her father came in in his blue workman's uniform. He looked up at the kitchen ceiling. He looked at the closed kitchen door to the balcony. He took a look at her mother sitting at the table in her apron. She was telling us about the work. He said something in French. He crossed the kitchen to the balcony. He opened up the balcony door. He wanted to save the paint. I'd seen him do it before.

He did it again. But he was a man who loved his food and the way that she cooked it. So there was nothing really to be done about it. He couldn't save the paint. He looked at the ceiling and he left the kitchen. Her mother got up from the table. She closed the balcony door to keep out the flies. We were done with our talk. We set the table with plates and silverware. Her mother had the cookers all shut off. The food was on the table. She called out to her father. Her father came to the table. He didn't look at the ceiling or at the closed door. He sat at the table before his food.

The four of us had a long serious lunch with sliced butter-fried potatoes and sliced cooked beets and green beans in a vinaigrette salad with hard boiled eggs and a special spiced sausage and the hard-crusted bread that went in crumbs all over the blue and yellow tablecloth when you broke it by hand to eat it and the cold purpled wine that you cut with water and ice to thin it when you drank it and a hard goat cheese at the end with a last glass of the dark purpled wine that stained your teeth then the sliced ripe juicy peaches. It was a serious lunch. We took our time. They had a radio in there on the counter behind us and they always listened to the news while eating. There wasn't talk during the meal. There were the politics and the weather on the radio and there was our own little time of talk with her mother before lunch with the beer or after with the coffee. Her father he didn't drink beer before lunch or coffee after with us. At the end of every meal he would cut one last good piece of cheese with his pocketknife and put it to a crust of bread on the table and fill his glass to the top with the dark uncut purpled wine and pick up the bread and drink down the entire glassful chewing the bread and cheese. He'd put his chair back from the table, get up, and put his cloth napkin down on the tablecloth along his emptied plate, and go off to take a short nap on the living room couch before he walked the dog. Then her mother would get up and put the food away in the cupboard to keep it, not in the refrigerator, the wine went in the refrigerator, and go off to her housework while we cleared and washed the dishes. It was a lot of work to cook and clean a kitchen each day when you'd cooked like that and we got up from the table and without talking started to clear off the table. The lunch was done. Her parents were gone off in the house. We two were there in the kitchen clearing and cleaning the dishes. We were just doing things in a house. That was all. Each day that was all. In that beginning time we went on each day doing what things must be done in a house.

61

THE THINGS TO BE DONE
TO MAKE A HOUSE A HOME

Her father rattled the chain leash and the dog came running down the hall past the kitchen door to the top of the stairs and her father went off from the house with the dog to walk out on the country roads in the light. Her mother came back into the house with the dried clothes she'd taken off the line in the garden. She came into the kitchen. The dishes were finished. They were washed and done.

She spoke to her and she said to me, "She wants to wash the floors."

Her mother she kept the whole house ordered and clean.

"Tell her, we'll wash the floors," I said and she told her.

Her mother went to iron. She swept the kitchen first, while I started in a clean corner on my hands and knees with a rag and a bucket of water. When the water was dirty, she poured it out in the toilet, ran the tub to fill the bucket, and got me fresh water. We washed the stone floors of the house. Her mother went to all the bedrooms and washed all the sheets from the beds and she hung them up outside to dry. Then when we were done with the floors of the house we took the fresh dried bed sheets off the line. We ironed them in the afternoon light coming long into the house. We stood at one end of the living room with an ironing board and a basket of the dried bed sheets. Her mother showed us how it was done. That washing and ironing was a lot of work. There was a lot of work to be done around a house to make it a home like that and I had forgotten that. Thinking about it I thought of how we'd two ourselves go off on our own from there to do the things like that one day. And in doing those simple things in that house I thought of all what we ourselves would need for a place to make it a little like a home. I hadn't thought about it until our doing it.

We were standing in the living room next to the ironing board and I said to her, "We'll have to get our own sheets and dishes. We'll get an iron and a mop, too. Maybe, you'll never go off again from home, with all this work," I said to her, and looked to her.

Her mother was ironing a handkerchief. She looked over.

Then I said to her, "I'll go off to work, and you'll be happy and home in a house," and she was looking at the sheet in her hand, hearing me say them kinds of good and easy words for our life. She had heard them before. She said nothing.

She was folding up a fresh ironed sheet toward me, and as I held the one end of it, she brought it up to me and she took the end I'd held, and I reached down and took up the hanging end of it, and we folded it in half again, and when we were all done with the sheets and the ironing and all the floors of the house were washed and clean, it felt like we'd been to work, and then we three went to the kitchen and her mother made coffee and got out little biscuits with chocolate tops. It was late afternoon. Her father was working in the garden. The dog was at our feet under the table. I was tired.

We were having the coffee. Then there was conversation.

"Do they ever go anywhere anymore?" I said to her because it seemed like they hadn't gone anywhere since I'd been there, but worked in the house or out in the garden, and she said, "No." Her parents they didn't go anywhere anymore off away from home.

She said her father would say, "*Je ne peux pas voyager a cause du chien*, that's what my father says," and her mother laughed at that. He didn't want the dog left alone. Then she looked at her mother, and said to me, "But my mother, she went once to visit Italy alone." She had her mother tell about that. Her mother told us all about how she'd seen Florence and Rome and she told about the beautiful architecture there in Italy and said how she wanted to go again but not to go alone, but her father was finished with places. He'd seen his places. He went once a week with her mother on Friday morning to the big market in La Voulte. That was all. It was the four kilometers away. On Fridays when they came back home from the market, they ate fish every Friday at lunch like good Catholics and they weren't Catholic, and no one went to church around there anymore not even the Protestants, but only the very old who'd gone to church before the last war in France, and who'd just kept on going after the war ended in 1945, as if it still made sense the way it had always made sense when not much else did make sense. Her mother told us that that war was the one thing that had happened to everyone round there in the South to change their lives to make up the kind of lives they now lived. That war was still the marker for new and old things and good and bad ways of doing things there in the South.

"But your parents weren't here—in France in that war?"

"No," she said. But she said her parents they had been

changed by it too, when they'd come to France to live the lives of these French. Her father was a *Pied-Noir*, a Frenchman born in Algeria. She said the French French, they called them 'Black-Feet.' And his father was a *colon*, a French settler from the South of France, who'd gone off to the North of Africa for the land.

Her mother heard those words. When she heard those words spoken between us two she began to talk. Then at that kitchen table her mother began to talk for good. Her mother went through a little history of conquest, war, and independence. Her mother told us about the long war in North Africa from 1954 to 1962. Her mother told us about the *Front de Liberation Nationale*. Her mother told us how the Algerian FLN fought the French for independence. Her mother told us they were killing Frenchmen in Oran in the broad light of day in 1962. In that time, that is when she'd come to them cut, and she looked to me, and her mother she told how she'd been afraid for her father, they were all afraid for good reason in those days, and she told how they'd cared for her in their house and I looked up from my cup of coffee and looked about us in the quiet of that kitchen with the nice French doors of the house opened out to the light and her mother said to us at that kitchen table, "We were not that young like you, but like everyone, we did what needed to be done," and she said, they only did the simple and necessary things, not always the good things, to live, and she drank her coffee and she went on with the little history of it all and she told us then about the massacres in Oran in summer 1962. She told us how the Independence was declared, how in one day in July 1962 a thousand or two Frenchmen were killed in the houses and streets of Oran. No one could tell the exact number. No one stopped it. The French gendarmes, the French soldiers did not stop it, they would not stop it, and that is true if you look in a history book. She told us, "It was exile or death, the suitcase or coffin—*la valise ou le cercuiel*."

She said, "For the people it is something about the land. It is something about what is right, and no one, after a time, can tell who is right," and I understood that, and I saw what she was saying, and by September 1962 two-thirds of the city of Oran was emptied out of the French *Pieds-Noirs*, they had to leave to live, and they couldn't take her with them, they wanted to take her, and when they themselves must leave to live she didn't have her paperwork, and they left for France without her with nothing left to them but their suitcases in summer 1962. They were exiled to France to live in the poor country of the Ardeche in the South of France, along with a million *Pieds-Noirs* who went to France, and she said then, they were foreigners speaking French in France far from home.

Her mother was done. Her mother took up her cup of coffee, and I turned to her beside me, returned there in that house to the box of biscuits on the table and the coffee cups sat before us on that blue and yellow checked tablecloth, and I said, "Then you went—*where*? Where did you go, girl?" I said to her and didn't want to hear how it was hard, and she told me how she went to live with the Catholics at *Notre-Dame du Salut* overlooking the sea at Oran, she said she was again with the Catholics, she was where she'd been before when exiled in the North, and she was quiet then about that, she didn't tell more about what was unhappy and hard with her mother there at the table, and her mother seeing her quiet like that, in hearing the name of that church, knew what it was about, and her mother then she'd started again on how they'd all come to home, and she went on to say to us that then without her in France everything they did was just them themselves doing things and that the things cannot ever be all done in a life you are not ever once and for all done with doing them things of a life and the days go on and you go on in them without end and they did go on without her with her father working in a factory and her herself cooking in a house each day and they'd wanted to take her with them when they'd come to France and couldn't, until then in time the Catholics had got her her paperwork at last from the Consulate for her to officially come, and she came on across the sea to them and they were already not that young when they wanted to make a home and they took her home to the house in Beauchastel to make what they had done and what they would have to do into something more than themselves doing things. They yet were to make a home in France. They would make that house a home. They made a home in France with her and when you're not that young it's hard to make a home in another new country. Her mother she said some things like that to us two sitting there at that kitchen table drinking coffee having a biscuit or two in the late afternoon light and we listened to her home there in the house when she told that kind of catalogue of what was lived in their life. And there is a lot more to it as there is in any life but we were done with our coffee and she was done with the telling of their lives. And we sat there round the kitchen table in the South of France and we looked at one another and away in the going light and another war was ending and we were beginning.

62

AN ELEGANT GIRL IN HER BLUE DRESS

In early rising light, I was awakened in my thinking of all what her mother had told us two over coffee at that kitchen table in the easy afternoon light about how they had come to France from out of a war to make a home and that it was hard to make a home when you were not that young. It was hard to make a home in another new country when you weren't that young and we were young.

In morning, I told her I wanted to go find the work

in the country. She told me she was to go off to Valance to the places that had advertised for work there in the city. She wanted me to go off to Valence with her to the city. That's why she'd cut and straightened her hair when I'd come to find the work in the city. Then her mother she had used some little money to buy her a nice new dress and a pair of good shoes at a little shop in the village of La Voulte. She had got her a hat for the summer sun too as she was very dark. She did not want her to get too dark. Her mother she wanted to buy her those things for her to go off to the city and she had wanted to do it herself to feel good about it but her mother knew all what needed to be done and she did it. She did it for her. She thanked her for it.

In Valence there was this office work in the city that was not that bad if you could get it. It was in places like hotels and travel agencies and in banks and law offices. There were these kinds of places like that that needed these special kinds of secretaries who could speak two or three languages. They were good jobs she said and she said she could do those jobs.

"Those kinds of jobs are not that bad—they don't sound bad," I said to her seeing the work and her there in it.

We lay there naked in bed in the coming light and she said to me, "But you have to be lucky to get one. I have not been that lucky, it is hard to get one, I think." She told me that once she had tried to get one and hadn't. Then her mother she had got her the haircut and the dress and the sunhat.

"I will take any kind of work—I can work," I said to her.

"But you do not have your paperwork," she said. "You must have the proper paperwork, to work in France—you must first get your paperwork." She told me that we must get the paperwork. We would wait on that.

"But—I can work," I said.

"Your French is very bad. We will go to the city," she said.

She lay there kept close beside me naked in bed and I saw her off in one of those nice places in a pretty part of the city at work in some large well-lit office with her purse put away in a desk drawer and her coat hung up in a closet, or maybe she was off in one of those old ornate hotel lobbies with the high painted ceilings where she'd sit out at a reception desk with all her work things laid out on it, and where she would then speak in this or that language to help the people who'd come in off a busy boulevard with their room reservation and luggage after long travel. Waked like that in bed beside her it was a happy sight to see her there off in one of those old French buildings with the rising black iron balconies and the tall glassed windows stretched nicely along a treed avenue in a pretty part of the city and that is where she began to look.

In afternoon, she got out the good dress from her closet. She held it before me on the hanger. She showed me it. I wanted to see what she looked like in it. "Try it on," I said. She tried on her new dress for me to see it. She undressed. She stood naked. She pulled it up blued and sheer over herself bared and black. She looked good in it. It looked expensive. "Zip it up," she said and turned her back to me. I did and she turned back around to face me. The fabric fit the whole form of her body. I looked at the whole of her. She looked strikingly good. She looked beautiful dressed up like that in her blue silk dress. She looked all elegant and poised with that new dress and haircut, and I said, "You look very good girl," I said to her and I was struck by her look, by how you wouldn't have recognized her from that girl I'd first met with the long black-braided hair, the blued shawl, the white pristine robe, but for the blackness and the cut, and I said, "Look," and she went and she stood in front of the mirror at the sink in the summer light in the heat of the bedroom to look herself. She took a good look at herself to see herself good with the window opened out to the flower garden in the strong summer light and it was true she looked very good even if she herself thought otherwise when so well-dressed.

"People will look at me strangely," she said.

"People will look because you look very good," I said.

She kept looking at herself in the room's little mirror at the sink.

"I look dark and different," she said and looked to the image.

"Let them look," I said. "You're beautiful," I said. I wanted her to know that to feel that and to feel good in going off. I didn't want her to feel unsettled about how she looked all well-dressed. She shouldn't feel worried or bad about it, to feel that in going off, not knowing that she was unusually beautiful and good to look at, and I said, "You'll get something good in the city," I said, and I felt better thinking it. I said, "I'll take anything, good or bad, in the country, in the city—and I'll be happy to do it—I'll find something, too," and I felt better thinking it and how we would go on good in the work.

"You will come with me," she said as a declaration. "I want you to come with me," she said and she turned from the mirror.

"I'll come with you, girl," I said.

"I don't want to be looked at alone," she said.

"But you're good to look at girl," I said. "I told you that. You'll be lucky girl. All will be good," I said. "You won't be looked at alone," I said and looked at her there before me all done up in her dress feeling unsettled about it and worried about her look and I could not imagine that anyone would not want her. I felt big things for her. You have to have hope for another you love and do. You must have hope and you do. You tell the people you love that it'll all go good. If you should love them you tell people that. I told her that.

"Sometimes, they do not take you," she said standing there looking like that.

"They will take you," I said.

"There are these people, they take a look at you, and they do not take you," she said. She took a good look at herself. She turned and took a look at herself then again in the mirror. She took a good look at her own black cut girl's face. "Sometimes you are not so lucky in a life," she said appraising that face of hers and the facts and she turned back to look at me. "I have been unlucky a long time," she said. "Don't you know that?" she said calmly and she was fixing her hair.

"You will be lucky girl," I said. "They will take you," I said. I said, "You are good to look at girl. Do not worry girl. Good things will happen for you, girl." I told her all that.

I told her that and I know you must tell people that if you should love them and you do tell them that when they are to go off into the world like that when you don't want them to go off anywhere at all worried like that let alone into the world.

63

A BOY AND A GIRL A LITTLE IN LOVE

The next morning we walked out the front door of the house on through the flower garden into the smell of the earth to the iron gate of the house to the street out into the rising light. We walked the asphalt village street rowed with the line of low-cropped plane trees. We felt the heat of the day to come and went beneath the cool concrete of the railroad bridge colorfully painted in an unintelligible alphabet of layered-over graffiti expressing what to the world we didn't know and would never know and went out from under the coolness of its concrete columns on our way along the bright lit main street of the village of Beauchastel holding hands walking along the little shop windows lining the main street for a block before the street became then again the highway where we came to the post office there to the public bus stop to wait for the bus to Valence. There it stopped along the edge of the highway at the bridge over the Eryiex River. There we stood waiting at the side of the road before the bridge over the Eryiex River.

It was good weather. The mountain rose against the blue. The river ran off the mountain into the Rhone. We heard the water run the river stones. She was beside me in her blue dress. She was holding her black little purse. She was wearing her sunhat in the strong light. She was all dressed up and I looked to her. "What is it?" she said when I'd looked to her. "Nothing," I said, "I am happy," I said. There were all them other girls held in her. I had all this feeling for her. There was nothing to say for it feeling it like that.

There was no one waiting with us. There was no traffic going on through the village street. There was no one in the street. A man and a woman came out to the street. They were carrying bread in wicker baskets from the bakery. They were to pass us by. They came toward the bridge up from the bakery to cross the river. I took her hand in my hand. They passed along us. They looked. They took a good look at us. They looked at her in her sunhat. It was a curious look. They looked off from us. She had her sunhat shading her face. She had her hand hard in mine.

"So I am good to look at?" she said in the look.

"Let them look," I said.

"How do I look? Do I look all right?" she said. I looked.

"Don't you know you are a pretty girl," I said to her in her hat.

She was a pretty girl. I wanted her to know that.

"The people will look—you told me they would look," I said, "—You're good to look at."

"But that is not why they look," she said. "Don't you

know that? You know that."

"You're a pretty girl."

She said, "You are too in love, boy." She called me boy.

"It is love, and it is not love," I said. "I like how you look," I said.

"I think you are too in love, boy," she said and laughed, but she liked it. She liked to use boy on me. I didn't at all mind it from her.

"Don't you know that you're beautiful girl?" I said. "You are beautiful with it."

"Why do you like it?" she said.

"It did nothing to you. You are prettier than it. You have always been prettier than it," I said.

"It did something to me," she said.

"I would not like you without it," I said. "I would not like how you look without it. I like how you look with it," I said to her.

"You do not know how I would look without it," she said. "I might look more beautiful without it," she said. "I might be more beautiful," she said as if she herself were thinking of how that would be.

"But you like it that way," she said as a matter of fact.

"I like it that way," I said. "I love it. I will always love it," I said.

"Now, I have to love you?" she said, playing with it.

"Now you have to love me," I said. "You see how it is?" I said.

"I see how it is," she said. We saw how it was with one another.

We played a little with it like that waiting. We said little things like, "You will always have to love me now. "But I have always loved you." We said, "Forever you will have to love me." We said, "I have loved you forever." "I have already always loved you forever." "I have loved you already always forever and it is the beginning and we could have loved anyone." "But we do not love anyone," we said. "We love one another," we said. "We could have loved anyone at all and we have already always loved one another forever, and it is only the beginning." It all sounded funny. We passed the time with it. We were not afraid of that then and one another playing with it. We were together for it.

64

GONE NORTH IN COUNTRY BETWEEN THE RIVER AND THE ROCK

The big shiny silver bus with all its glass and steel reflecting the light came up the road and stopped and we stepped out of the early wet smell of the side of the road onto it. We went down the aisle. The cloth-covered seats were empty. There were few people. We sat at the back where we had a good view out a window. It was one of those old shiny-sided diesel buses from the 1950s with the curved tinted glass windows and the comfortable worn seats faded from years of light and smelling of smoke.

Its large black tires were smooth on the road. It felt good to be riding up high in an old comfortable seat and to see the village of Beauchastel going all easily by behind you like that. The few buildings of Beauchastel fell quickly behind us. We left the weathered yellow stone and the white stucco of the houses that were strangely colored by the wide blue-tinted window. North to Valence the tree-lined road came away from the mountain and the white-painted trunks of the trees went by close along the bus window. We went beneath the green-leaved canopy of trees with the leaves in their high passing branches patterning-out the seats of the bus with transient spots of light and dark.

Then we broke out from the trees and away from the rock and we were close to the concrete embankment of the river. We saw the big blue-black sheet of the river running south. It was wide fast-moving water. It went on heavy in current spreading to swell against the iron pilings of channel depth markers and colored buoys fixed out in the light in the water where in green and red in their black iron bases they were anchored in the river to guide the barge traffic going south to the sea. We saw barges out on the water bearing canvas-covered cargo moving imperceptibly on with the current to the sea as they hauled on low and dark in their laden hulls heading south. There were seagulls hung above them.

North to Valence the highway ran flat as the river in its asphalt across the floodplain where the road was laid on between the river and the rock and we went through obscure little villages strung out in scattered stone buildings with the stone passing close by the bus window at the edge of the road. We passed out of one of them villages along the river. The road ran back from the concrete bank to the foot of the mountain rock. The rock rose high and shadowed above us in the bus.

I asked her about the people on the bus. There were not that many people going north on that bus with us. There were few people. There were the few people who had come down from the mountain country to the river plain to go on into the city. There were really no young people. When I asked her she told me the bus ran a circular route each day no matter how many people, heading south from Valence on the flat of the river, before going up west into the higher country into the Cevennes mountains, and on through all the little villages in that part of the Ardeche, where the route ended in a mountain city in the Cevennes called Aubenas, before coming back along the steep turning descents to the east, as the mountain road fell off to the flat of the river, to head again north on the highway back to the city.

North to Valance with us there were them few old people from the high mountain villages. Some of them were come from far back up on the land of the high plateau where there was snow in winter. They did not drive. Some of them looked too old to drive. Some of them had never driven. On that bus is how they got to the city for this or that provision no longer found in the country. On that bus with them the country felt remote. In the sight of them the country felt poor. It seemed sparse and isolated country. It could not be that remote or poor a country. It was the South of France. I hadn't felt that before about the people or the place. The people were dressed in dark wool clothing and wore flat black caps and it was summer weather and I said to her, "There are hardly any people—and everyone is old."

"The country is becoming dead," she said telling of the people.

"But these people, they are living in it," I said of the land.

"Can you say that, 'The country is dead'?" she said.

"Yes, you can say it like that," I said. I thought about the country and the people. There really were no young people.

"The young people have left it," she said of the land. The land was becoming unsettled. The land was being left for good. The young people had gone off for years now from the little villages and the land to go live. The young people did not want to become old and poor. They never wanted that. The old people were dying off. The young people were going off. She told me things like that.

We rode north.
"Will they come back?"
"They have not for years."
"Will they?"

303

"I think they will not," she said.

We went north.

The few people on the bus looked out the tinted glass of the window to the scattered villages. The countryside passed. There was all that land. To have land that is the thing. But there is land and there is land. There with them people on that bus I lost the feeling for the land a little. We were young in it and it felt for a time we were far off from it.

There is country and there is country. It was really not that remote a country. It was not that poor a country. It was beautiful country. No matter the people it was beautiful country. We went on through it between the river and the rock and we soon closed on into the outskirts of the city. We rode from out of it into the lit and lively streets of the city.

65

FINDING BOOKS IN ENGLISH
AND A VERY HAPPY-BEAUTIFUL GIRL

In Valence she went to all the places that had advertised work. She talked to the people there in them. I sat awhile on a wooden bench waiting beneath the green-leaved plane trees along a bright-lit street busy with traffic. I got up and walked a boulevard. I looked into the windows of shops. I came to the shop that she'd told me about that sold maps and magazines, books and stationary, where she'd told me to wait for her to come get me. It was called the *Librairie Fournier*, and was at 54 avenue Victor Hugo. I went in the shop. There were the stacked sheaves of paper and pens, and the bound and blank notebooks, and at the end of the aisle, there was a rack of French novels, and there next to them the Classic books in English she had told me about. She had once bought her

English books there for school. I stood at the rack reading off a couple of titles I knew. I didn't buy anything to read but read a few of the pages in them books remembering what it was like to be in those English words awhile. There were these little Classic books from American writers who had once lived in France. I read a few of the pages in a couple of them books to see what they sounded like, and in going from the one book to another, I found a short strange one that struck me. I went through its pages to pass the time until her return. I heard in its sentences the sound of the first book I'd just read from, from a later writer who'd written his book after hers, with now the one stylized sound found written out in the other, and I stopped at the words in a passage that caught my eye, and read, "But when Melanctha was alone, and she was so, very often, she would sometimes come very near to making a long step on the road that leads to wisdom. Some man would learn a good deal about her in the talk, never altogether truly, for Melanctha all her life did not know how to tell a story wholly. She always, and yet not without intention, managed to leave out big pieces which make a story very different, for when it came to what had happened and what she had said and what it was that she had really done, Melanctha never could remember right...," I turned the pages randomly, "James Herbert did not fight things out now any more with his daughter. He feared her tongue, and her school learning, and the way she had of saying things that were very nasty to a brutal black man who knew nothing. And Melanctha just then hated him very badly in her suffering. And so this was the way Melanctha lived the four years of her beginning as a woman. And many things happened to Melanctha, but she knew very well that none of them had led her on to the right way, that certain way that was to lead her to world wisdom."

It was a strange book. I closed it. I put it back on the rack. I heard it in my head. It had passed the time. I went back out into a nice large light. I stood along the avenue beneath the shade of a sycamore tree and watched the cars pass and the people pass getting on their way to all their things in the city. I still heard the sound of that book. There were all these books that you could read and when you picked them up to read in them awhile they passed the time in your life and even seemed to tell you something of you yourself and to tell something of the people in your own life, at times even more than you or the people so openly told, all of that which was never to be found in a book but only in a life, and right there in front of me were all the real people going on to do all their actual things in the light and I was seeing not them but hearing the sound of that girl in the book.

  I stood there on the street. I looked into the shop window of *Librairie Fournier* thinking to go back inside to buy that book to read it. There in the shop-front glass were the display books arranged in direct view of the street to interest the passer-bys, and across their covers now arrayed brightly in the glass the city passed, the people passed with their sunhats and shopping bags. The passing traffic of cars and buses travelled on brightly-loudly in the flat depth of the reflected glass, and I found that what was of interest in the liveliness of the glass, was not now the books, but the intimated interest of the street, where all the stone depths and heights of the congregated buildings people cars buses were illuminated in the lit surface as in another interior city extended and elongated within and across the sheer plate glass sheet of the shop window, where now in looking the city was oddly and profoundly animated in the flat-glassed sheet before me, all the city travelled on in glassed solidity in distorted perspective in that fixed shop-window glass, and in the congregation, animation of that reflected and livid sight, I turned from the images in the glass to face the actual things of the city, I looked off from the deep-lit reflections of the things of the city to the things themselves. I saw all what she had once told me of French cities. It occurred to me that it was the first time I had ever seen an actual French city. All along I'd only seen what she'd said to me of all the far-off French-looking places. In real cities I'd seen replicas. I'd never really seen a French city but in imitation or in relation. In the realization, I stood there beneath the real branched-up leaves of sycamore trees, before me were the weighted and weathered block-cut stone of the rowed apartment buildings, the forged and welded ironwork of black-painted balconies, with their scrolled fleur-de-lit ironwork of the high handrails exposed to the elements, framed there by slatted green shutters swung back on their hinges, locked against high walls of the rough-textured stucco, with the unlatched French balcony doors with the tall-laced windows here and there opened out nicely to the air and light, with curtains caught in light wind, where voices would fall to the street, when heard from out of the extended space of interior rooms, apartments going up floor upon floor in great height, to the red-tiled roofs set into blued sky, not at all now any of it pictured across the flat plate-glass of the shop-window behind me, or to be seen in the spoken or the written word of a telling however well-pictured, as that is all dimensionless image however clear or apt. There it was rising in worldly solidity from the avenue all a built thing given in its measurable distance. In the entire material arrangement of it risen above the asphalt of the avenue, in its actuality, it looked like a lively and interesting place, a city richly alive in its provincial architecture, and even as you would have imagined it existing as a far-off place invented in a telling, not readily given right before you in a life as it was, and I stood there and I had never once seen a real city so. It was not at all an uninteresting place. You could have a happy interesting life in such a city. I thought that. I looked to it. I saw all what she had said about the country. The country was dead. There right before me in the city the people went on to all what they must.

They went on in some given purpose and pleasure. I walked up the street amidst the life of the place. There were all the girls young and alive in the city street. They came to pass me by. I looked to their young girls' faces. I looked in some pleasure to them girls passing me by. I looked to see her. No matter their color in them I saw the sight of her. I did not yet see her. She did not appear from out of them. I found myself back at the shop-front of the *Librairie Fournier* and I looked out to the avenue to the passing girls. The girls came. I waited for her to come. It was pleasant waiting. There a girl came from out of that lit and livid distance up the avenue. Then she was the girl coming up the street in that blue dress of hers in the light. She became the girl. It was her. I stood there as she appeared dark from beneath the sycamore trees and she was the girl and she came up beside me and I held her feeling we were in the midst of our lives on that French street thinking of what it would be like for us two to have one of those happy interesting lives in such a city and she was finished with her going off to all the places to see the people in them for the good work in the city and she looked all dark in her dress in the lively light and we went to a cafe and we had a beer together outside where we could watch it all go by that life of the city.

"How are you?" I said to her. I had her hand at the table.

"I am happy," she said and she kissed me and she never said such things so openly. She never said such things so easily. She was happy.

"So, tell me what happened. What did they say?"

"They do not tell you right away," she said. "It takes time," she said, and I felt happy she was happy. I felt how the good would happen for her. I felt all the good to come for us. She was happy she'd gone to all the places. She'd been afraid to go and she'd gone and then it was good.

I'd not felt that good in a long time. I felt everything

we two would go do in France. I felt younger with her there then than I had in a long time and I was not at all that old. We were a little young some in the lively light. You got to let yourself be a little young and happy some. I was happy she was happy. She was a very beautiful girl when she was happy and we were sitting like that out in the light when good things could happen. There are always good things to happen in such a light.

66

IT IS LIKE THAT IN THE SOUTH

She never heard from any of those places or people in Valence. Then we went to La Voulte and she went to the places and people there. It was very close by Beauchastel and not a big city at all like Valence. But it was bigger than Beauchastel which is not even a name-place on some maps of France. There in La Voulte there was a baker who her father knew and there were a couple of cafes also that would put people to work when they were busy in the summer sometimes and needed help. These were the kinds of places where you could find work close by. They were not bad places and La Voulte was not a bad place. It was a small and simple place. It was a place you could think some in if you were to live there in it in a kind of simple little life. I thought about living like that.

She went to those places in La Voulte. I walked around to them with her and waited for her outside under the trees. It felt good waiting there for her under the trees. The trees were a very green green in the light of the going afternoon. It was a soundless afternoon. There was a voice now and then. You might hear a bird. The traffic was far off. She told me when she came out of one of those places that they'd told her right then and there that they didn't need anyone at all though her father had told her that they did.

I held her under the trees.

"I cannot tell my father," she said.

She would not tell her father. She did not want to hurt him.

He wanted to hear all about it. He had his friends he said.

She told him. When she'd come back and she told her father he looked away from her and us because they had turned her away and her father he did not talk to her or to me or to her mother the rest of that day. For a few days after that her father looked a little older than he was and I felt bad for him and for her mother who knew what it was all about but who'd had some hope for her.

"I'm sorry girl," I said and I held her to me in her room.

"It is like that in the South," she said in her matter of fact way to me. I saw old sights of the South. We broke off.

Her father lay there on the couch a couple days looking out to all that rock. He stayed on his own for a couple days. I saw how he was sick. He was sick of people. He'd lost hope in people. People had worn him out.

In that time, when he looked to us in the house he would look away. The place was very quiet in that time. We did the usual everyday things around the house and no day was unlike another. I watered the garden and walked the dog some when he did not. Her mother knew what it was all about but she'd had some hope for her no matter what. The good thing about her mother and the thing that had worn her out a little too was that she'd always had hope for people no matter what.

67

WALKING UP IN THE LIGHT

I shut up the French workbook. I stood before the window of her little bedroom. The mountain rose against the sky framed by the window of that little house. I turned from the sight of it. I went from her room. I found her upstairs in the living room. She was reading a glossy magazine. The curtains were pulled shut. The room was shaded in the heat. She saw me at the door. She turned a page of the magazine. She was sitting in the darkness of the couch. I went in. I took her by the hand.

"Come on, girl," I said. "We're going."

"To where?—where are we going?" she said and she turned a page.

I had her by the hand.

"Out of here—up the mountain," I said, "Out of the house."

I took the magazine out of her hand. It fell to the coffee table on top of the glossy pictorial covers of a couple others strewn there in no good order. I took her up from where she was sunk in the cushions of that couch. We walked out of the living room. We went down the hall of the house out of the house and into the light into one of those very late afternoon lights cast richly across the roofs of houses and strongly into the ends of streets.

We went up through the old stone village of Beauchastel walking hand in hand in that widely-cast nostalgic-looking light that makes everything appear to the eye vibrant and alive in look with our shoes hitting hard on the rising stone of five hundred year old streets. The bleached and weathered stone of the houses of the village were clearly lit in that lowering light hitting across the stone stained in the accumulation of ever increasing centuries of weather and wind. There high in the street we came to very old houses in the ancient-appearing village where the higher we rose up the cobbled-stone street laid in the ascending rock of the mountainside we passed by iron-forged hitching rings and rusted up hooks stuck out of the stone of the houses in strange bent shapes of frayed iron where it looked like animals had once been hitched and hung in another time.

There was a short solitary man who stood stilled in an opened door of a stone house smoking a pipe. He stood at the top of worn smooth stairs struck with light. The steps came up steep in lit stone off the street to a darkened doorway behind him into which nothing could be seen. He looked at us with no hint of recognition. He wore dark blue trousers. He had a faded blue work-shirt. His black leather shoes were caked in red mud. We went on past him framed out in the dark door blued in form at the top of the steep-lit steps to the house. The smell of pipe smoke trailed nicely up the village street.

We came to an aged woman in an apron. She leaned out an unshuttered window where she was hanging laundry on a wire line. The wire ran to the stone house opposite hers across the street and back to her at her window where there was a pulley at each house end. She hung a shirt on the wire line watching the two of us come up the steep street. We walked up into all that stone and light and she pulled on the wire to hang her fresh-washed work shirts out over the stones. She looked in some curiosity to us in seeing these two young unknown people come up to her hand in hand walking them old steep streets of the village in the summer light cast low and long across the hard worn stones.

We walked by her and them hung shirts and her face was familiar in its look of long work. Her face was unknown to us and she turned away from us to her work. We went beneath the shirts off from her. She would never be known to us. We couldn't put a life to that face of hers or to any one of them people there in that place to know what they'd long done themselves to live but for what was left in the look of them house facades of weathered stone in what life was left in them looks of passing faces.

We went up through the steep streets to the high end of the village to the last village houses to walk up the red-graveled path climbing to the fortification rising in ruin where it was laid since the time of Charlemagne a thousand years in strewn stone in the long grass in a clearing on a foothill overlooking the village. To get up to it we went on the loose-graveled path that rose out of the last village street over the rooftops of the ended village up along high wild brush grass grown dry along the climbing path scattered with pine and oak trees across the ascending hillside where walking we smelled the dried grass and the trees in the lingering heat of the brilliant afternoon hours of light hitting hard on all the mountain rock. We walked up in the light.

We made the ruin. We stood awhile amongst the mute and strewn stone to look from the rock of the ruin and the mountain out over the whole land of the river valley. It was a big view of things. We were high up round all of the country village and what little things of life went on down in it. We were high into the first hills that made the foot of the mountain with the valley and the village laid out small below us. It was all laid out little at our feet. Standing at the stone of the ruin up on one of them long fallen stones of a watchtower, razed-appearing as when wrecked in battle but now only deeply-etched stone long eroded by exposure to the elements, we could see far out over the whole of the valley of the river as far East as the first Alps laid out little at our feet. Charlemagne himself might have once stood so and there were no approaching armies to be seen and there had long been none and there was a sense of solitude and peace in the contemporary view. There was a

313

sense of civility. It was all a trick of the eye.

    Across the great flood plain of the Rhone River far to the East the high ranges of the first French Alps were rising snow-capped against blued sky as in an idyllic scene painted on one of those old Oriental dressing screens where as a backdrop to a room an immense land of mountain and sky is laid out on little folded-out panels in a few illustrative brushstrokes, while there on the valley floor at our feet in the near foreground far before the white-capped peaks of them distant-rowed ranges of the Alps, the Rhone River ran wide dark strong in current beneath a couple big-spanning bridges, on through the vast brown plain to the South where there at the edge of the wide-running river every great man-made thing that had been built after the last war in France, lay along the river ridiculously diminished to the eye with the kilometers of the great bunker-like concrete river embankments holding off the river surge from the tracks of houses set provisional-looking along the river floodplain, with the spanning hydro-electric damn built there in steel and concrete across the Rhone River at Beauchastel, constructed in its social necessity and there in its utilitarian immensity set out to shape and to confine the water and the land, it all sat toy-like in miniature as if permanently reduced in its scope and magnitude right there at our feet.

    The view was a trick of the eye. But it made a real feeling.

    There was this real feeling of the littleness of all things in their magnitude that I found I liked. Standing up there on that ruin with her all was reframed in easy perspective for the eye and, in the sight, there was the feeling of the transience of all, of all what the people had made that had all seemed just a short time ago so large and overcoming and immovable in its permanence. It was not. All what was made to last across the land would be lost and gone for good. For some reason I was not unhappy to think it standing up there on the stone of that ruin with her. There would come again and again another time to the land. The land would last in its time no matter what the people had made in theirs. The land would last to be rediscovered and known in another name. The land would be known again new. It is all an inconceivable thing to think and to think true looking to it there in your own time.

There at our feet were the little red rooftops of Beauchastel laid down along the named and numbered roads along the Rhone River with the houses put down a time between the water of the river and the rising rock. We looked from the ruin to them village houses rowed in their pleasant red roofs along the river, and I said, "Look—there it is," and we found her parents' house there just after the railroad bridge at the end of the little circular street on the river side of the village. That is where we lived amongst its rooms and our familiar things and I felt the briefness and littleness of all and us and it seemed unreal laid out like that at our feet and I turned in the feeling to look to her and she was close beside me and I took her by the hand, and I said, "Look, the village—the house, it's all so goddamned far-off from us, and small girl—it seems hardly real."

"It is—that is what is most real to us," she said.
"But what's wrong with people?" I said to her.
"Come on," she said to me. She was to go.
"Let's look awhile," I said. I wanted to stay.
"We must get back to the house."
"Let's look awhile longer," I said.
I didn't want the view to go.
"It will soon be dark," she said.
There was the all encompassing view. It would go.
We turned from the stone of the ruin.
We left for home. The light was going. I looked back up at the rock rising behind us to the West where it was eclipsing the last of the light streaming East, cutting it off with

its set stone ridge as we descended. In the receding view, the mountain seemed to rise to the sky from another time. Then before us, the light was gone to the East. The feeling was going. And in front of us the river ran South to the sea. And appearing far off to the South, there came then into view in the descent, the rising limestone monoliths brilliantly lit at their stone tops where they were fixed against the sky, risen from the valley floor to stand in the setting sun like icebergs set out to sea, so much stone anciently-eroded from the rock of the valley floor since that unrecorded time beyond antiquity when the last ice had left the land of the continent, there the stone of them stood in our time immensely lit a minute against the sky, with the river's little tributaries flowing in amongst them to the sea. The light went. The feeling went. The all-encompassing view was lost. The place and us in it was collapsed to our contemporary time.

We came off the stone back down on home to the house and the whole view of it went and was lost in going on down through the old steep stone streets of the old French village, descending past the shuttered-up houses, to the flat of the highway, to the flood plain of the river, to the tracks of houses set along the river. The village and the houses all closed in to come round us close in the descent. We came to the street to the house. We went in through the little gate to the front of the house and into the house to her room come round us. We cannot let that house and its history come too much round us. We lay on her bed in the last of the light and dark came.

68

A KIND OF UNDECLARED WAR

The next day we came off from the high lit rock of the hills down through the village and stopped at a cafe in Beauchastel to get a drink. We came back from a walk in those high hills in summer afternoon and I wanted to sit once with her in a French café before we went back home to the house. I wanted a nice easy drink with just the two of us sitting at a table in the light. I wanted to see what it was once like to sit in a French café.

I said, "We'll get a good cold beer. We'll have a nice easy drink."

"It is better to go home—it is not an interesting place," she said.

We had not ever stopped to drink in Beauchastel. She did not want to stop there now. We stopped. We stood in front of the wood-framed blue-painted façade of the place. There was a flower box in bloom on the window sill. It was a nice pleasant-looking place. Something you might have once seen on a picture postcard of France. If you were to buy such a card for a souvenir you might get one just like that if you were to write home something good about where you'd been and what you'd seen. You'd pick it up and sit at a desk in a room far from home and take up a pen and look at it awhile the glossily-shot cropped picture of the place and then you'd turn it over and write on the back some happily briefly felt sentiments about being in such a picturesque place far off from home. I will not say that I have never done it, and we stepped in and sat down at the table just inside the front window. The smoke of cigarettes hit with light hung along the dark wood of the bar where men stood smoking and drinking dressed in those blue work uniforms you'll see Frenchmen wear all around there in

France. Everyone had their little uniform.

The men stood drinking at the bar. They were loudly drinking. They were having themselves a good time. In a far corner two old men played cards. There was a dog on the café floor at their feet. The floor was white mosaic-patterned stone laid beneath iron-legged café tables and red-backed wicker chairs. The old men smoked pipes and drank wine at the table in the back. They had a half-full carafe of dark red wine on the café table. The dog got up and turned on around and lay back down again in the same spot beneath the table looking out across the dimness of the floor into the smoke and laughter of the room. The men at the bar looked at us. The light was coming in the window across us. They'd watched us sit down up there at the front of the place at the window in the light. They'd looked. We'd sat. We sat there at a table at a nice window in a café in a French village.

The old men turned back to the cards in their hands. The blue-uniformed men looked back to the bar to the pale sick-looking girl with the black short cut hair who was working the bar. Everyone in the café had their drinks. She stood behind the bar smoking a cigarette and reading a magazine laid open on the shiny bar top. I looked at her. She had the same hair cut. This girl had the same one she'd got when she'd gone to Valence to look for the good work. The girl put down her cigarette. She came to the end of the bar. She came on through the café tables over to us at the light of the window. She was not unpleasant.

She took our order. She told the girl what we wanted.

"Two beers, please," she said very politely in her perfect French. The girl went back through the tables and behind the bar. She carefully poured two beers. I watched her pour them out. They looked good and cold in the glass. When she had them poured out, she put them on a big round tray. She brought our beer to us while the men talked loudly.

We looked out the window at the passing traffic while the men talked loudly. They were looking-talking. They were having themselves a good time. We were any two people to them. We were any two people to anyone.

I said, "What do they say? I want to know what they're saying."

"They are talking. They are drunk. They say nothing," she said.

"They are talking about us," I said.

"You must not listen," she said.

We had the last of the cigarettes. I lit them. I listened. I caught some of it. I heard how it was said. You do not need to understand all of it when you hear it. The sound of it is enough. I stood up. They sold cigarettes at the bar.

"I'm going to buy cigarettes," I said to her. "We need cigarettes," I said. I couldn't see drinking that cold beaded beer with her there in that café without cigarettes.

"No, not here," she said. "Sit down," she said. I sat down.

"What is it?—we need cigarettes," I said.

"Sit down," she said.

"I am sitting down," I said and she looked at me.

She said, "What do you want with them?" and I looked away out the window.

I said, "I want cigarettes."

"You will hurt yourself?" she said to me and she sounded angry and as if she did not understand it. She said, "Why do you want to hurt yourself?" and I wanted to say that it was not so and that I didn't want to.

"So what if I hear it—I want to hear it," I said, "I'll get the cigarettes, and come back," I said.

"No," she said to me. "You want to fight—you want to fight."

It surprised me when she said it. I did want to. I

wanted to fight but I hadn't known it, until she'd said it. Then I could not say that it was not so and that I didn't want to. She saw that in me.

"You must not—you cannot here," she said and I watched the traffic pass out the window. I sat there and felt how I wanted it. I did want it. It's true that I felt like a fight. I felt like a fight no matter I couldn't win it. I did want it, I wanted it a little badly. She was right. I didn't know it until she'd said it. She was right to say it. I felt myself in it. I felt myself in that want of it.

Then I sat and thought about the place and us in it.

The traffic went on occasionally down the highway past the café out of the village of Beauchastel on along the river north to the city. The laughing-looking came to us. I sat there stopped with her in the café. I thought about the place and the people in it. The place was a good place to live in, but I think the people there living in it, they did not understand one another too good. There was all that beautiful country called the South of France. There were all the little picturesque villages. There were them lively and interesting provincial cities. There was all the great wide Rhone River and the whole of the valley of the river and all that rock and light and land to live in and there in that little room in the French café the people they did not understand one another too good. There are these people in these places and for some given reason they are against you. They are already against you and they do not even know you. They have only looked at you and they are against you. And you have taken nothing from them. And they are afraid of you taking something from them. There are these people in a place who are against people for no good reason and they feel justified to be so. And the funny thing is that the place needs people. The place needs people and has become unsettled. There are whole villages you could resettle in the South. There are thousands of high wild acres of overgrown orchards up there all across the high country beyond where we two sat there drinking down in the dim little room of the village café where the people did not understand one another too good. There's plenty of place and the place needs people and the people are against the people. There's all that land and light and no one fight left to be fought. And I thought then, that it is like a kind of undeclared war.

I sat there, and I thought some things like that, and I looked out the window and drank the beer cold in the glass, and that beer tasted very good to drink after one of those long walks in the summer light, and if you'd thought about it nothing mattered there in that café but to enjoy the beer. The girl came to us with another beer. The workmen laughed at the bar. The two old men kept happy playing cards at their table. The dog got up and moved round in its spot under the table. This is how these days must agreeably and pleasantly go in this place. The time passed in that feeling of lingering in a café. We had nowhere to go. We had time. The light was changing. The room in the back was darkening and dimmed from the mountain shadowing the village. I looked up to the light gone across the high mountain rock. It still hit us two at the window. I saw the far off hills above the village. She saw me looking up into those hills. We had walked together all easy in afternoon up there off from the house and felt good. Then she asked me about the running up there. Sometimes in morning I would study the French and then run up to the ruin before lunch. It was a good hard run.

She said, "Did you run there to it, this morning? Was it good?" she said. "Did you do it hard?" she said.

"I did it. It was good, it was hard," I said.

"Good. You have that," she said to me.

"I have that," I said to her.

I ran hard into them hills to that ruin. It hurt to do it hard. I'd do it hard and I'd look back over the land. Her parents thought it was unusual to do it like that when you were not training for a sport. She knew what it was about. It hurt bad to do it hard. It made me feel good. In that hurt I felt myself. I thought how I felt myself most when hurt. There was no self-strangeness to it. I was most myself in it. All self-strangeness was gone in it. All other sights of time and self were gone. The hard hurt part was good. I always felt good after it. I held it as long as I could. It was a kind of sport. It was more than a sport. You had to last in it. I felt goddamned good after it. She was right about it. I had that. It was hard and it hurt and it was good. I did want it. I wanted myself in it.

I turned from the view of the high rock to her. I wanted us to take our own good time in that French café. I wanted us to enjoy the time and one another in it. She was not having such a bad time. I don't think she was even unhappy she'd stopped. I wanted her to have a good leisurely little time in a café. I turned from them thoughts.

"Do you want another?" I said then.

"You will practice your French?—with the girl?" she said.

"You want me to order it?" I did have the words to do it.

"You may order it—tell her what you want in the French."

"Do you want one?" I said to her.

"If you want—you must practice your French," she said.

"I will practice my French," I said and looked to the girl.

The girl came. I ordered it. I did it as I should. I did it in the French. She listened to me carefully doing it. I did it correctly. I told her what we would have. The girl she understood me. I spoke the French and I sat there with her in the village café and she was looking at me from across that little café table and she was not having such a bad time there in it. We would take our time in it. We said nothing for a time to one another then at the little café table. The cars passed the window. The light was going.

The laughing came to us. I looked to it. She looked to me. She did not look to the laughing. She said to me, "Be happy."

"I am happy," I said.
"We must be happy," she said.
"We are," I said, "We are."
"Or the rest is nothing," she said, "You know that."
"This is everything," I said. "I know that."

We looked out the front window of the café into the street. We had our beer in the café looking easily into the street. Then there was the good feeling of simply sitting with one another. The good feeling came. It was simply the feeling of being there with one another at that café window. I did not feel lonely for us. She didn't look lonely. I wanted to keep all that good feeling as it had come on. I felt we were all right. We were all right. The people in the café looked and looked away. We looked. We looked away. We looked at one another. I felt close to her and that it was good. Once sitting there I wished someone had been there with us to see it all and to know that it was good.

69

IN A FRENCH CAFÉ

The beer was cold in the glass. The cigarettes were finished. We were having the last beer. I could not see drinking that beer in that beaded glass in that French café without the cigarettes. The laughter came loudly to us from the bar. I held her hand across the café tabletop. I let go her hand. I got up and I said, "Let me practice my French, at the bar, I'll practice my French—if I'm ever going to be a good Frenchman, I need to speak French," I said to her. "I'll get the cigarettes—we'll smoke walking home along the river."

"You will never be a good Frenchman," she said to me in some play. I felt a little pleasantly drunk. She let me go. She watched me go. I got up now to do nothing but get the cigarettes. We were to have the last drink and smoke and go. The rest was finished in me. I felt it. It had gone. We were to finish our nice easy drink in a French café. We were to walk back home along the river. It was a pleasant walk along the river. I walked on through a couple café tables, up to the bar to order the cigarettes. I saw us walking home along the river smoking. It was a pleasant way back home. There were the very green trees along the river. There was the wide dark water stretched to the far shore. We would walk it easy. I got up to the bar in the loud light. There were hunting pictures hung above the bar on the smoke-coated wall in dark wood frames. I ordered the cigarettes. I spoke it like I should to the pale sick-looking girl.

"*Un paquet de cigarettes—si'l vous plait—Styvesant*," I said that to her naming the cigarettes and she reached to get them and they were all looking-laughing. It was all loud and close. There was the dim drunk-talking up at the bar. The light from the window was gone. The street outside was becoming shadowed. She sat at the window looking out to the grayed shadowed light come across the village stone. She looked lonely like that. The loudest biggest one of them stood close in the din and dimness. The girl at the bar handed me the cigarettes. I reached for the cigarettes. The large loud one leaned into me a little against my outstretched arm with his drink in hand and his eyes all watery bright. He was having a good time. They were all having a good time. I saw him how he was having a good time. I took the cigarettes from her. I was beside him. I stood beside him. He looked to where she sat dark at the window. The last shadowed light was hitting across her arms black in the little light. She was a dark girl at a window in little light. Saying it I remember seeing it. He'd looked to her. It was what he'd said when he'd leaned against my arm in the look when I was still beside him taking the cigarettes from the girl. I remember when he'd said it she'd turned from where she sat looking out the window to the village street to look to him. She looked to him. He was loud. He wanted to be heard. She'd heard him. He wanted to be heard and was:

"So, that's the daughter of that *Pied-Noir*. I guess his feet really were black after all," he said to no one in particular he said to the whole of the room leaning against my arm with his bright watery look looking right at me as he hit one of them on the back and the laughter got loud and he raised his drink and I remember I swung hard on him the loudest biggest one of them lifting the beer glass to his mouth knocking him right straight to the wooden floor before he knew what it was coming to him. He didn't see any of it. He thought he'd seen something of her. He'd seen nothing of her. It was some thing in me I couldn't stop. I didn't want to stop it. I didn't. And in his getting it like that not knowing how it was coming to him I saw how he was all surprised by it as if he'd been at last waked badly from some happy sleep to the dim light of that loud crowded room and to us two in it and the men they looked round themselves and the laughing was stopped and the drinking stopped and the time was stopped and then in that quieted stillness there was a wild loudness in the place and I was down on him hard with my fists in his face in the wet stink of blood and beer with the glass cutting us two up in our faces and hands strewn across the stink and grit of the mosaic-patterned floor. It was wet everywhere from blood and beer. I think I tried to kill him. I wanted to kill him. They took me from him. The rest of them when they got their hands on me to stop me I didn't stop. I lasted awhile. In the stink of blood and beer I heard her in the loudness. I was sorry for it then. I was sorry for all of it. I remembered hearing her in it off in the room. Then I gave into it beat and bloodied until it was finished and I hated myself for it but I had wanted it. I'd wanted it. It had not felt bad but good. I remembered feeling it for days. I held it as long as I could. It is more than a kind of sport.

    They threw me out to the village street. There I lay. The mountain stood against the sky. I wanted to be up on it. We had had our easy little walk up there all happy in the high hills young a time in the feeling of all before us yet to be in a life. We shouldn't have stopped. She'd been right about things all along. I've been wrong a long time.

    The hurt was bad. I lay there in it. I felt myself in it. She got me up from it. She helped me on to home. In the village street, the people looked. We went on along the houses, one hung on the other as though two drunks looking to the stones descending before us. We came out from the last village street into lowering light to the flat of the river. We walked the floodplain home along the river. She washed me up some a little in the river. She tried to clean me up a little before getting home to the house. They'd beat me badly. I was hurt bad. I didn't feel that bad. I walked on with her badly beat. I held myself into her in nicely falling light looking to the river. The water went south to the sea. The gulls hung over it. The trees were very green in the going light. I smelled the water. It was wide to the far shore. I saw the place clearly. The dog had got up and moved round in its spot. I do not think the old men ever stopped playing cards.

70

HURT GOOD

She stayed away from me in bed. She would not talk to me in the night. I lay awake hurt in the night. The old things were in me. They played out in me richly bleak sights lit in the shuttered dark. There were the unsettled sights. I was badly waked in morning sick in half-sleep. I was wakened sickened. She got up from me. She put on her loose white robe. She opened the shutters to see me good. She folded back the brown-painted metal panels in the loud clacking noise of metal. The light came cast across me. The light hurt. The looking hurt. The big window was opened to the morning smell of the garden come in to the room. She stood white in her robe framed by the big window, and I said, "Come here, girl," and she didn't.

"I was wrong," I said. I saw her at the window like that. She looked lonely. I wanted her to know I was sorry. In the un-shuttered light she saw me good for the first time. She came to the bed, and she said a little hard, "You are hurt bad," and she was not happy. She stood at the bedside. I lay there on it.

"It's not that bad—it looks worse than it is," I said. "I feel good, not bad," I said. "I'm hurt good," I said to her. And it really wasn't that bad. I'd seen what was bad. I'd seen people hurt bad.

"Don't talk like that about it, to me," she said sounding hard. And she shut me up. I shut up about it.

She went upstairs to get some ice. I was a sight not to be seen like that she said. She didn't want her parents to see me beat bad like that. She came back with the ice in a towel. She gave it to me. I held it against my face. She said nothing and left. She was not happy with me. And it is not good to go on like that. I didn't want to go on with her like that. I never wanted any of that with her.

I didn't go up to eat lunch. I wasn't hungry. My teeth hurt. It was hard to move my jaw and I remembered then what that all felt like. It is strange how you can forget it once healed and feel as though you'd never felt it. She came down and said, "They asked about you."

No one ever missed a meal round there even if they were sick.

"I'm really fine," I said. "What did you say to them?" I said.

"I told them you were resting."

"They are not angry with me—are they angry with me?" I said and I was worried about it because I didn't want anything bad like that between us.

"No—it's not that," she said to correct me and she was not happy with me and she said, "They have already heard of what has happened," she said. "It is the village news. That fighting is nothing to them," she said. "They've seen neighbors hung in houses. They want to know if you need a doctor."

I said, "Come and sit with me, girl."

She came and she sat on the side of the bed. I lay my hand on her arm. I lay easy on the bed with her quiet beside me. I lay there on the bed with her in a comfortable easy quiet. That quieted stillness with her is a kind of peace. You want to leave yourself in peace with another in a life. You'd think that you could leave yourself once in peace in a life. But even after such fighting, for no good reason one cannot leave one's own self in peace. There is this disposition to war lingering on in one, and one contends in some continuous battle, and in time you'll feel yourself most in it, and you are most against yourself in it, you are not fighting anyone in it, you are fighting yourself. I wanted to feel what it was like to be left once and for all like that with her in some simple peace, and I couldn't, I hadn't. One must be left alone after all in peace and it seems one cannot be. It is hard to be. One must be. I know that.

"I was wrong," I said to her. "There is something in me," I said to her.

"Is it like before—is it bad like before?" she said and she wanted to help me. She had this care for me. She was unhappy with me and she wanted to help me and she had all this care in her for me and I wanted to let her care for me and for her to be happy in it for she felt a good for herself in her doing it and I felt I might.

"It is something bad in me," I said. "And I am afraid of it."

"But is it like before?" she said not now sounding hard.

I did not answer her. I did not know. I did not want it to be. I lay there badly hurt with her in want of lasting peace. I lay there a time wanting lasting peace.

71

THERE IS A CERTAIN PEACE

In afternoon in summer light come strong to the window of her room across us on the bed, we could smell the flowers of the garden in the heat. I had my head resting up on her pillow, leaned up against the bedroom wall. I lay against her pillow. I had my shirt and shorts on that I had slept in. She had the ice on me. She was beside me on the bed sheet with her hand to my forehead with the ice. I had slept some in afternoon. It wasn't a bad way to lay waked with her bent to me like that in the light. I felt some comfort in it. Her shirt was wet in the water come from the ice in the heat. Everything was wet. She wanted me to take off my shirt. It was wet. She wanted to look. I myself had not looked.

"Take your shirt off," she said to me. "You're hot," she

said in the touch.

"It hurts to move," I said. I didn't want her to take it off me.

"I must wash your cuts," she said. I didn't want her to wash me.

"I can't take it off," I said. It hurt to move to do it where I lay.

"Sit up," she said to me.

I sat up as I could. I sat up into her. Then she had me off the pillow case held close to her. I felt her wet in her shirt. I could smell her in the heat leaned into her. She took the shirt and she lifted the shirt up easy on me. The cloth came up across the skin. She took the shirt up across the cuts. She took it right up off my arms and head. She didn't want to hurt me. She tried not to hurt me. It hurt like hell.

She had the shirt off. She looked at the colored and cut up places.

"Goddamnit, girl," I said when she'd done it like that and I lay back with it come off and hurting like hell and laughed at how it hurt and felt naked there in front of her hurt like that but she'd seen it all before.

"Be quiet," she said all matter of fact in her way and she looked at me all uncovered to her and hurt. She looked at me uncovered and cut. She looked at me a little hard. She looked at me good and hard. She looked at them healed-up holes seeing what in them I do not exactly know. I didn't want to know. She looked at my cut and colored up face. She saw all what was new there, and she said, "Why do you want to hurt yourself?" she said to me. "You hurt yourself too badly," she said.

"I don't want to," I said.

"You do."

"I just did what's right. That's all."

"Don't think that you have done anything right," she

said.

"No—I have done nothing good," I said. "You're right."

"You cannot change these people," she said. "They are French. They are against my mother and father. It is who they are."

"But they're wrong about people," I said.

"They feel justified," she said.

"Can't they see what's wrong?"

"We are outsiders, foreigners to them."

"What is it to them?"

"They will be even against you," she said.

"But this is home—their house."

"It is a house."

"They never tried to leave it?"

"To go where?" she said.

She looked at me all cut and colored-up.

She had the wet cloth. The ice was gone. She washed me good. It hurt. She did it in some care. She did it in real care. She washed me and the bloodied blackened hurting places caring for me and them new wounds. The cloth was wet and reddened. She looked at it. Then she was a girl gone far off beside me seeing other places right there washing me like that hurt and hurting beneath her hand. I saw it in her look. Then she stood from the side of the bed. She looked to me as in some appraisal. Everything was black and blue. She held the reddened-dirtied cloth in her hand. She looked along me from my face to the old holes that went through clean. She had never looked at them that long in the light. I would not let her. I wouldn't let her look like that. I felt naked. I didn't want her to think it was so bad. Nothing was that bad. It was very late afternoon. The weather was good. The rose wallpaper was lit up all a golden red. Everywhere the people were thinking of supper. It was that time of day when all the things of the day

331

are finished but the day is not yet done. There is a large quiet in a place. There is some certain peace come between the things done and the things to do. It is in the look of things in the angle of the light. That is enough to feel it. I felt it.

She stopped her studied looking to me. She went to the sink and she rinsed out the dirtied-up cloth. She ran it clean in the water. She ran it in the water cold. She sat on the bed sheet bent over me wet in her shirt. She touched me. I smelled her touching me. She laid the cold cleaned cloth down against my forehead. She lay it down on my eyes. She put it on down my cheekbones. She held the wet cloth in her hand touching me in her simple care lightly about the face where the skin was cut and colored up.

"You have a fever," she said and she went on down my side along my legs with her hand and felt me and I was hot to the touch and she brought her hand back to my cheek, and she said, "It is an infection. You will see the doctor," she said.

"I'm all right," I said. "I don't feel that bad." I had felt bad.

"Do you want to be sick? You will be sick," she said and she had her one hand to my face, her other to the blackened and blued places where she felt me and she said I was hot.

"I'm really all right. It is nothing. It will pass," I said. "There is nothing to be done for it anyway," I said. I said something true like that to her. "Just sit beside me," I said. "Sit with me. That's all I need for doctoring," and her arm was there along mine and I said, "See we are almost the same," I said and played with it, I tried to play with it.

"No—we are never the same," she said, and she was not happy with me for playing with it, and for not seeing the doctor. I was sick. To her I was sick. She didn't want to play with it like that. She was serious about it.

She sat beside me and she was far off then.

"This will pass," I said to her, "Let it pass."

She said nothing. I went on. I was sorry for it. I was goddamned sorry for it all. She let me talk.

"It is good," I said to her, "Something bad has gone out of me—I *am* better," and in saying it, I felt it true, I felt it more than I'd ever felt it, that something bad had gone out of me. I felt something of the bad was gone out of me for good.

She said nothing. She let me go on.

"I feel good," I said to her and I was not trying to convince her of anything I was just telling her how I truly felt and it is hard for others to know that you can at last feel good in some real true way when you do not look it and are badly beaten and sickened.

"It is not bad like before, there *is* something gone out of me," I said to her. "It is good gone—I have gotten something out of me, girl," I said feeling the conviction of it in saying it true.

She let me talk. She'd told me to talk all along.

"There's something gone for good—gone from me in the fighting, and I am the happier for it," I said, so to make her herself happy again about it all no matter how badly I looked laid out there like that. I wanted her to know it true. That something bad was gone out of me and that now it wasn't like before and could not be. She must know that. That she'd helped me all along and that now it was good and I'd never said such things so openly to her, and I said to her, "You have helped me, girl, you have helped me, for good," I said to her, "You have helped me as no one can, only you can, you have, and no one can but you, no one ever will."

She'd let me talk. She'd wanted to hear it. I was tired in it.

"Be quiet now," she said and I stayed quiet and she looked at me in another way. She looked at me a little in her old loving way. She was the only one who could help me and had and in her hearing that that something bad had gone out of

333

me in her hearing me talk to her true about it in my confronting it the feeling of it she looked at me in another way a little in her old loving way and I saw all before us in that loving look of hers.

"Tell me that you are happy," I said, sorry for it all.

"I am happy," she said. "We must be happy," she said.

But she stayed far off in her look. She had a little of her old loving look back but she stayed far off in it seeing something now yet in her seeing me laid before her badly beat. Then I thought it is not enough to be happy. It is never enough to be happy. What a thought that is when it comes on you and she took the wet-cleaned cloth to the cut and blackened places to finish her washing me gone off in her touch of them wounds from the room to another place with me beaten and bloodied before her in that bed of hers in France.

She stopped with the wet-reddened dirtied-up cloth to look to it in her hand with her hand kept to me, and she said to me laid like that before her, "I had a mother and a father," she said, "I was once a girl called *Tintifawin*," she said speaking her own name, and in her saying the name, she said, "The French killed them in that war," she said, "They killed that girl, too."

She said, "You must not fight them," she said, "You cannot fight them," she said, "John, you will not fight them," she said, "We must be at peace, we must seek peace, you must," she said, "Or there is nothing," she said.

She said nothing more. I asked her nothing of it what she had said. I only wanted the peace of that place. It is all a hard thing to hear. I was not strong enough to hear it beat before her. It is a hard thing to hear in knowing all what you have done from which peace cannot come.

"Come here, girl," I said to her. Then there was only that.

I brought her close. She came down to me. She was far away from me. I let her stay far away from me. We stayed gone off on one another. We stayed kept one to the other far off from one another. I was hard against the whole of her. She lay herself down on me with her black against mine and we slept awhile in the light slanting low and long into the room. We rested some like that. There like that we felt some peace and waked come alive in the dark. Then there was that and we were most ourselves lost in it in the dark.

72

THE FIGHTING IS FINISHED

Her parents they were not that unhappy about it all. They saw me. They took a good look at me. They looked at me a little too long in the light. They looked at me differently and she said, "They look a little proud of you," she said and I didn't see it. But she knew and I did not. She knew them and how they were happy. Then she said to me of her parents, "When they first met you, they were happy and a little proud." She said that to me. She said when they'd looked to me and seen me, her mother and her father they'd been happy, and they were happy now she said. "They were happy you were light," she said. "They did not want you dark," she said. "They did not want you like me," she said and she didn't sound hurt or hard about it.

"Did they say that to you?" I said and they did not say that to her.

"They would never say that," she said. They never said that.

"How did they think I should look?" I said to her.

"They did not know," she said. "I did not tell them." She'd told them nothing about me she said. "I was hard on them that way," she said. Then they were happy. And I heard how she felt a little bad about it.

And now they did everything to ask how I was when they'd seen me beat like that and they asked if I were sure that I didn't need to see a doctor when they saw me for the first time all cut and colored-up in the face once it had blossomed up and come on out me like a kind of bad flower. And they knew what it was all about. And they knew a very good doctor they said. And I told her to tell them that I never went to see doctors.

"I do not see doctors," I said. "I'm finished with doctors." And I told them that this was a very little thing no one would ever see a doctor about. I do not know what she told them. But they understood it. They'd seen it. They understood all of it. She did not like them understanding it too much. She was proud of nothing, and in morning while she lay in sleep I got up quiet and I looked in the mirror in the shuttered light awhile and I saw how I looked, I saw what I looked like to the two of them and her and I saw it was not at all a very pretty sight. I hadn't looked that closely at myself. I saw for the first time how she felt about it. The funny thing was that my face had gotten all dark and yellowed in the places where there was not ever that kind of color. Beneath the eyes and about the bone of the jaw it was bad. I myself would not have wanted to see it, such color on someone I knew let alone loved. It was opened up and spread all about the face. I looked up to it in the morning light of her room. I did not shave that morning or the next. I tried. I picked up the razor. Shaving hurt the face. I tried to brush my teeth. The teeth hurt. You would not think that that is a very funny thing but I began to laugh, and she was not now in the room, she was just gone upstairs in morning, and I was left un-quieted in it alone, and it was funny, when I felt how the teeth they even hurt. I thought it was a very funny thing that even your teeth could hurt, and it was not at all that funny, and I stopped and took a good last look. I took a good look for once not just a passing look. And I saw how they saw me hurt and beat with the blackened and blued parts getting all yellowed-up, and there was something left to see of what it all was, and I was laughing, but in looking bad felt good. I felt good seeing how badly I looked and did not feel that bad. Then it was all of it very funny and I was laughing like hell and I could not stop it and I did not want to. It was a joke on myself. I hung my head on the sink. I felt the cold porcelain of the sink hard against my head. That's how they saw me beat and bloodied and all along I had felt good looking bad. What's even more funny, in feeling bad I felt better. You see how it is. They didn't see that part. She saw how it was, and when she came back downstairs to the door to the bedroom to get me for lunch, she saw me badly beat and laughing all alive like that, and in her seeing me hung up at the sink I saw she was afraid and she went and sat unsettled without me on the bedside and she said to me, "What is it, John?" and I know you cannot go on like that too long and have another love you and so I told her I was done with it and I stopped it and lifted my head and came back to the bed and lay down in it beat and blackened beside her.

"I'm finished fighting," I said. "I will behave myself," I said. "There's no one fight left to be fought," I said and that day it went away in me little by little and then it was as if it had never been and the one day it was gone and done and you could see none of it between us. It was gone from the face and I took a good shave and looked all young. She took a good look at me. She was close beside me. I looked all well-behaved. She looked not at all unhappy. We looked as we'd always looked to one another. We looked dark and we looked light and we never stopped anywhere anymore in Beauchastel. We were to get out of Beauchastel. We were done with Beauchastel. We took our long walks up into the mountain light above the little village where we were happy a time gone off from the house with all before us young in a life. We looked back down on it all laid out small. There were the red roofs of the village houses laid below the rock along the river. It was all too small.

We stood awhile up at the ruin gone off from house and home. We were beginning. We wanted to be a little home. There comes a time you've got to go off for good to get home. To be a little home you got to go for good. One day you've got to go for good if you want to be a little home.

73

ON A LITTLE HOLIDAY

There was no place good to go and no money to get there and her parents they didn't want her to go off anywhere for good. But one day after that fight they told her that we should go somewhere awhile. They said it would be good for us to go off from the house a time. In them days after that fight they said to her that they were young once too and that it is hard when you're young and when you're beginning to know one another and that they knew what two young people should do when they were yet beginning and that they should be alone together awhile. I don't know if it was really about that fight or about us but her parents they sent us off on a little holiday to camp and to swim along one of them famous and beautiful rivers in the South. Her father had a big green canvas tent and one morning after that fight he took it out of the garage. We rolled it out and cleaned it up in the light. We let it air in the sunlight a day or two. No one had used it in years. I still remember the smell of it. We put it in the old two-door red Peugeot they had with the rest of our camping equipment and the sleeping bags. They hardly drove the car anymore and they told us to take it. We went off camping like two young people on a European vacation.

We drove south. We drove in coming dark through the Rhone Valley to the south of the Gorges de l'Ardèche and turned north to go up a mountain. We went up a mountainside in rain. We drove in summer rain up a dark mountain rising in rock in the night and followed the treed edge of its ascending road where we came to a high turn in the road and crested the rise and the road descended down the other side in the dark. We went down in the dark. We came from off the foot of the mountain to the edge of the river and went along the road where it dropped straight off to the river gorge. We couldn't see the bed of the river in it. From there the road went into the village of Vallon Pont d'Arc.

In the night in coming off the mountain road in the rain we couldn't hardly see anything of what the land would look like in the day. We couldn't hardly see a damn thing in the bad weather beyond the headlights let alone the road or the rock in the dark. We saw nothing in the night. We saw the white-painted line of the edge of the road at the river gorge. The headlights hit along the pilings of the stone guardrail. We saw the blackness beyond it where the ancient openness of the gorge fell absently off beyond the headlights to the river. It was raining.

It was bad weather. We kept on and the road came away from the canyon and flattened. In a couple kilometers we came to a white sign with black lettering that said *Vallon Pont d'Arc*. We followed the signs and came into the village of Vallon Pont d'Arc along a little road lined with trees their trunks painted white to keep the cars from hitting them in dark with the rain hitting the windshield hard and we found the campground entrance along the river. There was a guard out front standing in the rain, stopping people from going into the campground and he wore a kind of blue uniform and a greatcoat. He was an Arab watchman.

"He isn't French?" I said to her.

"No he's an Arab," she said. "There are many men in such work in the south."

"It's strange," I said. "We're just camping."

"It's France. It is usual in France," she said.

"To guard a campground?" I said.

"He must check to see that you have a place," she said. "Then they do not let you in until morning, if you come too late." And then she told me that people would just show up in dark and leave before light without paying if there were no guard.

The whole place was shut down in the bad weather. She talked to the guard. She told him that we had a place and that we'd paid. I heard them speaking in a strange language. She gave him the paper to prove that we'd paid. He went into a little shack. He checked the paperwork. He came out. She got a piece of paper from him and a number for a site. He lifted the gate to the campground road. He let us pass and drive on in. The rain was dripping off the hood of his greatcoat. We drove the car in on the little gravel campground roads and counted off the numbers of the sites and we came to our campsite. We pulled up on the site and got out of the car and left the headlights on and heard the river in the night on the other side of a line of trees. The water was running hard across the rocks through the gorge. The smell of wet grass was everywhere. We rolled out the canvas tent lit up by the headlights. We hammered the steel tent stakes into the grassy wet ground. We stood the metal poles up and lifted the tent and the canvas came taut and the rainwater poured off and hit the ground. The thing was up. I hung a flashlight from a center hook in it. Our cots and our sleeping bags and our clothes fit into it without any problem and we stood inside it with everything damp and looked to it full of our things in the lit dark and I said, "Think of it, how it would be to go off, live out on the land," I said to her. "It's too bad, you can't go live anymore out on the land somewhere, not anywhere," I said to her, and I took up a towel from the end of a cot to dry my hair and I dried my hair a little.

"We can't," she said. "No one can."

"It's too bad," I said and I threw her the towel for her hair.

I got a warm beer from the metal cooler where we'd kept our sandwiches and water stored for the road. It was warm beer now but you didn't care that it wasn't cold. It was wet. It tasted very good when you didn't have one until late in the night all tired out like that after being packed up and moved out to where you'd got to get set up in a place out in some unknown country and I sat my beer bottle down on the green metal top of the cooler. She dried her short wet hair with the towel and our rain jackets were wet and we laid them out in the light coming across the ends of the cots. The shadows from the hung light were cast nicely across the canvas floor and our feet. The canvas of the tent hung above our faces darkened in the light. We sat there on cots like that arrived in the low light in the tent with all our things laid out around us with it raining like hell outside saying how we could never be people now who'd go off and live out on the land. But we couldn't say where we'd go live.

I drank the beer. She had one. We drank our beer and we listened to the rain hitting down on the tent as if two people, characters, in a scene from an old black and white movie that you've seen as a kid where late at night they'll get caught out in the rain in some dark country broken down and stopped along a unknown road in the night before coming on into the low lit room of a house to seek shelter, to have a drink and to dry off with their coats taken off and hung up on a hook by a mantle before a fire, and where in that kind of scene, as the main characters, they'd then be about to say something to one another that they'd might not ever have said before, and just as they were about to, then some minor character, someone from off-screen would come back into the room to break this kind of pregnant silence held in the scene, to stop them from speaking some central truth, to keep the film going on in a kind of deferred and intimated interest, and I think that it was just the rain and the lateness that gave me that kind of feeling of one of them scenes from a movie where something central is left off from and remains unspoken between two people who cannot get close now to something essential in one another no matter it is the moment because the day has been long and it is late and you only want the peace of the place, and so then there in that tent just as if I myself had turned from the promise of such a scene, and were now playing my own minor character, as though to deliver a line, I broke the quiet, but I said not one essential thing about what we'd gone off to talk about, about where we were now to go, what we were to do now in a life, I only joked about the beer to her. I said, "It's warm and wet, but it's good for you that way," I said, saying nothing important, and I drank half the warm bottle down I had in hand, and then I got another bottle out of the metal cooler, and closed its lid, and sat back down and she said, playing, perpetuating the continuity of such rhetorical aversion, "You shouldn't ever have it too cold," drinking hers slowly.

"Or drink it too fast—if it's too cold."

"When it is warm," she said, "You cannot get enough of it."

"I'll take it wet and warm," I said.

"When it's wet, I think you cannot get enough of it," she said.

She played with the joke of it. She had never drunk like that out in a tent. I had drunk a lot out in tents.

"As long as you can have it, it is enough," I said.

"And you will always want to have it?" she said.

"Yes," I said to her. "I always will."

"You will always want it—*tu es sur*?" she said to me.

"Always, girl," I said.

"You'll want it wet and warm?" she said. "You'll always want it wet and warm?"

"Yes, always," I said and that's how she was with me before we went to sleep. We said the important things playing. We were young. We were tired out. We went to sleep before we wanted. I felt I could've stayed awake all night playing, saying nothing. I never wanted to sleep again to wake to what must be done. I wanted to make the night last. I wanted to make that feeling of being young there with her last. I didn't want to wake up at the end of things. There are nights you could stay awake forever. I was strangely awakened and present to myself as I'd rarely been. I wondered how it would be if you could stay awake forever. It is a thing to think. You'll think there are yet these nights to come all like that night. And you get a few of those first nights. You don't ever really know when they come. You cannot know it. That is what makes them. They don't have to come at the beginning of things. You don't want them to end. They end.

74

A KID MADE ALIVE BY STORMS

I lay there and listened to the rain hitting down lightly on the tent while she slept and I smelled the wet canvas above us and the smell of the tent made me remember things I'd not remembered in a long time. I'd camped a lot as a kid. I remembered I'd camped a lot as a kid and liked it and I had not forgotten about those things, I'd just not thought about them lately when they were once and for all finished and they meant something else to you than they were. I lay there and I hadn't known I'd remembered being a kid so much. I lay there in the smell of that canvas seeing America, that childhood, my childhood, how it felt before it'd ended, as if it hadn't all ended. It had ended. It'd long ended. But we were kids. It's hard to think we were kids once.

The rain hit hard. I looked up into the tent. I'd camped up north along a great lake in a tent in a big old silver beech tree forest. I'd never told her that. It is all gone now. You can never get there now. I think I was born up there. You can almost get there in something like the smell of a tent. It is all kept in that. I looked over to her. There is always this going from home. I did not mind it. I grew up in it. That is all another life. The rain hit hard there in France. I remembered the big thunderstorms along the lake that could scare the hell out of you when you were a kid. There'd been big storms, not only hard rain. But they made you alive. I lay there beside her and I felt certain that you couldn't ever be that alive in good weather when everything was too bright in long stretches of blank light. I'd been made alive by storms when I was young. I remembered that, that storms made me most alive. I began to remember other things there in the rain in the night camping in that tent. The storms, they were the real things that had made you bigger than you would've been without them, and in only being kept too close to home safe and sound in some kind of big nice beautiful good weather. I remembered that, that in your being in them you became bigger than yourself. I lay there and it seemed that I'd grown up going off to camp out along a lake and to fall asleep in tents late in night beneath wildly blown trees in summertime storm and that it'd been an ordinary time, it'd seemed an ordinary time then, like this, but there was nothing ordinary about it, being gone off home from the house, gone always off again to an unfamiliar place and not to home and that was a nice adventure. Nothing was ordinary. Nothing had ever been so ordinary. None of it is ordinary.

It is ended. The low shapes of our scattered clothing

lay strewn about the tent. There was the outline of her body laid beneath the bag. In seeing those things in dark in the tent I saw my own old sights. I saw tents in summer, tents stacked with sandbags. I heard shouting in the night. There was far rifle fire. There are tents and there are tents. I was to be happy with her. She must be happy. I was in her. I lay and listened in the night to the rain hitting down lightly and nicely on the canvas above us. I looked to her, and she slept. She was right to sleep. She wouldn't think of what she didn't want to think of when she must sleep. She knew better than I to sleep. We must all sleep. I closed my eyes to sleep. Outside the rain went on lightly. The weather would be very good when it was good and not that bad when it was bad. She'd said that, and I was sure of it. I felt at home with her. I do not think I ever felt that way. I never felt that way. It all felt happily familiar and strangely new. I fell asleep feeling again possibility in the things to come. It's a feeling you're sometimes lucky enough to feel late at night when you're young enough and far off from things. We were far off from things and yet young enough. We were yet young enough.

75

A QUESTION OF PLACE

It'd rained hard in the night but in morning everything was already becoming light and dry. This was the country of sun and rock. Already the light had opened up the land. In the distance were low hills purple on top from the way the light hit the high pine. There were red-roofed and white-walled houses scattered up in the hills. Sometimes there was white smoke from the chimney of a far house. There were clouds making acres of dark and light patches moving across the tree and hill tops. I looked back from that to her, to where she was sitting in a lounge chair out on the grass beside the tent wearing a big straw sun hat. She was eating her lunch and reading a magazine in the sun. I was holding my plate in hand, to eat my lunch looking around, and the campground was a bright, hot, crowded place. The whole place was filled with colorful tents and caravans, and from site to site, there were folding tables and chairs set up on matted green and brown grass. Some of the camp sites had a tree, here or there, and we had some shade from a big sycamore tree next door to us. There were rope clotheslines hung with swimming suits and bright beach towels strung across the open stretches of dry dead grass between the trees. The whole place was hot and bright and crowded, but you didn't feel that it was badly crowded. There were blue and red striped awnings cranked out off the sides of silver caravans into the strong light of midday, with people sitting in lawn chairs under them taking it easy eating their lunch in the nylon-colored shade. I looked away from the colorful assortment of chairs and tables spread out before trailers and tents, finishing my lunch looking up to the high hills with the pine.

"We should get up in those hills—take a walk," I said to her. She was eating her lunch reading her magazine. On the cover of it was posed some well-known celebrity couple, incognito in sunglasses, and I didn't know who they were, and she looked up from that magazine she was reading.

"We can see how the land is laid out," I said looking to the high ground of that treed and rocky land rising round us. There were thickets of evergreen and brush grown out from rock. In the foreground there were vineyards rowed to the low foot of hills. I'd never seen it. I didn't know it. I looked to it in a kind of curious reconnaissance.

"Eat your lunch," she said to me. She had put it out for me on one of those regular kitchen plates her mother had made us take that she sat on the metal folding table that her father had made us take where she had laid out the food. It all felt in a way very proper and domestic. "*Mange,*" she said. She said it in the French. She was teaching me to say the simple easy things. She looked down again to read her magazine and eat.

"I am eating—I want to see where we are," I said to her. "Do you know where we are, girl?" I said.

"Do you think you are being funny?" she said.

"Tell me where we are," I said looking back to the campground closed round us. In the look of the tents and trees and lawn chairs and nylon awnings with the bright-colored beach towels strung out on lines you couldn't really tell. In the casual look we might've even been somewhere in North America if you didn't listen to the language or make further explorations of the land laid round the place.

She didn't look up from her magazine. She said, "We are here, John." She said to me, "We are here," and she read. She turned a page. She was a practical beautiful girl when she said such true things. She said such true things.

"You're right," I said. "I've not ever known things as well as you, you know that," I said. I looked to the hills. Them high hills would tell you where you were.

"Eat, John," she said. "Then we will go to the river," she said and I sat down at the table there in that campground then and I ate the rest of my lunch as she said I should and I could smell the cooked meat and campfires of noon in the campground that time of the day when the people were finishing up their lunches and going off to the river where they'd lie out in the light and wade off in the water to cool off. The smell of campfires and cooked meat hung in the air and I ate what she'd cooked me. I sat at the table. She looked at her magazine and I looked back to the dry rocky-colored country rising up in that place in France called Vallon Pont d'Arc. All round us the mixture of high pine and lightly-colored brush on the hills of limestone made the hills look purpled in the heat. Then I looked off from the rising hills toward the flat of the river. I couldn't see the river. There was a high line of tree tops at the edge of the campground along the river. All you could see were the tents and caravans with the tree tops hung tall over them and I was done with the plate and the campers round us had closed up their little camp stoves and were washing their dishes in plastic washtubs and drying their plates and cups with those yellow and blue cotton dishtowels. The people were taking their beach towels off clotheslines to go to the river. They were very well prepared and practical campers and it was all a very orderly and efficient process this kind of camping. It was a little like being at home in a house. There was a real sense of domesticity. It's not the way I'd done it as a kid and the lunch was done and we washed the dishes and dried the plates and silverware like everyone else and we hung out our dishtowels on the line and then we each took a beach towel to go to the river. She'd changed into a swimsuit. I had my cut-off shorts and tee shirt on. We came out of the tent, and I said, "Can we buy ice for the beer—put it in the cooler. We'll have a nice cold beer when we come back," and she said, "You do not buy ice in France, John," and I thought she was joking with me. She stood there in her swimsuit looking at me, and I said, "But you can buy it, right?" I said. Her towel was hung over her shoulder, and she was ready to get to the river.

"In France, you eat your lunch when it is cooked," she said. "You drink your beer that you buy warm," she said and I didn't know if she was being funny with me standing there all dark in her swimsuit waiting to go.

"So, it's as bad as that, where we are?" I said to her. "No ice? You would never get a real American to camp that way, these days."

She said, "If you do not know where you are John, I will tell you where you are. You are in France," she said. She was and she was not being serious with me, and I saw she was making some kind of point while having a little fun with me like the night before. I let her have it. I hadn't expected it, and I said, "All right—as long as it's wet and warm," I said, starting on what we'd stopped last night, remembering how we'd arrived in that talk the night before, and I know you got to play with one another after all, or in time there really is nothing but what all is practical and expected between two people, and that was not yet us.

"If you want your ice, like a real American—you will have to go to America, John," she said then and she didn't sound funny when she said that standing there all dark in her swimsuit.

"All right," I said, "We'll drink it warm," I said. "It's not that bad—wet and warm's all right with me—we are in France, and luckily I am not a real American," I said to her.

"But you want it cold, too?" she said to me. "Don't you? You don't want it cold, like an American?"

It wasn't play. She was making some kind of point about the place.

"I'll take it either way," I said. "Come on—let's stop it," I said.

"You must take it to the river then," she said, being practical in the way she was. She said, "The water there is cold," and the playing from the night before was finished, and the lunch was done, and we walked off from the campsite on down along the gravel road with our big beach towels hung over our shoulders, carrying warm bottles of beer to the cold water of the river.

76

ON THE SUBLIME

The road curved along through tall trees toward the river. We walked the gravel campground road where beneath the tree canopy we came to a brick bathhouse with toilets and showers. It was built of concrete blocks painted white. It had a tin roof. The roof was overhung with tall branched-up trees. At an outside sink there was a man shaving in full view of the people walking to the river. He looked into a mirror with his face all lathered up beneath the tree canopy. He was smoking a cigarette. We could smell his cigarette out on the road. He looked right at home with his things set up there on the sink. He had a bath towel hung on his neck. He had another one wrapped round his waist and looked as though he'd just showered. He held a razor up in the light. He pulled his lathered face with a hand. We looked away from him to the road.

The road curved to the river. The road was lined with tents put up beneath tall trees. The campground sites ended. We went off through a stand of trees where the grass turned to sand. We walked stretches of wild grass strewn with pine needles and sand. You could smell the needles in the sand. There were glimpses of stone and water between the trunks of trees.

We came out of the trees to a great yellowed wall of rising stone facing the far side of the river. There were the big white river stones sitting in the light up at the edge of the river. They made a stony river beach. We walked the sand and stone up to the water. We stood there looking across the water to the far side of the river. The stone cliff came right from out of water rising solid immobile and fixed straight to the sky from the running water. The heavy face of the stone was a great shadowed mass risen up from the clear running water to the sky. It was a solitary and enormous sight. I hadn't expected to see it. She'd wanted me to see it. The sight of it subsumed you.

"Look at it," I said to her. She'd seen it. She'd taken me to the river to see it. I looked to the high cliff of it where there was the green pine grown up in the yellow stone against the blued sky. "It's strange—you wouldn't have expected it was here," I said. I looked along the bottom of the stone face, upriver to where there was a white sand beach on the other side in a bend of the river that you could swim to across the clear cold water. The water moved good and fast before us. But the water was not that wide. You could have swum across it to the far side if you wanted to. I wanted to do it. The rain had mostly run through, and I said, "Let's swim it, girl—do you want to," I said to her and I stood with the beer bottles in hand looking to it.

"The water is too cold from the rain," she said. "I brought you to see it—you shouldn't swim across it," and I bent down beside her and looked down into the water of the river. It had a stony bottom and you could see all the stones in it going out deep and clear. Across the surface of it the cliffs were reflected up from the clear running flatness.

"Feel it," she said. "It's cold." I could smell it.

I put my hand into the imaged water. The water ran on and the images remained. It was cool. I felt its coldness but you could swim it. I left my hand in it feeling it run. I looked from the pictured water of the reflected stone running on in current across my hand to the actual stone rising in the light. That time of day from the high edge of the stone cliff there was an immense descending shadow cast down across the clear water of the far side of the river. The current ran my hand. The rock wall rose massive and mute above us. I was struck with a strange sensation. The whole place seemed to come out of time. I looked from the high shaded rock to the clear river water running across my hand beneath the blue and our own

351

contemporary time felt gone. The place felt unaltered since some long gone ancient time. There at the edge of the river with her beside me I was lost in a larger notion of things. It was that same strange sensation that'd struck me when standing with her up high on the mountain rock above the Rhone River where we'd looked out over the little rooftops of the village of Beauchastel far below us and I'd told her how I felt the briefness and the littleness of our own time. Our own time was nothing to that subsuming feeling of circumscribing immensity come round us in that rising rock along that running river. I took my hand from out of the water. I had a beer bottle in hand to put in the water. I stood there at the rising rock of the river gorge with her and I had that same strong unfounded feeling, I was struck by the unknown actuality of things, by an intimation of things so much larger and stranger than our familiar usual ordinary everyday things and thoughts that I briefly felt we belonged to a greater persisting time and place than to the given little things of our own life and that we'd only just forgotten it, that the land and the light came from out of another time that couldn't be perfunctorily comprehended let alone rotely counted. The face of that rock that water that sky that stone, that, it all came full round the transient look of tents and caravans and camp stoves and clotheslines and clothespins and pots and pans and folding plastic lawn chairs. The time came not in clocks and calendars. It came all otherwise to me, unformed and unfixed. And it really was a very short little walk by foot from the plotted-out campground sites to the river gorge where what time we were now in I couldn't tell you. No, I told myself that day, and in other words formed much after when I found the words for the feeling, this it wasn't a passing time of our usual ordinary things parsed out in the feeling of hours adding up to days and nights, to all that which we felt and thought we were most found in, when we were actually contained and caught up in another kind of confounding time that couldn't accurately be perceived but was everywhere intimated in the strata of that stone. It's a funny thing to think. It's a funny thing to think true. Standing there like that it's a thing when you think it, that'll take you out of the little story of your own life. It was the pleasurable eclipsing of the self in a sense of something sublime. I wasn't afraid of it. I was confounded by it, transported by it, it was that enlarging, self-annihilating, and striking sense of incomprehensible feeling found effected in great works. The long gone time of the stone stood before us. That past persisting time held on lasting unfinished enduring in impression in that stone before us. I stood there looking briefly to it in a sense of respite, one where the too familiar feeling of the so-called self was lost to the grandeur of the natural world in being caught and kept a moment off in another time not ever of one's own making, in a time which could not be accounted for in looking first too closely to what we'd made and put round us that told too easily and apparently of who we were and what time we were in, as if what material objects we'd made were the definitive one's which told truly of the time and who we were most accurately, and no matter that they do in our own short little history of such soon to be antiquated objects, and selves, it's still true that without the people there on their summer holiday swimming in their nylon bathing suits wearing their plastic sunglasses at that river gorge that you wouldn't have known the name or the time of the place. You couldn't. The stone stood before us without one name or time put to it. You couldn't name that mute persistence but in a kind of error. The stone rose in its untold time to the sky from that water. We stood in it in our little time of telling looking to it in its unfathomable own. Ours it is a short little time. We stood a little in it. We stood there holding them beer bottles looking to the shadowed river gorge. We could've never been in a place called France in a time called the twentieth century. All the stone stood before us in a place called France in a time called the twentieth century.

77

THE WOMEN HALF-DRESSED
IN THE STRONG LIGHT

I told her about the strange feeling. I told her of that sense of time that had struck me, and that I'd been worried about the power of it, that selflessness of it, come up in me, the sheer dislocation of it, and she told me not to be, and that it wasn't that unusual, that she'd herself felt it once too, and she began on a little history of the place for me then and on some aspects of aesthetics to explicate something substantive to me of the feeling I'd so strongly felt, so that I would comprehend what you might call my naive aesthetic sensation in some rigorous if not meaningful way, so not to worry about what I'd felt, and she said in some instruction, as was her way, "Yes, it is an ancient place," and we stood there beneath the rising rock in our little diminished perspective to its great magnitude, time, and she told me that the name *Vallon Pont d'Arc* came from the great stone arch risen high over the river to bridge the canyon cliff where the rock was eroded not far upriver from where we two stood, where the water of the river had cut straight down through the limestone of an ancient seabed five hundred thousand years ago. The water ran deep into the strata of rock to leave the great stone arch risen like an architectural wonder constructed over the river gorge and there were the ancient cave paintings too to be found right there in the subterranean stone of the gorge, the oldest art in the history of the world, thirty-five thousand years old and animated by no gods but great unnamed spirits, all that picture pre-historical to the cultural lateness and convention of iconic material image, the beginning of the sublime, the mythopoeic, the first beginning of story, she told me some things like that that day, she put some of them particular concepts to the general feelings

I'd uncannily felt, when that day she first gave me the formal words for them that I've often used in recollection, for, as in feeling all I'd felt I'd never known that there was such a thing as intellectual or aesthetic history, within which to pleasurably lose, in an ever circumscribing, wide-ranging conceptual reflection, the contemporary sense of one's own self, even in an act of narrative aversion in such abstraction, critical, analytical story you'll tell yourself of given things, and in her explication of the phenomenon, then no matter that it was yet strongly, atavistically fixed in me, I didn't worry anymore about the unfixed feeling I'd felt, that enlarging, transporting, and as though averring feeling. And then to make a comparison to other times she told me the Romans had built a great aqueduct across an ancient riverbed there in the South of France a couple thousand years ago and told me it was the highest one in the world not far off from where we two were now standing in Vallon Pont d'Arc, before any of the place was to be known as the South of France, in name let alone in idea, and that it was called the Pont du Gard in a place called Remuolins there in the South. Then she told me how upon their own seeing it rising from rock across the sky that, just as I'd been struck by such a sight in the rising rock of that river gorge, how the sight of the Pont du Gard had once struck Frenchmen like Rousseau and even the American Henry James when they'd come to see it wordless in its solitary enormous and unexpected magnificence rising in built stone crafted from the wilderness. At first sight, it is all to be inexpressible in word no matter the feeling she told me. She told me as in poetry, one must recollect the emotion of it in some late tranquility to find the expressive word for it. She told me some of them things.

So when I'd told her how I'd felt in the sight, she told me a little about this or that natural or historical fact of the land and the people that told you something known and distinctive, historical and interesting about the place, all that you couldn't have known in just arriving to it new like I had in some too-simple sheer looking, and now going past us, downriver on a kind of tour, there were the bright-colored kayaks we followed by eye in the river water, and close to shore there were a couple of kids with plastic sandals swimming in the stony water. There close on the sand were women round us laid out half-dressed in the high sun. We stood beside the large smooth river stones at the water looking back from the rock wall to the women. We felt the sand with our bared feet. It was hot and bright. I put the warm bottles of beer in the cold shallow water along the shore. I came back and sat on a rock beside her in the heat and light at the edge of the river. The women were topless. I had never seen it done like that openly as though without a thought. I looked to the women. She saw me looking. She looked at them.

She said, "Do you like how they look?"

The women looked dark. The women were getting very dark in the light. The bodies were darkened-up in the light. She was already dark. She looked good. "I like how you look," I said. "They'll never get as dark as you," I said, and when I said that to her the sight came as I said it with the stilled and scattered women laid out in the strong light along the river and no one looked to anyone and I looked off from them women's bodies laid out naked and alive in the light to the passing water of the river and I saw clear-coupled images of killing come lit across the women in the sand, they were in me, the living kept there within the dead, I saw bodies laid out in the grass, there were the houses burning against the sky, the bodies burned dark in the light, and I tried not to see it, and I looked off from the laid out bodies to see the river, I wanted to see the other inconceivable time of the stone and water and sky that I'd just seen because it made everything appear inconsequential in our own time but that time was gone for good from Vallon Pont d'Arc in the South of France in that time called the twentieth century. I looked to the river in a place called France in a time called the 1970s. It was 1972. I know you must live in your own time if you are at last to be happy. I looked to see the water pass below the face of the rock to see only the reality of the water and rock in that time and place. I saw the water and rock.

I got up from the stone and took a couple beer bottles out of the water. They were cool. It felt good to hold them in my hand. I came back and sat next to her on the stone. I opened the cold bottles. I handed her one. She drank a bottle with me. We drank in the light there beside the river. She looked very good in her bright nylon bathing suit. I looked to the women. I saw the bodies before me. I let them come. She'd told me to and I did. I held them before me and didn't flee the sight. You can't run in any actuality anyway out from your own head as you would from a room of horrors. It's too bad one's happiness is ever controverted in continual superimposition of past and present. But you do go on in the hope that in such conscious confrontation there is a peace to be found.

I said, "Have you ever done that?"

"No—I am already dark enough," she said.

"You're afraid of getting darker?" I said.

"How dark do you want me?"

"I want you *all* dark," I said. I only wanted to see all her.

"There is no good in it," she said. She looked at me in her looking-listening way that was a teaching if not a correcting. I said no other errant things. I said nothing more. She lay back there against the stone beside me. I watched the water pass. The women's bodies were laid out all about us stilled in the light as though so many other stones brought long ago by the force of storm to rest along the river. None of them moved. The river ran on by. The sun burned on into them half-naked scattered women's bodies making them look black against the white stones. She was dark in her swimsuit beside me. There were no new sights or scenes in my life but for her. I felt the beer. I looked to her blackness and her body in the bikini. I reached out and I touched her on the arm in the light. Her arm was hot and dark. The sun burned into her lit dark in the light. She looked over at me.

"What is it?" she said.

"Nothing," I said looking at her pretty cut up face. "I just wanted to touch you."

"Are you all right?" she said.

"I'm always all right," I said.

She reached over for my hand. She took my hand in hers.

We lay there and held one another's hands in the light at the river and we were young and alive and had plenty of time to live good lives. I felt that then true in that touch of hers, felt all the time before us, and they came once more at that moment when I felt most happy and lost in the good of her laid down there in the light along her, and she was alive and they were dead. She was beside me in the actual passing time of our own lives with the rest never now real anymore only recollections pictured persisting in my own living not ever anymore once real as she herself is real beside me as the river is in its passing before me. It is none of it real, and there they rose in their unreality, living on returned not unfamiliar in their form to me sitting on the stone a little drunk in the light in that congregation of the living and the dead, there they came in their recollected light running back on to me through the greened grass living all alive and as real as the readily given too apparent sight of what in actuality was in front of me, them stilled women's bodies laid half-naked round me, there at the river they fell in rifle fire, and to the rest done by my hand, the last of a whole history of killing by my hand, it is that they are the last in that lineage, to become so many strewn bodies laid disheveled expressionless left abandoned round me at the river, left dying and dead in me, seen more vividly and clearly now in remembrance, in significance, than those by eye, and I looked to the river and I saw the river, and I knew no recollection could come as substantively real as the river comes and goes across that rock, and the river ran on before me in current and the images remained, and the light was now shifted on across the stones and opened up all slanted across the water, and the water of the river was lit good and hard in front of me, with the persisting actuality of the past once more put against the presence of the place, come most strongly in such absent pleasure, in this unguarded leisure, formed from some dark unseen rich recurrent origin, as though one cannot let one's self have relinquishing happiness, and yet there was only the river water, the rock, the women's bodies laid out topless in the light, and I drank the beer sitting there on that stone amidst the half-naked women, and I looked over at her laid dark-lit beside me in the light, her feet in the sand, the bright colors of her beach towel vibrant in the summer light, and in the sight of her there was the promise of forgetting and living in what all was before me, of extinguishing ruinous acts, of eclipsing the past, and in that promise, there was hope of happiness, of time yet to come in which not to continually flee but to once and for all be freed.

She was the realized world.

In the sight of her there along me I wanted to watch her rise. I wanted to remember her herself rising. I wanted to get up and get to that water with her.

One must make new sights and selves.

I said, "We should swim. It's hot. Do you want to?"

"It's too cold still," she said. She had her eyes closed to the strong light. "Tomorrow," she said. She was lying face down on her towel and she looked to me. I had my shirt on and she saw that and she said, "It is hot in the sun—take your shirt off." In the strong light at the river she said that in her looking to me, she said, "You get dark easily—you'll get dark easily," and I hadn't taken my shirt off and she was in her swimming suit and she thought I was going to look very funny the longer it went on like that on holiday in the summer light all dark and light like that in the different parts of my body as though two different people put into one and I didn't take my shirt off.

"You're not going to take your shirt off?" she said to me and I did want to there at the river with her but I didn't want to be so openly seen, I didn't want to show myself like that in the light, to have anyone look at me like that in the light of the river when we were on holiday. All round us the people on their summer holiday were drinking and smoking and swimming and laughing in the light going on in and out of the cold water of the river gorge in their bright-colored bathing suits and sunglasses and I didn't want to see them seeing me like that.

"Take off yours, girl," I said to her and she had her bikini on and I told her that, that she should take off hers, and that I wanted to see her naked and alive in the light like that, "You'll look good like that," I said to her. I only wanted to see her in the light.

"I'm already dark. There is no good reason to do it," she said.

"I want to see you once all dark and naked in the light," I said.

"Do you think I'm afraid of it? You are the one afraid—I'm not," she said and she was lying there face down on the towel next to me and she turned over on her towel and she sat upright and she reached behind her and unhooked her top from off behind her and took her top off and she was bared to the light. She sat there bared to the light with only her bottom on. She did it right there in the light of the river in the South of France in front of everyone for me to see it to show me how to do it and she was not at all afraid of doing it. She did it and I didn't at all mind her doing it and showing me. I only saw her all naked and alive in the light.

"What if the people look?" I said and she was all black in the light.

"Let them look," she said. "*That* is not what matters—you know that," she said to me and she sat there on her beach towel not at all afraid of the people looking like that at that. That nakedness was not what she was afraid of and I know it makes no sense to be and the people looked and I don't think they'd ever seen such color and after awhile she turned on her side on her towel to face me and lay there like that with her top off in the light at the river.

"So, what about you?" she said.

"I'm all talk," I said to her. "You know that. I'm not as strong as you," I said. "I'm not—I never will be."

"You're afraid," she said.

"Yes," I said.

"But you will always be afraid, to be seen?" she said.

"Yes," I said. I did nothing.

"*Alors?*" she said. She waited.

When I sat up on my towel and lifted up my shirt and took it off me, I threw it to the rock and I was all white-looking in the light. I was all naked looking. I was too long whitened from the neck to the waist as though yet wearing some kind of uniformed dress but for half my arms. My arms were darkened up. I felt naked and all too uncovered and seen. She was all dark and naked and she didn't look at all naked or uncovered and seen. We lay awhile half naked and all awakened like that in the light in the South of France and I got dark some in the light. She was so very dark. She got dark dark in the light. We lay like that on holiday in the heat. The place was brilliantly lit round us. In time I got up from beside her and went to the water. I felt the clear river water. The water was cold no matter the heat that time of day. It came cold off the mountain.

"Come feel it," I said to her. She came to the water. She walked topless to the river to me. She was shining in the heat. She came and felt the water. She bent to it half naked as though from another time. We left our things laid on the stone. We swam in the river no matter it was cold. We swam across the river to the far shore to the little sand beach. We lay there on the little sand beach. We were waked by the water. We were alive in the light. We held one another half naked in the sand. The curve of her all of her body lay wet close along my side. We lay there as though in another time. That was the world. We swam back across to the stony side of the river. The swimming made us feel comfortable and clean. We got out cold and dried off in the light. We folded our towels. We took our things from the sand and rock. She put her top back on and I put my shirt on. We left the river and walked back beneath the trees along the gravel of the campground road. The summer light was coming down nicely through the tall trees in shady patches across us and the road.

78

A DARK GIRL IN A FRENCH CAFÉ

We walked back through the campground along the little gravel road to the campground café. We felt good from the swimming. All the campsites were filled with tents and caravans. We came out to the café terrace from beneath tall trees. The café was a little building set along the road into Vallon with tables set out in back. The iron café tables sat spread out on the gravel of the terrace in the light and the place was already crowded when we sat down at a table on the hot iron chairs in the light. We put our wet towels on the backs of our chairs. There were a lot of different languages at the tables round us. There was the Dutch and the Flemish, and she saw me listening, and she said while we waited, "Listen to how it is spoken," she said to me. "You can hear the difference," she said and then she told me that they were really the same language on paper but when the people spoke it the Dutch sounded throatier and harder and the Flemish sounded smoother and softer.

"I can hear it," I said to her, and I sat there and listened to it and to the difference and to how the same words said were sounding different and to how the people and who they were then sounded different in the saying the same words. There was a lot of German and French spoken too at the tables and she pointed it out to me and it was easy to tell that they were not the same language even if you knew nothing about languages for the people speaking those languages they sounded very unlike one another. There were a lot of people at that café round us saying things that sounded very different from one another and I didn't know what all they were talking about but I was sure that it was all pretty much the same.

Then I found myself feeling as if I were an actual American tourist waiting to order a beer in a French café. This is what it is like to sit on holiday in the light in a French café I thought. The sun was strong and everything was brightened by the good weather. The rain was gone for good. It was hard sitting there to remember how hard it had rained in the night. There were men and boys throwing heavy steel balls out on the gravel of the campground road. They were playing a game. The boys wore striped shirts. The men had cigars and I said to her, "What's that game they're playing, out on the road? Is it French?" I said looking at them men and boys.

"It is a traditional sport," she said, looking over to them.

"It's a strange sport," I said and the sound of the shot of one steel ball hitting off another came clear across the road to us at the café tables and a girl came up to the table to take our order.

She was very dark in the light. She looked black in the light. She spoke to her in French. She turned and she left with our order. The gravel under the table was very white and the black iron of the tables was hot to touch in the light. We heard the shots of the game from the men and boys out on the gravel road. I watched her go off. She watched me watch her.

"You are surprised?" she said. "They are all over the South, these girls," she said. "This is their work, the beautiful ones, when they can get it," she said.

The girl brought two glasses of beer. She had long black hair put up off her neck in the heat. Her arms shone darkly from the work in the heat. We thanked her. The golden-colored beer came cold in the tall beaded glasses. The dark girl waited the tables. She brought the beer in the light. We listened to two Dutch girls next to us. The Dutch girls were listening to us speaking in English. They were curious about us. The tables were close.

"Where are you from?" one of the Dutch girls said in French to her. They told us they were from Utrecht in Holland. We all began to speak in English. We said a couple meaningless things. They were interested in us. We were an interesting couple to them. We kept drinking beer and talking to the Dutch girls in English. One of them was turning twenty-one. She had a bright happy face. Her hair was a nice blonde blonde. The other one was quieter. She had a longer and darker blonde hair. They sat at the table in their bikini tops and I looked at them girls' hair hung long and straight down their brown darkened backs. It was very blonde hair in places and then browned in others. It was beautiful hair. They were pretty girls. They were not beautiful girls.

They wore bikini tops and cut-off shorts in the summer light and they were getting a lot of sun. They were getting dark in the light and they looked healthy and happy and the dark beautiful girl waited the tables and brought our beer. After the girl waited on us the Dutch girls came over and sat at our table with us. They drank a beer with us. They wanted to know where we were from. We told them where we were from.

"America."

"France."

We didn't really tell them anything of where we were from. You couldn't tell any of that there and with them two girls and us it was like the accidental convergence of lives that can never authentically meet and that have only one thing in common. We were young and drinking. Then they were going to the river and they wanted us to come.

"Do you want to swim with us?" one of them said looking to her then over at me. Now we were friends. They wanted us to go off to the river with them to go swimming in the light. They were really very friendly pleasant nice girls. But we had swum. We were drinking a beer. We were feeling what it was like to sit in some little leisure in a café.

They left us to go swimming. They walked down the little gravel campground road off out of sight past the men and boys playing at their little game and to the river to swim and we stayed at our table at the café to enjoy that time of day. There was really nothing to do in such a place at that time of the day if you'd already swum and you wanted to have a cold drink. There was only the drinking and playing. It was too late in the afternoon to read. It was too early to eat. You could go take a nap and sleep on easily into evening. But we were awake. We were in a French café and the dark girl brought us our beer.

We felt what it was like to drink in the summer light in the South at a café. The dark girl came to us. We watched her walk off in the light. We were interested in the girl. We were interested in the girl in a way we couldn't ever be with the pretty happy Dutch girls and we kept drinking cold beer and that is a feeling on a hot summer day after swimming in a river. The café was busy. The place was alive. The girl cleared the tables. She came to our table. The two of them they took a look at one another. She took our glasses. The two of them they spoke in French. I listened to it. Then they said something more familiar to one another. They spoke in another language. I understood none of it. Then the girl she left for the bar with our empty glasses. She had her work. The dark beautiful girl she walked off across the bright lit gravel to another table to take another order. I watched her walk away. She watched me watch her walk away.

"What did she say to you?" I said to her.

"She is a curious one," she said, thinking on her.

"She has a way of walking," I said.

She had a beautifully fine dark face and a way of walking across the stones and amongst the tables in the brilliant summer southern light cast down across the tabletops and emptied glasses of the people on holiday carrying everyone's beer speaking in French. There was this misplaced nobility in her.

"Tell me what you see," she said looking to her.

"She looks like you, girl," I said.

"You are struck by her," she said.

"She's a beautiful girl," I said.

"You might have loved her," she said. "She is a beautiful girl. She is young," she said, "She is lonely. There are all the dark and lonely girls like this one in the South," she said.

"But I do not," I said. "I love you," I said.

"She is too beautiful for you?" she said as if playing.

"Yes," I said and I looked at her. I felt how I loved her in the look.

"Yes, I know what you like," she said seeing me look to her.

"Tell me what I like," I said playing.

"You like me cut and dark like this," she said flatly.

"I love it," I said.

"That is what you love more than beauty," she said to me. "You like it that way," she said.

"That is what I like," I said. "I love it. I'll always love it," I said. But we were not playing now. I stopped it.

We weren't playing with it. There was something about it that had become too real. She'd said it too straight out at seeing the beautiful dark uncut girl. I felt bad about it. There was this unhappiness in her. It came on a little out of her. We'd just been happy in coming to the café from our swimming. We'd wanted a simple drink in a French café. We hadn't thought to see such a girl. In the look of her in her work the easy afternoon was changed. We'd just walked from the river to the campground café to get a drink. The place felt changed. It wasn't changed. There were the iron tables. There was the cold beer beaded in the light. Nothing was changed. We sat at the iron table. We drank in the brilliant light. The dark beautiful girl worked the tables.

We watched the girl. It was the girl. She changed it.

"What do you see, John?" she said to me. We were looking-drinking.

"I am confronting something. You told me to confront it," I said.

"You must confront it in yourself. Not in the looking to others—look to yourself," she said. "It is not in her, or me."

"I'm trying to," I said. "I am."

It was very hot there in the southern summer afternoon. The iron of the table was hot to the touch. She had her big sunhat on that she wore out there for the summer light. She sat there beautifully dark and cut in her big straw hat in summer light.

"We shouldn't drink so much in the light. It is dangerous," she said. "It is too hot, to drink so much.

"Madeleine?"

"What is it?"

"I love you."

"You don't even have a hat for the sun," she said. "But you are not afraid of getting dark," she said to me. "No, you are not afraid of that."

"I want it—I love it," I said. I tried to play with it. It's hard to go on playing saying nothing. You go on long enough and you start to say something.

"But it is not good for you," she said. "You see how it is not good for you?" she said as though playing and she sat there cut in her sun hat across the table from me and she looked over to the beautiful dark uncut girl carrying the cold beer out to the people on summer holiday in the café and I saw how we might've stayed longer at the river and swum in the clear cold water in the lowering light. We could've gone off to the river with those two happy Dutch girls where it would've all been some simple easy fun to swim and to lay out in the lowering light on the sand river beach talking of little nothings on our little holiday.

"We haven't seen the village," I said. "Do you want to walk into the village? Let's walk into the village," I said. The feeling for the café was finished.

"We must eat," she said. She was hungry from the swimming.

"We'll eat something in the village—we're on holiday," I said. We turned from the girl and stood up.

We got up from the table. We went off from the café. We left the sight of that girl to walk into the village of Vallon Pont D'Arc to walk the little streets lined with all the shops and trees in the summer light to forget about the girl.

79

ON PLAYING AND FORGETTING

We walked away from the river up the side of the road in the summer light along a line of trees into the village of Vallon. All round us were the hills rising above the village. There was a lot of high bared cliff rock rising between far stretches of high oak and pine trees. The rock was very high and bright and dry. The hills looked bleached in the heat. It looked as if it had never rained up there on that rock. It was barren and bright. There were far houses scattered up in the high pine. You couldn't see the roads that led to the houses but you knew they were there. You saw the roofs and imagined the roads.

There were far rowed vineyards rising to them low rocky foothills. It was hot and dry country of fields and hills. We came to an old stone path with its little stone walls leaning into the walkway. The path went through a vineyard up a low hill to another narrow street. Beyond the stone walls of the path stretched the green leaved rows of vines going out in the stony gravel. We came up the street to a village café. There was a terrace there in front where you could sit outside to look to the vineyards and hills.

We sat outside under the trees. There was a jukebox inside the cafe playing an American pop song. We could hear it coming clearly through the opened door of the café. It was a song I knew. I'd heard it home. All round us were the vineyards and rocky hills. A waiter came. We ordered beer. The terrace was crowded-in with iron tables and chairs. There were a couple of cropped sycamore trees giving it shade. There weren't a lot of people. They were at the river that time of the day. They were in the market square at the small shops in Vallon. There was little life. There was us at an iron table.

Across the street from the café the wall of a house was a faded and cracked yellow color and sometimes a red beneath where there were patches of plaster put down and painted over to cover the stone beneath. It was pleasant to look at like a painted-over painting in which you yet saw another scene beneath. It looked old. A song played. An old man came on a bicycle. He stopped there in the shade of the house beneath the plane trees. The beer was cold in the glass. He leaned his bicycle against the nicely cracked and shaded wall of the house. He went in through a plastic rainbow-beaded doorway to the house. He had bread. He did not come out. We sat in the shaded light beneath the trees. Nothing moved. It was that very still time of day. We sat on the café terrace in the quieted stillness of late summer afternoon in a little village in the South of France. In that stopped time in afternoon with nowhere to go and nothing to do there on holiday I listened very closely to the quiet of the place. There was a peace in the place. It was one of those afternoons where you felt a great or small thing would happen if it went on long enough. Nothing would happen. It was just the quiet of it and the feeling that the quiet would be broken into something else. Then there were cicadas in the trees. That is a sound on a hot day. And even in that sharp loudness there was yet an immense quiet. A passenger jet cut west across the high sky. Its great white jet trail streamed out in the sky. The jukebox played on. The cicadas were in the trees. A couple came laughing out of the café. Around us the sky was vast and vacant in clarity above the high bleached hills. The hills were bright and barren beneath the blue.

    The song was done.

    She said, "Play a song for me."

    "I'll play a song for you," I said. I got up from the table. I went in. I put on a song. I came back out. She knew the words to the song. She began to sing. I had never heard her sing. She sang sweetly in the heat.

"I didn't know you sang, girl," I said. She laughed. She was shy like a girl about it.

"It is a *kind* of singing," she said. "But there are many things you do not know," she said about herself.

"What things?" I said.

"Well—I studied it once in school," she said about her singing.

"You were a very good student in school, girl," I said. "You were a good schoolgirl," I said.

"You were never a good student?" she said, "A good schoolboy?"

"It was always too late for me," I said. "None of us listens to anyone at that age. Then it's too late."

"No—you are still young enough to learn some things," she said. "Do you know how young you are?" she said to me.

"But I don't feel it, I feel old," I said. "Make me feel young," I said. "I want to feel it. I don't feel it anymore," I said. "You know how to make me," I said.

"I will make you feel it," she said. "I will make you feel things again, like a boy."

"Promise me?"

"I promise. Tonight you will feel it."

"You will make me young again?"

"I will teach you something, boy."

"What will you teach me?"

"You must wait to know. You will know it in the night," she said. In that heat on that terrace we played. We could yet play. We played a little there on that terrace with the things that couldn't be easily said. It's all a way of talking without telling. It's a way of telling without talking.

"Tell me how I will feel it," I said. "I'm already ruined."

"I will make you good again," she said.

"How will you make me?"

"So that you forget everything."

"But I want to know something."

"No, you're a very bad student. You do not want to know really anything," and I couldn't tell now if she was playing with me. The things would turn.

"Make me forget myself, then," I said.

"Will you be happy then?"

"Happier than I've ever been."

"You just want to play," she said.

"It's all playing, isn't it?" I said and she looked at me. We were playing saying nothing. You learn things that way. We were learning things drinking in the light. There's a lot about yourself and another you can learn that way. It's not by any serious thinking in the day. It's by drinking in the light. It's by telling things in the night you don't in the light of day.

We got up and left the café to walk the rest of the way into Vallon. We walked down the street to the center of the village to the market square. We sat there at a table outside in the light in the square under the trees along a row of little shops. There were fancy little shops. It was one of those quaint French market squares with pretty plane trees you'll see on a postcard. We'd walked into Vallon to see the village. Vallon Pont d'Arc is really a very picturesque French village. The people on holiday were walking by going here and there in leisure in the summer light. The people passed. There was nothing new to see. There was the village. There was the two of us looking to one another in the light in a French village. We were sitting in another French village having gone nowhere and done nothing. We weren't those people on holiday. We'd played at it and being them. We'd had a couple easy drinks in a French café. We'd played at being a little French.

We sat there and ordered nothing. The playing from the terrace was gone. The feeling for it was finished. We'd said everything and nothing. We'd pushed off all in play like schoolchildren and kept on with it as long as we could.

Vallon was finished.

"We are losing our time," she said.

"We must go," I said, "It's no good."

"We must think carefully of where to go," she said.

"We must not hate what we do," I said. "Think of one thing to do without hating it," I said to her.

Sitting there in Vallon in that market square I didn't want her to hate it. I could not think of one good thing for her there in France to be happy in and not to hate.

"Everyplace is hard," she said.

"There's America," I said.

"Tell me about America. You never really told me about America," she said and I saw it then as I had before. It was the way she said it. The whole idea of it came in her spoken word. It came big there to that small village square. It came in its limitlessness. In her saying it sitting there in that little French village the sight of it came to us in some idealized greatness it came in some good promise. I felt something for it.

"Do you want to go to America, girl?" I said.

"Is it hard in America?" she said.

"We'll go to America, girl," I said. "It's settled," I said.

"There is no money to go anywhere, or to America," she said to me.

"We'll get the money, even if we hate what we do, we'll get it, and go," I said. "Where is the work, any work?—good or bad. I'll do the bad."

"There is Montpellier," she said. She knew the city.

"We'll go to Montpellier," I said. "There is work?"

"There is the University," she said, "The holiday will be over, the students will return to the city, there will be work," she said, "It might not be good work," she said, "There is the sea," she said seeing it. She said it. I saw it.

There was the water and the sky.

373

"We could go to Montpellier," I said to her, "It's not too far?" I wanted to get up from that table and go off to it with her.

"It is off from home—but a real French city not too far," she said and we sat there in the market square rowed-in with them close-crowded shops in the little picturesque village of Vallon Pont d'Arc seeing the city by the sea.

There was the water stretching to the far sky.

"I always wanted to go to the sea," I said.

"It will be hard I think," she said then.

"Everything is hard," I said. "We'll go there, we'll start out small. We'll get a room, a room is a place. We'll come back home to our own place. We'll be a little home in it—we won't hate it—no matter what we do. You don't hate the thing that makes you a little home," I said to her. "No matter what we do, we won't hate it, we'll be together in it," I said that to her at that table talking it up like that now about how we'd go get work in Montpellier and be together in it. It all sounded good. I didn't want her to hate it any of it. You got to tell yourself a story about anything good and hard to go do it. She knew it was a story.

"It is not so easy in France," she said.

"I know what's hard," I said, "I'll do what's hard."

"It is not so easy as in America I think," she said.

"It's not really easy anywhere for anybody," I said.

We'd had to talk of where to go. We had talked. We took a last look at the people at the tables in the summer light in the little village of Vallon Pont D'Arc far off from home and happy. The people walked along the shops in the light. The men wore bright shirts and the women had straw hats and wore sandals and carried paper shopping bags filled with what new things they'd bought. They ate out at the little iron tables on the cobblestone in the summer light talking long and easy. They did all the little leisurely things a long time late into the afternoon light.

We got up and walked out past the shops. We left the market square. We walked on out of the streets of Vallon. The hills were barren and bright about us. The village opened out into the fields and hills. We went back on along the village road to the café terrace overlooking the fields. We hadn't eaten. We were hungry. We sat out on the terrace of the café and there we ate in the early evening light deeply cast lit richly-golden across the stretching vineyards green and rowed to the low rocky foothills. We took our time.

We walked back down through the little leaning stone walls of the vineyard path cutting through the low hillside leafed-out in green walking on along them rows of big leafy vines cast in diminishing light back to the campground to the river to lay there on the stone listening to the river in the last light. We lay there late on the river stone in dark.

80

NEVER TO BE LONELY AGAIN

The next day one of those Dutch girls we had first met turned twenty-one years old and we saw her swimming at the river and we swam with her and she asked us to come that night to a party. That night they had a little party for her outside at the campground café. The Frenchman who ran the place had gotten to know the Dutch girls drinking in afternoon at the café and he'd got cake and champagne. It was to be a kind of celebration. We didn't really want to go there. We were going in morning. We didn't want to go there and we went there. The Dutch girl had had a beer with us and swam with us and she had invited us and we sat there drinking and laughing at jokes we didn't understand. The middle-aged Frenchman brought out champagne to the table. It was to be a kind of celebration. Everyone was happy. We sat at the long table. There was a red and white checked tablecloth laid the length of the table. There were Japanese lanterns strung in the dark around the café. The Frenchman opened the champagne. The Frenchman poured out the champagne. We all had a glass.

The dark girl came up to the table. She stood at the end of the table smoking a cigarette. We were drinking champagne. The Frenchman waved for her to sit down. The beautiful dark girl sat down beside me. I felt her against me. I poured out some of the Frenchman's bottle for her. I filled her glass. Then the two of them were talking to one another. They started up a conversation in French two dark girls drinking French champagne. They sat across the table from one another talking for a time in French. I drank champagne with the Frenchman. The half-eaten birthday cake sat on the red-clothed bottle-filled picnic table. I talked to none of them. I drank with them. After awhile the Frenchman tried out his English on me. I tried my French on him. We didn't understand one another too well at all me and him. The Dutch girls talked to one another in Dutch. Then I heard that unknown language across the red-clothed table. I understood none of it. It was strange and pleasant to listen to. I sat there listening to it. There was music in it. I heard how they understood one another in it. I saw it in their faces. She looked to me speaking in that all-unfamiliar language. I felt how I loved her. That dark girl was beside me. I was seeing strange and inconceivable places in their unintelligible talk.

When it was late one of the Dutch girls went off to bed. The one girl who had turned twenty-one stayed and sat there looking all pretty talking to the Frenchman. He had his arm around her with a champagne glass in his hand. The Frenchman had silver hair and thick-framed black glasses. The Frenchman didn't know me at all. I drank his champagne and he said nothing to me now. He tried to speak in Dutch to the girl. She spoke to him in French. He went on in his Dutch that was the farthest thing from Dutch as far as I could tell. I sat there with them all talking like that with me listening not knowing what was said by anyone. I heard all of it knowing none of it. It meant something that way to me in the sound of it. I've often never really wanted to know exactly what the things said are anyway in ordinary words. It makes them less.

Then the champagne was gone. We sat there finishing a drink. The talk was died out and done and the Frenchman said something to the dark beautiful girl. The girl got up from me to go. I wanted to stop her. I wanted her to stay. I didn't stop her. It was late. The Frenchman said something to her I don't know what it was he said. She was going. He was her boss and the Frenchman he got up from where he was sitting beside the Dutch girl. The Dutch girl sat on the bench drunk. We said good-bye to the Frenchman in English and he really knew no English. The dark girl went off with him to the road in the summer night. We were pleasantly drunk. The girl walked off into the dark of the road with him. I didn't want it to be so. The night was finished. The party was over. The whole place felt finished.

We said goodnight to the Dutch girl. She kissed us on our cheeks beneath the Japanese lanterns and she thanked us. It was her birthday. She walked off drunk on the road alone in the dark. We were left there alone. The café was deserted. There was the table filled with dirtied glasses and emptied bottles and strewn silverware and the half-eaten cake in the night on its silver platter in the light of Japanese lanterns. We left it all scattered from the celebration. We walked the campground road in the night to the river to smoke a cigarette. The wind was in the tops of the trees. The wind came hard in the trees. It was the mistral. It made the place feel wild and deserted in the dark. We listened to the blown leaves above us in the dark. There was the rocky gravel of the little campground road beneath our feet. We walked the road in the dark held close in the wind.

She said to me, "She hates her life."

"She cannot get out of it?" I said to her about the beautiful girl.

"No—there is no one left for her. There are only these men."

We left the road for the river. The night was big. We saw all the stars. We kept our arms round one another in the night. I said to her, "What can be done for it?" and we walked beneath the trees across the grass to the sand and stone and up to the water. "There is nothing to be done for it," she said and we sat beside the river and smoked. There was one sound there at night along the river. It was the sound of the water where it went over the stones in the bed of the river.

We looked into the running water of the river.

"She can't go home?" I said.

"There is no home."

"There is no one for her? She is lonely," I said.

"She is young. She will be all right, I think."

"What will happen to her?" I was worried about her.

"You cannot worry about her. We must worry about ourselves," she said to me.

"We'll be happy," I said to her. "I don't worry about us."

"But, we must make ourselves happy—we must make our happiness, John," she said.

"We will," I said.

The stars illuminated the river gorge in faint light. They gave the stone little light. We sat smoking in the dark light of the stars. We talked like that about the lonely girl. We'd left her and her loneliness. Something of it lingered on between us. The stars hung in the high blackness of the sky.

It was very late. There was solitude in the stone of the place. There was great solitude in that starlit stone of the gorge. I felt it there with her and I didn't want to feel it so present and large. There was a sheer emptiness. It was a sensation of nothingness in the dark. There was a sense of loss.

"I don't want you to ever be lonely like that," I said to her.

"I am not," she said.

"We can't be that way now after all the rest."

"But, don't think you won't ever be lonely again, John," she said to me.

"I know a way."

"What way?" she said, and then she knew what it was. I'd said it before to her. It is always something about children. It is always something about them children. I saw the children, I saw her with them children in the rooms of the old colonial school, with them children we'd never been alone, and she'd had a loving look for them, and I'd seen it. We'd never been alone with them. We'd never been left alone in the way you can be with another. You can be left alone with another you love but never with children.

"We'll never be lonely again, like that," I said. "That's the way to forget all, that's the way to forget the loneliness, and all. We'll never be left alone like that girl. Don't you want one, girl?"

"It is not a question of wanting—," she said.

"We'll have one, then," I said. "It's settled—did I ever tell you that you're good with children?" I said. "You are good with me, girl," I said to her. "We'll have one," I said. "You can't ever be alone in that," I said to her. "Do you understand that?" I said to her in the dark.

"I understand you," she said.

"We'll always be together in it," I said.

"We are together now," she said.

"You are not afraid?" I said, "For us."

"I am not afraid, for us," she said.

"There is a way at last to be happy," I said.

"You can yet be lonely," she said.

"There's a way to be kept happy together never lonely again," I said.

"Listen to me," she said. She stopped me.

"What is it?" I said, "I am listening, girl," I said sitting beside her in the dark.

"That is what you want from me," she said. "You have always wanted it—," she said. "I do not know if it is possible—not in the way you want."

We sat there in the stillness of the stone. The river ran the rocks.

"It must be possible," I said.

"I was sick once," she said. She stopped. "I was to tell you," she said and I felt afraid for us. She'd stopped me. Then she said it outright there at the river. "I was to have a child," she said. "I was to have a child once," she said right there in the night sitting at the river gorge, "I was to have a child," she said as though it were hard for her herself to believe that it was ever so and as if the realization of it could only come now in the repeating it to me to make it real to me and even to herself. "I was sick. An Arab doctor came," she told me. She was with the Catholics. They gave her a cross to wear around her neck and she believed in none of it. It came badly out of her. Then it was gone for good from out of her. That doctor told her she may have none now from what'd been done.

"What did you do to yourself?" I said to her.

"Nothing," she said. "I only hated it."

"But you hurt yourself?" I said to her.

"Are there not enough children?" she said to me. "Do you love me now?" she said to me.

"Yes, I love you," I said. "I have always loved you."

"But that is what you want from me," she said.

"What do doctors know?" I said. "Doctors they know nothing."

We were quieted in the stillness of the stone gorge.

The wind was in the tops of the trees. The wind came hard in the dark down the rock of the river gorge. We sat on the stone beneath the trees with the wind come hard at the whole place emptied and wild. The trees were loudly bent. The leaves were blown across the river stones. The wind took the leaves down to the river to the dark water. We were sitting there looking across the dark water. I took her hand in mine and I got her up from the stone. I felt how she'd been hurt and I held her. She'd been hurt badly. I saw what it was how it'd been in her and I didn't say it. I held her in the dark of the river gorge. The wind beat into us. The river ran on.

"Let's go. It's late," I said.

We walked from the river gorge up the bank into the trees onto the road to go sleep.

We came to the tent.

"I cannot sleep," she said at the tent. She felt badly. She was awakened from what she'd said.

"Then we'll walk awhile," I said. "You'll feel better. You'll sleep."

We walked on a time in dark. We wandered into the village on along shuttered streets. The houses of Vallon were all shut up against the wind. It was late and everything was closed. We felt the hour and its lateness. We walked along the closed shops in the market place with the iron bars locked over the dark windows. The chairs were stacked and chained in the night against the trees where the crowds had been in the day. We sat down on a wooden bench under a tree in the square. We were awakened. We needed to sleep. A car came along the village square. Its yellow headlights hit up on an advertisement for Pernod painted on the stone wall of a building. The car drove out of the village. There was no one. There was the wind in the tops of the trees. We stood up from the bench to walk. We shouldn't fall asleep in the square. We needed to sleep. We walked the little picturesque streets in the dark. They led nowhere. We stopped. We stood in the dark street. We looked to the sky. We held to one another in the night. We stood stilled in the street. We looked down the dark shuttered street. There was nothing new to see. There was the sky and the blackness. We held one another and there was us and the dark. The sky was immense. We looked up into it without end. There was a loneliness come down from it to us. We were nothing to it. We stood on the stones of the village street. There was us in the dark under the unending sky. There was the present and vivid sense of the real. There were all the brilliant and burning stars.

She closed her eyes to it. She laid her head on against my shoulder. She could not now stay awake. She had walked it off out of her. I kept her close and I said, "We won't walk back, we'll go get a room—I'll put you into a nice big bed with one of those big soft pillows and in the morning we'll wake up all rested and we'll have a big breakfast brought to us out on a terrace in the morning light."

There was a street of holiday hotels. We went to find a room. Our shoes hit across the cobble-stone. Our footsteps echoed in the dark ends of streets. There was a street of nice old hotels with those courtyards you could eat out in with all the other people in a nice morning light. It was July or August. The month doesn't matter. Everything was full. There was no room.

We walked back down the shuttered village street out of Vallon. We kept close to one another and went on held into one another beneath the sky. We went on down through the leaning stone walls of the garden path on past the green-rowed vineyard descending the hillside in the night to the river and everything was big in the night and we felt older than we were in the lateness. We walked on through the campground road beneath the trees in the far light of stars. There were all the stars. We came to the tent.

"Let's sleep under the sky," I said. "I don't want to sleep in a tent." We didn't sleep in the tent. The walk had wakened us.

We were reawakened to the night. It was the last night. We took our sleeping bags from the tent. We went to the river. We laid the bags out on the riverbank. We put our bags together on the bank of the river to make a bed above the stones that went down into the water. The smell of wet grass and pine needles was everywhere beneath us. Above us the sky was very clear and tall and we saw all the stars. We lay there in the bag awakened awhile. The river made its little sound.

The light came. In morning it was cold and wet and we got up naked in the cold and put our clothes on when people started to come down to the water. We went to the bathhouse and made love in the shower. When we ran out of coins the hot water stopped and we got out wet and cold and left shivering in the wind wrapped up in our towels carrying our clothes. The mistral was blowing. We dressed in the tent. We were going. It was a good feeling to know that we were going for good. There I told her I loved her. Then she said it to me. We said it because we knew it was true. It was easy to say it when it was true and you were naked and holding one another alive and cold in the light.

We drove up out of the Ardèche river gorge into the hills all around Vallon and everything there behind us got small and we could see far to the north and all across the horizon again and I was surprised at how small Vallon looked down and in back of us. Once the river and the houses and fields and the vineyards outside it all could no longer be seen to be clearly separated from one another all we could see or anyone would

383

see against the far sky was sometimes the rising white chimney smoke high in the hills above the place where a house or home might be.

Works Cited

Stein, Gertrude. *Three Live*s. New York: Vintage Books (1909): 100-103.

Textual Paraphrases

Milton, John. *Paradise Lost*. New York: W.W. Norton & Company, 1975.

[Volume II Forthcoming]

ABANDONED BY THE GODS

VOLUME II

CONTENTS

BOOK THREE: THE GOOD HARD WORK

81 The Long-Vanished Faces Of Like-Named Girls
82 Epiphany In A Train Station
83 On The Discovery Of A Country, Or A Framed and Narrated View
84 The Concierge, Kitsch Aesthetic, and The Rooftops Of Montpellier
85 اسنرف يف تايرئازجل ةيرح
86 On The Relation Of Dreams To Waking Life
87 A Room Is A Place, A Place Is What You Make Of It
88 The Idea Of Tomorrow, Is The Promise Of All The Good To Come
89 The Work Was There
90 On Lost Time
91 The Remains Of Reverie
92 A Clean Break
93 The Good of Unending Unmindful Repetition
94 The Relinquishment Of Recollection
95 A Famous French Poem and A Girl Who Once Loved Her
96 The People Of Vietnam
97 The True Story Of A Name
98 The Look Of Authority, Talk Of Law, and The Authorized Self

- 99   A Kind of Undeclared War
- 100 A Dark Defeated Girl
- 101 The Money For America, Or Every Man Has A *Property* In His Own *Person*
- 102 On The Theory Of The Leisure Class, Conspicuous Consumption, and Hunting Deer
- 103 The Underdetermined and Redetermined Self
- 104 A Castle In The Sand
- 105 Joyuese Illuminated In Nostalgic Light
- 106 The Good Hard Work
- 107 What Is To Come
- 108 The Village Doctor
- 109 A Happy-Beautiful Girl In The Late Autumn Light
- 110 An Intimation Of America
- 111 Last Days In A Simple Little Life Lived In A Simple Little Place
- 112 Scene Of A Farewell In A Train Station

BOOK FOUR: A KIND OF HOMECOMING

- 113 The Remaking Of Americans
- 114 A First Look Of America
- 115 The Unreal Actuality Of Arrival
- 116 A Kind Of Homecoming
- 117 On Being A Little Home In A House
- 118 The Look Of America Is An Idea Of America
- 119 *Michi Gama*: The Recorded History Of A Name
- 120 *Ominitago*: The True-Given History Of A Name
- 121 To Go On Good In A Place Of Great Sights and Grand Impressions
- 122 On Self-Making
- 123 The Snowman and The Angel
- 124 A Life For Want Of Work

125 To Live In A Time Of Great Spirit
126 A Real American
127 A Good Work
128 The Remains Of Reverie
129 On The Consumed and Attenuated Life
130 On Everlasting Life and The Catholic Priest
131 The People Of Vietnam
132 A Husband and A Wife
133 To Go On Only Reading, Or *Little America*
134 Epiphany Of An Authentic Self Shut Off From The World In Winter Storm
135 Snowbound
136 Two People Go On Together In A Telling
137 We Walk There In The Light Along Big Water
138 Real Americans
139 An Absurd and Official End
140 A Moment In A Life Unmade By History Or Place
141 A Kind Of Homecoming
142 This Is The Beginning
143 Indian Summer Days
144 We Go Forward In The Light
145 Scene Of A Farewell In A Train Station

Made in the USA
Lexington, KY
30 March 2014